NEON
PANIC

CHARLES PHILIPP MARTIN

NEON PANIC

A NOVEL OF SUSPENSE

~ Oct. 2011

To Zari:
It will be wanting
for you. Best wishes.

Charlie

vantage
POINT

Vantage Point Books and the Vantage Point Books colophon
are registered trademarks of Vantage Press, Inc.

FIRST EDITION: October 2011

Published by VANTAGE POINT BOOKS
Vantage Press, Inc.
419 Park Avenue South
New York, NY 10016

www.vantagepointbooks.com

Manufactured in the United States of America

ISBN: 978-1-936467-13-6

Library of Congress Cataloging-in-Publication data are on file.

0 9 8 7 6 5 4 3 2 1

Cover design by VICTOR MINGOVITS

To the memory of
Ruth and Thomas Martin
who made the vernacular
spectacular

Ping
O world ...
Pong
O world ...
Pang
O world ...
Ping, Pong, Pang
... full of madmen in love.

—GIUSEPPE ADAMA AND RENATO SIMONI,
LIBRETTO TO *TURANDOT*, ACT II

AUTHOR'S NOTE: All of the Western first names given to Chinese characters in this book are true names, having been borrowed from real Hong Kong people. The Hong Kong Symphony Orchestra, however, is a fictitious institution.

There are about eight Hong Kong dollars to one U.S. dollar.

The time is 2003, five years after the handover.

PROLOGUE

MONG SPRINTS TO the water as if rushing to the aid of his critically injured career. Sooner or later he'll redeem himself. Today, he hopes, let it be today.

He charges past some pilings, clears a Stonehenge of cinderblocks by several inches, and touches down on the expanse of land that juts into the bottle-green waters of the Yau Ma Tei Typhoon Shelter.

Someone—a young woman—has called to report a body drifting near the new reclamation project. Mong's Emergency Unit team must check it out. They're treading slowly over the reclamation, Maglites in hand to dispel the growing shadows. Mong plans to use their caution to his advantage; the faster he covers ground, the more likely he'll make the find himself.

Mong is overdue for a change in luck, but despite his fervid offerings to Kwan Dai, he's had none. He has no wife, no girlfriend, and few friends, for reasons that elude him. In the Emergency Unit he barely has a name. Since Day One he's been known as Mong, short for *mong cha cha*. Airhead, dope.

He trails up a gravel slope to get a better view. If only that stupid girl had shown up to direct them to the body, instead of screaming anonymously into a cellphone from the Lantau Ferry. She'd been afraid; they always were. Probably a teenager from one of the numberless troupes that camp on the beaches and barbecue chicken wings, strum guitars, sing Canto-pop anthems, and eventually congeal into couples to *pak to*—snuggle, kiss and, if they can find shelter in the bracken up from the cove, do things that Mong only dreams of in shame-soaked nightly vignettes.

Mong sees no bodies living or dead, only confined, restless harbor waters before him and haze-clad skyscrapers behind. The man-made shore is wreathed in jetsam: ice-cream sticks, condom foils, candy wrappers, and other mementos of good times. The corpse could be anywhere, or nowhere at all, and night is coming on. He hears only the *plok-plok-plok* of an old diesel tug engine, the sound borne on damp salty air. Word has seeped out that death is near, and people want none of it. They've gathered up their chicken wings and guitars and moved on.

He descends the slope and moves onto embryonic land where no cop, for all he knows, has ever been. On the station's map this ground is blank, a white space marked NBD. No Beat Defined.

The reclamation explodes into light. Mong utters a yelp.

"That you, Mong?"

Constable Sinbad Ho, perched on a gravel mound, is leveling a flashlight on him.

"Yeah," Mong says, resuming his breathing. "Find anything?"

"Nothing. Damn, I could use a smoke now."

Mong doesn't smoke. He bought a pack of *Ma bo los* once, after it dawned on him that the rest of his team smoked, but he ended up missing two days of work from nicotine poisoning.

"There's no body here," Sinbad says. "It's probably a phony report. Bastards do that sometimes..."

Mong can't see a damn thing thanks to the flare of Sinbad's

Maglite. He looks toward the water to regain his night vision, and spots something.

"What's that?" Mong says.

"What's what?"

A quiet, rigid presence is bobbling in the water. They focus their two beams upon the form, a torso in a T-shirt. Head still beyond the piling. Legs below the opaque waters.

A thought builds like a Mahler crescendo in Mong's brain. *I've found it.*

"Shit, look at it," says Sinbad. "That thing's been in the water a month."

"I'll radio in," Mong says. "Then we'll mark the area off as a crime scene." He's almost dizzy in his triumph.

"Don't do that," says Sinbad. "It's late. Let the Marine Police handle it."

No, please! Sinbad would sabotage Mong's one fragment of recognition.

"We can't do that ... can we?"

"Sure—the body isn't on land."

As if defying them, the corpse wobbles closer in, nudging against the polystyrene afterbirth of a newborn Toshiba.

"It's too late," says Mong. *Please, let it be too late.*

"We don't want this," says Sinbad. "You feel like standing guard while we wait for Urban Services to collect it? Probably just an II that didn't make it. A waste of time for everyone. Let's call Marine now, while we still can."

As Sinbad grabs his radio, the corpse's head and shoulders ride a wave onto the bank.

"Shit!" says Sinbad. He douses his light and looks at his colleague.

"Mong," he says. "Do you want to be a hero?"

The question is designed to get Mong's attention, and it does.

Sinbad continues. "Just go down there and kick it back in the water. I'll tell them to radio Marine."

"Me?"

"Just do it!"

Mong checks and sees he's mostly hidden from street level observers by a mammoth Mitsubishi crane and hills of concrete piping. He walks toward the waterline, squats, and extends his foot, but he falls short of the corpse by a few inches. When he tries to creep forward, his legs freeze.

"Come on," says Sinbad. "Just give it a shove. Beer's on me tonight. Everyone'll thank you."

No one has ever thanked Mong. The thought makes his head float.

For a moment he wavers, first imagining his acceptance into the troops, then watching the body, oozing with bad luck and malign spirits, rock on the water. Finally he gains control of his limbs, slithers up to the body, and plants his foot against its ribs.

He pushes.

His foot sinks ankle-deep in the flesh of the torso, which sub-tropical sun and brine have pickled to the texture of a well-done brisket.

The howl from Mong's throat ricochets back and forth between office towers and fades into the moist ether that is the city's September air.

He tries to clamber backwards, but his heel snags a rib, and the body follows him up the slope, boosted by the wash from a passing ferry.

Mong gasps three words in a hitherto unknown language and pries off the embedded shoe with his other foot. He runs away and cries out once more as his stockinged toes bash a cinderblock. The body now lies on dry ground, Mong's shoe projecting from its ribs.

He hears a scream behind him. For a moment he thinks it's the first of the ghosts he's freed, coming to haunt him, drive women even farther away from him, lose him money, deliver misfortune in wholesale lots.

But it's only Sinbad laughing.

"Hey, everyone, over here! Get over here!"

Mak and Cheung sprint over, sweep their flashlights onto a corpse with a size 8 oxford in its flank, and then over to Mong, still hopping on one foot and clutching his bruised toes.

"We'll get results now," says Sinbad. "Mong has stepped in!" They're all doubled over laughing now.

So much for his career. The demons have started their first shift.

"CONSTABLE, DO YOU know what we have here? Please don't say 'a dead body.' That would depress me. What we have here is the body of an unknown female, Asian, aged between twenty and, oh, twenty-five. She was found Saturday afternoon floating in the Yau Ma Tei Typhoon Shelter, probably having been in the water for about two weeks, judging by the condition of the skin."

PC Sinbad Ho tries not to listen to Doctor Lee. He feels assaulted by the unfairness of it all. For one thing, he didn't discover the body; his idiot colleague Mong did. For another, the van didn't arrive to collect it for two hours. The driver dawdled over his dinner while Sinbad stood guard by the rotting corpse. As the evening breeze died down, the smell got worse. You can only post yourself so far from what you're supposed to be guarding.

Worse, Zoba heard that he'd spent that evening with a cadaver at the Public Mortuary, and canceled their date. Who could blame her? Bad luck, bodies are. Out in the open he could laugh at Mong. But in a closed chamber it's not funny. Ghosts can be trouble.

He's alone with Doctor Lee in the special room reserved for working on decomposing bodies. No official name, but they call it the Smelly Room. Twice already Sinbad's gorge has threatened to erupt from the stench, which easily overpowers the Vicks underneath his nose.

Pulling on his latex gloves, eyes on the corpse, Doctor Lee speaks long, detailed sentences in Cantonese, punctuated with occasional questions to Sinbad in English. Is that to throw him off?

"Now, Constable, the subject is dressed in worn shorts and T-shirt, cotton underpants, and brassiere, all cheap, standard Chinese-made garments. What does that tell you?"

"Uh, not much money."

Doctor Lee pauses, exhales. "A stellar deduction, Constable, and no less irrelevant for that. I ask you again, what *relevant* facts does her clothing suggest to us? Such as where she is from, and how she ended up on the beach?" He removes a scissors from a tray and snips through the shirt.

Sinbad grapples for an answer. The doctor is now cutting the brassiere, which has remained eerily in place during her travels through Hong Kong Harbour. "Not exactly Victoria's Secret, is it, Constable?" Damn this inquisition. Damn Doctor Lee. What will Sinbad be thinking of the next time he and Zoba spend the afternoon in the Mongkok love hotel and she removes her blouse?

He looks away, and finds no relief—everything here is custom made for the dead: the stainless steel table on which the corpse lies, no pillow, no railing to protect the occupant from a fall, just a drain underneath. Fluorescent lights and the pungent tang of formaldehyde.

"Time passes, the Constable thinks, but no words issue from his mouth," says Doctor Lee. "So we will tell the Constable what we who have been observing have observed. It would appear that this is an illegal immigrant, or maybe a fisherwoman off the boat. No Hong Kong professional woman would be caught dead in those clothes. This woman, however, was." He clips the shorts, places them in a tray, and she is bare.

Sinbad eyes the floor. He's racked his brain for an excuse to leave the room, or at least catch his breath outside. In a timid voice he's requested to make a phone call. Doctor Lee has denied the request, as he always does, on the grounds that his exam might give rise to some questions regarding the discovery of the body. None of the PCs recall Doctor Lee ever asking them a question to which he didn't already know the answer.

"Now, this, Constable, I've not seen before. A foreign object embedded between the sixth and seventh ribs on the left side. From what I understand, it's been identified as the shoe of one of your colleagues, whose position on the Force is, one would hope, temporary." Doctor Lee removes the shoe and places it in a basin on a nearby table, then scans the corpse's face. "Both eyes are missing, which you expect when the body floats face down. So many marine predators."

"Will...we get an identification?"

"Good question, Constable. See this?" Sinbad looks briefly at the hands, and jerks his head away. "No possibility of fingerprints, as all ten fingers are missing. It's those marine predators again. By the way, were you taking your lady friend out for crab tonight, by any chance? I recommend Ocean Palace, in Aberdeen."

A few minutes of blessed silence follow. Once, overcome by curiosity, Sinbad moves his head to catch the body in the corner of his eye. He sees where the doctor is poking around, and instantly regrets having looked. Just as well Zoba canceled the date.

Doctor Lee turns to face Sinbad. "That's it. Note the parallel lacerations on the left shoulder. Those are postmortem, obviously from a boat propeller. Given the state of putrefaction, we'll probably never determine cause of death. It does look as if some poor girl from up North fell off the back of her fishing boat and never made it home. The currents would have brought her down here."

"Can I make a phone call now, please?" Doctor Lee has turned back to the cadaver, and studies the pitted, bluish-black face with its sightless eye sockets. A few white teeth poke through a hole in the jaw.

"Dental work not bad, but you get that in South China nowadays..."

"Doctor, uh..."

Doctor Lee bends over the corpse and stares at the face for a long quarter-minute. Gingerly he places a latex-coated thumb above the cheekbone.

He stands erect. "Get the duty officer."

Sinbad expels a lungful of air he didn't know he was holding and trots out the door.

———

DOCTOR LEE UNDERSTANDS the Chinese fear of death. Funeral colors or the sight of a coffin are enough to make people avert their faces and shudder. Even the number four, which sounds like the word for death, causes some of his countrymen to cringe. He, however, has spent priceless years of his youth in Edinburgh, studying medicine. A cold country, Scotland, and a wonderful place to bring you down to earth and teach you the cynicism you need for this job, for this world. Just about all of the unfortunates who were wheeled into the doctor's room had taken care, in life, to dodge ghosts and avoid the symbols of death. They were wheeled in nonetheless.

She'll be hard enough to identify without fingerprints. And no one will want to waste time with this kind of murder case. But murder it is.

He draws a scalpel across the forehead below the hairline and peels the woman's face downwards, lingering at the eyelids to confirm his suspicion. Nothing in his life compares with this, the thrill of being right, of seeing what no one else sees, of being the first to say *I know what happened*. He removes a stainless steel saw from a drawer and lays the blade parallel to the eyebrows. A younger pathologist would let the diener cut into the head with an electric saw. But power saws have a mechanical whine, and in any case Doctor Lee is a do-it-yourselfer. He presses the blade against the forehead, feels the bone yield subtly. A few even strokes, and he's cut a trench in the cranium. Ten minutes, and he'll be through.

No, modern gadgets are fine in their place, but for opening a skull, there's nothing like the *feel* of a hand saw.

PART I

CHAPTER 1

Your purpose is unclear to those who carry weight, so you carry none. To the working public you're an anomaly, a moment of static, a fragment of cosmic interference. To the economy of Hong Kong you're a subatomic particle that appears for a nanosecond and then disappears so fast that its very existence can be doubted. In Hong Kong cash terms, you are a speck of dust, a quark, a lepton. You add up to less than zero. You are a musician.

—LEO STERN

THE STRINGS BITE into Hector Siefert's fingertips; six weeks without playing have softened his calluses. The fiddlers and flute players will have practiced every day during their summer holiday. But Hector is a double bass player, and though he's not getting old—he's twenty-six—lugging the bass on planes is. So he needs to get back his chops, which won't take long. A few days, perhaps. In any event his tone is still warm, the pitches true as ever.

He begins with scales, from the low E up into the highest regions, where the bass begins to sound like a terrified rhino. Then a few exercises, and finally whole bleeding chunks of Strauss, Mahler, Mozart.

His long and knobby fingers have known the notes for years. Once, while performing Beethoven's Fifth, Hector turned to the second page of his part to find a photo of a female nude taped over his music—a trombonist's prank. Hector played the symphony from memory, while the woman in the picture urged him on with all of her airbrushed charms. That's everyone's second-favorite Hector Siefert story.

After he tires—his body clock is still synced to New York, after all—he rests his bass in a corner, picks up the phone, and punches the keys. A feeble tune sounds, one he's tried to forget all summer. *E, D, F-sharp, D ...*

"Hi, Zenobia. Hector. This is the last message, okay? Not that I'm getting tired of leaving them. It's good hearing your voice on the recording ...

"But it hurts. I just want you to know that, the way you don't call back. If you're trying to hurt me, then fine. You're doing a great job. But if you're not ... call me." He hangs up.

Leo will make it better, he thinks. *Got to see Leo.*

Out in the hall he finds Mrs. Lam returning home with her rust-colored Pomeranian. Fiftyish and plump, Mrs. Lam walks with the side-to-side hobble of those who have tried forward motion in their youth and found it overrated.

"Back from holiday?" she asks in Cantonese.

"Yes. USA."

"Who pays for the ticket?"

"My employer."

She nods, presumably recalculating the relative deals life has cut them, and ambles to her door.

———

TWENTY MINUTES LATER Hector is in North Point. It's late afternoon, a time when trams clatter and hum down King's Road every two minutes, commuters' flesh pressed against their windows like bean curd in glass jars. Blue double-decker buses spew humanity onto the pavement and ingest more at every corner.

Hector turns down Tong Shui Road, weaving past people clutching newspapers, lugging briefcases and shouting lies into BlackBerries. He enters a storefront, Poon's Restaurant to readers of Chinese, anonymous to Westerners. As he seals the door against the rush hour madness, a brass bell sounds.

A-natural.

Inside it's serene and dark. No light except from the streetside windows and a red five-watter radiating upon Kwan Dai, the big-brother god who smiles placidly from his post above the cash register.

Poon's is cavernous by modern Hong Kong standards, one of the old, high-ceilinged storefronts that became obsolete when air-conditioning came into fashion. The floors are unpolished wood, the walls cheap paneling to shoulder height, with dusty seafoam-colored plaster above. Ceiling fan blades twirl languorously on filth-coated poles.

Most of Poon's pew-like benches are empty in the dead hours between lunch and dinner. At a front table two old men in polo shirts sit playing Chinese chess, Tsing Taos fizzing at their elbows. One player studies the board soundlessly; the other taps a spare piece rhythmically on the glass tabletop. *Click ... click ... click.* I'm back in Hong Kong, thinks Hector. A Western chess player would have strangled an opponent who made that much noise.

Apart from the twitching hand of the chess player, the only visible movement in the room is a rill of smoke from a figure puffing away in a back booth.

"Leo! You bastard!" Hector calls. The figure jerks to attention and waves Hector over.

"I was surprised you're here," Hector says as he slides into the booth. "It's not the last minute yet." When he can, Leo Stern boards a plane before midnight on the night of the last performance, and returns scant hours before the downbeat of the new season. A few of the players mistake his attitude for contempt of orchestral playing in general, but it's merely Leo's dislike of transitions, of waiting around.

"I've been here all summer. Ran out of money." Leo stubs out his Camel. A copy of the *Post* sits folded by his elbow. "What about you? How's Zen? Heard from her?"

Hector shakes his head and the subject is dropped. "So, what's so important that you've been leaving messages for me?" There had been four, all of them a simple *Hector, man, call me when you get in. I'm at Poon's.*

"Hang on. *Poon sin-sahng, Lam Mui!*" Blue Girl, the Chinese name for Leo's beer of habit. Like Hector, Leo slips easily back into Cantonese when he returns to Hong Kong. Leo's is better, though. He listens more, uses it more, has had more local girlfriends teasing Chinese words from his lips.

"Seen this?" Leo says. He slides over the paper, open to page three.

Symphony Conductor's Ability and Character
Sour Notes to Dissatisfied Performers
BY TWINKIE CHOI

As the Hong Kong Symphony Orchestra tunes up for a new season, dissonant rumblings are being heard. A number of players want to sack Shao Din-yan, the orchestra's Music

Director. Mr. Shao, a graduate of the Guangzhou Conservatory of Music, was appointed following the departure of Klaus Schofeld, who resigned due to health problems in the middle of last season.

"Morale has never been worse," says Chiu Shun-fu, a French horn player. "Shao is a terrible conductor. No wonder people are deserting the orchestra." Last May two English players left in mid-season without giving notice.

Bonson Ng, General Manager of the orchestra, discounts the anti-Shao statements. "Most of the orchestra is solidly behind Maestro Shao. They realize his goal is to improve the orchestra and get the best possible performance out of the musicians."

Roger Snell, chairman of the Players' Committee, the de facto musician's union, would not comment on the matter.

Poon, a slight, bald seventy-year-old, brings the beer. He beams at the sight of Hector.

"Mista See-fat! Ho loy mo geen!" Long time no see. At the mention of Hector's name, one of the chess players looks over and grins, flashing a row of yellow teeth.

"Did you ever read such bullshit?" asks Leo, lighting another Camel.

Hector skims the article again, and smiles. "Twinkie, eh?" He delights in Hong Kong's tradition of taking whimsical English names. "Well, maybe they'll give Shao the boot."

"Not a chance. Shao's got some weird hold on things. Can't figure it out."

Across the restaurant the chess player is still at it. *Click... click... click...*

Leo looks tired. Most of his face hides behind his brown beard and unwashed brown hair. His green eyes are aflame as always, but the sockets surrounding them are grey and puffy. His age could be anything from mid-twenties to late thirties. He wears jeans and an olive drab T-shirt, the sleeves of which have been torn off to display rippled arms. Hector has never known Leo to work out, but women notice his body.

They drink in silence.

The conductor Shao is a phony, and they both know it. The resignation of Schofeld, a washed-up hack himself, paved the way for something that the board had craved for years: the hiring of a Chinese music director. In post-1997 Hong Kong, it doesn't look good for a *gweilo* to be in charge. Hong Kongers had to put up with Westerners in high places for a century and a half. Brits in the civil service, European professors in the universities, Americans running their firms' Hong Kong offices, all of them using talented locals to run interference because they can't put two Cantonese words together.

Hector breaks the silence: "I'm surprised you're still here, to be honest."

Leo smiles. "Hey, it's a living. Earn money to give away."

Leo married a voluptuous flautist a decade ago, then left without bothering to divorce her. Claudia eventually sued for child support, even though the child was from a previous marriage. She threatened to turn him over to the IRS, assuming correctly that he wasn't declaring his Hong Kong earnings.

"You should get away this year, do some auditions," Hector says. "There are always viola openings. You could go to the States again, Europe."

"Can't afford to take any auditions this time around, how about that? Eight hundred U.S. each time you fly to the States. Play ten minutes and hear them say, 'Thank you, that's all.' The bank canceled my VISA card, can you believe that?"

He takes another drag on the Camel. "Whatever. Listen, Hec. I called you because I need you to do something." He tops up both their beers. "This is serious. There's an opening in St. Gallen, that's in Switzerland, small place but a nice orchestra. I can get you in. I need you to take the job." He puffs again and exhales upwards, adding fresh smoke stains to the fresco of cobwebs. The health people fine Poon regularly for his filthy ceiling. Poon is too old to wield a mop so high up himself. He priced a cleaner, but decided instead to pay the fine.

"Right."

"No bullshit. I know the principal bassist. She'll trust my recommendation."

"You know her that well?"

"Shaved her pussy once."

"Thanks for the information."

"Picture's worth a thousand words." He drains half his beer.

"What do you mean you 'need' me to take the job?"

Another drag, and the words come out in a torrent of blue smoke. "A week from now you could be playing real music. It'd make me feel I'd done at least one fucking worthwhile thing in Hong Kong."

Switzerland, Hector thinks. Pristine, bland, organized. About as different as you can get from Hong Kong, except that both are places money goes to misbehave in private. *The Swiss would care about his music*, he thinks. They would worship quality there. But it's out of the question.

Leo reads Hector's mind, slams down his empty glass. "Come on, Hec, screw the contract. You know a good thing when you see it. And you can't go back to the States, right?"

Hector shakes his head. "It's okay here."

Leo locks eyes with Hector. "Look, man, it's not going to last. Now's the time to get out."

Hec shrugs, exhales. "Maybe I'll put away some money this year. We can get out together. I'll spot you the plane fare. How does that sound?"

Leo thinks, then says, "Yeah. Let's drink to that." He orders another Lam Mui. The discussion is over. Leo never beats a dead horse.

"Did you catch what we're playing on tour?" Leo says.

"*Turandot*. It's chasing me, Leo. To the end of my days." How Puccini's last opera got Hector booted from Tulsa, and how he'd made it to Hong Kong just ahead of the news, is everyone's favorite Hector Siefert story.

Halfway into the third beer, the clang of the North Point tram bell filters through the windowpane.

"Whassat?" says Leo, nodding toward the sound.

"G-flat."

Leo looks at Hector. "Shit, Hec, get out of this place. Take the Swiss gig. They'll get a replacement. One phone call." He downs his beer.

"Got to get back now," Hector says, standing up. "Doing anything next couple of days? Play some duets?"

Leo nods.

"I'll get this one," says Hector.

Leo breaks a smile. "It's your life."

"Later, Leo." Hector slaps Leo's bicep.

Leo hardens into his smoking pose again, the way Hector found him. Hector drops a couple of bills on the counter and leaves.

CHAPTER 2

TO: DI Herman Lok
Re: Service Enhancement Campaign
Phase II: Teamwork in the 21st Century

On 18 September the Department Commissioner's Office will hold a seminar on Teamwork in the 21st Century. The seminar is designed to complement the material covered in the previous seminar, Empowerment through Win-Win Relationships.

The program provides a new paradigm for creating effective teamwork by focusing on clear communication and sharing values. Participants will also benefit from a set of benchmarks designed to create a work culture focused on value-added community service.

Topics Covered:

- Moving from Top-Down Culture to A Teamwork Culture
- Communication—Teamwork's Lifeblood
- Rewarding Team Players
- Creating a Feedback Loop
- 21 Tips for Potent Collaboration

Seminar will be held at the Police Training School at Wong Chuk Hang, 9am to 4pm. All are expected to attend. Please arrange your schedules accordingly.

DETECTIVE INSPECTOR HERMAN LOK strokes the delete key as he reads, then whacks it down hard enough to startle Fu, the hoary station sergeant, who's padding down the corridor outside Lok's office.

"That's the way I feel about them too," says Fu in a low rasp, before he disappears. Lok smiles, amused at Fu's assumption that the computer, rather than the message on it, had set him off.

Lok stands and rubs his eyes. He's stayed late this evening to write up the headwaiter who drowned his wife's lover in a bathroom sink, and add notes about the loan shark who turned up dead behind a stall at the flower market. With those reports done, he's turned to his e-mail, something he rarely bothers with during regular office hours. The killers won't e-mail you their confessions, he tells his men.

Outside Lok's window is the Tsim Sha Tsui peninsula, at this hour the tawdry carnival of neon glorified by guidebooks in fifteen languages. Up close, he knows, those lights are traps, luring men to bars where marked-up drinks are watered down, and then to whorehouses where wallets vanish and microbes linger. On more wholesome streets the names of fashion designers radiate from shop windows, hawking goods as genuine as a pimp's promise. Day after day tourists from drab cinderblock towns, dropped into this ocean of neon for the first time, feel their hearts dash ahead of them. They race through the streets to catch up, for fear they won't be able to shed their money fast enough. Young men, just cut loose from cramped warships, breathe faster as they give their billfolds a prurient squeeze.

But Lok is immune to neon panic. At a distance, the play of the colors is restful to his eyes.

"Ah Lok, sir?"

The voice at the door brings him out of his thoughts, makes him aware he's been leaning on the table behind him, breaking a police taboo. That's how you bring on new cases, everyone knows. He straightens up.

"What is it, Ears?" His youngest Detective Constable stands in the doorway.

"Ah Lok, sir. The ADC wants to see you."

Lok nods. Serves him right for sitting on a table. "Thanks. Shouldn't you be getting home?"

"I'll be leaving soon, sir."

Not a chance, Lok knows. Cops get wound up so tight by the sixteen-hour days in Crime that everything else seems like a quaint hobby that time won't allow anymore. "Ears," he says, staring again out the window. "What the hell is a feedback loop?

"Sir?"

"Never mind."

Down the corridor Assistant District Commander K.K. Kwan, one ear to the phone, gestures him in. Lok knows to sit down, something a PC would never do. The faded chair has served eight years, Lok twenty-two.

Kwan is shorter and slighter than Lok, perhaps ten years older. He wears wire-rim spectacles which fail to shield the world from his piercing stare. His skin is clear, his bald head glowing with health under the institutional fluorescent lights of the Yau Ma Tei—Tsim Sha Tsui District Police Station—Yau Tsim for short. A nameplate on his desk, half buried by manila folders, says ADC CRIME K.K. KWAN.

Kwan hangs up. "We've got a body, Herman. Unknown female,

turned up in the Typhoon Shelter Saturday."

"Jumper or drowner?"

"We don't know yet, but the pathologist thinks something's wrong."

"Cause of death?"

"Nothing yet. I've just said as much to Regional."

"And they don't want anything to do with it, of course."

Kwan smiles. "They said, and I quote, 'Have you got a chopper cut, knife in the heart, bullet in the head? If you don't, then what are you calling for?'"

"So this one's ours?"

"This one's yours, Herman."

Until we get a suspect, thinks Lok. While the case is a long shot, Regional wants nothing to do with it. None of the footwork, the man-hours, and, of course, the likelihood of failure that goes with a job like this. It'll all change if Yau Tsim District comes close to solving it. Regional will take the case over, thank them for their work, make the arrest, and bask in the credit.

"Let's get an ID first," says Kwan. "Get your team together, go down to the mortuary first thing in the morning. Have a look, find out exactly what Doctor Lee's talking about. Talk to the UB men who found her."

Kwan removes his eyeglasses, wipes them with a cloth he keeps in his desk drawer. "Too late for the Uniform Branch to do much tonight," he says. "They've marked off the scene."

"We'll do a search at dawn, then."

"No. I'll send out the PTU."

"Do you think that's necessary? The death could have happened anywhere. Possibly the mainland." He'd never think of calling out the Police Tactical Unit for less than an emergency.

"Herman," says Kwan, replacing his spectacles and looking

straight at Lok, "From what the doctor told me, it's not going to be easy identifying the body. It'll take time and resources I'd rather put elsewhere. In short, I hate this case. You're going to hate this case. It's a hot night, and Bravo Company hasn't done anything in weeks. Let's make them get out their torches and earn their money. Then they can hate this case, too." He snatches up the phone.

"Who knows?" he says, punching an extension. "Maybe they'll come up with a finger."

———

THE CORPSE FLICKERS white and black, a supine phantom, as the photographer closes in on the face, the chest, the remains of the hands with his strobe.

Inspector Lok looks up from Doctor Lee's neatly paragraphed notes, the pathologist's attempt to fill in the many missing parts of the naked, eyeless, fingerless, putrescent thing on the table. Where an organ has vanished, Doctor Lee has supplied a reason, or at least a speculation. He's also filled in her age, her income bracket, her probable city of origin. They fit together like parts of a puzzle, the last of which, Lok fears, will be his to find.

"And it was just the eyes that convinced you?" Lok says, hoping against hope that Doctor Lee will reconsider an opinion for the first time in his career. They both know what lies ahead: a body, no identification, no motive, another unsolved case to blemish the force's clear-up rate.

"The woman has had her eyelids surgically altered—what we call an upper blepharoplasty, though it's commonly known as Westernization of the eyelid. Her nose has been built up as well—made more pointed. Add to that the fact that her dental work is top-quality. The woman is clearly a well-off Hong Konger, but she was dressed in the cheapest Chinese-made clothing imaginable. There is no way a woman who spends thousands to look like a *gweipoh* would wear a Chinese Emporium cotton T-shirt and shorts."

Inspector Lok thinks of Dora. No surgery, thank God, but his wife wouldn't own so much as a handkerchief that didn't have an Italian name on it.

"So you're saying someone dumped her in the water, and wanted her to look like an II or a fisherwoman in case she washed up on shore."

"I'm not saying that. I'm describing salient features of the body and the clothes. As far as I can tell, the two don't match. One fits a well-heeled Hong Kong girl, the other an illegal immigrant. The rest is up to Crime."

Inspector Lok looks once more at the rotted figure on the table. Doctor Lee's judgment will be in his report to the Coroner. It would take a rash man to hold out against the Doctor, who dines with the big balls, who hears the gossip and complaints from men higher in the force than Lok will ever be.

The Doctor continues the examination as Lok watches.

"Pity about the missing fingers," says Doctor Lee. "The body hadn't been in the water long enough for degloving to occur. We might have had a fingerprint for you."

He's slicing open the neck. Lok knows what he's looking for.

"The hyoid bone is intact," the Doctor says.

"So she wasn't strangled?"

"We can't say that, unfortunately. This is a young woman. Our hyoids are tough in our twenties. A good strong hand can cut off oxygen without breaking it."

"Bruising on the throat?"

"Too much flesh gone, alas. I can't tell."

"Any evidence of defensive wounds?"

"No, none. Which is not to say that none existed. From the deteriorated state of the hands, it's impossible to say if there are any."

"But without defensive wounds…"

"I do not detect wounds, Inspector," he says in clipped tones. "Nor do I detect a lack of wounds. There is simply not enough flesh left on the hands to draw a conclusion. Please don't infer that I am dismissing the possibility of defensive wounds."

How like the Doctor to consider that a satisfactory answer. While Lok prides himself on his ability to apply logical reasoning to problems, the Doctor has made it into a religion. The result is good forensics but poor company.

Doctor Lee works through the body systematically, examining organs and placing tissue samples in vials. Finally, he steps back from the body and sheds his latex gloves. "That's all I can do now," he says. "Nothing out of the ordinary as far as I can see. We'll have to wait for toxicology. Of course, with a body in such a state …"

Lok reads a small sign, printed in English, pinned to a bulletin board behind the Doctor's desk.

The internist knows everything and does nothing.
The surgeon knows nothing and does everything.
The psychologist knows nothing and does nothing.
The pathologist knows everything and does everything—two
    weeks too late.

"So you're saying that you have no physical evidence for murder?"

"Not yet. But we have a girl who probably never did a day's hard work in her life turn up in the harbor, dressed like a fishmonger.

You'll agree that the circumstances are extremely suspicious."

I will indeed agree, thinks Lok, like it or not.

"When do you think the surgery was done?"

The Doctor doesn't have to look at the body again to offer an answer.

"Not too long ago. Within six months at the most. That must be of help."

Lok welcomes any help he can get on this one. He walks out of the Public Mortuary and steps into the Ford Laser that will take him back to the Yau Tsim District station.

He's not convinced the victim is from Hong Kong, doesn't see why Doctor Lee is so suspicious. The doctor isn't the one who will have to dredge up an ID, a motive, a suspect. It's the worst kind of case, one that starts with nothing. The kind of case he'd give up in a second. And then, as he has done countless times before, he begins to sketch out the case in his mind.

CHAPTER 3

HECTOR'S RIBBON OF eighth notes, crisp and even, unrolls like a silk carpet beneath Leo's melody. After the last note dies away, Leo says, "Let's do the last eight again, and put a little ritard on it." The second time around, the tiny slowdown lays the minuet to rest a little more gently.

Leo puts down the viola and uncorks a fifth of Wild Turkey with a musical *doonk*.

"B-natural," says Hector.

"Bastard."

"No big deal."

Hector places his bass back in the corner, and they assume their usual breeze-shooting positions, Hector sprawled on a faded leather chair, and Leo on a set of pillows on the floor.

"Nah, it's a gift," says Leo, filling two glasses. "Can't deny it. Like mathematical genius, or real tits."

A gift, all right. Hector comes at the world ears first: he never forgets a sound or its pitch. As a child, it was his mom's blender in F natural, the vacuum cleaner's G-sharp hum, the ping of his spoon on the cereal bowl in the morning, sometimes a slightly flat D, sometimes an E, sometimes dead between E and F, depending on which bowl his mom set out.

To Hector, each of the twelve tones has a separate personality. An A-flat isn't just lower than A-natural; the notes have different sounds, as plums and oranges have different tastes. A C-natural sounds clear but narrow, like the call of a seagull. D-sharp is full and kind of fuzzy, D-natural hard and shiny, like polished chrome. A couple of years ago he tried to explain it to Leo. Leo just shook his head.

The keys are all unique as well. Hector's B major is cold, a dark blue, like a winter's twilight in New York City. D minor is a warm crimson; mulled wine. And G major. Oh man, G major is hot yellow, a carnival color, the luminescent feathers of some wild-ass tropical bird, the flaming burst of a Roman candle at midnight. Nothing feels as good as G major. It's like hanging out with your best friend.

Hector knows that his neurons map differently from most people's; some lobe or other is slightly fatter than average, physical evidence of the extraordinary way his grey matter processes music. Only one in ten thousand has his gift. To Hector the aurally imperfect masses are like the color blind, afflicted with something sad beyond his understanding. How can they not recognize a pitch by name? It would be like forgetting the same faces again and again. He'd go mad.

Hector and Leo sip without speaking, lost in the echo of Beethoven and the aromas of Hector's flat: ginger flowers, next door's cooking grease, mildew, Kentucky sour mash. The flat is furnished sparsely, with hand-me downs from former HKSO players. Hector's suitcase, cracked open and overflowing, sits by the door. The colorless rumble of Kowloon traffic, rebounding on oceans of concrete fifteen stories below, pours in the window.

Eventually Leo speaks.

"So much music being played, and no one doing it for the right reasons."

"You are."

"Yeah, you, me, Clem, Porvin. Chiu. The rest, man, why do they bother? Why do they fucking bother?"

"They bother because they love music."

"They don't know what music is, and you know it! Last season they played the *Pathetique* as if they'd never seen the music before! And so they blame everything else—the shitty salary, the incompetent management, the General Committee. Anything to keep from having to pull their finger out of their ass and start practicing."

"So let's get you out of here. As soon as I save the cash, I'll bankroll your auditions. You can pay me back when you get a real playing job."

Leo laughs. "Here we are, each trying to spring the other from the Hong Kong Symphony. That should tell you something." He lifts his glass in a mock toast.

"To escape!"

"Escape!" Hector says.

Leo knocks his drink back. "Let's hear some music," he says. "Do the cork."

Hector refills their glasses and pops the cork on the bottle one more time. Whatever note comes out, that's the key of the next piece they listen to.

"F-sharp."

"Shit. Tough one."

"Nah. Korngold symphony."

The phone bleeps. *Rapidly alternating F and A natural.* As if in response, Leo says, "I need a smoke." He rises and heads to the balcony as Hector grabs the receiver and moves to the bathroom.

"It's Roger, Hec." Roger Snell is the Symphony's tympanist and chairman of the Players' Committee.

"Hi Roger. What's up?"

"How was your summer?"

"Fine, Roger. What's up?"

"Zenobia? What's she up to lately?"

Hector takes a slow breath. "Roger ..."

"Look, Hec, I need your help. You saw the paper yesterday? Well, it's getting worse. A petition to get rid of Shao is circulating now."

"Great," says Hector, flipping up the toilet seat. "Where do I sign?"

"That's not funny. This could backfire, Hec."

"So what are you saying?" Hector starts to piss. If Roger hears, he doesn't acknowledge it.

"What I'm saying is that Chiu Shun-fu and a bunch of people are out to dump Shao. They've written down what's wrong with him in a petition ..."

"Must be one long petition."

" ... and when everyone signs it they'll give it to the Committee. If this gets out there will be trouble—they might even cancel the tour. They hate bad publicity."

"Isn't any publicity good publicity?"

"Trust me, Hec, the Committee's full of businessmen, doing this for public service. If we throw it back at them, it's a big loss of face. We don't want that."

"We don't?"

"No. And stop doing that! Look, am I the only one who feels this way? Tell me if I am, and I'll quit. Really, I will."

"You're the only one who feels this way."

A pause. Leo, still on the balcony, is shouting something into his cellphone.

"Shit, Hec, thanks a lot," says Roger. "I was hoping that you'd be sensible."

"That's your problem, Roger. You're sensible. If I were sensible, I wouldn't be playing music in this place, or any place, for that matter. But I am, and I like playing under good conductors who know what the hell they're doing. You know what Shao is. Is that what you want? To play shitty concerts because Shao doesn't know how to rehearse an orchestra? That's your idea of a career?"

"Hec ..."

"Why are you in the orchestra anyway? So you can get free plane tickets and see the world? I'm doing it for the music, Roger, and anything that makes that better, including firing a shithouse conductor, is fine with me." He punctuates the last word with a flush of the toilet.

Roger mumbles a good-by. Hector shuts off the phone—*B natural*—zips up, and washes his hands. "Roger Snell is spooked about the petition," he shouts over the rushing water. "Wants me to help him calm things down."

He returns to the living room, towel in hand. "Anyway, where were we? What about F-sharp minor? Haydn's *Farewell*, Mahler's Tenth ..."

Leo's bourbon sits by the pillow, gathering pearls of condensation from the steamy air. The viola case lies open on the coffee table. And Leo is gone.

CHAPTER 4

MILLION MAN IS the last to arrive. Lok marks his entrance with the briefest glance as the younger man peels off his cashmere blazer and takes a seat across from the other DPCs on the team.

They're in the Hot Room. Ten years ago, when a crime wave had Kowloon East scrambling to cover their territory, the Station Sergeant brought in a *feng shui* man to find the problem. The geomancer, an elderly gent who made his reputation freeing up the *chi* in the town's major bank headquarters, frowned and clucked his way through the consultation. It turned out that a new satellite dish atop a nearby hotel was deflecting half the city's evil spirits down Canton Road into the room where they now sat. The room, sadly, was no match—the window opened inwards, drawing in all the destructive energy. A poorly-placed door, moreover, was letting good *chi* escape.

It was a tough job. For a stout fee, the expert repositioned the station's fish tank. More important, he declared that this room's windows needed to be shut, and blinds drawn, at all times. In went a jade plant to slow down the good *chi*, and a *ba gua* mirror to bounce the bad *chi* back to the hotel.

In three days crime was down, a few key arrests were made,

and policemen were getting home in time to see their children before bedtime.

Now the Hot Room is used rarely, and only by those who know how to keep meetings brief.

To Lok's right is Old Ko, short and beefy, with sullen eyes traced by black hornrims. He's Lok's age, too old to be a constable and still hold dreams of a promotion.

Next to him is Big Pang, six inches taller than Old Ko, ten years younger.

Opposite the older team members is Million Man, still in his twenties. According to station gossip he's had his nickname *man yan mai*—"millions fall in love with him"—since secondary school, when he started beefing up his playboy act with hair gel and loud shirts. Later came silk suits and cars, the latter of which he couldn't afford but which he bought just to hear women squeal when they jumped into the leather and chrome cockpit.

Sitting on Million Man's right is Ears. The source of his nickname is obvious.

"We have a girl in her twenties," says Lok. "Washed up Saturday in the Typhoon Shelter. Cause of death unknown, but it's possible that she was murdered and dressed like a fisherwoman to keep anyone from getting curious. We know she's not really an II because she had cosmetic surgery to her eyes and nose."

"Ah Lok, sir," says Million Man, "I heard a PC did some surgery on her at the scene." The DPC's laugh. Lok smiles.

"Million Man," he says, "you'll check missing persons. She's been dead two weeks to a month, so we need a list of women age 23 to 30 reported missing in that time."

Million Man nods.

"Don't count the ones that are still at your apartment sleeping," says Big Pang. A few more laughs.

Lok turns to Ears. "I'm told that a lot of girls who go in for this kind of surgery are the topless waitress type, so we'll have to make the rounds of bars, see if anyone stopped showing up for work recently." Ears smiles and lowers his head, slightly embarrassed.

"Ears might faint," says Million Man. "Better give that job to me."

Lok ignores the remark. The same thought crossed his mind, but he needs to bring Ears up to speed. "Old Ko, you can accompany Ears."

"There's the surgery," Lok continues. "It was probably done in a Chinese private hospital. So Big Pang, you'll check the doctors who do this operation, and get lists of recent patients. Check if any have disappeared recently. That's all."

Lok rises to leave the room. Million Man says, "Too bad she didn't get her tits done. That's my kind of investigation."

Old Ko finally spoke up. "Yes, it is. One fake ought to be able to spot two."

LOK ENTERS A landscape familiar yet alien. Slowly it dawns: his chair, the comfortable one he sits in to read the paper, is gone. Lok ransacks his mind to think of some reason for the missing furniture—a new sofa on the way, perhaps—but if Dora told him, he's forgotten.

Dinner is long over, and he sees no movement in the living room apart from churning images on the television. There are sounds, though: Esmeralda clattering dishes and whacking cabinet doors shut. A bathroom faucet gushing. Dora's telephone voice. The air-conditioner's hum.

Lok moves to the bedroom to change his shirt, which has already moistened and cooled in the short hike from the carpark. Of some seventeen thousand breaths he takes each day, perhaps two or three hundred have not been filtered and refrigerated by Hitachi, Samsung, or one of the other giant electronics firms of Asia.

In the bedroom he finds Dora standing by her dresser. "Herman," she says. "come here."

"What is it, Dora?" She's poking through her jewelry box.

"She wore my earrings on Sunday!" she whispers.

"Who?" He can't bring himself to whisper himself.

"Esmeralda. She's been getting into my jewelry and wearing my pearl earrings. The little ones you gave me." Lok gave Dora the single-pearl earrings many years ago, when they were newlyweds and money was short. He'd saved for six months. Now she owns some clusters and a necklace, which she bought for herself. She never wears the single pearls anymore.

"Are they gone?"

"No. But when I first suspected her, I started leaving one earring on the post, and one off. That way, if she returned the earrings with both backs on the posts, I'd know she'd used them. See? These have both backs on the posts."

Lok looks at Dora. She is his age, still exquisitely slim, still a very acceptable facsimile of the beauty he married nineteen years ago. And like all inspector's wives, a better detective than her husband.

"Maybe we should fire her," she says.

"No, Dora. It takes ages to get a good amah. She's doing fine."

"But Herman, I can't have her going through my things!"

"No, of course. But sometimes a talk is enough. Let me say a few words to her later."

She pats his arm as he slips his shirt off to wash up.

Afterwards he sees Kitty is at the dining table, textbook and notebook out. She's eleven, as round and pudgy as a Shanghainese soup dumpling, with braids dangling from either side of her genial moon face.

"What happened to the chair, *dao see*?" Lok asks her.

"Mama took it away. She doesn't like it. It was too old and soft, and she said it made you look old and soft when you sat in it."

He can always get the straight story from Kitty, who is alarmingly sincere and open-hearted. At school her nickname is *fei-fei*—fatty—but at home they call her *dao see*, or black bean, because she was born tiny with a full head of black hair.

"Well, then, where's Kelvin?"

"At the movies."

"Edna?"

Kitty says nothing.

He scans the room and reviews his furniture options. There's the leather sofa, which he doesn't much care for. A club chair, but it doesn't face the television. That leaves a cane chair, not the most comfortable, but at least he can draw up a footstool and relax with the news.

As he flips on the TV, Esmeralda walks in.

"Would you like something to eat, sir?" she asks in English.

"Yes. Nothing big, though."

"Fine, sir."

"And no need for all the dishes when it's only me." Dora insists on a full setting.

Halfway into the market report Lok hears the door unlatching. Edna walks in and treads silently past Lok. Conscious that he's being avoided, he glances in her direction. Immediately he's on his feet.

"What ... when did you do that?"

"Today," she says in a casual tone, but her eyes avoid his. "It's very popular."

Her hair is now platinum. The blonde color transfigures the seventeen-year-old into something foreign, as if she's somehow deserted her family and her race.

"But why?" is all he can say.

"I like it."

"I don't. Get rid of it."

She turns away from him, walks to the kitchen. Lok suspects she is handling him, refusing to get into an argument, which infuriates him.

"I see girls with hair like that every day in the station," he says, raising his voice to be heard. "Triads' girlfriends, all kinds of women you wouldn't want to look like."

"How do you know who I want to look like?" She opens the refrigerator, grabs a carton of chrysanthemum tea.

"That's enough! Look, what will they think of you at the University with hair like that? Your professors want serious students, not ..." He's afraid to choose a word from the ones that come to mind.

"I don't want to talk about it now, *Ba Ba*. It's done."

"We'll talk about it Sunday on Cheung Chau."

She pauses. "I won't be there."

Lok stares at the stranger in the kitchen.

CHAPTER 5

HECTOR AWAKENS SWADDLED in limp, sweaty sheets. The air-conditioner having died before the summer, he has nothing but an open window and a desk fan to get him through the nights.

Slowly he becomes conscious that something has disturbed his sleep, something beyond the heat and the clammy bedclothes, beyond the stiff neck from the fan and the teary eyes and raw throat from the mattress mold. Beyond the mosquitoes and beyond even the throb in his left temple, a throb he recognizes as a hangover when he sees the bottle sitting upright on the table. It was a question that awakened him, the one he'd tried to answer last night, getting nowhere but drunk.

Where the hell is Leo?

He'd dismissed his friend's quick exit with a shrug at first. Out of cigarettes, perhaps.

At nightfall Hector tried calling Leo's cell number, but that, said a recorded voice, was no longer in service. Yet Leo had been using a cellphone on the balcony. Nothing made sense.

He trudges to the bathroom, stares in the mirror, imagines Leo's voice. *What's really getting to you Hector? That I've disappeared? Or just that your ass has been left behind?*

Nothing left but to go to rehearsal. Leo might well be there, he knows. Leo's done that before, pulled a beer-soaked all-nighter and then blown everyone out of the water the next day, nailing every note of Shostakovich's Tenth at the first read-through. Hector dresses, grabs Leo's viola case, and exits his flat.

BACKSTAGE AT THE Grand Theatre he's unlocking his bass trunk when a voice speaks to him.

"Did you hear they were doing a pops concert of 'Fifties favorites? The program said *Holiday for Strings*, so none of the viola players showed up."

Hector laughs, turns to face Porvin Yeh, whose heart-shaped face bears rimless spectacles, round as dollar coins, and a pathetic moustache. He wears a Chicago Bulls T-shirt, and carries a violin and bow.

"How did the Cleveland audition go?" Hector asks, raising his voice to be heard amid the pre-tuning cacophony.

Porvin shrugs. "How do most people's Cleveland auditions go? A guy from Utah got it. I heard him, he was tremendous. Makes you think. In what other profession can you be better than anyone and still be in Utah?"

"What about the viola opening?"

"Still open. I thought Leo would go for it."

"So did I, but he couldn't afford the trip. Have you seen him?"

"Wish I had," he says, moving off. "He owes me a couple of hundred." Leo is nowhere in sight.

Hector opens the white fiberglass bass trunk, which is as large as a New Kingdom sarcophagus, and extracts his bass, a booming Czech five-stringer. Some sort of film has condensed onto the fingerboard during the summer, making the strings grimy to the touch. Hector wipes them with a cloth, then checks over the bass for seams that might have loosened in the summer humidity.

The climate always wins in the end, Hector. The humidity is the vanguard of the eroding force of Hong Kong. First it destroys your things, then your soul. It takes your books. Then your shoes, belts, any clothes you forget to take out and wash once in a while. And finally, your fiddle starts to come apart at the seams. You think that's the worst it can do, take away your art and your livelihood, but that's only a shot across the bow, my friend. The rot has only begun.

Leo could mix metaphors like no one else.

It's five to ten. The musicians, with their instruments, music stands, open cases and various rags and bottles, pack the stage from end to end. The stage is awash with multi-tonal riffs and multi-lingual conversation. Everyone who isn't warming up or practicing a tricky passage is catching up on summer news and gossip. The last of the bassists to take his place, Hector moves to the stool beside Clement Farraday, who is repeating a two-bar phrase in the bass part, one of the famous traps in Mozart's *Jupiter Symphony*. One of those licks you get down when you're young, or you never master it. Clem tears through the eighth notes, his fingers a blur.

"This seat taken?" Hector asks.

Clem looks up and slaps a warm, heavy hand on Hector's shoulder. With fingers that size, no wonder he makes that passage look easy.

Hector presses his cheek to the neck of the bass, letting his skin and bone conduct vibrations to his inner ear. That's the only way to tune a bass when the brass jockeys are going hogwild in the back.

"Welcome back, all. I hope your summers were good."

The General Manager, Bonson Ng, has mounted the podium. He is a slight, thirtyish man, dressed impeccably in blue blazer and khaki trousers. Rimless lenses add a touch of maturity to his youthful face.

"As you know, this is shaping up to be a big year for the Hong Kong Symphony. After our opening concert we begin rehearsals for a production of Puccini's *Turandot* in Shenzhen. We're accompanying a roster of singers from Europe. Rather than use a local orchestra, they want the extra prestige of our group. I couldn't say no."

A few cheers, a few laughs. Bonson continues.

"There's more touring coming up, of course, and we're looking into recording possibilities, so I hope that we can all work together for success." Some feet shuffle in applause at the mention of recording.

"You'll see a couple of new faces on the staff. We took the opportunity to hire a professional instrument mover and crew. As I said, this is a very important year for the Symphony, so I hope that we can make wonderful music and have great fun. Thank you."

Applause and whistles, cloaked in sarcasm.

A voice from the back. "What he means is, behave yourself and shut up."

Hector notes the remark, remains quiet. As Bonson repeats the announcement in Cantonese, Hector leafs through the music of the new piece, looking for traps, passages that might be harder to play than they look. His teacher taught him the habit back at Juilliard. *Never, ever play a piece for the first time*, is how he'd put it.

The conductor emerges from the wings. He's tall and lean, with a narrow face and prominent cheekbones. His hair, though wispy on top, is long at the back, and his skull blazes in the lights of the Grand Theatre. "Welcome back," he says. "We'll do the Mozart now, and the Fong after the break."

The heavy brass disperse, leaving the core of strings and winds, and Shao raises his baton. For a moment Hector entertains the fantasy that Shao might have learned the art of conducting over the summer. But when the downbeat comes, it's the usual slow, useless sway of his arm in that bowl-shaped arc, a gesture made without the slightest regard for those who have to follow it. With no way to tell when to come in, Hector instinctively follows the concert master's bow into the opening of Mozart's 41st Symphony.

———————

AT THE BREAK, Hector lays down his bass and takes a seat beside Chiu Shun-fu, who plays third horn. Their hands meet in a fierce grip. Chiu's was the voice he'd heard before, translating the real meaning of the general manager's words. He's Hector's age, with close-cropped hair and a small goatee.

He should be playing first horn, Hector knows, but Shao won't give him the position, preferring to keep Chiu in the third horn chair and dangle the higher-paying position as bait at overseas auditions. Chiu stays where he is, taking orders from a procession of inferior players who happen to audition well.

"Make it to Munich this summer?" Hector asks. Chiu studied in Germany, speaks the language, loves the Bavarian countryside and the beer.

"Played the festival. Doerner wants me to come back. I might take the job."

"Great. When do you leave?"

"Not sure, Hec." He picks up his horn, sprinkles on a few drops of polish from a tiny bottle, and begins to stroke the surface with a chamois rag. "I have things to take care of here first."

"So I've been reading in the *Post*."

"It's time to get rid of Shao. Past time."

"He's bad, all right."

"It's more than that. I hate what he stands for, Hector."

Chiu polishes the horn's bell in slow, even strokes till it glows like a Bali sunrise. "I work damn hard at this thing, Hector. I don't care that conductors get the money and the glory. I really don't. They even live longer than orchestra players, did you know that? They live into their nineties while we die of ulcers or heart attacks about the time our grandchildren are born. But who cares, as long as the music is good?

"But then I see this *scheisse kerl* Shao in front of the orchestra, dragging it down, making us sound rotten. He's only on the podium because he's Chinese. He makes us all look bad. People hear us, they say, 'Is this the best the Chinese can do?' I won't take that, Hec. I'm getting Shao out of here."

Hector stands and faces the viola section, sees Leo's instrument on the chair, lying closed like a casket at a wake.

"Listen, I need to know something. Have you seen Leo anywhere?"

Chiu shakes his head and blows a quick scale.

The players begin to take their seats again. The sounds of tuning, the subtle boom of Roger Snell's kettledrum, and the current of babble all subside as players turn to their parts and rehearse passages.

Hector calls over the trumpet section. "Guys, any of you seen Leo?"

They shake their heads. "Probably in Manila," says a trumpeter.

"Locked in a Makati whorehouse," says a trombonist. They laugh.

"He's here. I saw him a couple of days ago, but he hasn't come near the orchestra."

"No shit. Then he's just smart." They laugh again.

Hector takes up his bass, strokes the strings with his bow to make sure they're in tune. The bass has been with him for eight years now, his longest intact relationship. He loves the speed of its response at the slightest touch, the evenness of its tone as he descends from one octave to the next, the lack of buzz and harshness in the upper register. And most of all, he loves that low C string, the fifth string that most double basses lack. It's a passport to a region of sound unknown to most musicians.

When Shao rises to the podium and the room quiets down, he notices that he's been humming an old tune: "Holiday for Strings."

CHAPTER 6

DOCTOR THEXDER YU sinks back into his leather chair, a gesture meant to calm the girl, give her confidence in him. Nothing matters more to the doctor. Skill and knowledge are vital, but careers in cosmetic surgery are made by those who can inspire a patient's faith. Deft as he is with the knife, if he can't get young women to go under it, he'll be out of business in a week, left to pay his $95,000 monthly office rent and the mortgage on his Repulse Bay flat, perhaps forced to surrender his Jaguar or his wife's Benz, call his sons home from Stanford, and lose face with his colleagues and friends at the Hong Kong Country Club.

This one's name is Windice Lai, a twenty-two year old who chatters in a small, animated voice. Doctor Yu nods patiently at her words, but in his mind he is already cutting, reshaping, and stitching her flesh. She's lovely, full of the cheerful radiance of youth, with a face that many girls would give up twenty years of their life for.

"Believe it or not, it was my hairstylist who told me about you," she says.

Dr. Yu raises his eyebrows and cracks an ironic smile, as if to say, *Now I've heard everything*. As if the hairstylists he operates on commission weren't vital to his business. There are six of them, and they're good, thanks to the training his nurse Edith Chan has given them. *First,* she tells them, *you strike up a conversation with a young customer, compliment her on her good features, give her beauty tips. Then, if the girl is unmarried, work in some man talk. Tell her about a girlfriend who snared a CEO after she got bigger breasts. If she's not trawling for a husband, find out her career goals. The more ambitious, the better. Say she's an aspiring model or actress. You wish her luck, tell her you knew right off that she had that special quality. Reflect, however, on how big producers all want girls with pointy noses, like Evergreen Mak.* Evergreen's face, a meter square, stares out upon the customers from the wall behind the styling chairs, reflected in the salon's mirrors so you can't escape her. Clear skin, big, round eyes, and an elegant, sharp nose. Hong Kong's gossip magazines can't get enough of that face.

Tell her you know a secret—you know that Evergreen went to a Doctor Yu in Central. In Prince's Building. You don't know much about it, but your sister knows someone who went to him. You'd be happy to call and find the number.

Edith knows her stuff. Girls all over Hong Kong are skipping lunch, postponing shopping trips and eating dried cup noodles in order to stash away dollars for Doctor Yu. Ten percent of them will end up in her Moschino purse, another five in the pocket of her persuasive beautician.

"You're an excellent candidate for the operation, you'll be glad to know," the doctor tells Windice.

"That's good," She lowers her gaze to the carpet, unaccustomed to talking about her body. "I'm just a little nervous ..."

"Of course. That's natural. Think it over. And when you come back ..."—he catches himself—"and if you decide to have the procedure done, bring some photographs. Show me how you want to look. We can discuss the possibilities."

Windice beams as Doctor Yu nods a modest good-by. *Possibilities.* In her mind is the image of Evergreen Mak, eyes big and round as Sailor Moon. What had the hairstylist said? *If you don't look like Evergreen, you might as well be ugly.*

She leaves the doctor's office, breezing by Edith. Windice, almost breathless, promises to call.

"That's fine," says Edith. "And that's for a breast enlargement?"

Blushing, she hides her face from the two men who have just walked in. "No, eyes and nose."

"Oh, of course. Sorry."

Windice pauses at the elevator, looks down at her body. *Possibilities.* Maybe if she skipped breakfasts for a few months she could afford a pair of those as well.

DOCTOR YU HANDS the morgue photo back to Lok. "If it's who I think it is, she was a patient of mine," he says. "I did a blepharoplasty and augmentation rhinoplasty on her this July. She scheduled a breast augmentation, but never kept the appointment at the hospital."

Lok and Big Pang accept the Doctor's gesture to seat themselves. Pang has been on his feet since eight, hitting all the cosmetic surgery practices in Central. When he called in to report a lead, Lok crossed the harbor to join him.

"Did you try calling?" Lok asks the Doctor.

"Let me check with my receptionist." The doctor excuses himself for a moment.

Lok turns to Big Pang, who's busying himself with his notepad.

The constable flips a page, checks something, and taps his pen on the page as if evaluating some pertinent fact. He appears to be in deep concentration.

"Don't bullshit me," says Lok.

Big Pang smiles.

Lok says, "You just don't want to look at your friend over there."

They both burst into laughter. It's obvious that Big Pang has been avoiding a staring contest with the bodiless head on the desk: a model of a skull, revealing a web of facial muscles on the right side, and bare to the bone on the left, grinning like a hungry ghost.

"It's creepy, if you ask me."

"You've seen worse. And not plastic either."

Big Pang nods, whispers, "I hate these places, that's all." He pulls at his collar like a school kid in his first suit.

Lok enjoys Big Pang's company. The man rarely stumbles when talking to pimps, loan sharks and other *lan jai*, yet he seems awed by Doctor Yu and his framed certificates, his spotless Berber, his shelves of medical books, and the eerie thing on his desk.

Usually it's Big Pang who makes others nervous. The nickname is recent; there were two Pangs at the Police Training School, and at six-two, he was taller by an inch. The other trainee, to his dismay, became Little Pang.

One hundred seventy pounds, and more handsome than a cop needs to be, Big Pang is remembered wherever Lok sends him. That gives him a certain usefulness. Everyone on the team has seen women emit a slight gasp when Big Pang appears at their door to check an alibi. They've seen housewives invite him in and talk readily, going into surprising detail, sometimes even working in that their husband will be out of town on business next week.

Men, unless they have big balls indeed, hop down a rung on the dominance ladder when Pang shows up.

"Sorry to keep you," says Doctor Yu, placing a sheet of paper on the desk, then taking a seat. The doctor is perhaps forty-five, with a tennis body, tailored clothes, designer glasses. Lok studies the sheet, a form that has been completed in poorly-formed English letters.

"This is it?" Lok asks. A name—Milkie Tang—address, cell-phone number, and a string of "no's" next to questions about health problems. The address is Tuen Mun, way out in the New Territories. "That, and some pictures. My receptionist is digging them up now."

Lok sends Big Pang to get the pictures, and turns to the Doctor. "She gave no Chinese name?" he asks.

He shakes his head with a smile of resignation, as if to say he slipped up on that one.

"When was the operation scheduled for?"

Doctor Yu flips through a desk diary. "That would have been August 17th. Milkie didn't show up. We tried to contact her."

"How?"

"We phoned, no answer. We sent a postcard that was returned."

Lok takes a breath, releases it. Time to move on. "What can you tell me about her?" he says.

The doctor purses his lips, pauses, assembles the words. "Just between you and me, Constable, I'd say she was pretty bright, not educated, but determined to get her way. As you can imagine, I keep patients well informed about every aspect of the proce-dure—concerns, risks, discomfort. She wasn't interested in that. To tell you the truth, if she could have had the surgery done right here the day she walked in, she'd have agreed, I'm sure of it. She even wanted me to do the breast augmentation at the same time as the eyelids and nose. Of course I said no, but I've never met someone so fixed on a course of action. She couldn't wait to get under the knife."

"Do you know why?"

The Doctor pauses. "I think so. She didn't discuss it, but she brought a picture of Evergreen Mak. She wanted to look like her. I think she had her heart set on a movie career."

"Is that unusual? The picture, I mean?"

The Doctor smiles. "Hardly." From a drawer he pulls out a copy of *City Screen*, one of the scores of fanzines that gush about Hong Kong movies and their stars every week. A sultry Evergreen Mak fills the cover. "I keep it in my desk to save time."

———

EDITH CHAN IS thirty, and has never gone near Doctor Yu's knife, Big Pang judges. She doesn't have much to say about Milkie Tang. Apparently the girl had little interest in waiting room small talk. No boyfriend talk, certainly.

Big Pang stares at the photo. The girl has a broad, pleasant face—attractive enough, but no knockout, at least not in this point-and-shoot doctor's office photo. No makeup, her hair pulled back in a pony tail to give a clear view of her features. Eyes forward, expression tough and serious, like a photo he'd once seen of a Chinese soldier during the Japanese invasion. Whether the assaults she confronted were imagined or real, past or future, he cannot tell.

"Any other photos?" Big Pang asks. From a shelf Edith pulls a photo album as thick as the Hong Kong phone book. When she opens it, Pang catches his breath.

Six pair of eyes stare at him.

The photos are close-ups, from just above the eyebrows to the midpoint of the nose. On the left, three pairs of young Asian eyes with smooth, unfolded eyelids. On the right the same eyes, made larger and rounder. The eyelids now bear a fold, like a *gweipoh's* eyes. It doesn't do a thing for Pang, but he knows that Western look captivates some women. European blondes prance across Hong Kong TV screens each night, selling perfume, cognac, diamond-studded wristwatches.

"Number 8322. That's her."

All the cases' numbers begin with 8, the lucky number. A ploy by the Doctor, Big Pang realizes, to reassure and encourage his patients. On the left, 8322 has the same small Chinese eyes, the one he sees every day on the faces of his friends. On the right, new, transformed eyes. They not only look less Chinese, they're clearer, more relaxed, more confident. But not happy. Not these eyes. Big Pang draws back unconsciously, as if a tiger has stared him down.

The constable tries to compare the flinty gaze in the photo with the vacant sockets in the morgue picture, but the pictures drift apart in his mind, unreconciled.

The nose photos are just as unilluminating. On the left, a flat nose typical of the Han race. On the right, a pointed one.

Edith hands him an envelope. "We only have a before photo for the breasts. She never got the operation." Despite its irrelevance to the investigation, curiosity overpowers him.

The views, front and side, are from the neck to her belt. She is wearing a maroon skirt. Her breasts are pale in the office light, small, with protruding nipples, like his own wife's. "Too big," Eva had said of her nipples, self-mockingly, the first time Pang complimented them. Too big for what? Where do women get their ideas?

Embarrassed by his own intrusion, he hands back the picture. "She didn't give you an ID number?" he asks.

"No, I'm sorry. She didn't fill it in, and I must have overlooked it. I'm sorry." Nothing else occurs to Big Pang, so he says good-by and rejoins Lok.

As the policemen approach the door, Edith pokes her head through the receptionist's window. "She came back after an appointment one time, said her car got stolen. Do you think that's important?"

CHAPTER 7

HECTOR ENTERS LEO'S flat with a key Leo gave him ages ago.

The place is little more than one room, with a tiny bedroom off to the side. A worn green sofa, bookshelves filled with music, and a dehumidifier whose flashing red light shows that, like Hector, it's had all the Hong Kong humidity it can take.

Smells: old cigarette smoke, mold.

A music stand, stamped Property of Curtis Institute of Music.

Everything is there: the metronome, the ashtray, the lacquered bowl in which sits a photo of the two of them: he can see the two bearded faces from halfway across the room. Hector shaved just before the summer.

He takes in the entire room, closes his eyes to conjure the space as his memory knows it, then scans the room again. Something is amiss. The sofa has been dragged a few inches away from the wall. So has the bookshelf.

He moves to Leo's desk, pokes in the drawers, the cabinets, the refrigerator, not knowing what he's looking for, not finding it. Nothing out of the ordinary until he steps on the pedal of the trash can and finds a couple of small mountains, brown and white. Someone has dumped out Leo's coffee and sugar, obviously looking for something in the canisters. The flat has been searched. Not recklessly, not violently, but carefully and methodically.

Now he sees more things askew. Slips of paper are scattered on the floor—bookmarks that escaped when the books were turned over and shaken. Clothes in his closet have been shoved to one side, to reveal what might have been stashed behind them. No telling what they found, if anything. Whoever they are.

He runs out of Leo's apartment and down the stairs, punching the corridor wall in anger, imprinting the dust.

Once in the street he charges swiftly towards Nathan Road, oblivious to everything but his dread. Leo wouldn't leave like this. People just don't leave.

People just don't leave. Did he really think that? That's just plain false.

You're up to your nose in warm flannel sheets, the door open because dark rooms scare you. John Siefert is in the next room, talking too loud; he's drunk again. He didn't used to be drunk all the time, but it's happening more and more.

"We'll lose everything!" he's saying.

"John, you can't say that yet." His mother talking now. "Your customers like buying from you."

"With a superstore a block away, they'll damn well buy there! What do they fucking care if we starve?"

"John, please, the kids."

Oscar's voice from the kitchen. "Yeah, the kids."

"You shut up!" he shouts. "What good are you? Useless bastard, you think you're smart ..."

Oscar walks in toting a beer. "I'm smart enough not to be a loser like you! Selling your stupid irons and washing machines. The superstore is just an excuse. You drink so much, no wonder your fucking business is going under."

You hear a slap, then a punch, and the sound of a family picture skittering to the floor.

"Get out!" says John. "Get out now!"

"That does it! You can all fuck yourselves. I'm going."

"Oscar!" their mother calls, but Oscar is in his room now. You hear a drawer open, slam, then another.

"Let him go!" says John.

You want to speak, but before you can the front door slams and your brother's gone.

You close your eyes and draw your head deeper into the covers. Oscar will be back tomorrow, you think. He'll walk in the door while you're practicing, he'll grind his knuckle gently into your arm, saying, "Hey, my man." Oscar will come and make Dad apologize. And then Dad will stop drinking.

The bed rocks slightly. The cool air strokes your neck as the blanket is raised. It's your younger sister Bernadette, who heard the shouting from her own room down the hall. She climbs in and curls up like a dying leaf. You lie together, her breathing quick and rhythmic, yours slower and interrupted by stifled sobs. Soon Bernadette is asleep.

A pinstriped shoulder slams Hector's arm. A briefcase grazes his knee. At some point he's come to a stop in on the sidewalk. There's no telling how long he's stood there, letting tourists and commuters buffet him, but he knows why he wandered to this corner of Tsim Sha Tsui. He walks to the Symphony offices on Canton Road.

———

ZENOBIA CHAN SITS at a metal desk, copying markings from one cello part into another. Hector glances over her shoulder.

She looks up, and her face darkens. For a few moments they remain silent, transfixed by the sight of each other's faces. Finally, Zen speaks.

"I'm very busy. You shouldn't be here." She turns back to the cello part, marking little v's for up-bows, little inverted square u's for down-bows.

"Look, Zen, I didn't want to come."

"Then why did you?" she asks, eyes on the music.

"Why are you acting this way? I'm the one who should be angry, right?" To emphasize that he's not, he riffles idly through a pile of string parts that lie on a table opposite Zen's desk.

Zenobia Chan is thirty, which in Chinese society is old for an unmarried woman. She's also radiant, with mysterious brown eyes and a soft, graceful body. The sight of her transports him back six months, sets his brain running a loop of old sensations: a whiff of perfumed neck, the touch of warm lips, the sound of muffled, agitated breathing.

"Forget it, Zen," he says, conscious that her forgetting it is precisely what he fears most. "I came to ask if you've seen Leo around in the last couple of days."

"No, not since last week." She places a few slurs and bowings on the last page of the part, closes it, and takes out the next one. Six stands, six parts.

"He didn't show up for rehearsal today. He's not at his flat, hasn't answered the phone." He decides not to mention the search of the flat yet. "It's not like him," he says.

"Isn't it?"

"He's nuts, but he's reliable."

"Is he?"

"Christ, don't you hear what I'm saying? Something's wrong, Zen. He left his viola at my place, hasn't returned, didn't show up at rehearsal. You don't give a shit about him or me, do you?"

Her hands scribble away, but he can see her eyes shut tight. From one of them escapes a tear, glistening in the fluorescent light. He walks behind her and clasps her shoulders.

"Zen ..." he says, softly.

She wipes the tears from her eyes. "I don't know where he is. I'm sorry. I'm being selfish, I know."

He strokes her shoulders, whether to bestow warmth or draw it from her, he can't tell. "I miss you," he says in a half-whisper as if, told softly, the truth will surreptitiously take root in her mind.

"Please," she says.

He lets go and backs away as if she's suddenly become radioactive. "Right, Zen. I'm good for a while, just not permanently. Nice to have around, but you can't get serious about a *gweilo,* can you?" He tries to hook her gaze, but she looks away.

"Stay away from Americans," Hector continues, "that's what your Grandmother said. Their marriages don't last. You want a nice, dependable Chinese guy who'll make steady money."

"It's not the money..."

"Right. You told me already, it's your family ..."

"Hector, you came to Hong Kong to get away from everyone who expected something of you. I don't have that luxury."

"Fine, Zen," Hector says. "Give my regards to the family. May your first child be a boy." He stomps out, heedless of the stares from the cubicles.

Just months ago he'd had it all: friends, music, and the love of an extraordinary woman. Unwilling to trust his own instincts, he tested himself constantly, trying to confirm that his feelings for her were not just more evidence of his attraction to Chinese women. The attraction was real enough: he hadn't pursued a *gweipoh* since walking off the plane in Hong Kong. The allure of Chinese women, the way they wore their femininity without guilt or endless self-examination, and of course, their skin, their eyes, lips, their delicate frames were all concocted, as far as Hector could tell, to drive him out of his mind.

Zenobia's gift to him was a constant, almost hypnotic state of happiness. When they found out she was pregnant, marriage made a kind of crazy sense. To hell with youth. Having wrung an extra half-decade of adolescence from life, he was ready to be a four-star husband and father. Reckless, perhaps, but decent, and perhaps the first decision he'd ever made that involved a life other than his own.

It was Zenobia who postponed her answer. A week later she aborted the baby and told him not to call her again. No reason why. Hector felt he'd been aborted himself.

He'd come to Zenobia today to save what was left of his family—his real family, not the pathetic creatures he'd left in New York. Leo and Zenobia are everything to him.

THE UNIFORMED TWENTY-SOMETHING introduces herself as Scarlett Pak of the Miscellaneous Enquiries Sub Unit. She takes down Hector's details on a clipboard, suppressing a smile at his name, and listens with a quiet, professional sympathy as he describes Leo's disappearance.

"Has anyone telephoned him?" she asks.

"I did, a couple of times. I even called after two a.m. to make sure."

"Have you spoken to anyone at your workplace?

"No. I know him a lot better than they do."

She nods. "When was the last time you saw him?"

"Four days ago. At my house. He left his viola there, and just disappeared."

"I'm sorry. He left his ..."

"Viola. His instrument. *Chung tai kam.*" She smiles at his use of Cantonese, writes down the Chinese words for "middle fiddle."

"Does Mr. Stern drink alcohol, or use drugs?"

Hector pauses, perhaps a bit stunned. "Beer," he says, with a shrug. "He's not on a drunk, if that's what you mean."

Scarlett Pak lowers the clipboard. "We'll make some enquiries. If he does show up, please let us know."

"There's one more thing."

"Yes?"

"His flat. It looked as if the place had been searched."

"Searched?"

"That's right. Things were upset, pushed aside. Someone had been there."

She considers that for a moment. "Are you sure Mr. Stern wasn't looking for something himself?"

Hector pauses to think. "There was coffee and sugar ..." His words trail off.

"Coffee?"

Another pause. "Never mind," he says. He walks out, certain that she'll do next to nothing. As far as she's concerned Leo is sleeping off a drunk on Lamma Island, or else he's gone scuba diving in the Philippines and forgot to leave word. Missing *gwei-los* aren't a priority here. Hector had explored Constable Pak's face for a sign of compassion, found only professional dedication. Does she know what it really means that Leo is missing?

We're all here for one reason or another, us expats. I left to get

*away from my ex-wife. But you know why you came here? To find
your brother. All you know about home is that your brother isn't
there.*

He's never spoken to anyone but Leo of the chill that engulfed
him the night that Oscar struck his father. No one ever saw Oscar
again. It's his father's fault, he's been told. John Siefert poisoned
everything with his bitterness and self-pity.

But Hector knows that he himself is to blame, not his father.
He should have been strong enough to keep the family together.
He should have found a way to keep Oscar home.

CHAPTER 8

LOK ENTERS K.K. KWAN'S office, where murders are compiled, counted, and distilled down to harmless colored lines on spreadsheet graphs. All the crime in Hong Kong is here, neatly arrayed on wall-mounted clipboards. robbery, pickpocket, rape, assault, each jagged scrawl implying how well the police and the criminals are doing their job.

Most of the lines are fairly even, descending slightly toward the right. The one showing the steadiest decline is TVWA, or taking a vehicle without authorization, a polite term for the ruthless car thefts that had plagued Hong Kong a few years back.

Lok cannot figure why Kwan summoned him. Usually a telephone report does the trick at this stage of a case.

"Lok *jai*," Kwan says, "I hear you got a name on the floater." He uses the diminutive when he's in an affectionate mood.

"That's right," Lok says. "Turns out she's not an II. Doctor Lee was right."

"He'll be pleased to learn that. Anything beyond a name?"

"It's coming. I'll need some information from Traffic."

"Traffic, you say?"

"Yes, sir. She drove a car, apparently, and had it stolen or towed while she was at the surgeon's. Ko's checking on that now."

"All right, good work. There is one other thing. You're planning on attending the seminar, aren't you?"

"Ah sir, I'm not sure I'll have time to go."

Lok sees Kwan's face tighten. "I think it would be a good idea," he says.

This is the conversation Lok has been dreading, the one he cannot win. "Look, sir, I'm too old to change the way I work."

"Maybe so," says Kwan. "But you're putting yourself at risk."

"How do you mean? I'll stand behind my record."

Kwan pauses, tapping his fingers on the desk. "Herman, think about this. Our *Ba Ba*'s life is gone. The way people do business, what children learn in schools, everything is different from when we entered the force. Our effectiveness depends on our being able to gain the trust of the people. I know you understand that. Remember how it used to be? My great-grandmother was born in the Qing Dynasty, Herman. She was robbed of her life savings by con men, but she never thought of calling the police. It was no one's business, she said, least of all a stranger's. Few people reported crimes, or trusted a policeman. As for getting witnesses to talk—you can imagine."

Conscious that Kwan is studying his face, trying to read his reaction, Lok says nothing.

"It used to be that most Hong Kongers were born on the mainland, suspicious peasants who kept to themselves and expected nothing from anyone. Not anymore. The people we're working for now have been born and bred in a modern city. The police need to change, adapt, find new ways of working that fit with today's Hong Kong. If you don't change with it, you risk becoming outdated and useless."

The words burn like acid. The Force loves to portray its recruits as young, university-educated, tech-savvy. They're out to make him feel like some crazy old uncle who's kept in the back room when company comes.

"I don't think things are changing that much, sir. The girl in the harbor didn't die in any modern 21st Century way. She's just dead, and instead of finding her killer ..."

"Herman ..."

" ... I have to go to school..."

"You read the memo ..."

"I read the memo, sir. I'm drowning in memos—we all are. 'We need to enhance operation flow and continue our upward thrust.' You should have heard Old Ko when I told him about upward thrust."

Kwan smiles despite himself. Lok continues.

"All this HR bullshit is getting in the way of the job, and you know it. We can't call arrested persons APs anymore. It's 'customers.' Like we're running a department store ..."

"Lok *jai*, I'm trying to help."

"Then don't put me in that classroom and waste my time. I feel like a dog chasing rats in there. Sitting watching some computer presentation..."

"You know, it wouldn't hurt to build up your record of service a little." The irritation shows through in Kwan's voice now.

"What's wrong with my record?" Lok says. "I do what I'm hired to do—go out on the street, ask questions, bring in the killers. A good mark in Human Resource Management isn't going to change that."

"All right, that's enough," Kwan says. Then, less sharply, "I understand how you feel, but if you're the only one in the district who doesn't attend, I'll have to explain it to the DC."

Once again, pressure from above explains it all. The career

game, Lok knows, doesn't take only the ass-kissers and climbers. Even good cops like Kwan feel the need to impress the Big Balls.

Lok leaves the ADC's office and walks into the Hot Room, where most of the team is gathered for the case conference. Old Ko sits alone on his side of the table, Big Pang having gone to court on another case today. Million Man and Ears sit opposite him.

"As you know," Lok begins, "Big Pang and I spoke to the doctor who did the operation on the victim's eyes. He's a Gold Rolex type. But the girl is a different story. She was shy about giving out embarrassing personal details, like her correct address. So far we only have her English name, Milkie Tang."

"No CCC?" asks Ears.

"Didn't you listen?" asks Old Ko. "With ears that big, you should hear everything." Laughter.

"Not yet," says Lok. In Chinese the spoken name is not enough. The Chinese Commercial Code lets business and government pin down which of the many written forms of Tang, Wong or Lau a person uses. "She filled in her name in English, not Chinese. And she's done her best to make herself hard to trace. Believe it or not, she paid cash for the doctor's visits and the hospital, so we don't have a credit card. Her cellphone number comes from a rechargeable SIM card you buy at any Watson's. Can't trace it either.

"We did get a break, though. The nurse remembered that Milkie's car disappeared that day. Old Ko, I want you to check with Traffic, see what cars were stolen or towed in Central, near Prince's building, on July 2nd. Then see if you can find a driver's license for a Milkie Tang." He turns to Ears. "How did it go in the titty bars?"

The face of the young policeman flushes red, despite his obvious determination to hide his embarrassment. "No luck so far, ah Lok, sir. I still have ..."

"Get back on it," he says. Lok dismisses the team.

———————

OLD KO PUNCHES the phone number while taking a sip of tea.

"Vehicle Pound. *Wai?*"

"This is DPC 19831 Ko Man-man, RCU one KW. I need some information about a car that was stolen or towed on 2 July this year, in Central, reported around 11:30 a.m."

"Right. This is Sergeant 33173 Chan Din-yan. What do you need to know?

"Who it's registered to."

"Make? Color?"

"Lexus. Don't know the color."

"You want me to find a stolen car, and you don't even know what color?"

"I don't want you to find a car. We can do that without your help. I want you to look up the report."

Traffic cops hate CID, Old Ko knows. While Crime people are busy doing real police work, catching crooks and advancing their careers, what are Traffic doing? Flagging down motorists, giving tickets, and arguing with morons about whether or not they've made an illegal right turn. If they want to salvage their careers after a detour in Traffic, they'll find themselves a couple of years behind. Not that most of them have a chance. If you're in Traffic, chances are you deserve it.

On the phone Old Ko hears the sounds of an office much like his, however he might despise its inhabitants. Computer keys click, men chat, a copier churns. Someone has put fifty on City

Dragon for tonight's race at Happy Valley. Been slow this season, someone says. Didn't place last week. But he finished three lengths to the winner, says another. He has a chance of breaking through this time.

The traffic sergeant finally speaks up. "Here you go. There was a hired Lexus that was parked in a restricted area, towed at 10:15 a.m. Registered to Brilliant Fortune Car Hire, North Point. The owner picked it up, said it had been stolen, but never reported it."

"Makes sense," says Old Ko. "A $400,000 car goes missing, they don't report it. No wonder our job is so easy. Thanks. And tell your friend to save his money. City Dragon is a dog. He'll make more betting on his mother instead."

"City Dragon's mother or his own?"

"No difference."

Old Ko shows Lok the results from Traffic. "Want me to check it out?" he asks.

Lok shakes his head. "No, get Ears. I want him with me. You can take the girlie bars."

Old Ko returns to the big room to find Ears. "You're in luck," he says. "Lok wants you to stay a virgin a few more days. You're going with him."

He watches Ears leave to the sound of laughter in the big room.

CHAPTER 9

"OKAY, WE'VE GOT a few items on the agenda, shouldn't take long." Roger Snell addresses the handful of players who remained behind for the orchestra meeting. Clem is teaching at the Academy. Porvin is at Grand Hyatt, serenading fat American tourists as they rest between bouts of shopping. Many players simply have no interest in the Players' Committee, and a few actively loathe it. Hector sits in the front row, one ear on Roger's Midwestern drone, his eyes on today's *South China Morning Post*, his mind on Leo.

"First, they finally got in a real moving team for the instruments. Mr. Yip Tak-tak, who worked for orchestras in Vancouver, will be supervising a crew of three to ensure that all the instruments and stands are moved safely. I know you'll be pleased with the results."

"Too late to save Mindy's harp," says Chiu Shun-Fu, who sits in the back, unscrewing the bell of his French horn.

Hector turns to watch the movers wrestle the tympani offstage. The boss Yip, with Rolex and sport jacket, doesn't look like any instrument mover he's ever seen before. His two assistants, decked out in dyed brown razor cuts and gold jewelry, appear to be adrift in a world of strange new objects that defy their under-standing. Yip directs them to the glockenspiel, his impatience showing. They are clearly mystified by the contraption.

Gold watches, Hector thinks, expensive haircuts, gaudy designer shirts with long sleeves to hide their tattoos. These guys are triads, members of one of the Chinese criminal societies that support the drug and prostitution trades, and infest the city's heavy labor pool.

One crew member is not working. He's lean, tall, and sullen, older than the others, propped against the wall, chewing on sun-flower seeds. This one has a face like a stone idol, and not one of the benevolent ones. Hector hasn't seen him move so much as a drumstick. Not working, not giving orders. What the hell is he there for?

"Now, there's also a matter of the tour," Roger says. "We want to make sure that we get paid a per diem while we're in China, to take care of our expenses. We need to come up with a figure to propose."

"Ten thousand," says a bassoonist. Laughs.

"Seriously," Roger says, frustration already in his voice.

"Five hundred?" asks Penny Chang, a violinist dressed head to toe in red leather. "Anything less would be a hardship." Hector smiles. Penny's family owns four shopping malls and a parking garage in Mongkok.

The meeting crumbles into a dozen localized arguments, and for a moment Hector pities Roger, who spent the previous year earning the contempt of the players for his inability to make the slightest difference in their lives. Bonson doesn't return Roger's calls. When he manages to beg a few minutes with the General Committee on Saturday mornings, Roger in his suit and them in yachting jackets or golfing shirts, he faces amused condescension.

Not much we can do. We take your point. Our hands are tied. I'm sure you understand.

Chiu Shun-fu stands and speaks, quelling the mumbling instantly. "You're not paying attention to what's important. The problem is Shao. This man has no talent. He's bad for the orchestra, he's bad for music in Hong Kong. Let's get rid of him."

Murmurs of agreement. "Fuckin-A," says a trombonist.

Roger hesitates. Immediately Chiu stands up, waving his own clipboard. "Here's the petition to dump Shao. Once I get your signatures, I'll take it to the General Committee. Let's do it, people!"

The orchestra erupts in cheers.

"Don't you think it's a bit early for that?" Rogers says. "No one's crazy about Shao, but the season's just starting. Having a petition hanging over things …"

He's stalling, thinks Hector. Roger's term ends in a couple of weeks. He wants to postpone the petition so the next Player's Committee has to deal with it.

A knot of musicians forms around Chiu as the petition passes from hand to hand. Roger's voice is lost in a tide of animated conversation.

Hector stands up, shoves his newspaper in a trash bin and takes the petition from Chiu. Chiu gives him a thumbs-up.

"Are you really going to sign that?"

The voice comes from behind him. Chinese, he guesses, female, probably Western-educated, and short. He turns to look at the woman who spoke. She's certainly petite. Her head, topped by radiant jet-black hair, barely reaches his chin.

"Why shouldn't I?"

"Don't you think it could cause trouble?"

He hands the clipboard to the first oboist. "No. You're not a new player, are you?"

"No. I'm with the *Post*."

"Great. See you." Hector turns to the exit, but feels a soft hand on his arm.

"Wait, please. Could I ask you about what's going on?"

"No."

"Why not? The petition's news. Aren't you interested in having your side of the story told?"

He draws his arm from her. "First of all, it's not my story. I just play the bass. Second, you're not trying to tell anyone's story, you're just hired to write stuff that'll sell papers. Third, there are plenty of people here that love to talk to reporters, so you'll have no trouble getting what you need. Thanks anyway. Bye."

He turns to move away. Yip's troops are picking up the steel music stands, which occasionally strike each other like dull gongs. *F-sharp. G-natural.* The two flashily-dressed assistants begin hauling a bass case offstage, while Yip Tak-tak, cellphone in hand, barks orders. One of the movers drops the bass case with an ominous *klunk* that causes every musician in the room to freeze.

"Jesus," Hector says. He and Yip stare at each other for a second. The reporter interrupts them.

"I heard that Leo Stern is missing. Did you know him?"

Hector whips around to face the woman, who's now far enough away that he can take in her whole figure. Slender, slight rounding at the breasts, legs thin but handsome in black jeans. A true Chinese beauty, one that Leo and he would have rhapsodized over during a session at Poon's.

"What do you mean 'did' I know him?" Hector says. "I still do."

"Do you know where he is?"

"No. But he's fine."

"What makes you say that?"

"I know him better than anybody. He's fine. He's just on vacation."

"The season just started. How can that be?"

"It's a viola thing. You wouldn't understand." Again he turns to the exit. The two men, having made it offstage, set the bass trunk down, still uncomfortably hard. Yip shouts at one of them.

"Leo Stern called me," she says. "He had something to tell me about the orchestra, something important."

Again Hector spins around to look at her. "When?"

"Last week. He had a fight with somebody, and sounded pretty worried."

"A fight with who? What kind of fight?"

The reporter glances at several people within earshot. "This isn't the place." She pulls a card from her jacket pocket. "Call me tonight," she says, and dashes toward the back exit.

The card says *Twinkie Choi, South China Morning Post.*

CHAPTER 10

"**HONG KONG HAS** never finished out of the money—never! Sure, there have been rough times. But here's my advice—never, ever tear up your betting ticket before the race is over. Hong Kong will be out in front of the pack before you know it."

It's Ambrose Wan's third newspaper interview this week, and he feels like a prisoner of war eating his daily meal of boiled grass. Worse, he's regurgitating it, one inspiring aphorism at a time.

"In the Seventies and early Eighties a couple of the big U.S. banks tried to get in on the action," he continues. "Back then things were more volatile—you could move the market with a transaction of five million U.S. dollars. Those American banks couldn't take it. They tore up their betting ticket before the race ended, and let others cash in."

A memo recorder sits on the table between them. The reporter, an intern at a regional business magazine, makes some marks on a steno pad. *This one looks as if she's just out of college*, Ambrose thinks. Good legs, shiny blonde hair. *What could she know? How could she imagine what I'm going through?*

"Are you worried about competition from Singapore and Shanghai?" she says in a clipped British accent.

If only his worries were that insignificant. Ambrose chooses a knowing smile from perhaps a half-dozen in his repertory. "Not in the least. If a company is serious about doing business, Hong Kong is where they want to be. No city has a work ethic like ours. Add to that the communications, the sheer financial power, the superb infrastructure. More than that, Hong Kong is the capital of China."

The girl looks up from her pad, puzzled.

"Overseas China, I mean. This city is the nerve center for the millions of Chinese living outside of China. It's where they get the scuttlebutt, the skinny. 'So-and-so is starting a real estate venture in Beijing, he needs to go in with a bank and a construction company'—you'll find it out here first."

Ambrose has said this a million times to feature writers. Don't they ever read each other's stuff? He casts an eye at the clock across the meeting room, next to his treasure, the Braque still life he paid two million for. His father-in-law exploded when he read about that in *Sing Tao Daily*, but Ambrose loves the picture. Of course, that was at the zenith of the boom. "We had pictures on the wall when the Japanese came," his father-in-law Octavius said to him. "They didn't do us any good."

The interviewer burns up another half-minute studying her cheat sheet. "Has there been any news about Valiant Plaza?"

"No comment there, I'm afraid," he says, a bogus smile lighting his face. "It's still under litigation." Not for long, if things work out the way they're supposed to.

Ambrose isn't a bad manager, but he's no entrepreneur, and his record proves it. There was the business of the Jakarta office building, which Octavius had advised against: those are Muslims, after all. But there was so much to gain if he could just get in and out quickly. He lost a bundle.

Then came a string of tech investments, and everyone knows

what happened with those. But he was cursed with impatience, which leads to mistakes. His father-in-law wouldn't understand; Octavius came up back when the fruit hung low from the tree: bribery was easy, labor cheap, governmental regulation a happy joke.

Valiant Plaza was Ambrose's last chance. Desperately short on cash, he knocked up the residential/commercial complex in Shenzhen as cheaply as he could, urging his contractors to cut every imaginable corner. Sure, there would be complaints, but he could sell the place or fix things after the cash flow started up.

He hadn't counted on the San Francisco partners coming and taking a look around. They hated what they saw. Third-rate fittings. Electric not up to standard. Construction so poor the place wasn't fit to be occupied, much less marketed to tenants. Ambrose tried to stroke their balls, but the lawsuit came anyway.

If he can just make the suit disappear, the cash will come.

"Intellectual property is a hot issue too," the woman says, and Ambrose forces himself not to sigh. He just spoke to the *Post* about this. She must have seen the article.

"As I've said, that is an issue that Hong Kong needs to come to terms with."

"Do you think it's going to happen?"

"It won't happen overnight. Remember that we have a reputation as imitators. They say Hong Kong is where you can have an idea in the morning, register your business at noon, start making money in the afternoon, and have someone copying you by evening." He beams as if the cliché were the last word, as he hopes it will be. When he pushes his chair away from the desk, preparing to stand, he's relieved to see that she takes the hint. They rise and shake hands. Ambrose disappears through a door before she can shut off her recorder and gather her papers.

In his office, Ambrose pours a tall glass of water and gulps half of it, hands trembling. He tears his jacket off, loosens his tie, and flops in his chair, breathing heavily.

His watch emits a tiny peep: five o'clock. The sound seems to activate him, move his muscles against his will, force him to draw a cellphone out of the bottom drawer of his sprawling ebony-and-glass desk. With weak mechanical motions he presses keys to summon the one number that's programmed into it. A man answers.

"*Wai?*"

"Any news?" Ambrose asks.

"It's good. You're a lucky man."

Not the word he would have chosen.

"You're certain?" Instantly he regrets questioning Greeny's competence, robbing him of face.

"Didn't you hear me? You'll get official word in about a week. The judge will tell the Americans to go home and eat shit."

Ambrose feels a hand around his throat loosen.

"I can't thank you enough ..." He almost says Greeny's name, stops himself.

"I did it for your father-in-law, not you. Just see that you do this job better than you did the China venture."

Far from insulting, the words sound like a reprieve to Ambrose.

"It will be fine," he hears himself say, and the phone goes dead. He drops his arms to his sides and the phone tumbles to the floor.

A minute later Winsome strides in, yellow pad in hand. She's thirty-four, top of her class at Hong Kong U, joined the secretarial pool at Wan Industries thirteen years ago and by sheer intelligence and force of will made it as far as a woman could get in the company. "That didn't go too badly," she says. She means the interview, which she caught on the intercom.

Ambrose collects himself, begins to button his collar. "Same old, same old," he says. "Jockey Club dinner now, right?"

"One more here first. The people from the Hong Kong Symphony. They're in Conference Room Four."

"What's that about?"

"Some players. They asked for fifteen minutes, and I thought it would be a good idea to give it to them, considering the situation." She brushes a hair off the shoulder of his blue chalk stripe suit.

"What situation?"

"The players want to fire their conductor. They've all signed a petition, and they want to hand it to you personally."

Why me, he thinks. Realizing he's asked himself a legitimate question, he says, "Why not Whatshisname?"

"Bonson Ng is only the General Manager, in charge of administration of the orchestra. You're head of the General Committee, so you hire and fire the conductor."

A knot congeals in Ambrose's gut. This is not good.

"What do you think I should do?" There was a time when he sought her counsel in a roundabout way to save face. Lately he's too desperate to keep up the pretense.

"Listen to them, nod, reassure them, tell them you'll discuss it with the committee. "

"Listen, discuss. Right." His mind is far from the meeting room, on events happening miles away, events which might settle his own future.

"Conference 4, you said? All right, let's do it. What are their names?"

She looks at her yellow pad. "Roger Snell and Chiu Shun-fu."

After Winsome leaves, Ambrose retrieves the cellphone from the floor, shoves it back into the bottom drawer, makes sure it's locked tight. He heads down the corridor, picking up speed, so he can burst into the room with the energy one expects of a director of Wan Industries.

CHAPTER 11

IN A COFFEE SHOP on Peking Road, over a steaming tea laced with condensed milk, Hector reads Twinkie Choi's account of strife within the orchestra. It must have been a slow news day; the story covers half the front page. Hector searches the text for exaggerations and lies, finds none. *Trouble is brewing in the Hong Kong Symphony Orchestra. Yesterday 91 of the orchestra's 102 players signed a petition asking the General Committee to fire musical director Shao Din-yan ...*

The litany of complaints takes up most of the article, but only one player has agreed to be quoted. "Hong Kong deserves a better orchestra than this," says Chiu Shun-fu, outspoken French horn player and author of the petition. "Shao is holding us back."

General Manager Bonson Ng said he was "surprised and disturbed" by the petition, but declined to comment further. He is expected to respond later today to the accusations of the players. Roger Snell, the chairman of the Players' Committee, was unavailable for comment.

To the side of the article is the petition itself, with the accusations listed in dignified Roman type. *Mr. Shao's conducting technique is inadequate...his rhythm and pitch are poor ... his*

*rehearsal technique is extremely enervating for the orchestra.
Rather than fix problems and "get on with it," as most good conductors do, Mr. Shao merely repeats passages and movements*
ad nauseam ...

Below the petition is a list of names, Chinese and English,
scrawled in anger and frustration. This could get ugly, Hector
knows. Pathetic as he is, Roger spoke the truth about the General
Committee. People like that don't like to be pushed around.

Leaving the paper on the table, Hector exits the tiny restaurant and walks toward the music store where Twinkie Choi will
be waiting. She'd suggested meeting at a coffee shop, but Hector
refuses to trap himself. On his feet, flipping through compact
discs, he can be in control, even a little rude, if it suits him. Above
all, he can avoid appearing to cooperate with the press. He wants
to find Leo, not supply the papers with fresh gossip.

———————

WHEN TWINKIE APPEARS at the music store, Hector greets her
and turns back to the compact disc he's holding. Palestrina motets.

"Are you interested in this kind of music?" he asks, keeping his
eyes on the disc.

"Da da da daaa," Twinkie sings. The first four notes of
Beethoven's Fifth, but she's in A-minor, and flat at that.

"I see you got your story."

"You sound angry. Was there anything unfair or untrue in it?"

"No," Hector says. "I just don't think it'll help anything, that's
all."

"Some people disagree."

"Sure. I bet Chiu couldn't wait to talk to you."

"Don't you like Chiu?"

"Sure I do. He's a good horn player."

"Well, it's not only him. A lot of players think it will be good to get this in the open, put pressure on the Committee."

"Ah, so your motive is to help out the orchestra."

Hector flips over another CD to read the personnel. *Da da da daaa.* The same tune just about anyone in Hong Kong would sing to describe what Hector does for a living. Reducing four hundred years of musical history to four notes. *That's Hong Kong for you, Hec, they size you up and move on.*

"I don't need a motive," she says. "It's my job."

"Well, it interferes with my job, so I don't give a shit about it."

"Fine. I don't need to give a shit about you."

Startled, he looks up. That's a fair amount of confrontation for a Chinese girl. "Sorry, I've been rude," he says. He extends his hand in an exaggerated gesture of conciliation. "I'm Hector Siefert."

"Hector ..."

"Siefert. See-fat."

She bursts out laughing, not even covering her face as so many Chinese women do. Hector's found that most Cantonese talk loudly but laugh quietly.

"You should come to America with the name Twinkie," he says. "Then you'll see laughing."

"Yours is worse."

"Makes my life interesting." A cellphone tune sounds from the pocket of a shopper behind them. *C-natural.* Okay, look, I understand you're doing your job. Just don't print anything I say, okay? I don't want to be part of it."

She smiles as a signal of acceptance. "All right. Then why are we here?"

"You said you knew something about Leo."

"Not really. But I talked to him when all this started. I was calling as many orchestra people as I could find, and he answered the phone."

"When was that?"

"A couple of weeks ago. Before most of the overseas players came back. He told me about something that happened at the Cultural Centre."

"Leo? At the Cultural Centre before the season's start? Doesn't sound like him."

"There was a concert there. He sneaked into the second half, so he wouldn't have to buy a ticket."

"Okay, that sounds like Leo."

"He told me he went backstage to talk to one of the players. While he was waiting around he must have poked into a couple of rooms. Yip Tak-tak spotted him."

"The mover guy?"

"Yes. Yip got angry about something, and they had a fight."

"What kind of fight?"

"He said Yip pushed him a couple of times, he pushed back."

"Jesus. What was it about?"

"He didn't say. But Saturday he told me he was going to look around, get a better idea of what's going on, then call me."

Saturday was the day they'd met at Poon's. Monday they played duets, and Leo hasn't been seen since. For a moment the image of Leo's violated flat comes to mind.

"And did he call you?" he asks.

"No. I was hoping you could tell me where he is."

"Are you trying to find Leo," he says, "or just get a story?"

"Both. Is that so bad?"

He's silent.

"Oh, come on," Twinkie says. "Leo must have said something that made you curious."

"No. But he wouldn't."

"Why not?"

Hector looks at her again, north to south. "He's not trying to get in my pants."

She wheels around and storms out. Hector watches her jog down the escalator and vanish. A needle of guilt stabs him. *Why so cruel, Hector Siefert?*

See-fat. When Hector first arrived he'd seen the bemused stares, heard the stifled giggles as Hong Kongers pronounced his name. Siefert became *See-fat,* Cantonese for asshole—literally shit-hole. It wasn't auspicious, but he's made the best of it. The ten-year-old son of one of the bass players asked him if the name had been intended to keep away bad spirits. Parents still do that sometimes—name babies things like *Gau-see*—dog shit—to mislead kidnapping ghosts.

In better times Hector's father nurtured the myth of a family with its own standards, its own pride. *Act like a Siefert, and you'll be treated like a Siefert,* he'd say to the boys. So far it's worked just fine.

He makes his way to the Cultural Centre, dawdling on Nathan Road to avoid catching up with Twinkie. When he reaches the door he pauses, pulls a name card from his wallet, dials a number on his cellphone.

"Hello? WPC Pak? This is Hector Siefert. I'm calling about Leo Stern. Yes ... I understand. All right, I'll call tomorrow. Thanks."

Pulling out the name card has dislodged a photo from behind his Hong Kong ID. He removes the photo, opens it. It's a folded post card, soft and dog-eared, portraying a sunlit beach with an upended skiff weathering in the background. Hanging in the sky, the words *Sag Harbor, Long Island.*

Hector flips over the card, reads again the printed words. *Hi,*

Hec. You should be here. Love, Oscar.

His brother had gone to camp that one summer. He sent no letters to the family, just one post card each to Bernadette and Hector. Soon afterwards their father's store went under. There was no more camp, no escape from the summer heat of New York. And Oscar left, but never wrote again.

Hector folds the post card, slips it behind his ID, and walks in to rehearsal.

CHAPTER 12

BRILLIANT FORTUNE CAR HIRE CO. is registered to Yorks Ma, but up to now Inspector Lok has heard mostly from the proprietor's wife. Cynthia is well into her forties, with a thick, pillar-like body, chemically blackened hair, and a generous appliqué of crimson lipstick. A string of pearls encircles her neck.

"The police called one day and said that the Lexus was found— it was waiting for us out at Ho Man Tin, in the pound. We didn't even know it was missing. Tell him, Yorks."

Yorks, looking on from behind the counter, nods with a faint smile.

"I went back to the lot, and sure enough, the car was gone! That was a shock. The keys were missing too. Right from this drawer." She points behind the counter. The office is large, lit by fluorescent tubes, with floor-to-ceiling windows affording views of the lot and its cars. Mercedes, Lexus, a few vans.

"Do you have any idea how it could have gone missing?" asks Lok.

"No," says Cynthia. She looks Lok straight in the eye. "We're very careful. Someone must have grabbed the key when we weren't looking, but we don't know when."

"Had this ever happened before?"

"A car stolen, you mean? No." Again, Yorks shakes his head in concert.

"Does the name Milkie Tang mean anything to you? A miss Tang?"

"Which Tang? How do you write it?"

"Not sure." Milkie's driver's license hasn't turned up yet.

She shakes her head. Yorks's eyes trace the counter. Ears pulls the plastic surgeon's photo from his pocket.

"Do you recognize her?"

They look at the picture. Cynthia shakes her head, Yorks gives it a cursory glance, defers to her.

"That about does it, Ma *tai-tai*." He pauses to take in the whole office. "One thing. Is the car in question here?"

"Let me think ... no, it's rented out."

"Well then, can you show my detective constable your carpark, where the gate is, how it's locked?"

She pauses and shoots Yorks a puzzled glance, then accompanies Ears out the door. Once they're gone Lok hands a card to Yorks, respectfully with both hands. His back is to the window, blocking Cynthia's view of them.

"I'd like you to call this number today," Lok says.

Yorks says nothing.

"Ma *sin-sahng*, this girl is dead. She was found floating in the Yau Ma Tei typhoon shelter. Right now, I don't think you had anything to do with that."

Yorks's skin whitens like a steamed pomfret.

"Of course I didn't! My wife told you. We don't know the girl." His voice is thin, tentative, as if his tongue is out of practice.

"Listen, Ma *sin-sahng*. This is a murder investigation. If you cooperate, we'll get this cleared up, and you'll be rid of us. However, if you prefer, you may come with me to the station, and we'll discuss this matter there. I'll invite your wife, too. I'm sure she'd want to hear what you have to say."

Yorks continues to pale, as if someone pulled a plug and everything he's made of is draining onto the floor.

"That's not necessary! Please..."

"Then please help me on this matter," he says, giving Yorks face at last. "When can you get away?"

His shoulders collapse slightly. "In the evening."

Lok takes back the name card, writes on it, passes it back to him. "Meet me here at nine."

Yorks nods in resignation.

In the van, Ears tries to hold back his findings till his superior asks, but he bursts out before the van pulls into Austin Road. "Ah Lok, sir, I took notes on the car lot."

Lok nods, absently. Ears continues.

"I figure two men came in, and one went with Yorks to look at the car. Meanwhile, the other one stole the keys. They came back later and drove the car off. Or else they could have stolen the key to the padlock that locks the gate at night, and done it that way ..."

"Then why didn't the owners notice it was gone?" asks Lok.

Ears is silent.

"And why would two men steal a Lexus and give it to an aspiring actress?"

Silence.

The inspector continues. "You should have realized they were lying. Or at least, he was. I don't believe they both could overlook a missing Lexus."

More silence, a mortifying one for Ears.

"Did you watch them when you showed the photo?" asks Lok

"I think so. They said they didn't know her."

"Did they? Ears, in Crime we hear more lies than anyone on earth. If you believe what people tell you, you'll get nowhere."

Getting nowhere is precisely what Ears dreads. He has always been a terrible liar himself, and is still not used to a world where people bullshit you as a matter of course.

"So what do we do?"

"First, we separate them. Yorks didn't look very hard at the picture, because he was afraid of his own reaction. While you were out with the woman, I set up a meeting with him."

The constable understands immediately that he'd been nothing but a decoy, his tour of the parking lot merely a diversion for the wife while Lok worked on the husband. His eponymous ears redden like Autumn Festival lanterns.

Ever since he was old enough to hold a toy gun, Ears has wanted to be a detective and nothing else. Back when his classmates traded cards and stickers with Canto-pop stars and kung-fu heroes on them, Ears curated a shoebox collection of police badges. He could tell a PC from an Inspector by his insignia, and delighted in surreptitiously tailing the policemen who monitored the street hawkers and patrolled the Wanchai market in pairs.

His chances weren't good. The Inspectorate wanted university graduates, and there had been no money for university. He had to work after school at his uncle's stationery store, a cubbyhole sandwiched between an ironmonger's and a noodle shop. His uncle couldn't read or write, and when his aunt died, Ears had to do the accounts, order supplies, pay the bills, renew the business license, read the tax forms. In return, all he got was his nickname, *dao fung yee*—"change wind ears"—referring to the way that breezes blowing toward the boy's face would be deflected sideways by the amazing appendages on each side of his head.

The day Ears was accepted into Police Training School, he felt that Kwan Dai had repaid all his offerings. He did two years in Uniform Branch before applying for a transfer to Crime Duties. Skinny as a rail, with no degree and, let's face it, those ears, he didn't impress the interviewer at first. But the recommendation from his superior made his application glow like a thousand candles. He answered every question thrown at him, and knew his procedures backwards. No interviewer throws away that kind of motivation.

But lately, in Crime, motivation just doesn't seem enough.

CHAPTER 13

THE CELLPHONE, fused to Ambrose Wan's ear for the last hour, has been relaying one stinking piece of bad news after another.

"They can't pull out," Ambrose says.

"Technically they can. They're saying they've got too much on their plate, and can't fulfill the conditions of the agreement."

"Bullshit."

"Of course," says Ronnie Ho. "But there's nothing we can do. It's going to be like this until the suit is settled, and people find out we're still afloat."

Ambrose wants to reassure Ronnie, but he can't let on that the outcome of the suit is assured, not even to his own CFO. Meanwhile, he gets to watch his only other major real estate venture fizzle away like water in a hot wok. He knows why New China Quest shook hands with Wan Industries in the first place—to connect with his father-in-law. But no one will stick with a company that's being torn apart by lawyers.

Rule of law was Britain's gift to Hong Kong, a gift he'd gladly shove back up their asses right now. When Wan Industries is caught doing shoddy work, some American company screams foul and unleashes a pack of wild lawyers on them. But when a local partner wants to back out of a deal that might have kept him going, it's all very Chinese and civil: of course, you understand, conditions have changed, this isn't the right time. He's being screwed front and back by two different civilizations.

Ronnie Ho utters a few comforting words, promises to find a way to cover the shortfalls for a few more weeks. Ambrose signs off and rubs his throbbing temples.

"Are you all right?" asks Brenda. Ambrose didn't hear her enter the room.

"Fine," he says.

"You should see my acupuncturist for the headaches."

"I said I'm fine."

"All right. Dinner's almost ready. Won't you come and see *Ba Ba*?" She lays her hand on his arm tenderly, as if the pain were there instead of behind his eyes.

"In a minute." He slips away from her, trudges to the bedroom.

Hong Kong society writhed with envy when Ambrose Wan married Brenda Wu, daughter of Octavius Wu. They'd met overseas while at Harvard, and after announcing their engagement, gave up their private lives with grace. Everything from Ambrose's daily swims to Brenda's grades ended up in the Hong Kong gossip rags.

The excruciating irony, which only Ambrose sees, is that his life is not good. Until his father-in-law's death he heads his own company, Wan Industries, which has been incorporated for the sole purpose of giving Ambrose a way to prove himself. So far he's botched it. And now this goddam lawsuit, dragging his name— and his father-in-law's by association—into the papers. He prays that Greeny will make it all go away soon.

In his bureau drawer he finds the vial of pills, swallows two, sips some water from a paper cup in the bathroom. By the time he enters the dining room the knife in his brain is a little duller. He finds Octavius holding forth on one of his favorite subjects.

"Where are my grandchildren? That's what I want to know."

It isn't enough to rule a company, beat the drum for Hong Kong, be the object of every man's envy. He must also bring his very seed into service on behalf of the firm.

Of course, Brenda hasn't conceived a child yet. Ambrose suspects it is his fault, and in any case he doesn't love her and rarely touches her. But there is no question of seeing a doctor: his father will cut him off if he finds their marriage barren.

Fortunately Lourdes, the Filipina maid, chooses this moment to announce dinner. Brenda takes her father's elbow and ushers him into a dining room filled with the aroma of roast pork.

Brenda helps Octavius to the head chair. He's thinner these days, Wan notices. The suits bag on his frame. And he stoops more.

"It's lonely here," Octavius says. "Not like at my sons' houses. No grandchildren here to greet me."

"There will be, *Ba Ba*," says Brenda. "These days we plan kids carefully."

Octavius grunts.

Lourdes sets out a fragrant dish of pork and bamboo shoots on the immense rosewood dining table. She didn't cook it: the Wan family keeps a Chinese chef on call for family nights. Octavius, never one for steaks and salads, won't eat anything but Chinese food anymore. Raw meat, raw vegetables, he said. Why can't the *gweilos* learn to cook?

Thin he might be, but the wizened man devours his rice heartily. "You might as well live on the Mainland," he says between bites, "where they're not allowed to have kids. Is that why I built this business? So you could live like a worker in Swatow?"

Ambrose smiles in a way he hopes is sufficiently servile. "I'm a little busy now, *Gong-Gong*."

"That lawsuit horseshit? All this suing going on! During my first ten years in business I only met one lawyer. And that was just to read contracts. We settled our own business then."

Indeed you did, thinks Ambrose.

It was Octavius's father Harold who started exporting paper goods in the nineteen-thirties. During the war Harold collaborated with the Japanese, not from necessity, but from a shared hatred for the British. The money he earned betraying the Allies helped him emerge stronger than ever when the Japanese were finally driven out. He founded Goldway Industries as a tool for his patriotic ambitions. Of course, for a Chinese, there was only one kind of patriotism: loyalty to China. The Hong Kong Government, with its rule of law and capitalistic ethos, was mere soil in which his enterprise could grow and serve China.

Then Mao swept through the mainland and claimed it for the people. Wu found no contradiction in supporting a China that executed landlords and turned factories over to workers. After all, Mao spit in the eye of the British, the Americans, the West; that was the important thing. And there were the Chinese people, starving inside the world's largest labor camp, who needed his help.

Back then an embargo kept strategic goods out of China. Materials like cobalt oxide, used in enamelware, and thorium nitrate, needed to manufacture light bulbs, were not permitted, on the grounds that the Chinese could use them to make weapons. It was unfair, and Harold Wu knew it. As far as he could tell, the Brits were trying to keep China poor as well as weaponless.

Fortunately, the inspectors at the Strategic Control Licensing Branch were paid like peons, and welcomed extra income. That's how Harold smuggled medical supplies, food, machinery, car parts, diesel engines, and tires into China—a dangerous gamble that made him millions.

During the Korean War Octavius joined his father Harold's business. He started sending arms and ammunition into China at an astounding risk. Other tycoons and small operators did the same, of course. Some were patriotic, and some just greedy, but all of them got rich.

Gradually Octavius took over Harold's company. Not nearly so patriotic as his father, and much warier of communists, Octavius removed Goldway from the armament business. It was no sacrifice; as far as smuggling goods into the mainland went, out-of-date medicines were just as profitable as World War II–vintage Tokarev rifles, and a good deal safer.

Something was always being banned somewhere, and Octavius set out to supply it. He shipped industrial diamonds and watches to India, flouting import duties. He sent shiploads of Marlboros and Camels to the Philippines, where foreign brands were taxed to boost the local industry.

Harold Wu died in the mid-Sixties. On his deathbed, he made Octavius promise to fight to keep Hong Kong World War II veterans from getting a pension. *"They fought with the British; they should all starve,"* he had said.

Goldway Industries became Goldway International. Octavius branched out into real estate and shipping, in plenty of time for the territory's heyday as a financial and export center. The system of government land auctions, which parceled out insanely valuable real estate to a small clique of businesses, brought wealth that even old Harold could not have imagined. Goldway's empire grew, and by 1970 all of the old smuggling operations had ceased. Octavius understood that once you're big enough, once you own a quarter of Central District, you don't have to break the law any-more. Why steal money when you have a license to print it?

Brenda excuses herself, walks out of the room. Octavius looks up from his pork, turns to face Ambrose for the first time tonight. A smoker until the 1980s, he speaks in a hoarse whisper.

"Need some rhino horn? My man gets the best stuff. Tiger penis too. A little every day and ..." he raises his chopsticks until they stand vertical, and cackles. To Octavius, any man who doesn't have children is either impotent or queer.

"No, *Gong-gong*, I don't need any rhino horn," Ambrose says. The fact that rhino hunting is banned isn't worth mentioning.

"Well, get to work. I take a little of the powder every day. Costs me five thousand a month, but I can still ..." The chopsticks go vertical again.

Brenda returns, sits down. "What did I miss?" she asks.

Neither man speaks.

Lourdes brings in a bowl of sweet corn soup and ladles it into bowls.

"All this food for just three people," says Octavius.

CHAPTER 14

ONLY THE STRINGS occupy the stage. Hector and the other basses sit patiently while Shao attempts to fix a passage in the piece, *Threnody for the Victims of the Nanjing Massacre*, a new work by Phileas Fong. The passage is a cascade of eighth notes requiring awkward string crossings from the violas.

"Play four after C," says Shao. The violas saw out a phrase. Shao halts and stares at them.

"Not good," he says. The silence in the room deepens. "You were supposed to prepare this music. You had the parts before this rehearsal, I know. How can we get any work done when you don't know the music?" He speaks in clear English, his Cantonese pronunciation changing "were" to "wuh" and "work" to "wuk."

"Just the first two stands," he says.

The four violas closest to Shao play, making it through with a decent sound. *An exhibition of staggering adequacy,* Leo would have called it.

No one starts out with dreams of playing viola, Hector. That's all you need to know. You begin on violin like everyone else, and after a while someone—your teacher, your parents, the school orchestra leader—decides that you're not going to make it. They shove a viola in your hand and introduce you to a world of reduced expectations.

So you're playing this instrument that's fatter than the violin, but not much longer. On the viola, the exquisite proportions that give the violin and the cello their sound are kludged into something that's low enough to support the violins, but small enough to fit under your chin. A $20,000 instrument that sounds like a rubber band. A violin with a head cold, if you're lucky.

So you're a violist now. Forget about the high passages, the solos. Most of the time you're covered by the fiddles or backed up by the cellos, since composers aren't stupid enough to inflict your naked sound on the audience. Forget about the main melody that brought everyone into the concert hall in the first place—you're allotted some crazy mirror image of it to fill out the harmony. You live your life as a noodle in the orchestral soup, sopping up the flavors around you and being swallowed along with them. Second-raters in front of you, failures behind you. That, Hector, is why viola sections bring misery to everyone.

"Now the rest of you," Shao says.

The five back players—Leo would have been the sixth—fall apart during the passage.

"Just the last stand."

Edison Ki and his stand partner Mok Bong-ho have sat in the back since the orchestra was founded, sharing no glory and feeling little pain. Their weak sounds are usually buried in the wash of volume that the section produces. Few things frighten them more than having to parade their abilities naked in front of their peers.

"I don't like this," Clem whispers in Hector's ear. "He smells blood."

Bong pauses to tighten his bow. Ki draws a breath, and they

play a shabby version of the phrase, barely managing to end on the same pitch.

"Again," Shao says. They repeat it. Ki's neck glistens with sweat. At some point their bows go out of sync, so they look as ragged as they sound.

Shao stops and points to Edison Ki.

"Just you," he says.

The violist blinks, and starts to play. He lurches to a halt when he misses a note, then continues with his pitiful approximation of the notes on the page.

Shao lowers his baton and stares at Ki silently for a half minute borrowed from some ice age in which time barely crept at all. "You play like that," he says softly, "you should save your money."

Ki's tan flesh blazes red. He trains his eyes on his music, avoiding everyone's gaze for the remaining quarter hour. Then, when the break is called, Edison and Bong disappear to the dark corridors upstairs.

Chiu Shun-fu, who's been sitting in the audience, bounds to the stage.

"So you think you can make everyone afraid of you?" he shouts. "Make us back down?"

Shao glares at the horn player, then pushes through the empty chairs to his dressing room.

Clem lays down his bass. "This is insane," he says. "I can't believe Shao did that. And did you hear Chiu? The man's out of control. This place is going nuts, Hec."

"Something else is going on," says Hector. "Did you see Bonson in the back with the notepad? He was jotting things down while Shao was drilling the violas."

"There's a man comin' round takin' names ..." Clem sings in a resonant baritone.

"Right. Shao wants to clean house. This is payback for the petition."

Clem shakes his head in resignation and loosens his bow. "We already lost our best viola. Where the heck is Leo?" Clem, a Baptist from Nebraska, never curses.

Hector explains about Leo's disappearance a couple of days ago.

"Think he just had enough? Folded his tent and stole away, like Rick and Emily last year?"

"Without his viola?"

"Maybe he decided to chuck it. He's probably hanging out in some topless bar, figuring out what to do next."

But if he is, thinks Hector, *who searched his flat?*

He watches the crew wheel a bass trunk off stage. It's Clem's trunk—the wheel squeaks in D-sharp. As usual, Yip is watching, not lifting.

Twinkie had mentioned an argument between Yip and Leo. He tries to imagine them nose to nose: Leo's Semitic beak up against Yip's broad Chinese mushroom. Leo is slightly taller, Yip a bit wider in the shoulders. Neither would be a pushover in a fight.

The crewman has a poor grip on the side of the trunk. His right sleeve creeps up his awkwardly extended arm, revealing the tail of a meticulously-inked dragon.

Chinese freemasons, Leo had called the triads.

As he pulls the trunk up a ramp the mover turns a little too fast, and one wheel drops off the side, sending the case tottering to the left.

"Maan-maan," Yip says, a knife edge in his voice. *Slowly.* The man rights the case, steers it out the back service exit, and returns for Hector's case. Hector trails the man and watches till his bass is safely strapped to the wall of the truck outside.

"Got a problem?" Yip says in Cantonese. Part question, part

taunt, same as in English.

Hector says nothing.

"Take a look," Yip says. He walks up the ramp of the box truck, a twenty-four footer, and gestures Hector to follow. Not rudely with a crooked finger, but politely with a scooping motion at hip level, the Chinese way. Hector follows him up into the truck.

The tympani are already packed in next to the rest of the percussion. Metal trunks are filled with music stands. And on a stool sits the other mover, the man with the face like a voodoo mask. He looks up at Hector, eyelids at half mast, as if musicians climb into the back of the truck every day. He draws a sunflower seed from his pocket, splits it in his teeth, spits out the shell. *How much do you charge to haunt a house?*

Yip yanks down the door of the truck and faces Hector.

"You don't like our work?" he says in English. He's gym-fit, with moussed hair.

"Did I say that?"

"You were watching my man. That's my job."

"Sorry. I didn't mean to offend you."

"Do you think I don't know my job?" Yip draws close, a bit too close. Hector knows about jobs and face. Never imply that someone can't do his job. Never tell someone his job. Never confront people directly about the lousy job they're doing, unless you're a superior and the permission is implied. Oblique hints are better. Blaming it on yourself works. *Sorry, I forgot to mention that you're not supposed to drop musical instruments on the ground. I should have been clear, but I must have been too busy. Forgive me.*

Hector is silent.

"Why don't you answer?"

The tall man with the face splits another seed. Yip turns to him.

"Skinwic, what do you think of this guy?"

Skinwic doesn't move. The whole scene is something out of a Cantonese melodrama.

"You and that horn player Chiu, you're trouble," Yip says. "I tell you what I told him. Learn how to behave."

"I'm not trying to make trouble," Hector says in calming tones. "But these are fine instruments. Mine was made back when Hong Kong was a fishing village ruled by the Qing Dynasty emperor. It cost a lot. And it has to be moved carefully."

"Don't worry so much."

"May I go now?"

Yip rolls up the steel door. Hector walks down the ramp, turns and looks back at the man in the truck.

"Skinwic, huh?"

"No trouble, okay?" Yip says.

CHAPTER 15

AT THE YAU TSIM canteen, Lok ponders his Singapore noodles, chopsticks untouched at the side of the plate.

"This help?" Will Pullman delivers a jar of hot sauce to the table and takes the chair opposite Lok. His plate is heaped with pork chow mein.

"I hear you got the floater," Pullman says. He's a Detective Inspector, about Lok's age. "And they're saying she had breast implants?"

Pullman has been outside recently. Beads of sweat dot his brow and plaster his thinning mouse-brown hair to the pink dome underneath. One of those Brits who never gets used to the heat. Though you wouldn't suspect it by the gouts of chili sauce he's pouring on his dish.

Years earlier as DPCs Lok and Pullman brought in the murderer of Russell Wong, a Macau casino owner who'd turned up wrapped in his own intestines in a trunk behind a seafood restaurant in Yau Ma Tei. The team's every move was front page news for a couple of weeks. The resulting prestige and commendations boosted their careers.

And then came the new era. The force wanted university educated cops, and suddenly Lok was looking old-school. And Will Pullman, of course, was a *gweilo*. Good record, spoke Cantonese like a native, but 1997 was over and done with. The British element of the force, once prominent, was being squeezed to the sidelines. The ready-made excuse was that the force had little use for cops who couldn't read and write Chinese.

Still, Lok likes him. You learn to treasure good friends, because if you're doing a good job, they're the only good people you ever meet. Everyone else is a loan shark, murderer, or other all-out shit, or else an informer, pickpocket, or some stupid kid from an international school caught stealing gin from a supermarket. Even when you're thrown up against good people, it's at the worst time of their life. You're the one telling a mother her son's been caught selling pills to school kids, telling a husband that his wife has just been killed by a runaway bus.

"You know better than to believe what you hear," says Lok. "She had her eyes and nose done, that's all."

"Bah! The rumor's always better, isn't it?" He swallows some tea. "I saw Dora the other day at the Club. She seems to be enjoying life. How are the kids?"

"Not bad. Edna's being difficult. She colored her hair yellow. I don't know what to do."

Pullman smiles. "What makes you think you can do anything?"

"I don't know. It's not just the hair, it's everything. She's ..."

"Growing up?"

"More than that. I know they grow up, Will. But it's as if she's trying to show me how daring she is, how disobedient she can be."

"Is it really as bad as all that? She does well in school, you said."

He ponders, tries to draw away from his own emotions. Would he consider the same behavior as worrisome in someone else's daughter? All the kids are more Westernized nowadays. They listen to Western music, parrot English song lyrics, wear American fashions. That doesn't mean they'll all do drugs and get pregnant. "Maybe you're right," he says.

Pullman spears a wad of noodles, lifts them to let them cool. "Well, my oldest made my life hell for a while. I figured if I just set some limits, and accepted what she did, she'd eventually grow out of it. That's pretty much how it worked out."

Ironic, Lok thinks. When Edna was born Lok's brother Edwin tried to give him face by playing down the disappointment of having a first-born girl. "Girls are much less trouble," he'd said. "And they'll take care of your next ones."

He needs to do better with Edna, be big about it. Kwan had it right: change with the times, or become outdated and useless. China, having refused to change for centuries, is still tormented by the humiliation its stubbornness brought on.

"See you at Wong Chuk Hang? Week after next, right?" says Pullman.

"Not sure if I can make it. Too busy."

Pullman raises his eyebrows. "They're really pushing this sort of thing now. I doubt it's wise to stay away."

Lok nods and picks up his chopsticks.

CHAPTER 16

IGNORING THE KEENING of vacuums and the clatter of chairs, Letitia Wheately-Craven taps out the opening of her concert review. Apart from her, the press box at the Grand Theatre is empty, the Chinese critic having written his review during the finale and e-mailed it during the applause. Such haste strikes Letitia as improper, so she's waited, as usual, till the house is quiet.

Friday night the Hong Kong Symphony soared to new heights with a performance of Mozart's Jupiter Symphony that demonstrated fully the players' ability to tackle the complexities of this most demanding of scores. From the opening bars, it was clear that Maestro Shao Din-yan was in control.

The door squeaks open. That reporter, the one with the absurd name, pokes her head in. Twinkie. The very idea.

"So how was it?" Twinkie asks.

"Very good. Didn't you hear it?"

"Yes, I sat in the audience, but I don't know much about this kind of music. I thought I'd get your opinion."

Unsure of whether she's being complimented or manipulated,

Letitia says only, "It was excellent."

"And Shao? He's good?" Twinkie walks in, sits in a chair opposite Letitia, glances through window of the press box to the stage, where two men in dress shirts are stacking chairs.

"I'd say he's good, yes," Letitia says.

"He sure jumps around a lot."

"That's his way of drawing music out of the players. All good conductors do that."

"The orchestra doesn't like him."

"So I've heard." Now Letitia is on guard. Twinkie scares her—all the real journalists scare her. All those facts they know, all those connections they cultivate, all that familiarity with newspaper politics. Letitia avoids the reporters, preferring to deal only with her editor.

Beyond that, Twinkie is one of the Pretty Young Chinese Things, a group to which Letitia feels she owes nothing but revenge.

"The horn player, Chiu Shun-fu? He wants them to cancel the tour. He says the orchestra is playing so poorly, it would present a bad image."

"That would be a shame," says Letitia. "A tour would be a wonderful thing for the orchestra, don't you think?"

Twinkie shrugs. "If you say so. I'm just trying to figure this out. People have been writing in to the paper. Seen this?" She pulls a printout of an e-mail from her bag.

Hong Kong is a Chinese city. The Colonial era is over, and we no longer need Westerners in key positions to show us how to manage our affairs. If those expat players are such great musicians, let them get jobs in their own countries. Hong Kong will do fine with a Chinese orchestra and Chinese musicians.

Letitia shakes her head in disgust. "This is what happens when a few troublemakers make noise. Shao just needs some time to improve the orchestra. Things will get better, you'll see."

Twinkie stands. "Okay, that's what I wanted to know. Thanks for your help."

"Anytime," she says, unsure of what help she might have been. Letitia follows Twinkie's movements as the younger woman strides confidently out, before turning back to her laptop.

Letitia Wheatley-Craven came upon her chosen career through a lack of talent and a surfeit of spare time. Seventeen years ago she arrived in Hong Kong from Brighton with her banker husband; fourteen years ago Nigel boarded a 747 back to Brighton with a promotion, a new Pretty Young Chinese Thing of a wife, and a blue-eyed, raven-haired infant.

The unscheduled spawning and departure of Nigel Wheatley-Craven forced a decision of a magnitude Letitia was unaccustomed to making. She could return to share a cottage in Brighton with her divorced mother and aunt Georgina, and pass her life steeped in the shame of two generations of abandonment. Or she could stay in Hong Kong and try to assemble a new life. Like many expatriate women whose marriages have fallen to Yellow Fever, she chose to stay.

Some advantages stayed behind with her. The flat was paid for, and Nigel, in what passed for magnanimity in his eyes, gave her a parking space and a lovely big car. The children (their children, not the issue of Nigel and that bitch) were in boarding school in England, where they were spared the bitterness that attended the wreckage of their parents' marriage.

Letitia was also attractive, she believed, with natural blonde hair and a body that had not yet begun to swell or sag. Nice breasts. There have to be some men in Hong Kong who appreciate real breasts, she thought. She would get a job, meet someone new, and live life on her own terms.

Letitia was not alone in her belief that her proficiency in written and spoken English entitled her to a career in Hong Kong; many Westerners believed so, and often willed a career of sorts into existence as a result. In Letitia's case what materialized was an English-language tabloid, which happened to be hiring from the pool of part-time English teachers and underoccupied expat housewives that supplemented its regular crew. She began writing fawning profiles of visiting clothes designers, actors, and other notable English speakers on a freelance basis. When the position of music critic came open, Letitia jumped for it. As a child, she'd sung in the church choir, and more important, she possessed a genuine Musical Sensibility. Reviewing concerts wouldn't be difficult, she thought, once she got the hang of it.

Her first review used up all the musical adjectives she knew. A thesaurus taught her to describe nice playing as lyrical, strong bowing as incisive, loud voices as robust, sweet tones as angelic. But soon she was struggling to find something new to say week after week, performance after performance.

More distressing was the letter that some irate music lover wrote, and which the paper saw fit to publish. "Your reviewer is obviously not aware of some basic facts about music," it began, and went on to cite her confusion of "crescendo" with "climax," "arpeggios" with "double stops," and so on.

Letitia was mortified. Seeing the letter as a threat to her livelihood, she set out immediately to boost the authority in her writing voice. The more professional she sounded, she was convinced, the less likely that readers would challenge her.

Books on music were no help. She found them boring and hard to understand, full of terms like *secondary dominant* and *sforzando.* A better source of ideas were the music reviews in newspapers from back home, which taught her how to create the illusion of familiarity with a work. *The evening opened with a glittering version of Glinka's overture to* Russlan and Ludmilla. *Performing at breakneck tempo, Shao drew a spectacular variety of colors and textures from the orchestra, surmounting the technical difficulties of the piece without surrendering the truly Russian feel of the piece, as conductors sometimes do.*

Newer composers were problematical, but she found a way around that.

Phileas Fong's Threnody for the Victims of the Nanjing Massacre *is a challenging work which uses the full resources of the orchestra to portray what the composer terms, "the existential questions arising from the role of history in Chinese life." The violently clashing textures and evocative sonorities make it difficult to take the measure of the piece in one hearing, though the work clearly owes a debt to Penderecki and others of his ilk. The orchestra gave a spirited reading of this arresting, enigmatic piece.*

The language of reviewing was a gold mine for Letitia's self-esteem. She loved using the word "reading," which sounded so much more professional than "performance." She never felt more secure than when stating how players "acquitted" themselves that night, how a conductor brought out "inner voices" resulting in "unexpected colorations" and "compelling sonorities." This golden vocabulary, she felt, earned her an invitation to quit her tabloid and become the *Post*'s music reviewer. Four years after launching her career, she'd reached the top.

From that day, Letitia assumed she was in control of matters musical. She might never have learned otherwise had not someone—obviously a discontented musician—mailed something nasty in a tissue to her, along with one of her reviews, neatly scissored out of the Post with one sentence underlined: *The Symphony musicians did not play very well, but the conductor was brilliant.*

Isolated on a sliver of newsprint, the sentence did look a bit, well, silly. But what made some crank single out those words, among the thousands she'd typed over the years?

After an hour's study of her bulky scrapbook she came to realize what had angered the reader so much. Without exception, Letitia described conductors favorably when they danced frantically on the podium, and unfavorably when they were reserved. The conductor's physique also came into play. Reports of conductors who were short, stocky, or old—with the exception of very handsome elderly men with wavy white hair—invariably led readers to believe that they'd not missed much that night. Women conductors puzzled her, and when writing an account of their performances, Letitia rarely said more than that the maestra "did a fine job" or "proved equal to the material." Shao, with his slim figure and masculine bearing, and his habit of waving his arms in wide, samurai-like sweeps, generated constant and extravagant praise.

A horrifying thought occurred to her: was her genuine Musical Sensibility not adequate for the job of music critic for the paper of record in a city of six million? Her predecessor, after all, could read music and had even taken lessons on the baritone horn.

For weeks she agonized over the anonymous attack. During that dreadful period she tried to really listen to the orchestras she reviewed—listen hard from start to finish. She pored over her dusty collection of second-hand music books, and tried to penetrate deeper into music's dark, mysterious core.

All that penetrating made her tired, and frankly, didn't improve her reviews at all. Eventually she decided not to let one complaint from an orchestral malcontent ruin her life. Letitia went back to enjoying concerts as she had before, writing about them in the way she knew best. And no one complained again. So how badly could she be doing?

———————

THE AUDIENCE IS gone. So is Twinkie, and everyone else save a couple of women in smocks, sweeping the floor and gleaning discarded programs. With no critics, reporters, or Pretty Young Chinese things breathing down her neck, she taps out the rest of the review.

All in all, the concert was a splendid season opener, and one waits with bated breath to see what wonders Maestro Shao will work with his baton next week.

CHAPTER 17

THE FLAT IS empty when Lok returns. Dora must be at the gym. Edna at University. Kelvin at basketball practice, perhaps. No idea about Kitty. Esmeralda at the supermarket, surely. These days the apartment is less a home than a terminal where roaming inhabitants come to rest during the evening hours. It was different when he was a child out on the island, where a grandparent and an aunt or two were always gossiping in the yard or pottering in the kitchen.

He grabs a Tsing Tao and enters the living room, only to be confronted once again by the void where the soft chair used to be.

His puzzlement at the quiet of the flat is tempered by some relief at not having to confront Edna right away. The girl is going to have to listen to reason sooner or later, but right now she's too rebellious and thin-skinned, too prone to bridle at his advice.

He flips open the paper.

Ambrose Wan to Appear in Shenzhen Court
Ambrose Wan, CEO of Wan Industries, will testify today in a lawsuit brought against him by Elkon Industries of San

Francisco, California. Wan Industries and Elkon were joint venture partners in the construction of Valiant Plaza, a multi-purpose residential/commercial complex in Shenzhen. The American company accuses Wan Industries of providing substandard construction which renders the complex "useless for its intended purpose."

Esmeralda is the first to enter, toting some pink plastic bags from the market down the road. One of the bags twitches: a grass carp is suffocating in the Hong Kong air. She vanishes into the kitchen, and soon Lok hears the whack of the chopper and the hiss of the wok, sounds which begin to re-weave the frayed tapestry of his life.

Halfway through the business section Dora breezes in, gym bag on her shoulder. She greets Lok with an affectionate pinch on the arm.

"Where's everyone?" he asks.

"Kitty is at the library studying with Man-wai. She has a math test tomorrow. Kelvin is at the game arcade."

Lok loathes those places, with their barking machines and teenage triads bullying protection money out of kids.

"I think I found out something about your friend Rocky Cheu," Dora says, zipping open her bag and unfolding her fuchsia gym suit. She's been working out at the Police Sports and Recreation Club.

"What's that?"

"He's cheating on his wife."

"He said that?"

"No. But he told me he went golfing in Shenzhen on his day off yesterday."

"And?"

She drops her bag in a closet and picks up the TV remote. "You know how sunny it was yesterday. But he had no dark spot on the back of his hands, where golfing gloves are open. Whatever he was doing in Shenzhen, it wasn't outdoors."

Lok nods appreciatively at Dora's deductive skills, and they sit down to watch the news. Neither of them mentions Edna.

Kelvin and Kitty are home by the time the fragrance of steamed carp and ginger fills the air. Edna arrives at the last minute and keeps silent during dinner. Lok steals a few glances at her blonde hairdo but talks about work. Only after the meal is over and Esmeralda has begun clattering dishes does Edna speak up. "What boat are you taking next Sunday?" she asks.

"8:45," says Dora.

"I thought you weren't coming to Cheung Chau," says Lok. Most weekends they take the one-hour ferry trip to Cheung Chau Island to visit Lok's parents.

"Herman ..."

"It's a fair question, isn't it? She said ..."

"I want to come along. Is that all right?"

"Of course," says Dora, her voice radiating a defensive cheer. "Why wouldn't it be?"

Lok has a moment to savor the restoration of order to his life before Edna speaks again.

"I'll be bringing Julian."

"Who?" asks Lok.

"My boyfriend. He'd like to meet you."

"What boyfriend?" Lok says. "When did you get a boyfriend?" His voice gets louder with each word.

"*Ba Ba* ..."

"Herman ..."

Lok stands up. "I have to go out," he says.

———————

"I DIDN'T DO anything wrong," says Yorks Ma. "I just lent the car to her as a favor." His voice carries a little more authority now that he's out of his wife's shadow, but the proprietor of Brilliant Fortune Car Hire is clearly petrified.

They're sitting in a booth at a Mongkok tea house, a quiet spot away from the window.

"Calm down, Ma *sin-sahng*," says Lok, using the title to give him some face. "No one said you did anything wrong. But a girl has died, and we need to find out what happened."

"I didn't know! I swear! It has nothing to do with me."

"All right, all right. Now, her name was Milkie Tang, correct? Do you know her Chinese name?"

"Yes. I saw her driver's license. Tang Yee-fun."

Finally Milkie is on our radar, thinks Lok. Now it's a matter of pulling up the documentation that tracks Hong Kong people from swaddling clothes to funeral urn.

"How do you write that?"

"Tang like Tang Dynasty, Yee-fun." Yorks sketches "Yee" and "Fun" in the air. Lok writes them down.

"Do you have an address?"

"No. I think she lived around here and passed by the shop. Maybe that gave her the idea."

"What idea?"

"Getting a ... free car." His head settles into his neck like a turtle's.

"You let her use a car for free?"

"Only a few times."

"And what did she give you?"

No answer. Lok puts away his pad, looks up. Yorks resists his eyes, stares into a corner.

"Ma *sin-sahng*," says Lok, "Did you sleep with her?"

Yorks closes his eyes in shame. Yet he's almost relieved that the admission is over with. "We went to a love hotel in Mongkok a couple of times," he says. "Only twice." He raises two limp fingers for emphasis.

"Is that how many times she borrowed the car?"

Yorks reddens. "No, there were more times after that. First she'd say she needed the car right away, and she'd take me to the hotel later. I had her cellphone number, but after a while, she ignored my calls. She'd just come in when she needed the car, when my wife was gone. I ... I told her she'd have to go back to the hotel if she wanted to keep borrowing the car. But ..." The last words jam in his throat.

"She threatened to tell your wife," Lok says.

Yorks is dismayed. "How did you know?"

Lok resists the urge to burst out laughing. "Still have that phone number?" he asks.

"No, I tore it up."

That showed her. "What can you tell me about her, Yorks?" He pours them some tea, seems to concentrate more on the pot than his interview.

"About this tall ..."

"Yorks, I've seen her. I'm asking what kind of girl she was."

Yorks doesn't appear to like the question.

"She was nice to me at first. She was ... very passionate. But I suppose she was using me." No surprise there, thinks Lok. A couple of hours in a short-time hotel with Yorks is not many women's idea of hot sex. Yorks is skinny as a chicken's foot, patches of black dye in his hair where he's attempted to conceal the grey.

"Did she have anyone with her when she came for the car?" he asks.

"Just a dog, sometimes. One of those little, noisy dogs that young girls seem to like. I was always worried the car would come back full of dogshit."

"Ever any men with her?"

His eyes narrow. "Once. He was tough-looking, maybe thirty, one of your triad types for sure. Didn't like him, but I just saw him through the window. I never met him. She gave him a ride back here, and then they went off somewhere. Didn't even come in to say thanks for the car. Will this have to get out? It's very ... I mean ... I'm so ..."

Lok nods reassuringly. "We don't know yet. We're still investigating. Maybe your name will be kept out of this, if it turns out the car isn't relevant to the investigation. But we might need to talk to you again."

"What shall I do about my wife?"

"Lie to her, Yorks. Think you can manage that?"

CHAPTER 18

WALKING INTO THE auditorium, Hector sees Chiu and Twinkie in a back row. He flops into in a nearby seat. Chiu waves to him but keeps speaking to Twinkie. On stage, Shao is rehearsing the woodwinds.

"It's a massacre," Chiu is saying, under his breath to keep from disturbing the musicians at work onstage. "Shao is trying to fire troublemakers, clean out the orchestra."

"But the people in danger, it seems to me, are the ones that can't play well, not the troublemakers."

"Don't you see? He's got everyone scared. Even good players are being careful now, watching what they say. No way they're going to push for a better conductor. That's always the way incompetent people stay in power, through fear."

"Do you agree?" Twinkie asks Hector. She points a memo recorder his way.

He sighs. "I suppose you're going to quote me. Just don't use my name, okay?"

"Wouldn't dream of it," she says.

"I've got to run," says Chiu. "Need to warm up." Chiu rises

and jogs backstage.

"Look, Twinkie," Hector says. "I apologize for yesterday."

She nods, says nothing. He continues. "I was rude. You're serious about your job, I understand. It's just that I know Leo, I know how he relates to pretty women."

She ignores the compliment. "Why don't you do more to get Shao out, if you dislike him? Afraid to be a troublemaker?"

"Are you kidding? I've just been called a troublemaker officially, by the head of our moving staff."

"By Yip? You're joking."

"Nope. He threatened me. Got me alone, told me to behave."

"What did you do to him?"

"I think I insulted his crew. Whatever. Look, Twinkie, forget Shao. I'm worried about Leo. He wouldn't have ducked out on me. Anyone else, maybe, but not me. Something's wrong."

Her eyes leave his for a moment. She seems to be weighing his desperation.

He continues. "If I tell you something, will you promise not to print it?"

"No."

That stops him.

"Well then, will you promise not to print it until I'm sure that Leo's safe?"

She pauses, apparently thinking the deal over. "All right."

"His flat's been searched."

Her eyes widen. "You're sure about this?"

"Yes. I know his place. Closets opened, stuff dumped out. Something's happened to him." A vague fear stirs inside him, but he can't summon the courage to give it a name.

"Why are you telling me this?"

"You can help me find him. He was going to tell you about something important. You're a reporter, you know how to look for things in this city.

"And I'm a Chinese speaker."

"*Yat deng hai.*" Absolutely.

"Very good accent," she says, without smiling. Immediately he regrets showing off his mediocre Cantonese. Most Chinese in Hong Kong praise Westerners for the skimpiest accomplishments in the language, like a father complimenting his toddler for tossing a ball an arm's length. Hector loathes the implicit condescension, but he knows it's well-earned by the Hong Kong expatriate community, the largest group of functional illiterates outside Calcutta: thousands of adults who can only say "good morning," "coffee no sugar," and whatever taxi drivers need to take them to the office and back. Full-grown *gweilo* executives, journalists, administrators, and teachers who communicate with the residents of their adopted city on a level below that of a native three-year-old. What can Chinese think of the many-hued, multi-shaped kindergartners who mill among them every day?

"Twinkie, help me find Leo. It might be a story for you."

"I doubt it. What's he like? Does he drink?"

"The police already asked me that."

She looks amazed. "The police? You spoke to them?"

"I filed a missing person report."

"Did you mention the search?"

"Not really. It sounded kind of, well …"

"*Chi sin.*" Crazy.

"Right."

"And what did they do?"

"Nothing, just took the report."

"That makes sense. Missing *gweilos* aren't a big concern, usually. Kids, maybe."

A reedy voice cries out in Cantonese. "All right! We need everyone!" The rest of the musicians file onstage.

"So what do you say? It could be a story."

"Okay, I'll see what I can do. But it seems like you need him more than he needs you."

Saw through me, didn't you, Hector thinks.

"Meanwhile, stay out of Yip's way," she continues. "Chinese people don't like direct confrontation, did you know that?"

"Yes. Does that mean I shouldn't confront you?"

She smiles, slips her memo recorder in her bag, and says good-by.

Everyone is a puzzle. He watches her walk up the aisle. *Everyone is a maze, and I'm lost.* One night he asked Zenobia what she saw in him. He'd pondered his own attraction to her, knew the subtleties of yellow fever, though he hated the expression. But why would a Hong Kong woman choose a *gweilo*? Zen made fun of his Cantonese, laughed at his hairy chest. What in hell did she see in him?

Maybe you're better off not knowing, she'd said.

———

NOW LETITIA WHEATLEY-CRAVEN sits on a sofa across from the Maestro, who wears dark trousers and the turtleneck that conductors the world over are issued before being released to do interviews. His hair—what there is of it—is neatly combed, and she notices at once that his shoes and watch are those of a man with taste. The late afternoon sun seems to ignite the curtained balcony doors of Shao's Kowloon Tong flat, whose enormous size leads her to conclude that conductors do well.

"Does it worry you, what the musicians are doing?" she asks, in a muted, respectful tone.

"The petition? No. That's all politics." His voice is thin and not particularly pleasant, but his English is good.

"I'm not a politician," he continues. "I'm a musician. My loyalty is to him." He points to a ceramic bust of Mozart on the mantle. "Perhaps I should learn to be more political. All I know is that I care how the music sounds, and I do whatever I can to make the performance good. I've always wanted the Hong Kong Symphony to be a good orchestra. Apparently a lot of people prefer it to be a happy orchestra."

The beginning of a question forms in Letitia's mind, but it escapes before she can finish writing Shao's response in longhand. She checks her list of questions, wishing they still seemed as pertinent as they did this morning when she compiled them.

"I don't know if you want to speak about the specific issues in the petition ..."

"I don't mind at all."

"There's something about the baton ..."

"Baton technique, yes. I could go on for hours about how you can use a baton to bring music out. Every conductor's beat is a personal signature." He sweeps his hand in the air in a gesture one could only call conductor-like. "I've developed my technique as a way to transfer my love of the music to the orchestra, and to the audience as well. My job is to put fire in the players. A conductor is a messenger, bringing the good news of Beethoven and Tchaikovsky to all."

"Well, that does make sense, doesn't it?" says Letitia. She wants to leave the topic of the petition, and listen to more of Shao's theories, drink in more of his musicality, but she does feel some journalistic responsibility to cover the pressing matter. One more question, and that's it, she decides.

"And how about that 'out of tune' business?"

"What do you think, Mrs. Wheately-Craven? You go to the concerts. You listen, judge the performances with professional ears. I've read your reviews, and I don't think very much gets by you. Does the orchestra sound out of tune to you? Do you think I'm not doing my job?"

Thrown by the question, she pauses. "Well, yes, I do. I mean, I think you are doing it. The concerts are wonderful." Gathering speed, now. "You know, Maestro, I really don't know what these players are on about. Are you angry about the petition?"

He shakes his head slowly. "No, of course not. It's not an easy job, being a musician. I feel for them. But it's not easy being in authority either. My first responsibility is to the composer, to realize his vision. Or hers. I suppose I irritate some players, and that's unfortunate. But the spirit of Mozart is what's important." He points to the ceramic head again. "Old Wolfgang is demanding. I can't serve him and also please every ego in the orchestra."

They chat on more comfortable topics for another half hour. At the close of the interview, Shao grasps her hand warmly and thanks her for her time. "It's wonderful to know that music criticism is in such good hands," he says. She is speechless, blushing all the way back to her professional ears.

CHAPTER 19

"I'LL TELL YOU what happened. Someone stole the car from Yorks and held it for ransom. He paid it. No big deal." Million Man is holding forth in the Hot Room, which lives up to its name today.

"Why not?" asks Ears.

"Happens all the time. It's a racket. You steal a car, and then call up the owner and offer to return it for twenty thousand or so. Most people pay the money. It's easier than doing all the paperwork, insurance, police. It's better for the crook too— quick profit. I heard about one guy in Wanchai who gets his car stolen three times a year."

Ears give him a skeptical look.

"No, these things happen. A guy reports his Benz stolen, and the next day he calls up Inspector Pullman and says, 'Guess what, I was taking a walk in Tuen Mun, and I just happened to find my car. Can you imagine that?' And here's the best part—the guy only has one leg. And he just happens to be out taking a walk in the New Territories two hours from his home, without his car."

He limps theatrically across the room. Ears and Big Pang laugh. Old Ko turns back to his notes, clearly unimpressed with the attention Million Man is getting. "Come on," Million Man says. "That's a good story, admit it."

"Heard better."

"So let's have it." says Million Man, a hint of challenge in his voice.

"No one tops Old Ko's stories," says Big Pang.

"That's the only benefit of being old, you have more time to hear stories," says Million Man. No one laughs.

Old Ko picks up a few stray sheets of paper, taps them three times on the table to straighten them, and lays the pile down squarely in front of him. He places the pencil parallel to the sheets, clearly reveling in having stolen the spotlight from Million Man.

"It happened in '91. You two were shitting in your diapers." He nods toward Million Man and Ears. "The time of the car thefts. A man goes down to his carpark in Tsuen Wan, finds his BMW 7 Series gone.

"He walks in to Tsuen Wan District, reports it. Suddenly he remembers that he left his cellphone in the stolen car. This gives him an idea. He calls his own cellphone number from the police station. And a guy from the gang answers."

Ears starts to ask something, then stifles it. Old Ko ignores him.

"The gang man just says, '*Wai?*' The owner says, 'what have you done with my car?'"

"'I'm stealing it, what do you think?" the guy says. The owner tries to make a deal—he'll pay the crook to bring it back. But the crook says, 'Too late, we're in the boat, we're on our way to China. You'll never see your car again.'

"The owner tries everything—begging, more money—but no luck. Then something happens. The owner hears shouting above the din of the engines.

"The crook says, 'The Marine Police are chasing us,' but he doesn't sound too worried. Remember, they've got four *dai-feis* each." The 400-horsepower engines that pushed the smuggling boats were called "big fats."

"Then BOOM! And he says, 'Shit! One of the *dai feis* has blown.' They're down one engine, and the boat is slowing down. And the crook keeps reporting what's going on. He's getting a thrill telling the owner what's happening with his stolen BMW.

"Now, the crooks decide to scuttle the car and escape on another boat that they've got riding alongside, which has four good engines and which can beat anything Marine has.

"Marine are closing in, so the pilot of the boat with the BMW takes his AK-47, shoots a full magazine into the floor of the boat, ripping a hole the size of watermelon into the hull. It starts to fill up fast. The pilot jumps to the other boat, and they're off.

"The only thing is, this boat's a car job special, custom built to have a BMW or Benz driven on to it. There's no extra space on the sides, so the guy who drove the car on the boat—the guy on the phone—can't even open the doors. There's no clearance to crawl out the windows. So he's trapped, watching the seawater fill the boat and pass the windows.

"All time, the owner is still on the phone in the Tsuen Wan police station. He hears the driver scream, 'Help me, the bastards are drowning me!' The owner doesn't say a word, just listens maybe five minutes, while the guy yells, curses, begs for help, and finally the phone cuts off.

"What happened was, the other boat held the cops off with machine gun fire for a couple of minutes till the car was half underwater. Then they took off like a rocket, too late for the cops to do anything. By the time Marine reached the boat it had flipped over, and car and driver were at the bottom of the South China Sea."

At that moment Lok walks in carrying a printed sheet. The

team falls silent. Big Pang smiles at Million Man, as if to say *I told you no one tops Old Ko's stories.*

"Yorks Ma owns a car hire company," Lok says. "He and I had a conversation last night. It seems Miss Tang was a piece of work. She gave Yorks a couple of Mongkok quickies in exchange for use of a Lexus. Then she threatened to tell his wife, so she didn't have to screw him anymore."

"Clever girl," says Old Ko.

"He remembered Milkie's Chinese name," Lok continues. "Traffic gave us her CCC and ID number."

The sheet, headed Tang Yee-Fun, bears a date of birth and the Chinese Commercial Code for her name. Underneath are printed some addresses.

"Ears," says Lok, "check out her last address, in Causeway Bay. It comes from the driver's license application, so it's not too recent, but you never know. Old Ko, I need you to check Immigration to see if she's been out of Hong Kong recently. Big Pang, see if you can find some employment records."

"Why don't you check the Shell stations?" says Million Man. "Maybe she got free gas, too."

Lok says, "Million Man, you and I will visit her parents, if they're still around. She'll have gone home for the festivals, so maybe they'll know something."

"Sounds easy enough."

"Think so? Good. You can be the one to tell them their daughter's dead. Be ready to go in two minutes." Lok walks out.

Old Ko moves to the computer to enter the results of the traffic enquiry. Despite years of computerization on the force, he types slowly and laboriously, eyes on the keyboard.

"Too bad they don't use ink and brush anymore," Million Man

says. "You'd be able to keep up better then." For whatever reason, Old Ko got passed up for one promotion too many. He is permanently off the track, never to receive a Detective Inspector's warrant card.

"If you think working a computer makes you a detective, you're as stupid as you look."

Million Man laughs the laugh of the invincible and says, "Say, what does Ah Lok like?" He makes the change of subject sound casual.

"'Like?'"

"What does he do on his time off?

Old Ko thinks a minute. "Golf," he says. "Loves it, goes golfing every chance he gets. Lately he's been complaining about his clubs—needs new ones, I think. You know how golfers are about their equipment. Don't play the game myself."

Lok appears at the door and motions to Million Man, who grabs his jacket from the chair and walks out. Old Ko keeps pressing the keys.

———————

TANG MAN SITS on the worn sofa, staring at a television muted but still aglow. His wife Ah Mei weeps. Lok has given Million Man a break, announcing the death of their daughter himself in one quick, compassionate sentence. Now the policemen stand silently till the two compose themselves.

Tang Man speaks first. He looks older than his wife, has short cropped hair and the dark, blotched, precancerous skin of one who toils under the Hong Kong sun.

"You don't know who did it?"

"No, not yet. We were hoping you could help us."

"No, I don't know," says Tang, "but I'm not surprised. She

was *lap sap.*" Ah Mei squirms in torment at the word for "trash." "The girl never listened to me, refused to obey me. Do you have a daughter, Inspector?"

"Two," Lok says.

"Then I feel sorry for you. A son can make you proud, carry on your name, support you in your old age. But a daughter? Only trouble. She was thirteen when she started seeing boys. Thirteen. A neighbor caught her with a man in the electrical closet near the stairs. That's where they go nowadays."

An image of Edna slips into Lok's mind. He's not sure he welcomes Tang Man's pity.

"She had an abortion a year later, too. Didn't she?" he says, turning to Ah Mei.

She says nothing.

"Didn't she!" His shouting tenses her spine, and she nods to ease it.

"I told her to stick to her studies. Shouted at her, punished her constantly. And nothing did any good."

"She had a good job," says Ah Mei through the sobs. "Sent us money."

"Bah!" says Tang Man.

"What kind of job?" asks Lok.

"She worked in a travel company," Ah Mei says. "She was so busy all ... "

"Who'd give her a job?" His roar resonates on the unadorned walls and tile flooring. "You should have seen the way she wrote her characters—worse than me, and I left school when I was ten. We sent her to school, because the law says we had to, and what did she learn? To wear makeup and sleep with men! Just like her mother!"

Ah Mei turns her head away from the policeman to hide her humiliation and pain.

"Did she have a boyfriend?" asks Million Man.

Tang Man shrugs. "How do I know? We haven't seen her in months. Not since *Ching Ming*."

"She said she was moving, and she'd give it to us when she could," says the mother.

"That's a lie. She didn't want anything to do with us. Ungrateful bitch. Now look at the trouble she's caused us."

Ah Mei is breathing slowly and deeply now. Her eyes are shut, and one might think her sleeping but for the agony pulsing beneath her closed eyelids.

"Our generation has the worst fortune in Chinese history," says Tang Man. "We obeyed our fathers, respected our elders, did everything we were supposed to. When we had children, they grew up in this new world. This place where kids drink and take drugs, where virginity doesn't matter, where children won't work in our businesses, or marry who we tell them to. We grew old waiting for our time of respect, and it never came."

Ah Mei finds her feet, pads unsteadily into the kitchen and returns with a slip of paper, which she hands to Lok.

"This was her number. Usually I left a message. But she always called back eventually. Until this August." Together they walk the five steps from the sofa to the door. Tang Man presses a button on the remote and the TV thunders.

"It was my fault," she whispers. "I should have … done something." They all glance at the man on the sofa.

Outside the flat, Lok and Million Man pace the corridor of Block 12, 15th floor, one of a few hundred such corridors throughout the estate. More than twenty thousand people—a good-sized Chinese town—had been shoehorned into sixteen hastily-built towers.

These shoddy buildings never appear in the tourist literature except in hazy photos that emphasize their height and underplay their decrepitude. Close up, the grime-coated walls are too squalid for the lenses of the guidebook photographers. The people who live here fuel the city's prosperity, certainly. They hawk vegetables and meats in wet markets, sell crickets for bird food, load and unload bags of rice, mix cement, and haul pallets of cinderblocks at the numberless construction sites. When they get too old and unemployable, a government stipend gives them enough money for meals, a couple of changes of clothing a year, even a haircut allowance, all carefully meted out by bureaucrats who track the prices of such things for a living. And the residents rarely complain, at least publicly. They've played the game, lost, and are mostly content to rot in this holding tank for Hong Kong's defeated.

"We're slowly getting the facts," Million Man says, just to make conversation. They pass gated doorways just like the Tangs', and peer through the bars at lives furnished with prefab shelving, fed by bubbling pots and steaming woks, accompanied by deafening televisions, and informed by the occasional shouted word above the din of it all.

"Facts?" says Lok absently. He'd patrolled estates like this in his young days. The worst ones were filthy, crowded breeding dens for every kind of crime, from loan sharking and drugs to rape and robbery. Small wonder kids try to grab a few minutes of bliss in a dark corner somewhere.

"Milkie worked for a travel company. Maybe a boss or co-worker ..."

"I doubt she told the truth to her parents about the job. No, I think Milkie had something else going."

"Then we haven't found out much, have we?" From the floor above the sound of phlegm being raised and expelled resonates on tile.

We found out what she was running from, Lok thinks.

CHAPTER 20

AMBROSE WAN WELCOMES the sight of his chauffeur Koo nosing the car up the drive behind Academic Community Hall. Ambrose has just been subjected to one of the newer torments in his life, a symphony concert. That last piece was awful, just a lot of noise. But it was the enforced idleness, the inability to escape from his thoughts, that threatened to drive him insane in his third-row seat.

Winsome urged him to appear interested in the fate of the symphony. He couldn't make the show last night at the Grand Theatre, so tonight he hauled himself to Kowloon Tong. There are always seats available for the chairman of the General Committee, he's found.

When he enters his car he finds Greeny Ma in the seat beside him. He nods to Greeny, somewhat stupefied by the presence of the older man. They've never met on Ambrose's own territory, much less in his own car. Ambrose dismisses Koo, who gets out, props himself against the fender, and stares into space with the mastery of a chauffeur ten years on the job.

"These calls …" Greeny, somewhat theatrically, is wearing sunglasses, though it's dark out. He clutches a Chinese daily in his fist.

"I'm sorry, Greeny. I suppose I panicked."

"Didn't I say I had it in hand? Didn't I tell you not to contact me?"

"They're calling people to testify. The electric contractors, suppliers ..."

"Fine. Let them. Doesn't matter who they get."

Ambrose and Greeny stare at each other. They are as different in temperament as they are in appearance. Greeny is sixtyish, squat, with a broad face, fleshy lips, and a mole on his cheek from which two long hairs sprout like ostrich plumes. Ambrose is young, slender, with clear skin and delicate features. Greeny wears a black silk shirt, Ambrose a quiet grey business suit.

But Greeny Ma is his father-in-law's man, the man Octavius calls whenever there are problems to be removed. Fruitful cooperation with the triad societies was behind every Hong Kong success back in his day, and Greeny is the link between Octavius and the Sun Yee On. Greeny is very high up in the organization, so high that Ambrose shivers at the thought of displeasing him.

"But they'll testify that I was responsible for the construction ..."

"Shut up and let me do my job. Worry about the music band."

"That's all going fine, Greeny," says Ambrose Wan, stinging from Greeny's rebuke. "Bonson has it under control."

"Under control!" He waves the tabloid at Ambrose. "You call this under control?" He unfolds the paper and reads. 'Hong Kong is in China now, and the money that supports the orchestra should be spent on Chinese culture, instead of a group of spoiled, whining overpaid children.' They printed that today. You didn't know I could read, did you?"

"I ... of course ... ."

"You go to college, you think you can tell me how to do my job?"

"I'm sorry, Greeny."

"Suppose they break up the music band? What happens to you, then?"

"They won't do that. You don't have to worry."

"I always have to worry. And until you take your seat on the board of Goldway, you're going to work, too."

Ambrose is silent.

"Okay. Keep cool, and you're fine," says Greeny. His temper has subsided as suddenly as it erupted. "In a few weeks the crews will be back to work, and in six months you'll be selling the shittiest office space in Shenzhen at top market price. But if I'm to do my work, you must do yours. I want everything smooth."

"Got it."

"Smooth. Like a duck swimming on a lake. He taps on the window to signal Koo. "Take me to Tsim Sha Tsui. Let me off at my club." A loss of face for Ambrose, having his chauffeur ordered around by someone else.

This is getting complicated. Why won't Greeny simply take a payoff? Ambrose knows all about payoffs. His father-in- law Octavius is a legend in that line of work.

But what Greeny came up with —what he wants from Ambrose—isn't like the old days. It's just insane.

CHIU SHUN-FU IS beginning to agree with Leo Stern. *Chiu, this would be a great job except for five things: winds, strings, brass, percussion, and that son of a bitch with the baton.* Tonight's concert at Academic Community Hall was torture, right up to the pretentious final chord of Phileas Fong's *Threnody for the Victims of the Nanjing Massacre.* Now Chiu is walking back to the MTR, avoiding the noise of Waterloo Road by threading through small residential byways with names like Cornwall Terrace and Devon Road.

It's not the music that's tying your stomach in knots, he reminds himself. *It's just the Hong Kong Symphony.* Whatever you do, don't start hating music itself. Hating all men because Adam sinned, was how Clem had put it.

A few friends have kept Chiu sane during this trough in his orchestral career. Hector Siefert, bassist and all-round musical encyclopedia. Clement Farraday, bassist and truth-seeker. Porvin Cheung, virtuoso. Leo Stern, madman. Disappeared madman, make that.

Chiu loves those guys, but he's not sure how long he can take this orchestra.

The woodwind players are beginning to chafe. All they want to do is play fast and high, never mind the music. Flute players think if they're loud, they get the prize. The bassoonists spend all their time screwing around with their reeds to avoid confronting their rhythm problems, which are serious. The oboes—don't get him started on the oboes. Control freaks who think they're saving the goddam world.

Leo understands. *No one gives a shit about the music, Chiu. Don't you get that? These people would rather play bad music where they shine than good music where they don't. No one gives a shit. Not the players, not the audience, least of all the goddam conductor."*

Don't forget the strings, the plankton of the orchestra, particles of torpid protoplasm wandering through the music without will or motor control. They stumble along, grateful that seventeen other players are on the same part to cover their mistakes.

And percussion? Kill them all.

Walking diagonally into the middle of the road, lost in contemplation of Leo Stern's words, Chiu ignores the rumble of the motor. By the time he hears the gunning throttle the metal beast has rammed into him.

The thump is terrifying. It's the sound of bones splintering and flesh giving way, a sound transmitted through his very spine to a consciousness that is aflame one moment, fading the next.

Chiu slides against a parked van to the pavement. The car, once again rolling at a sober pace down the quiet road, turns a corner and disappears into the current of light that streams down Waterloo Road.

PART II

Q: What do you do when a viola player dies?
A: Move him back a stand.

CHAPTER 21

YELLOW TAPE MARKS off a small isle of tragedy in the Kowloon roadway. Dawn hasn't arrived, but the bleeding, comatose wreck of a man has already been hauled away, leaving little for Mong and Sinbad, now of Kowloon West Traffic AIU, to work with.

"Locate any witnesses?" asks Sinbad.

Mong shakes his head.

"Then take a look around. See if you can find something." Though they're equal in rank—still constables—Sinbad speaks to his partner as to an inferior.

Shortly after they bungled the discovery of the floater in the Typhoon Shelter their EU commander kicked them over to Traffic, making sure they were assigned to the same unit. *"I want you to remind each other of what stupidity does to a career,"* he'd said. There was nothing Sinbad could do but accept the transfer and blame Mong for it, which he does in the form of periodic withering glances.

"Maybe the victim will be able to ID the car," Mong says.

"Don't think he's going to wake up." That means they'll have to resort to public appeal, which will fall on the indifferent, preoccupied ears of the Hong Kong masses. Worse, a public appeal alerts the press that Traffic has nothing to go on. That brings pressure.

Sinbad scans the road for a tire mark, a chip of fiberglass, something to get his first genuine traffic investigation off to a start. Thinking about tomorrow and the next day—that was never necessary in the Emergency Unit. There, you made the rescue, made the arrest, and were out on the street again an hour later. None of the paperwork that other branches stuck you with.

Yet perhaps change will be good, Sinbad thinks. Perhaps investigation is what he's suited for.

Just then he's reminded of why he queued up to join the EU in the first place. District Commander Knowles is stepping under the yellow tape to see what's what. Knowles won't get in the way— he's content to supervise and make sure things get done. But he's brass, and brass breathe down your neck.

"Who's the inspector in charge?"

"Leung, sir. He's around the corner."

"Well, what have you found so far?" Knowles casts his gaze over the implied answer: essentially nothing, a hundred square feet or so of asphalt, cordoned off as if for a concert, bathed in floodlights but empty of any apparent meaning. The DC is a slight man with salt-and-pepper hair knit into a tufted nap.

"Hit and run, sir," says Sinbad. "Man in his twenties. He's at Queen Elizabeth now, in a coma. No witnesses. The body was found right there, where you're standing. The vehicle probably came from there, hit him here, and went that way to Waterloo Road."

"I see. You're done here, then?"

"Almost, sir." As he says this a glint on the pavement catches his eye. He is about to speak but Knowles beats him to it.

"Looks like bugger-all to me, but keep at it. We'll want to see some results soon. The press are on it." Knowles turns to walk to a couple of reporters stalking by the tape boundary.

"Oh, sir, one minute, please." Sinbad's voice is taut with con-cern.

"Yes?" says Knowles, apparently startled at Sinbad's urgency.

"May I see your shoes, please?"

"My what?"

"The soles of your shoes. May I see them?"

"See here. What are you ..."

"Please sir."

Knowles eyes narrow as he takes in Sinbad's face.

"Of all the nonsense ..." Knowles mutters, but he offers first one sole, than the other, to the inspection of the constable.

"Hold it there, sir."

Knowles places a reluctant hand on the constable's shoulder to steady himself as Sinbad pries something from the sole's treads, and holds it up till it catches the gleam of the high-intensity lamps. A chip of glass, about the size of a five-carat diamond, and much more valuable to Sinbad.

CHAPTER 22

"IT WAS A Mr. *See-fat* who reported him missing," says WPC Scarlett Pak.

"I see," says Bonson Ng. He forces a chuckle at the name. His emotions, except perhaps fear, have been false ones of late. And now the police are calling to dump an extra measure of misery on his life. This morning Chiu's girlfriend Amy called and asked him, in words shaken apart by sobs, to tell the orchestra that Chiu has been hit by a car. He gathers that Chiu won't live another day.

And now this.

"Were you aware of Mr. Stern's absence?" asks the police-woman.

"Yes, but to be honest, we're not terribly worried. Mr. Stern was not very dedicated to his job. And anyway, some players have been known to break their contract like that. Last year two of our expatriate musicians left without giving notice."

"Left Hong Kong?"

"Yes. They're in the UK now, so we decided not to pursue it."

"Why do they leave?"

"Constable, the Hong Kong Symphony Orchestra is a young organization. We're not in a class with some of the better-paid orchestras. We just don't have the funding. Most of the musicians are content, but there are always some troublemakers who don't like the salaries or the director. You understand how that is. Mr. Stern was one of the troublemakers. My guess is that he decided to leave, and wasn't courteous enough to tell us. As I said, it's happened before."

"I understand. Mr. *See-fat* was concerned that Mr. Stern left his instrument behind."

A pause. "Well, I wouldn't pay too much attention to what Hector Siefert says. He's no prize himself. He was fired from his last job for fighting, we found out."

"Fighting?"

"Yes, he assaulted a member of an opera company. Not what you'd call a very reliable person. In any event, we'll let you know if Mr. Stern contacts us, but I'm sure he's back in the States by now."

Bonson pockets his cellphone and leans against the wall. *I don't need this*, he thinks. *What in hell is* See-fat *doing*?

———

HECTOR IS IN the auditorium, stretched out over two rows, ears fixed on Puccini's orchestration. Shao is rehearsing everyone but strings in the opening of *Turandot*. Hector loves hearing the piece broken down into parts. First winds, then brass. It's like a CAT scan of the music.

Suddenly Twinkie is beside him. "How's it going?" she asks.

"Terrible. He's making them play the passage again, but he doesn't correct anything."

"What should he say?" She's watching the conductor. So far she hasn't looked at Hector.

"Well, if he could hear worth a shit, he'd say that the second oboe is out of tune, for starters. The tympani are too loud. The people aren't all playing the accents the same way. Find anything yet?"

"I'm checking up on Yip. Bonson said he used to work in Vancouver. Any word from Leo?"

"No."

"Well, since his flat was searched, I'd like to see it."

"Right. Meet me after the rehearsal. I'll take you there."

She looks at the stage. "This music sounds Chinese, kind of." The harmony is slightly dissonant, unsettling. Hector knows it by heart, mentally fills in the missing vocal parts.

"It's about China," he says. "A mythical China, anyway. Do you know *Turandot?*"

She shakes her head, setting waves of onyx-black hair into motion.

After the break Hector joins the strings on stage. Within minutes Shao has found a passage he thinks needs mindless repetition. Three, four, five times, and it sounds worse each time as attention spans fracture.

Leo should be here, Hector thinks. *He'd be looking back at me with that sneer on his face. I'd roll my eyes. Afterwards we'd take off for Poon's, order beers and talk about Bjoerling and Toscanini, Michaelangeli and Starker, Robert Merrill and Renee Fleming and that wild Czech violinist we heard in a tavern in Graz. To hell with the Hong Kong Symphony, dull rehearsals, bad conductors, and audiences who clap between movements and bring bags of groceries to concerts.*

Hector is checking the bulletin board for announcements when he hears a loud, sharp *whack*. He runs outside and sees his bass trunk lying on its back. Yip Tak-tak is unleashing a torrent of profanity at the two men who apparently let it slip off the ramp to the truck. Some of the women and more decorous men slip away, shamed by Yip's language. Others gather around to watch.

Hector raises his voice. "What the fuck happened?"

"It fell," says Yip. Not defensively, just a statement of fact.

"I know it fell!"

He hears Yip tells his men in Cantonese to leave the *gweilo* to him. One of the movers turns and leaves. Skinwic, sitting on a stool in the corner of the truck, does nothing except reach into his pocket and take out a sunflower seed, place it in his teeth, and crack it. Calm as a Buddha who's just placed twenty on a fixed fight.

Hector falls to his knees, unsnaps the locks and throws open the case. From behind him rises a chorus of anguished groans. The scroll and fingerboard of the bass have been sheared off brutally at the neck.

Hector explodes. "Jesus Christ! You fucking ... you shitass! You can't even move a goddam instrument ..."

"It was an accident," says Yip.

"It wasn't an accident," Hector says, rising to his feet. "Your people don't know what the fuck they're doing!"

On his feet in seconds, Skinwic shoots down the ramp and grabs a handful of Hector's shirt. *"Diu le lo mo!"* he shouts in a voice so hideous no one would want to hear it twice. *Fuck your mother.*

Hector knows he's robbed Yip and his men of face. But to back down would be to surrender his own as well. He clamps his hand on Skinwic's arm to restrain him. The man's superstructure is iron.

For a moment, Yip does nothing but watch the two of them. Then he tells Skinwic to wait in the back. The taller man releases Hector's shirt and walks off.

Yip draws forward and leans into Hector's face.

"I know your name now. You're *See-fat*. Listen, *See-fat*, it was an accident."

"You're hired to prevent accidents, remember?"

"You're trouble. Just like your friend Chiu."

They glare at one another a moment longer. Hector walks back inside to find the players talking in somber tones.

"Christ," he says to Porvin. "These guys just smashed my bass. I don't ..."

"Hec," says Porvin. "Chiu's been hit by a car."

CHAPTER 23

"NOT GOOD," IS Lok's summary of his progress. He's reporting to Kwan. "The cellphone number the plastic surgeon gave us is dead. It's the same one her mother gave us. So we're no closer to finding her residence."

"You had an address for her, didn't you?"

"She gave a false one at the doctor's office. We checked out the one on the driver's license application. That building was torn down a couple of years ago."

"What building hasn't been lately?" Kwan says. "That's all?"

"Big Pang couldn't find any employment records. Milkie was flying under the radar, it seems. Immigration turned up a couple of trips to Macau, so we're showing her picture at the big hotels and casinos, to see if anyone remembers her or if she was with a man. A man with a woman ought to stick out in Macau, after all."

Kwan smiles ruefully at the joke. For a moment they silently share the familiar feeling of staring at a Dead End sign.

Kwan speaks. "Parents any help?"

Lok thinks of that sour tyrant and his helpless wife and shakes his head.

"So," says Kwan. "No witnesses, no motive, and you don't know where the victim lived or worked. You'd better grab onto some-thing, or you'll be out of luck."

I was out of luck when I took this case, Lok thinks.

CHAPTER 24

QUEEN ELIZABETH IS a government hospital, where the city's poorest can gain a bed and lose an appendix for the price of a ricebox lunch. Walls are in need of paint, and floors are too scarred to ever again convey the impression of cleanliness. Room, time, staff, money, and sympathy are all in short supply.

Hector spots Bonson Ng seated on a bench in a corridor, briefcase in lap, BlackBerry in hand. The place smells of formaldehyde, the incense at the temple of human misery.

"What's the story, Bonson?"

He glances up at Hector, looking drawn, pale. "He's still in critical condition."

"What about the driver of the car?" says another voice. They both turn to see Twinkie, memo recorder in hand. "Did they catch him?"

Bonson looks away from her as he speaks, if her eyes will sap his will. "When I wish to speak for the Symphony, I'll call your editor. This is a private matter, and I don't want to intrude upon the family's grief."

"Fine, then," Twinkie says. "But I didn't think the Symphony had reason to be hostile to the press."

"Hostile, no. But lately your articles have cast the orchestra in a rather unpleasant light. You seem to be satisfied printing one side of the story." He glares at Hector. "And without reliable information."

They walk toward Chiu's room. "Why are you here?" Hector asks.

"I cover the Symphony, remember?"

Chiu's girlfriend Amy, crumpled in a chair outside the ICU, leaps up and hugs Hector. Her eyes are raw from weeping. Amy is a secretary at the Canadian Commission, with reddish-blonde hair and a Titian cherub face now drained of its rich color. Next to her is Porvin, his supporting arm wrapped around Amy's waist.

"I'm so sorry, Amy."

"I wasn't there ... the car didn't stop. They left him for dead." She begins again to weep, collapsing onto Hector. He holds her tight, letting her warm tears splatter onto his neck. They breathe together for a minute or so, eyes closed, oblivious to the harried nurses charging from room to room, the old men in pajamas shuffling down the hall, the orderlies wheeling carts and clanging bedpans.

"What does the doctor say?"

She composes herself, wipes her cheek with a limp handkerchief. "Who the hell knows?"

"You'd better sit," says Porvin. He helps Amy to a seat, rubs her shoulders for a moment, then ushers Hector down the hall.

"Internal bleeding," he whispers. "Fractured skull. Ruptured spleen. I tell you, it's really bad, Hec. Who is this sonofabitch? How can he just drive away and leave Chiu in the street?"

"Is he going to live?"

"I don't think so," he whispers. "No one's said anything, but I keep listening for one word of encouragement. You know, 'not as bad as it could be, fifty-fifty,' that kind of thing. Nothing." Then:

"Hec, I think they killed our guy."

"Who?"

"Dunno. But Chiu's been in everyone's face, pissing off people, talking to the press." He stops walking and faces him. "Am I being paranoid, Hec?"

Hector recalls Yip's words. *You're trouble. Just like your friend Chiu.*

"Can I see him?"

"No visitors yet."

Hector rejoins Twinkie, and they head for the elevator. On the way they pass Bonson, who's still answering his e-mail. "This works out nicely for the orchestra, doesn't it?" Hector says. "No more petition, no one making trouble."

Through his spectacles Bonson glowers. Then Twinkie speaks. "Ng *sin-sahng*, one question. Who is Yip Tak-tak?"

The question clearly startles him, but he says nothing.

"He's no instrument mover, is he?"

Bonson studies her face, then looks away and sighs. "I assume Mr. Siefert has told you what happened to his bass. We're very sorry about the accident. However, we're arranging to have it repaired, which is all we can do. But this isn't the time to discuss that, is it?"

"His résumé is a fake," she says. "I checked every orchestra in British Columbia. No one named Yip Tak-tak ever worked in any of them, either as a mover or anything else. And who are those people with him?"

Bonson looks ready to strangle her, his limbs tight and trembling.

"*Gau see gan*," he says. Then he's on his feet, storming off.

Gau see gan. Hector rummages through his Cantonese vocabulary as they descend in the elevator.

"What's all this about Yip?" he asks Twinkie. Amy's tears are still cooling on his skin.

"I've been making calls."

"So Yip's a fake. Big surprise. And those creeps with him, no doubt. Listen, I need to tell you something. Today Yip said something to me. He said that Chiu was trouble."

"That's all?"

"It's the way he said it. As if he'd got what he deserved."

The elevator opens and they walk out into air thick as kettle steam. Hector speaks again.

"What did Bonson mean about 'old times'?"

"What?"

"*Gau see gan. Gau*, old. *See gan*, time. Does that mean something like 'old times?'"

She rolls her eyes. "Your Cantonese is terrible."

"I know. What's it mean?"

"*Gau see*, dogshit. *Gan*, rod. He called you a stick that stirs dog shit. Someone who makes trouble."

They join a taxi queue. There, she pops open her ballpoint and asks, "What's Chiu like?"

"You met him, didn't you? He's a good man." Immediately he detests himself for choosing such a dim cliché, something from a British spy novel.

"How about as a player?"

"As far as horn players go, he's very good."

"What does that mean?"

Another stab of guilt, for discussing orchestra gripes now of all times. But he continues. "When you play an instrument for enough years, it changes you," he says. "You become whoever your instrument needs you to be. The horn is difficult. When you play a note you never really know what will come out. So a lot of horn players spend the whole concert thinking about not screwing up their next entrance. When the notes come out right, they think they're hot shit. When they don't, they bitch about how hard the instrument is. Where's the music in that?"

"Is Chiu like that?"

He thinks. "No. He's one of the better ones."

Twinkie smiles and opens a taxi door.

"What's so funny?"

"That's what Chiu said about you a couple of days ago."

"What?"

"That you were one of the better ones. Come on. I want you to take me to Leo's flat."

She speaks only once as they ride. "'Old times' ... why do *gwei-los* even bother trying to learn Cantonese?"

CHAPTER 25

HOCKEY LIANG'S EYES trace the seams of the elevator car first up, then down, in an effort to avoid the gaze of the EU team officers next to him. He inspects the inspection sticker, then the emergency phone, and notes that the "door close" button is worn to a nub, as befits this impatient city.

Police make Hockey nervous. Not that he has anything to fear from police anymore. Long ago he rented out his top-floor flat on Yee Wo Street, living all the while in an illegal shack he'd knocked together on the roof. After three years the hut had been discovered and he'd been ordered to vacate, but by then he'd bought another apartment, and installed the hut there. The money he saved enabled him to buy a third flat, and now the cash is rolling in. His outlaw days are over.

The key to 3F Prosperity Court is in his hand. A neighbor called the management company, who called Hockey, told him to come over now. The police said not to unlock anything till they got there. No danger of that. Not with that smell.

He's been pacing the faux marble tile in the lobby for fifteen minutes, waiting for what he knows will be bad luck. That's what's coming, he is sure of it. The presence of the police proves it.

Third floor. The lift opens onto a corridor that was last painted after Bruce Lee but before Jackie Chan. He leads them down the hall to 3F, one of three apartments which pay him a total of forty-eight thousand Hong Kong dollars a month in rent.

Hockey scrabbles the key into the door and opens it. After the policemen file in, he tries to remove the key and make a fast retreat. But the key sticks, and he's forced to inhale a nauseating lungful of contaminated air. It's too much; he gags and falls back, heaving.

A constable flips on the light, revealing a room abuzz with a thousand flies. There's a painting of a sunset on the wall, a sideboard holding a boom box, a large TV, and some movie and television fan magazines on the coffee table.

The smell comes from the bedroom. A policeman waves aside a few flies and leads his men inside, with Hockey Liang at the rear.

The double bed's sheets are rumpled, but no one is in the bed.

"Underneath," says the constable. He kneels down, pulls a Maglite out of his pocket, shines it under the bed for a split second. Then he grunts and jerks himself backward.

"What is it?" says one of the other cops. Together the four men push the bed to the wall to reveal what's rotting below it. Clutching a tissue over his nose and mouth, Hockey Liang elbows his way past the team for a look, then averts his head.

"I told the bitch no dogs," he says.

———

LOK IS THE first senior officer to cross the yellow crime scene tape that barricades 3F Prosperity Court. Ears and Old Ko are with him to help make sense of the two-and-a-half rooms that were home to Milkie Tang. The putrefied bichon frise has been removed.

"She didn't cook, I can tell you," Old Ko shouts from the kitchen nook. "Just a microwave and a stack of cup noodles. Chopper's dull and rusty."

"She had enough money to eat out, I think," Lok says, poking in her dresser drawer. "Nice TV, some good jewelry here."

"Just a busy girl, then" says Old Ko. He's in her bedroom now, at her clothes closet. "She had money, all right. Or a sugar daddy."

Lok walks over and handles the dresses. "Do you notice something?" he says. Ko stares hard at the clothes, and then it hits him. "They're all evening dresses. If she were a fancy dresser, she'd have some good coats, sweaters, jackets. This is all evening stuff."

"Right. And nothing from China Products."

This is where the murder investigation really begins for Lok. The victim's home is a snapshot of life as it was lived the moment it ended. It's the arena for family fights, a scrapbook for memories, a revealer of habits, passions, fears. Read a room carefully, and you can write a book about the one who lives within.

Ears walks in from the bathroom. "Sir, does this mean anything? Birth control pills, but she also has a box of condoms by the bed."

"Large or small?" asks Lok.

"Just condoms. I don't know about size ..." He blushes. Ko guffaws and goes back to poking through the shoes at the bottom of the closet.

"The box," says Lok, smiling despite himself. "It was a large box, correct?"

"Oh, yes."

"How'd you even know what they were?" says Old Ko.

"The pills are for pregnancy, the condoms to prevent AIDS," says Lok.

Ears points to a soft leather purse by the bed. Lok nods. Ears draws out the wallet, opens it.

"One red fish, three big cows," he says, using the slang for the one- and five hundred dollar bills, " ... total sixteen hundred dollars. Gold watch on the night table, so whoever did it didn't rob her."

"What else?" says Lok.

Conscious of Lok's eyes on him, he checks each item with care, almost ceremoniously.

"ID card, Tang Yee-fun. Credit cards, receipt from Wing Hung video shop, name card for hairdresser ... lipstick ... hang on." A tiny plastic box is reluctant to open. "Ah, eye makeup ... three more condoms ... a small case with her own name cards ... ." He pulls out one of the cards, reads it.

"She was some kind of office worker," he says, handing the business card to Old Ko.

The card says:

VSOP Nightclub
Milkie Tang
Public Relations

"No, Ears," says Ko, reading the card. "She was a whore."

BACK AT THE station Million Man hums an Eason Chan hit as he emerges from the lift carrying a long, slender package. A couple of DPCs turn as he walks by, clearly curious about the wrapped box. He ignores them, peeks in Lok's office, and walks out to the desk where Station Sergeant Fu sits. Fu is older than Million Man, even older than Old Ko.

"Where's Inspector Lok?" he asks.

"Still at the flat of the girl they found floating. He'll be back any minute. What's that? A rifle?" Fu scans the package with security-conscious eyes.

"A golf club. For Inspector Lok."

"A what?"

"A new driver. It's a beauty. Cost almost twenty-five hundred."

"What's this about?"

Million Man smiles his beat-the-system smile. "Lok loves to golf. Old Ko told me he plays every chance he gets. This should make his eyes pop out."

Suddenly Fu bursts out laughing. It's not a pretty sight, with Fu's furrowed brow and crooked bamboo forest of yellow teeth.

"You idiot!" Fu says. "You give him that golf club, your career is over. Ah Lok will stick it so far up your ass you'll have to send an EU team in to find it. Then you'll be arresting pushcart vendors in Sai Kung until you retire." His laughter has drawn a few officers out of the rooms.

"But I thought ..."

"You think Lok is that easy? That he'll favor you because you give him presents?" More laughter. "Old Ko knows how to pick them, that's for sure. What a dimwit!"

Flushing, Million Man swivels on his heel and strides to the lift to disappear. The doors to the elevator open, and suddenly he's face-to-face with Inspector Lok. Million Man fumbles the package to his side, but a preoccupied Lok pays no attention to him.

Down at the barracks Million Man tries to jam the club into his locker. The metal locker is too small, having been selected for CID personnel, who don't wear uniforms. He ends up shoving it behind a towel hamper.

CHAPTER 26

TWINKIE AND HECTOR weave through crowds of tourists who have crossed an ocean to experience being cheated on Nathan Road.

"There's something I've been meaning to ask you," Twinkie says.

"Yeah?"

"What made you become friends with Leo?" A reporter-type question, Hector guesses, calculated to spur a story and maybe a little insight.

"We've always been friends. Leo's my man." They're in Granville Road now, a teeming thoroughfare filled with tourist shops and restaurants.

"Can you be more specific?"

Hector takes a breath of the Kowloon air, warm and dense with hydrocarbons, and thinks. "Leo's alive, that's why I like him. He's not always rational, but he cares about what he cares about."

"Which is?"

"Music, first of all. Playing it well. He knows what matters. He doesn't care about all the bullshit that impresses everyone, like money and status."

"What's he doing in Hong Kong, then?"

Hec ignores the remark. "Last year the wife of the Venezuelan Consul General called him, asked him if he'd play in her string quartet. He told her he had better things to do than fuck around with spoiled housewives who play fiddle. She went ballistic, almost made an international incident out of it."

"So he hates amateurs?"

"No. He hates people who think professional artists are just there for people's amusement. Would she have asked the top chef in town to come over and help her make dinner? Why do people think they have a right to treat musicians like servants?"

"Or even equals ..."

Hector shrugs. They approach the building, which goes by the name of Golden Promise Mansions. The gated door, unlocked during the day, stands between the Hoi Kwan Mongolian Barbecue restaurant and a leather shop piled with fake designer handbags and luggage. They walk to the third floor and enter the flat.

"See what I mean?" Hector says.

"Yes. It's been searched."

"So what are we looking for?"

"Whatever they were looking for."

"What's that?"

"How should I know?"

"I don't like doing this," he says.

"Feel like an intruder?"

"I am an intruder."

"I'm used to it. All reporters are *bat gwah*." Literally, "eight directions," or someone who'll stick her nose in anything, no matter what direction it comes from.

While Twinkie peers behind the stove in the kitchen, Hector

reads a paper on Leo's desk. "This is weird," he says.

"What is?" She walks in, plucks the slip from his hand, scans it. "So that's what musicians make."

"Hey, that's too personal," Hector says, holding out his hand.

Twinkie hands him the slip. "*Gweilos* are funny. You tell everyone about your sex life, but you won't discuss your salary ... what is it?"

Hector stares at the slip. "The amount ..."

"Now you're *bat gwah*."

"Leo's getting some extra pay ..."

"Is that important?"

"I don't know. It says 'Library Duties, $2000.'"

"What library?"

"Must be the orchestra library. Where we keep the music."

"What duties did he have?"

"No idea."

"I thought you were good friends."

"We are, goddammit! This is all completely new to me." He walks to a cabinet, takes out a bottle of whiskey, pulls the cork. *D-natural.* Humming the first movement of Beethoven's Second, he grabs a glass and pours a drink.

"Want one?"

"Whiskey? Ugh!" She screws up her face.

Hector replaces the cork, then pulls it out one more time. *D-flat.* He's poured a perfect half-step. Carefully balancing the glass, he lowers himself onto Leo's sofa for the three hundredth time.

"Does he need extra money?" Twinkie asks.

Hector rolls his eyes. "Desperately. He's paying child support. He has no savings, and no money to travel and take auditions."

"Why can't he save any, keep a budget?"

Hector smiles at the idea. "Twinkie, Leo isn't that type. When he has money, he spends it."

"*Yee sai jo.*" A second-generation spendthrift, one who has a rich father.

"No, he was never rich. He just has contempt for money."

"Like I said, what's he doing in Hong Kong?"

We're sing-song girls, Hec. In old China they made no distinction between musicians and whores. So what else is new?

Twinkie sees the photo of Hector and Leo in the Burmese lacquered bowl. Taken more than a year ago, it shows the two of them bare-chested under the Thai sun. For the first time he notices how green Leo's eyes look, even in a simple snapshot.

"You're better without the beard," Twinkie says.

"Don't you care for beards?"

"No. They make men look like monkeys." She puts down the photo and gathers up her bag.

"It hasn't hurt Leo. But I admit shaving it off helped my case."

"Maybe Leo has a better personality." For a while they rifle through papers, pull open drawers. Twinkie upends a pencil can, finds a key with a tag bearing the letters HKSO. She dangles the key in front of Hector.

"Nice work," he says, grabbing it from her.

"Nothing else I can find." she says. "Let's go. Maybe you should empty the dehumidifier first."

Nice thought. Hector pulls the tray from the back of the machine, carries it to the sink, dumps it out.

"Hey, Twinkie," he says.

"What?"

"There's something here." She runs to the kitchen. In the sink, where it fell from its hiding place in the dehumidifier tray, is a plastic bag, tied shut. The bag holds a few sheets of paper.

He pulls open the bag, carefully withdraws the sheets.

"What is it?" says Twinkie. She moves closer to Hector to read the document with him. For a moment he's distracted, as her body touches his. But the sheer strangeness of the document overwhelms even her warmth and scent.

"It's the minutes of a General Committee meeting. The people who run the orchestra. What in hell is Leo doing with this?" He reads.

Bonson Ng said that Yip Tak-tak was the answer to his prayers. He considers Mr. Yip an excellent worker with more than adequate experience moving orchestral instruments.

Mrs. Albrecht stated her hopes that there would be no more accidents.

Right, lady, thinks Hector.

Twinkie sorts through the other papers. She shows him a sheet of Hong Kong Symphony letterhead bearing a single underlined name:

Mulqueen

"What the hell does this mean, Twinkie?"

She scans some other pages, shakes her head. "I don't know. But this must have been why the place was searched. Let's get out of here."

They lock up and move to the stairwell. Hector begins to descend.

"Hold on," says Twinkie. She pads up the stairs to the fourth floor instead, peers into the corridor, then looks down at Leo's door.

"What are you doing?" says Hector when he catches up with her.

"Just checking. I don't know, really."

"Find anything."

She shrugs. "Just a few sunflower seed shells."

Hector freezes.

"What?" she says. "Is that important?"

CHAPTER 27

FONG YING DIAMOND CO. LTD, founded 1964, sits on Hankow Road, deep in a swamp of tourist outlets in Tsim Sha Tsui. Halogen lights illuminate diamond-speckled earrings and necklaces, heightening their radiance till they sting the eyes.

Hector pauses at the threshold and greets a tall, swarthy man who cradles the shaft of a Remington shotgun in his muscular arms. The security guard beams when he sees Hector.

"Mister Hector! How good to see you!" He extends an enormous brown hand, and clasps Hector's warmly for half a minute.

"How are things, Khan?" Hector says. "I've missed you."

"Me too, sir. I sometimes ask what you are doing, but Miss Zenobia says she hasn't seen you."

"I'm pretty busy nowadays." A lie, but he must confirm Zenobia's story, uphold her honor. Such things are important to Khan, a Pushtun from the barren hills of Waziristan.

Back when they ruled the world the British identified Sikhs and Pushtuns as "martial races" particularly suited to carrying arms and doing the Empire's dirty work. Khan's father guarded the Hong Kong border until after the Second World War, when the government decided that the China–Hong Kong frontier was tense enough without adding a couple of extra races to the situation, much less races known for their willingness to kill and die in combat. The regiment was disbanded, and Khan's father retired. Khan became one of a legion of guards that intimidated potential thieves in front of the territory's jewelry stores and banks.

Khan is burly, with a pockmarked face, yellow teeth, and a thick mane of wiry black hair. He wears a khaki safari suit and Nike running shoes. Still smiling, he waves Hector in to the store.

When Hector began coming around to visit his employer's daughter, Khan hinted his approval, which meant more to Zenobia than she admitted: Khan had guarded the Chans' livelihood since before Zen was born. He was as protective of her as of the gems that gleamed in the velvet-lined showcases. There had been one boy before Hector, Zen told him, one that Khan didn't much care for. The boy complained that Khan gripped his shotgun a little tighter whenever he approached the store.

Zenobia is behind the counter, where she always goes after finishing work at the Symphony library, so that her parents can take a break and eat dinner. He feels some guilt about the entrapment; Zen can't leave the shop, no matter how he upsets her.

Zenobia looks a bit stunned, a bit weary, when she realizes who Khan has bid enter the shop. "What do you want now, Hector?" she says. "I'm busy."

"I need to know something about Leo. Was he working for you?"

"That's why I'm so busy. He took a summer job as my assistant. He was supposed to help me mark parts, but he ran off. Now I'm buried in work. Sometimes I have to go back to the office at night after we close the shop."

Hector tries imagining Leo Stern sitting at a desk opposite Zenobia, pencil in hand. "Leo actually took a job there? Marking parts? Leo?"

"Is that such terrible work?" She reaches behind her for a box full of earrings, each in a tiny plastic bag.

"Not at all. I didn't mean that." He waits a beat. "Zen, Leo is gone. He disappeared a week ago. No calls, he hasn't shown up for work. I'm worried about him."

Zenobia upends a bag, lets the earrings fall into her palm, places them a velvet-lined tray. "What do you want me to do?"

"I need to find him. Can you tell me the last time he was at the Symphony?"

"He showed up a few times. The last time he was at the office would have been Sunday."

"Sunday …" A thought occurs to him. "The offices are open on Sunday?"

"No, not normally, but he said he had Sunday free, so I lent him the key. He did a little work that day, but he left most of it for me." The word *bastard* isn't in Zenobia's vocabulary, or else she'd be using it now. He turns to leave.

"How is Chiu?" she asks. "Have you seen him?"

"No visitors yet. I'll let you know when I find out anything, okay?"

She nods.

Hector manages a wave and leaves the shop, passing Khan on his way out.

"May Allah bless you, sir," says Khan. "I am always at your service."

"And you," Hector says.

"And please say hello to Mister Leo," he says.

Fighting the rush of emotion the name brings on, Hector walks to the corner, takes a breath of humid Hong Kong air.

It takes him a minute to get his feelings under control. He handled Zen much better this time. There's much besides her on his mind, after all. Leo is still gone. Chiu is lying in intensive care. There's Twinkie Choi. Skinwic Sze and his threats. Those sunflower seeds on the landing above Leo's flat, suggesting that this Skinwic goon had been hiding there. Things like that will take your mind off a broken heart.

Or maybe he's getting over Zenobia Chan.

CHAPTER 28

"SO HE DID IT, did he? Fucking bastard."

Mary Ma, in her fifites, wears a jacket and skirt ensemble that would pass in any corporate boardroom. She is also, Lok judges, the single most profane speaker of Chinese he has met in his twenty-two years of daily contact with the thugs and perverts of Hong Kong.

Mary is the mama-san at the VSOP Nightclub, one of the few Chinese ones left in a profession comprising mostly expatriate talent nowadays. Lok can see immediately the sign of one who was once in the trade herself: the disillusioned stare of a woman for whom the male race can never hold a mystery. Probably she's one of the smart ones: saved her cash, got out, decided to stay where the money was. Maybe her pimp had been murdered, setting her free. Maybe she'd done it herself. If so, more power to her.

"Who are you speaking about?" Lok asks.

"Yip Tak-tak. Her fucking boyfriend. He's shit. But I'll deny it, so please don't write anything down."

"Tell me about him."

"He runs the valet parking. Sun Yee On. I think he's Red Pole." She knows her triad rankings, this one. "We pay him every month, he gives us a couple of kids to park cars. What can you do? Fucking crooks."

"How do you know he did it?"

"Who else? He was fucking her, giving her money."

"Did they fight?"

"Not that I saw. Yip treated her the way all those fucking triads treat their women, like dirt."

"And she took it?"

"They always do, don't they? Being connected to the big man, that's what matters. But she didn't like him."

"How do you know that?"

"You get to know those things, Inspector. It was about the coldest pairing I've ever come across. And I've seen them all."

Big Pang approaches Lok. Mary appraises him with one sweep of her eyes, nods her approval.

"The back room is ready," says Pang.

"So are my girls," Mary says. Pang smiles.

The VSOP Nightclub is neither more nor less ostentatious than any of the other clubs on Canton Road. That is to say, it's as garish, vulgar, flamboyant, and pretentious as the mind of man can make it. One enters by descending a staircase from street level, beneath a neon sign announcing its principal offerings: drinks and girls.

Inside are plush-upholstered booths, a bandstand where a group of tuxedoed, strobe-lit musicians sing the latest Canto-pop songs and the odd Sinatra hit, and a mahogany bar that's been dipped in a half inch of polyurethane. Neon-trimmed shelves behind the bar are packed with Cognac, still the preferred drink of high rollers out to impress their friends.

Hostesses are scattered about the room like painted dolls in a nursery ready to be picked up for some casual amusement. They're all comely, with crimson lips and polished fingernails.

Most are Filipina, a few Chinese and Russian, plus some scattered English, Japanese, Thai. They parade through the rooms in *cheongsams*, the traditional long Chinese dress, slit up the sides to reveal thighs and hips.

To one side of the hall are private rooms with U-shaped benches large enough for three businessmen to fondle and flirt with three hostesses behind etched glass doors.

The only rule at the VSOP Nightclub, apart from not having sex on the premises and not abusing the hostesses, is that the customer must order wondrously overpriced drinks. Usually that means Hennessy XO or something comparable, at $350 per glass. The hostesses sip a cocktail of colored ginger ale for $200 a shot. An executive for one of the Japanese electronics companies, out to woo a local partner, can easily drop ten thousand on a night's drinks.

The manager, Steinway Fung, is in the back room. He's at least fifty, with a face flabby as a geoduck. Thirty years ago a Police Constable's truncheon left three gaps in his top front teeth. The black-and-white effect led to his nickname. He's wearing a grey tailored suit over a black polo shirt.

"You want the sign-out book, right?" He shifts nervously from foot to foot, as if their visit is interrupting some vital business.

"And your credit card statements for the last year to match up some customers' names," says Big Pang.

"That's private information."

"We're not Inland Revenue, Fung," says Lok. "We're just trying to find out who was taking out one of your hostesses."

"That's even more private. I can't have you calling our customers."

"No? Surely they're not ashamed of patronizing a fine business like this."

"I could get in big trouble."

"Steinway, one of your whores is dead. If that isn't trouble enough, then we'll be back tonight, flashing our badges, talking to customers, taking down names. What do you say?"

Ten minutes later Big Pang and Lok are checking credit card slips and scanning the sign-out book, taking careful notes. Customers who enjoy the company of a particular hostess can sign her out for the rest of the evening, paying the club a fee of $2,000. The girl doesn't get any of that. If she wants to profit more, she needs to negotiate her own price for whatever the customer has in mind. For everyone's protection, the sign-outs are logged by Mary, boss and protector of the girls.

Lok reads the signatures, a roster of men who invaded Milkie Tang's body for money.

One of the girls brings Pang a coffee, asks if he needs anything else, turns away. Lok looks up and catches a glimpse of her back. He runs to the door, catches her, whirls her around.

"What is it?" There's panic in her voice.

It's the wrong face. The right height, and blonde hair just like Edna's, but it's a stranger.

"Nothing." He walks back, as shaken as the girl.

"Know her?" Big Pang asks.

"Never mind." Lok picks up the book again. After a few minutes he speaks. "Wednesday nights. Always around seven. Someone named Leung. Check your slips for Wednesday the 12th and 19th, around that time."

Pang pores through the slips. "Here we go." He writes down the card number and summons Mary Ma.

"What can you tell me about Leung Hing-kwok?" Lok asks. "He was a regular Wednesday night customer, signed Milkie out on a number of occasions."

"One of the nice ones, very gentle. He was only interested in Milkie. He came a couple of times after she disappeared, asking for her. Hasn't been in here since."

"Did they get along?"

"I couldn't tell you, but I imagine so. We don't put our girls into dangerous situations—you know that. If she kept seeing him, he was probably all right."

"What does he look like?"

She thinks, directing her eyes to the ceiling, which is covered in reflective black tile. "Not too tall. Thirties, roundish face, glasses, wears a beret and a cashmere coat ... and he doesn't bet on horses."

"How do know that?" Lok asks.

"Because he comes on Wednesday nights." Race night at Happy Valley.

Lok offers thanks and leaves a name card. Mary holds him back with a gentle touch after Pang walks out.

"Your officer, the one who just left?"

"Big Pang. Yes?"

"He's welcome in here anytime. My girls like him."

"I'll be sure to tell him."

CHAPTER 29

THE TAXI ROLLS up to the corner of Portland and Mong Kok Road, where Hector is waiting. Twinkie emerges from the car and greets him with a smile that is faint but real, and thus encouraging.

Twinkie has awakened something in his being. He'd drifted through the summer in New York, paying little attention to women, still ripped up inside from Zenobia's cruelty. This had not been the practical exit that he'd managed with other women. It had been abandonment, betrayal.

Since meeting Twinkie, he's walking a little faster, talking a little more, standing a little straighter. Maybe losing Zenobia is not the end of the world.

They pass a restaurant window in which a pile of turtles slowly roasts on a brazier. Next to that, bordering Hector's building, is an old four-floor commercial building. The only sign on it is one of cardboard, hanging from a wire, cheap enough to be replaced easily when the police confiscate it on their regular rounds.

The sign, scrawled in Chinese characters with marker pen, says:

local girls 340
wild vietnamese 320
hot western 690
mainland girls will do anything 350
malaysia—philippines

price for 45minutes.
price includes everything.
4 kinds of service

"Interesting neighborhood," she says.

"Well, it's cheap. They can't get women to stay in my building. When they walk down the street, people assume they work in one of the whorehouses."

Hector nods at Ah Tai, the security guard, who's seventy and maybe six pounds heavier than Twinkie. Ah Tai's job consists of nodding to people who enter and following the races on a radio that mumbles behind him on a shelf.

The elevator shoots them to the fifteenth floor.

"How was rehearsal today?" she asks.

He shakes his head. "Lousy, without Leo there."

"He makes a difference in your life, right?"

"Listen, Twinkie. I talked to the librarian. Leo did take a job with the orchestra library, but he didn't do much work. I think he just took it so he could get a key and go in on a Sunday, when no one else was in the office."

"So that's how he got those papers. He sneaked in, photocopied documents."

The door opens to reveal his bare walls, dusty floors, the suitcase by the door.

"You seem to have the same decorator as Leo," Twinkie says.

"I get ideas from magazines. Seriously, it's not my place, so why bother?"

"You should buy a flat."

"Me? I'm one of life's great renters."

Twinkie smiles at the phrase. His eyes race around the contours of her face, taking in the imaginary lights that flicker when she's pleased.

She lowers herself onto one of the immense pillows, Leo's favorite, while he brews a pot of tea.

"Here's my idea," she says. "We'll get into the Symphony office the same way Leo did."

"What are you talking about?"

"Find out what he was looking for. Look, Hector, Leo's gone, and Chiu has been hurt. You can see what happens to troublemakers in this orchestra."

"Leo didn't make trouble. At least, not the way Chiu did." A vague feeling of distress grips him as he realizes he's using the past tense.

"Maybe he was caught snooping."

"And they kidnapped him? Stuck him in a trunk and threw him in the harbor?" Despite the preposterousness of the theory, Hector finds the words are chilling.

"I doubt that. My guess is they had him arrested and deported quietly. The point is, something made him get out of town. He didn't even take his viola, and that means he either left very fast or was kicked out very fast. We need to know who did it. If he was deported, there must be some document."

They both glance at Leo's viola case, propped against a shelf in a shadow, a silent proxy.

"We also might find out why Bonson lied to the General Committee and hired a bunch of thugs to move instruments. How about we search the offices this Sunday?" Twinkie reaches in her purse, pulls out a key with the letters HKSO on a tag.

"Isn't that against the law?"

"It's the way you find things out."

She sips her tea, while Hector takes slow pulls on his Blue Girl, as the sky darkens.

"Tell me something," she says.

"What?"

"Why do you play that instrument?"

"*Dai yum dai tai kam*," he says. *Deep sound big fiddle*, the Chinese name for bass. "Low sounds. I love them. In school they needed a bass player, and I already knew the bass clef from piano, so they stuck me on it. After that, I never wanted to play anything else."

"Did they fix it already? It looks okay."

"This is my practice instrument. My real one is broken."

"Play me something."

He guzzles the last of his beer and walks to his practice bass. He pulls up the stool, tightens and rosins his bow, and draws it across the strings, one by one.

Then he begins to play "*Moo Lee Wah*," an old Chinese tune. First in the low register, taking his time, letting the low notes vibrate and fill the room. Then an octave higher, where the sound is sweeter, less dramatic. The last note fades away into nothing.

She applauds. "You're good, I can tell. I don't know music, but you look like an artist."

He nods in gracious acceptance of the compliment.

"It's so low. And so big. Do people like it as much as they like the violin?"

He props the bass in a corner, loosens the bow, comes back to sit on the pillow beside her. "What you mean is, do I wish I had taken up flute instead? That's what people ask. The answer's no."

You are a bass, his teacher Morgan had told him. You stand at the foundation of the entire system of sounds that makes up the most glorious musical achievement that human civilization has produced.

Where does harmony come from? It's based on overtones that ring in the ears of the audience.

Why do the overtones ring? Because you strike the bell.

Without your bass, deep harmonies turn shallow. Melodies lose their bite. Beethoven's chords of doom wimp out into impotent thirds and fifths. Brahms—where the fuck is Brahms without a bassline?

Take away the bass, the physics of harmony evaporates. Keys can't take hold, uncertainty reigns. Our musical world spins into chaos.

You are Atlas.

"Well, you sound nice," she says. There's a pause that neither of them knows how to fill. Finally Twinkie asks, "Are there other musicians in your family?"

"My family?" He repeats the word with a sneer. "No. We all had piano lessons as a kid. I'm the only one that liked music."

"Tell me about them."

"Not much to tell. I've got a sister Bernadette. She's a dental assistant, still lives with my mother in New York. My father's dead."

"Just two children?"

"I have an older brother. He left home when I was a kid, never came back."

She nods, apparently contemplating this. "Do you miss your family?" she asks. "You're far away."

He shakes his head. "I don't think about them much. My father … didn't make us too happy. We didn't stay very close."

"Is that why your brother left?

He nods, stands up. "Need another beer," he says. "More tea?" Twinkie shakes her head. Hector walks to the kitchen, finds a beer, then stops, thinks of Oscar. He's told no one in Hong Kong about his missing brother, no one but Leo. Yet he feels Twinkie should know. Or maybe it's just been a secret long enough.

He draws his wallet from his back pocket, slips out the postcard of Sag Harbor, with Oscar's gleeful message to him. He fastens it to the refrigerator with the edge of a magnetic hook.

"What about you?" he says when he rejoins Twinkie. "Family in Hong Kong?" He settles himself on a floor pillow beside her. "No. My mother died when I was six. My father's dead too. Also my sister. Just me now."

"Christ, I'm sorry."

The music, now finished, seems to have taken the sounds of the world with it. For a second they look at each other. Then Hector leans forward to touch her lips with his.

Twinkie jerks her head away as if burned by a blowtorch.

"Sorry," Hector says.

She appears more disappointed than angry. "I'm not like a *gweipoh*," she says. "I don't do those things."

He takes a long pull on his beer to hide his frustration, and tries to guess what she means by that.

CHAPTER 30

YIP TAK-TAK throws down the card with force that, were it a mahjong tile, would have cracked it in half. Groans of disgust erupt from his men.

"Nine! Should have known."

"Bastard."

Yip doesn't even enjoy winning at cards anymore. CC and Small Eyes play too poorly to give him any satisfaction. But there's no one else right now. The three men are sitting at a card table in a room backstage at the Cultural Centre. CC, on Yip's right, scoops up the slim, finger-sized cards to deal. He's well-muscled, with delicate features and a flat-top haircut. Only a turtle-like facial expression ruins his otherwise good looks.

Small Eyes is stockier, plainer, and with a face even less animated than CC's. Thinking himself something of a fashion plate, Small Eyes dresses in black to an obsessive degree.

They're both punks, and Yip has no illusions about their talents. They started out the same way Yip did, forcing the doors and trunks of cars, stealing radios and handbags from inside, prying off the mirrors and selling them to triad-owned garages. That's what you do when you're growing up, you steal what's easiest to take—

cash, gold, the odd Rolex. CC and Small Eyes grew into typical 49s, foot soldiers with no direction, no ambition, and no hope of attaining a higher rank. Their inert faces advertise their prospects.

Unlike his two flunkies, Yip came to realize early that the real money lay not in stealing what people own, but supplying what they cannot get. At twenty he started furnishing babies to wealthy Chinese couples in Thailand and Canada. The upper-class Chinese might be too conscious of lineage to buy a kid, but there were plenty of infertile middle-class parents who would pay a hundred thousand for a boy, fifty for a girl. He did pretty well: some parents even preferred girls, believing them to be less trouble. Turnover wasn't what you'd call brisk, though. You had to seek out pregnant teenagers and pay them a few thousand, arrange the delivery, and transport the baby.

Impatient with the rate of return, Yip started shipping girls to Thai whorehouses—less money up front but better turnover, and you got a percentage of the earnings. There were parents in China and even Hong Kong who would part with their brat for fifteen thousand or so. And he got to sample the merchandise himself.

But kidnapping whores was no picnic either: the package could give you trouble. He took to smuggling other goods, but now that too is over. There is bigger, faster money to be made, in a trade that has it all: boatloads of cash and repeat customers that don't rat on you.

Footsteps. Yip pauses, recognizes Skinwic's slow, deliberate tread moments before he appears in the doorway. That face still gives Yip a jar sometimes, though he won't admit it to anyone.

"Policeman downstairs, wants to see you," Skinwic says.

Yip pauses, betrays no expression to the men in the room.

"Are you going to talk to him?" asks CC.

In reply, Yip stands, checks his hair in the mirror.

"Shit," says Small Eyes. "Tell them to kiss your ass."

Yip ignores them.

CC turns to Skinwic. "Want to play?" Skinwic shakes his head and lumbers off.

"Cards bore him," says Yip. Just as well. Suppose they got into a disagreement? What then? No one would want to anger Skinwic Sze. Employing him is like buying a viper to guard your house.

YIP KNOWS THE station, knows the drill. Even some of the faces are familiar, though their ranks and offices have changed. Young cops get old, lose their uniforms and become detectives, and new young cops appear, staring self-righteously at him over the shoulders of the old ones, hungry for their own chance to make arrests and trade their own uniform for street clothes. For all his police encounters, for all the impertinent questions, he's never been convicted of anything.

The Detective Inspector walks in, takes a seat. Barrel chest, average height, middle aged, quiet-looking, but not someone he'd pick a fight with. Very deliberate in his motions, this Lok. Not like the kid with the big ears, who launches himself all over the station like a New Year's rocket. Lok doesn't move much. He waits for others to come to him. *Not a man to lose track of,* he thinks. Then, without preamble, Lok speaks.

"Your name is Yip Tak-tak, is that right?"

"Yes, sir." Keep a straight face, no smile yet. Take it seriously.

"Your work?"

"I'm employed by the Hong Kong Symphony Orchestra."

"The what?"

"It's the big classical music band. *Da da da daaaa.*" Lok nods.

"Do you know Tang Yee Fun?"

So that's what this is about. "Yes, sir, I do," he says.

"Can you tell me her English name?"

"Milkie."

"How do you know her?"

"She works at a club ... a place I go to sometimes."

"Which one is that?"

"VSOP. On Canton Road."

"Did you know she was dead?"

He keeps his expression blank. "No."

A pause. Lok is studying his reaction, he knows.

"How well did you know Milkie?"

"I knew her. I told you. She worked at the club." Careful. Don't slip too easily into past tense.

"When did you see her last?"

"It's been a long time. I don't know ... a month? Maybe more? I thought she quit."

"Were you sleeping with her?"

"Yes, sir."

"Was she sleeping with anyone else?"

"Inspector, she was a prostitute."

"Outside of work, I meant. Did she have another lover?"

"I wouldn't call her my lover, exactly, sir. It wasn't that serious between us."

"Just answer the question. Did she have any other lovers outside of her customers?"

"I'm sorry, sir. I just don't know."

"Did you have insurance on her?"

He has no trouble looking surprised. "What? No!"

"Miss Tang wanted to get into the film business. Did you know about that?"

"Yes, sir. Her and all the other girls in the club."

"She was serious about it. Did you know she had an operation?"

"Yeah. She wanted to be a big hill woman." He frames two gigantic breasts with his hands.

"Just her breasts?"

"Her eyes, too. She wanted to look like a movie star. I said okay ..."

"What do you mean, you said okay?"

Mistake. Too much information. But don't look defeated, don't make it into an admission of guilt. "I thought you knew, sorry. She needed money for the operation, so I gave it to her. And that bastard in Central is expensive."

"How much did you give her?"

"Forty-five thousand. Fucking thief. And that's just his fee. There was the hospital, too."

"Why did you give her the money?"

"She needed it. We were friends, and I'm generous."

"What did she do in return?"

"Excuse me?"

"Did she sleep with you in exchange?"

Looking slightly offended. "Inspector, do you think I need to pay for it?"

"Then why?"

"I told you, sir. I'm generous."

"That's a lot of money, Yip. Your job pay you well?"

Yip smiles. "I get by."

Lok looks down at his sheet again. "Indeed you do ..." Then he puts down the paper and looks Yip straight in the eye.

"Still smuggling, Yip?"

"What?"

"Duty-free VCRs into China, it used to be, silver dollars out. Maybe people out too."

Yip is surprised anyone has any information on that. Of all the people he ever worked with, the boat people were the best; they threw informants into the sea.

"Someone questioned me once about that, sure. But no one arrested me."

Lok looks down at the record in front of him. "The word is, you used to run guns from Vietnam, M-16s and Brownings left behind by servicemen after the big pullout. Brought them to the Philippines."

Those were profitable days, Yip recalls. The coastline from Vietnam to Hong Kong is long and impossible to police. And the NPA welcomed his deliveries, though they never managed to win the Philippine nation back in the name of the people.

"Never," he says. "I'm sorry, Inspector. Your informants are mistaken."

"When did you give Milkie the money?"

"I'm sorry, I don't remember exactly. A few months ago. You can check with the doctor."

"Did you give her a check?"

"Cash."

"Did you see her after the operation?"

"I saw her after she had her eyes done. But not after the tits."

"She never had the breast operation."

"If you say so."

"What happened after the eye operation?"

"She stayed away for a few weeks. Bandages, you know. Then she came back to work for a few days."

"To work where?"

"At the club."

"How do you know? Do you work there?"

Caught. Shit, Lok is good. "I do some management consulting for them," Yip says. "I'm there often enough."

"You run the valet parking, right? Those are your followers parking cars. The bouncer, too."

Yip shrugs with good humor. "I just help them out. Business advice."

"Didn't it bother you? You give all this money to a girl, and she quits and leaves you?"

"Maybe. But have you seen the club? Plenty of girls there."

"But you gave money to this one."

The biggest smile he can manage. "Happens sometimes."

"Did she say good-by to you?"

"No, she just stopped showing up, a few days after she started work again."

"That's because you killed her. You killed her and then you dumped her in the channel."

Calmly, now. This was sure to come, after all. Look a little surprised, but not frightened. "Why would I give her money for an operation and then kill her?"

"Maybe she dumped you. Maybe she found someone else."

"Maybe. But I didn't kill her."

"Were you running her? What percent of her fees did you take?"

"None, sir. You said yourself, I gave her money."

Lok is silent for a minute. Then: "Yip *sin-sahng*, we need to take a look in your flat and your car." A good sign. They're still scratching around for evidence. This is all preliminary.

"You want to do a search?"

"Yes. You're not going to make us go to a magistrate, are you? We'll do it if you insist. But we're not going to be happy. It would be easier if we had your permission."

"Go ahead, Inspector. I'm delighted to cooperate."

WHEN YIP IS gone, Lok reports to K.K. Kwan.

"He showed respect, did he?" says Kwan.

"The *lan jai* always do," says Lok. Crooks, triads, and creeps know better than to misbehave in the interrogation room. But get an innocent person in here, and it's a different story. They'll complain about the waste of time, threaten to call your superiors or the papers.

"So do you think he did it?"

"I don't have a feeling yet. He's triad, I can tell you. A Sun Yee On 426, my guess. Runs the valet parking. Management consultant, he called it. But that doesn't make him our killer. Milkie was in a nasty business, lots of dirtballs around the place."

"You're checking her customers, I take it. Do you have the sign-out book?"

Lok nods. "We can't trace the cash customers, the ones who came in after scoring big at Macau or Shatin, but we're checking credit card receipts. There's one regular who came up pretty fast, a man named Leung Hing-kwok. We're also talking to the other girls, to find out if she fought with Yip.

"Good. Suppose it doesn't pan out, what's your next step?"

"Find out more about Yip. He's still the most likely."

Lok doesn't need to say anything more; Kwan knows he's planning to watch Yip for a few days, find out how he lives, who he hangs out with, how he pays for his Porsche. Legally Lok is supposed to apply to the Regional Surveillance Support Unit for coverage, but he won't bother with them yet. Without evidence, he might even be refused. But the only practical way to get things started is to find out who Yip Tak-tak really is.

───────────

MILLION MAN EMERGES from the Hot Room, about to leave for Yip's flat, when he passes Station Sergeant Fu snoring in his chair. He stops, considers the moment. Old Ko he can humiliate anytime. But Station Sergeant Fu is different—his tour ended a couple of years ago. He's been brought back on contract, so no one's sure how long he'll be at Yau Tsim.

And Million Man owes Fu. The Station Sergeant wasted no time in telling everyone about the golf club Million Man bought to butter up Inspector Lok. And Lok, he's since found out, is not a golfer. During the past few days a number of PCs and even Inspector Pullman have poked their head in and yelled "Fore!" prompting a predictable outbreak of laughter. If he's going to make Detective Inspector, Million Man can't be laughed at.

He's heard about people like Fu. A karaoke cop who'd start drinking Friday lunchtime and end up shitfaced at five a.m. in Wanchai. Old dross that would never have made it in the new Hong Kong Police.

And now, Fu has been delivered to him, asleep in his chair. With exquisite delicacy the younger man lifts Fu's service revolver from his holster, plucks the cartridges from the cylinder, and then empties the speed loader. He replaces the emptied weapon and loader with the delicate hand of a surgeon.

CHAPTER 31

HECTOR OPENS THE door a crack. The lights are off, confirming his hunch. It's Sunday afternoon, and even the most conscientious workers at the Hong Kong Symphony offices are gone by now.

Hector and Twinkie split up and begin opening file cabinets. Even with the lights off, the floor-to-ceiling windows illuminate the room well enough to read by.

The first drawer he opens is full of correspondence. He finds nothing of interest except for an unusual number of letters from music fans requesting Mozart's Haffner Symphony. Hector knows that they were all forged by the first clarinetist, who likes time off, and hence tries to push the orchestra to program works without clarinets.

The next drawer he opens is marked General Committee—Minutes. He pulls out the thick file folder and begins to leaf through drearily paraphrased conversations about benefit concerts, personnel matters, contract details. One name stops him.

Mr. Mulqueen stated that Mr. Shao was an excellent choice, and it would be foolish not to hire him now, as he is a strong conductor and Chinese as well.

Mr. Wong disagreed, stating that it was not necessary to appoint a permanent Musical Director right away.

Mrs. Albrecht pointed out that Mr. Shao was not well known outside China, and therefore would not be able to attract much interest from overseas.

Mr. Mulqueen said that Mr. Shao's plans for recording and touring would raise both his profile and the orchestra's. He would be able to line up sponsorship for the recordings, if need be.

Mr. Wong said it was not wise to commit to Mr. Shao, since the orchestra had not yet played under him.

Mr. Mulqueen said such a situation was not unusual. It was more important to make sure we do not lose Mr. Shao to another orchestra ...

He calls Twinkie over, asks her what it means.

"I'm not sure. Looks as if a couple of people on the General Committee were dead set on hiring Shao. Ambrose Wan and someone named Mulqueen—his name was on a sheet of paper at Leo's place, remember?

"Is that John Mulqueen?"

"You know him?"

"From the business news. He runs a communications agency, Mulqueen Tangent. Something happened to them, I think."

"Good or bad?"

"I don't know. But I'll find out."

Hector reads the document through to the end. "This Mulqueen character is like a dog with a bone. No matter what anyone says, he keeps promoting Shao. What's his problem?"

"Why is it a problem? I don't understand."

"Later," he says. "I want to see something else." Hector walks to Bonson's office and tries the doorknob. It's locked. He takes a Swiss Army knife from his pocket and works back the spring bolt to force his way in.

Inside, he opens the blinds and surveys Bonson's tidy kingdom. A coat rack, empty. A desk, almost so. A small shelf behind the desk, with a few books and some sort of musical award: a bronze treble clef. *To the Hong Kong Symphony Orchestra for Community Spirit 2001.*

One wall is cork, covered in notices, memos, photos, and reminders. Another is an immense white board laid out in a spreadsheet-like grid: the orchestra's schedule for the next two years. Some of it he recognizes. There are Cultural Center performances, school concerts, recordings. In red, Bonson has marked some recent additions. In January, Guangzhou—Paris. April, Guangzhou—San Francisco. June, Bangkok—Los Angeles.

The drawers in Bonson's desk are locked too, and once again the knife is all it takes.

Nothing out of the ordinary in the top three drawers. In the bottom one, however, under an old datebook, is a candy box. He tilts up the cover. Chocolate creams, stale ones. On a hunch, Hector lifts the plastic tray that holds the chocolates. Beneath it, safe from all but the most unselective candy lover, is a pile of credit card receipts. He draws them out.

VSOP NIGHTCLUB.

COVER	500
BEVERAGE	2,800
ENTERTAINMENT	2,000
SERVICE	530
TOTAL	$5,830

Hector reads through the slips. $5,360, $3,920, $6,670, one after another. All from the same club. Sometimes the drinks are less, sometimes more, but there is always a $2,000 entertainment charge. Altogether some eighty thousand Hong Kong in receipts, he thinks. About ten thousand U.S.

He jogs to the copier in the main office and switches it on.

"Good thinking," she says. "You should be a reporter." She's still leafing through meeting summaries.

"Why did you become one?" He starts to arrange the receipts on the glass and copy them.

"It fits my personality.

"That's for sure."

"I'm *bat gwah*. I'm not afraid to confront people and ask questions."

"I know. I like that."

"Really?" She looks up from the summaries. "You didn't like it before."

He rolls his eyes. "My mistake. I make a lot of them, right?"

She looks off to one side, unsure of how to answer.

"Twinkie, I'm sorry again."

"You're used to Western girls, aren't you? Did you think you could just have me?"

"No. I don't consider you like that. It just seemed the right thing to do at the time."

All at once he's ashamed. His answer was glib, too self-assured.

She stares at him a long ten seconds. "I'll tell you when it's the right time."

CHAPTER 32

AFTER BRIEFING HIS replacement, Station Sergeant Fu stretches, dons a cardigan to ward off the chill of the aircon, and makes his way downstairs to the exit, stopping once at the bathroom and once to check the racing section of an evening paper that lies on a vacant desk. His last stop is the armory, where he turns in his revolver and speed loader and bids the PC behind the window goodnight.

"One moment, Station Sergeant Fu," the constable says.

"What?"

"The cartridges ..."

"What are you talking about?"

"The gun's not loaded. Do you have the cartridges?"

Fu looks at the empty Smith and Wesson thirty-eight, spins the chamber, peers at the loader. "What the hell ..." is all he can say. He stares at the PC, a kid who doesn't look old enough to take a piss by himself. The PC stares back.

"I'm going to have to report this, sir."

"What the hell are you talking about?"

"Sir, I have to account for ammunition ..."

"You think I lost the ammunition?"

"The gun and the loader are empty, sir."

"I can see that. Do you think I'm blind, too?"

"No sir."

Fu slams his hand on the counter and stomps off in a fury that startles all of the onlookers except Million Man, who dashes to the Hot Room.

———————

LOK WATCHES A beaming Million Man slip into the Hot Room.

"Glad you could make it," says Old Ko.

"Sorry, sir," Million Man says, making it clear his apology is for Lok's ears only. He closes the door, takes a seat, peels his jacket off.

"The search of Yip's place turned up nothing," Lok continues. "No surprise there. If we think he's worth pursuing, we'll need to do some surveillance. Old Ko, you and Pang will start on it when you've finished checking through the receipts."

"Almost done," says Old Ko. "Pang is on it now. This Leung seems to be the only real regular so far."

"What's the point?" says Ears. "He's just a customer, someone who pays to take her out. Why should he want to kill her?"

"Depends, Ears," says Lok. "You get a lot of different characters in these bars. Most of them are pretty detached about the sex, but you find twisted types who get emotionally involved, start to think they own the girl, or imagine that the girl loves them. Or else they're just sick whore-haters.

"But you've got a point," Lok continues. "We're looking for people who matter in this case. Who's that, apart from regular customers?"

"Anyone who would want to kill a prostitute," says Million Man.

"No. Anyone who would want to kill Milkie. We don't know it

was her job that killed her."

"Everyone hates them," says Million Man. "Even the customers."

Lok nods. He doesn't much like prostitutes himself. He's never used one, and he knows that wherever they are, the triads are not far behind, spawning a constant crossfire of spite and cruelty. Sooner or later every whore steps into it.

Yet he's never met a cop who wants to rid the world of them. They provide a service, an outlet for lonely and frustrated men. It might not be savory, but try to stamp it out, all that happens is the price gets higher and the criminals get more desperate and ruthless in their efforts to control it.

"It could be a betrayed lover," says Old Ko.

"Yip's logical for that," says Million Man. "She could have shot him down, and he got angry."

"Not likely," says Old Ko. "A triad caring enough about a woman to kill her?"

"You're not thinking about the case anymore," says Lok. "You're just trying to pin it on Yip because he's there."

"Because he's a piece of shit," says Million Man.

"How about Yorks, at the car hire place?" says Ears. "She was pretty cruel to him."

Lok shakes his head. "You're forgetting what this case is about. Who matters most?"

They're silent.

"Who is the most involved in this case?"

He looks at them all, sees the expression on Old Ko's face.

"Tell them," Lok says.

"Milkie," Old Ko answers.

"That's right. Milkie Tang is the only player in this we know about. We need to sort her out first. " He looks down at the file, at this point still little more than a name, a driver's license, a couple of grisly photos, a few resentfully told tales transcribed in that stilted police language that manages to further deaden the dead.

Yet Milkie was more than that. She was a woman who wanted something badly enough to pay a surgeon to carve up her face and reshape her looks. Who needed money enough to sleep with strange men for pay. Yet who shielded her parents from her life by lying about her profession.

Men gave Milkie what she wanted. Yorks Ma is a classic fool—no problem guessing his desires. But Yip paid for her surgery. Did he buy Milkie's dream of stardom, too?

"We need to get Milkie's habits, her hangouts," says Million Man.

"More than that," says Ears. "Someone wanted Milkie dead. Someone dressed her body in cheap clothes to mislead the cops and dumped her in the water. We can't figure out why. That means we don't have a clue about what her life was really like."

"Good, Ears, you're catching on. You and Million Man get back to Milkie's flat, talk to the neighbors."

"No one saw anything, sir."

"Someone did, Ears. Someone always sees something. You can't do anything in a city like this without being spotted by people. They're everywhere, all the time, on every street, in every building, staring out of windows, getting out of taxis. Someone saw something, but they don't know what it was, or that it matters. Find them."

The team breaks up. Lok returns to his office, pours himself a tea, moves to the computer.

He types "Milkie Tang" into a search engine. A long shot, but the name comes up three times: today's report, which mentions her name and a few noncommittal sentences from Lok to the press. A second version of today's news story. And something from the *Post*.

CHAPTER 33

THE MTR TRAIN glides on welded rails under the harbor. The gleaming steel benches are almost empty, but Hector and Twinkie prefer to stand.

She shoves a bag in his hand. "You're a photographer today," she says. "Can you figure out the camera?"

Hector peeks under the flap. "No problem."

"And here," she says, pulling a laminated card from her pocket, "is your ID." The card shows a Westerner, a man about his age with a thin face, spectacles, limp curly hair and a six-day stubble. Hector's face is full, clean-shaven, and unbespectacled, his hair straight.

"This is supposed to be me?"

"It's the best I could do. Don't worry, you all look alike to us."

Hector watches Twinkie gaze modestly at the floor. He's been thinking about her lately. Lying in bed, trying to remember her scent, her smile, her voice. *What else is there about her I haven't memorized,* he thinks. Her ears, small and delicate. Eyebrows that arch with the tiniest of points interrupting the graceful curve. Her blouse is demure, buttoned close to the throat, so he must be content to imagine those mysteries. As he has, a number of times.

Last night they exchanged innocent waves as their good-by. This morning neither has mentioned his failed seduction.

The train slows and pulls in to the Wanchai station, signaling a return to business for them both.

"What did you find out about Mulqueen?"

"John Robert Mulqueen, born in Greystones, County Wicklow, Ireland, studied journalism in London. Came here in 1971. Worked as a reporter for a couple of years at the *Post*, then as a PR representative for a few multinationals. Started his own communications agency, and did well during the boom. He even bought out another firm called Tangent, doubled his staff. He had lots of business from Jardine's, some real estate developers, airlines."

"Has he been on the General Committee for a long time?"

"Yes, about six years. He's does the charity balls, society fundraisers, that kind of thing. Well known, member of the Hong Kong Club, et cetera, et cetera."

"And he wanted Shao to be Music Director."

"Listen to this. Two years ago the airlines merged and Mulqueen lost the account. Then Jardine's pulled out, went with a new firm. So Mulqueen was in very bad shape."

"The point is ... ?"

"He'd fired half his staff, got behind with his office rent, the whole thing. Then, six months ago, Ambrose Wan saved him. Gave all his firm's business to Mulqueen."

"So Mulqueen owes Wan—he'd probably do anything Wan asked. Do you think it's Wan who wanted Shao to be conductor, and Mulqueen is just going along with him?"

"Yes."

"Why?"

"Let's ask him."

THE TAI FOOK Commercial Building, twenty-two floors, is an elder among Hong Kong skyscrapers. Once the pride of a great metropolis, buildings like this are falling all over the city, so that massive towers with fiber-optic cabling and rooftop satellite dishes can ascend from the rubble.

Hector and Twinkie breeze through a lobby which exudes a 1970s sense of style: mock crystal chandeliers, beige travertine. In less than a minute they're on the eighteenth floor. The receptionist barely blinks at their ID before announcing them.

John Mulqueen emerges to greet them. He's tall, stocky, with thin grey hair and a slightly pockmarked face whose sunburst of red veins advertises a dedication to drink. They shake his meaty hand and follow him into a conference room.

"Is this for a *Post* article?" he asks. "About the conductor business, I take it?"

"Not exactly an article yet," Twinkie says, unpacking her memo recorder. "I'm trying to find out more background about the controversy. There's a lot of talking, and not a lot being said, if you know what I mean."

If the comment is calculated to draw Mulqueen in, it works. He nods and slaps his hand on the table for emphasis.

"Exactly. That letter to the editor today? It's out of control, if you ask me. The Committee has only one goal in mind: making the orchestra a success. The way people are going on, you'd think we were plotting against them."

She nods. "The orchestra seems pretty clear about Shao," she says. "People have told me they don't like him."

"I understand he wasn't immediately popular. But you need to give someone time to work into the job. Did you get to choose your boss?"

She smiles. "No."

"Not when I was at the *Post* either. Denny Carroll was my editor then. Retired now. Good newsman, taught me a great deal."

"Sherman Fai told me about him."

"Oh, Sherman and I had some times together. Just mention my name and Lockhart Road, and see if he doesn't turn red."

Twinkie laughs. "I'm sure you know where the bodies are buried at the *Post*." A pause, to let the sham levity fade. She's doing beautifully, Hector thinks. "Now," she says, "why do you think Shao was chosen in the first place?"

His nose twitches, as if he's caught a whiff of smoke from a distant fire. "He was the best man for the job. No doubt about it. We found out who was available, looked at resumes, got the lay of the land, checked the opinions of colleagues, read reviews, everything. Maestro Shao came out on top, by a good margin."

"What do you think will happen? Will this all blow over?" She's pulling back, asking an innocent question to string him along.

"I'm certain it will. The orchestra is sounding good, despite what some people say. It would be a shame to dismantle all that's been achieved since Maestro Shao came."

"Where do you think the complaints are coming from, then?"

He pauses to think, smacks his lips. "I suppose … I hate to use the word 'troublemakers' … no, don't use that word, please. I suppose there are some young and very unrealistic people in the orchestra who are trying to make the job an ideal one all at once, and they're very persuasive about it."

Oh, you are slick, thinks Hector.

"I've heard that not everyone on the Committee agreed that Shao was the best candidate," says Twinkie.

The nose again. "Where did you hear that?"

"Wasn't it you and Ambrose Wan who were most enthusiastic about Shao?"

His eyes narrow. "Who told you that? That's nonsense."

"I'm just asking because Wan Industries is a client of yours—a new client, and ..."

It builds slowly, beginning in the depths of inchoate rage, boiling up like a sulphurous lava pool. "Bloody hell ..." Then he takes a breath, gets his temper under control. "I don't know where you get this stuff," he says. "Don't you know Ambrose Wan and I are old friends?" The smile is gone now. "Just because we happen to agree about a conductor, that doesn't mean there's some kind of conspiracy. Let's be reasonable, shall we?"

"So you're saying you didn't insist on Shao just because Wan told you to."

Mulqueen stands. "That does it. I'm prepared to answer reasonable questions about the orchestra, but this is insulting. My receptionist will show you out."

"Can we just get a picture?" says Hector.

Mulqueen looks at him. "I've seen you ... where was it? You're no goddam photographer." He exits the room, a one-man stampede.

HECTOR DABS A piece of cold chicken into a pungent mash of ginger and scallions. They're dining at Hop Fat, in winter one of the finest snake restaurants this side of the harbour. During the warm months the snake boxes in the window are stashed away, replaced by a flock of halved birds destined for plates of Hainan Chicken.

"What a lying bastard. 'We looked at resumes, got the lay of the land, read reviews, Shao came out on top ... '"

"'By a good margin.'"

"Bullshit. He's frightened, I can tell. How do you think Leo figured out that Mulqueen was being bribed?"

"I don't know," Twinkie says. "Does he follow Hong Kong's gossip? Read the business pages?"

"Leo? He doesn't do newspapers."

"Then he saw it in the orchestra files. But it's obvious that Mulqueen was bribed by Ambrose Wan, and he's frightened."

"So we need to find out why Ambrose Wan wanted Shao in."

"Maybe he owes Shao something."

"How could Wan and Shao have known each other?" In the background, the chopper thumps again and again through flesh and bone. "Wan doesn't strike me as someone who even went to a concert before he joined the General Committee. He's just doing his civic bit. I spoke with him at an orchestra party once. He doesn't know anything about music."

"You could tell?"

"Doesn't take long."

"But now he has Mulqueen ... what's the word ..."

"Under his thumb."

"Yes. Wan probably did his homework, looked around for the most bribable man on the committee. Mulqueen doesn't look happy about it, either. Must be tough, almost losing your business, then becoming someone else's toady to keep it going."

"Why did he come here in the first place?"

"Probably the usual. Some enterprise went bust, so came here to start over."

"FILTH," Hector says.

"Failed In London, Try Hongkong," they chant in unison.

"Did you notice that about Hong Kong?" says Twinkie. "We send our successes overseas, but the West sends their failures to us."

"Thanks a lot, Twinkie."

She laughs. "I didn't mean you."

After an awkward silence, she asks why he came to Hong Kong. Hector pauses before answering. "*Turandot.*"

"What?"

"The opera we're playing now. *Turandot.* I was playing it in Tulsa. That's in Oklahoma. I got in a fight with someone, got thrown out of the orchestra. Couldn't get a job anywhere else."

"What?"

He puts down his chopsticks, takes a sip of tea, and explains how an ice-cold murdering princess caused his expatriation.

The Tulsa production was a very fashionable update—set in LA instead of China, TV screens all over the stage, disco lights. *Rethinking Puccini's Last Opera* was the Arts section headline. The director was Joseph Calitri, ex-rock video, a man addicted to scandal and jarring visual images. The characters Ping, Pang, and Pong, originally ministers, were now in the Crips. Timur, specified in the libretto as an exiled Tartar king, walked on stage with motorcycle helmet and gang tattoos. Turandot herself, the Chinese princess, was transformed into a whip-wielding dominatrix.

At the opening night party Hector spotted Calitri lining up at the buffet table, *sans* entourage for the moment, and asked him what the whole thing meant.

"Remember it's a problematic opera," said Calitri. "You have Turandot, a princess who hates men more than anything else. Who can blame her, right? So she makes her suitors answer riddles, and kills them if they fail. This is one bitch on a power trip. And there's Calaf, a prince who's determined to marry her anyway. That's his power trip. He answers the riddles, and naturally Turandot is pissed off.

"In the final scene Calaf is triumphant. He sings of love, grabs her. And with one hot kiss, her hatred of men disappears. It's hard to say what's more bizarre—Turandot's reversal or the fact that Calaf wants a woman that twisted. The plot doesn't make sense."

"Then how do you fix that?"

"Ah," in the manner of a professor answering the key question. "You can't, if you keep it in the world of straight love and decency. *Turandot* only works in an atmosphere of depravity. Like the gangs of LA."

"Okay," Hector said. "But you still have the music. It's meant to evoke ancient China, and instead you give them broken bottles, littered alleys, machine pistols, junkies nodding out."

"Exactly. The straight production has been done to death. What I did was find something new in the story."

"But people were laughing. You must have noticed. When a tenor sings a high B and carries a Glock, it looks weird."

"I love weird. Opera is always weird."

Hector says nothing. The director stares back, nods, his suspicion confirmed. "I get it. You're one of those 'venerate the artist' types. 'Puccini can do no wrong, the masters knew best.' Listen, my friend, I'm not doing this to serve Puccini. He's dead. I'm the star, and Puccini is my bitch. So fuck off."

Hector's fist shot into the man's gut before either of them knew what was happening. Uttering a strangled "Oof!" the director clutched his abdomen and fell to his knees.

In lieu of police, whom Calitiri generously declined to call, the director summoned his press agent. Thanks to Hector Siefert, Joseph Calitri sailed into the national arts press with a new scandal. But those articles that reported Hector's name got no quote from him. The General Manager said only that he'd "left the state."

"Why did you do it?" Twinkie asks.

"Why did I hit him? Don't know. I guess it was the arrogance. I don't care if people think they're better than me. But when they think they're better than Puccini, that makes me mad. It's what kills art—people without understanding, but also without humility. They don't bother to learn or understand, and then they bring everything down to their own crappy, sensational level."

She shakes her head. "You lose a job, flee your country, and you don't even know why you did it."

"What do you mean?"

"Loyalty. You were being loyal to the composer. That's all."

"Loyalty ..."

"That's why you do everything."

The waiter brings the check. Hector, shaken by her words, is slow to grab for it. He finds her soft hand underneath his.

"I'll get this," she says. "My contribution to the arts."

He nods, but surrenders her hand slowly.

CHAPTER 34

"ARE YOU COMING?" says Sinbad Ho.

"Just a minute." Mong lights a stick of incense, bows three times in thanks to Kwan Dai, then exits the room with his partner. He has much to be grateful for. The government chemist has come up with all the information Traffic AIU needs to find the driver. Apparently when the car bashed into the unfortunate musician, a few flecks of blue paint rubbed off on his horn case. Analysis has revealed the paint to be Westminster Blue, a formula used by British Leyland on various models through the late 1990s.

There are hundreds of cars in that color plying the jammed streets of Hong Kong. However, finding the chip of glass in District Commander Knowles's shoe saved them weeks of work. The report states that the color and composition of the glass match the headlight of a 1996 Jaguar XJ6, Sovereign, or XJ12 saloon. There are less than two hundred such cars registered in Hong Kong, and only nine are Westminster Blue. They've spent the morning alerting garages in case someone brings in a 1996 Jaguar saloon. Mong, however, wants to make the arrest himself.

"This just might be an easy one," Sinbad says as they exit the building. They've gone over the instructions. Visit the owners and

They thank him and leave. Back in the van, Lok scans the article one more time.

Star Watch

Milkie Tang is another face to watch out for. Fatman Leung has given her a part in his latest comedy Double Girlfriend. "It's my first film," she says. "I don't know what to expect. But I know I'll be a hit." Asked if a fortuneteller is behind her confidence, she said, "No. I don't believe in fortunetellers. I tell my own fortune."

"This is a dead end, I think."

"Not so sure, sir," says Old Ko. "He said he doesn't usually cast small parts, can't remember where he met her."

"So?"

"Then how did he remember her at all?"

CHAPTER 35

"**MISTER HECTOR!** How are you, sir?"

Hector smiles and pats Khan on a burly shoulder. "Good. Everyone still safe?"

"Always, sir." As Hector enters the jewelry shop, it dawns on him that he does indeed feel safe. A Pushtun with a Remington will do that.

Zenobia is behind the counter, showing a teenage girl a jade pendant, doughnut-shaped with a gold inlay bearing the double happiness symbol. She glances at Hector, quickly turns back to her customer. Across the room Zen's mother is talking pearls with a young couple. He nods to her, but she's absorbed in her sales talk about color and sheen.

When the girl moves on, Zenobia says "I'm busy, Hector."

"That's not too friendly. I just want to ask you something."

"Hector, I said I'm busy."

"Why can't your brothers help out?"

"Alfred is in school. Ricky has a job."

"So do you. Why can't he come here on his lunch hour once in a while?"

"You know why. It doesn't work that way."

"I know. You're the dutiful daughter."

"If you like Chinese girls so much, why can't you understand the culture?"

He holds up his hands in defeat. "I just wanted to ask you, does anyone at the Symphony go out to clubs?"

"What?"

"Does Bonson do some entertaining? At an expensive place?"

She looks at him, clearly puzzled. "If I tell you, will you leave?"

He shakes his head. "I don't get it, Zen. You don't want to marry me. All right. But why can't you stand being near me? Am I that disgusting?"

She turns away, hiding her face.

"Never mind. I'll leave right away. Promise."

She faces him again. "A few times Shao's father has come to visit. He …"

"Wait a minute. Shao's father?"

"Yes. He lives in China. He comes to visit his son. But he spends more time with Bonson. One time Mr. Shao boasted that Bonson took him to a club in Tsim Sha Tsui and spent more than he made in half a year."

"VSOP Nightclub?"

Her eyes widened. "Yes! How did you know?"

"Never mind. What's Shao's father like?"

"Old. I don't like him, the way he looks at me and the girls at the office. *Hum sup lo*," the last words spoken under her breath. A dirty old man.

"Hmm," is all he says.

"Please Hector. Go away." She walks to another counter and begins to polish silver bracelets.

Hector walks out, saluting Khan, and hits the sidewalk, cell-phone in hand. He reports Zenobia's words to Twinkie. "It doesn't make sense," he says. "What's Shao's father got to do with it?" Hector crouches in a corner, pressing the cellphone into his head to hear the reply through the rumble of trucks and taxis.

"Maybe nothing," says Twinkie. "But Bonson is spending thousands of dollars at VSOP. Big businesses do that to make a sale or bend a public official. But orchestras that exist on government money and private donations aren't supposed to do that, right?"

"Right. So what now?"

"Find out who Shao's father is. I have the feeling he's a big part of this."

"Why?"

"When this whole thing started, it seemed to be about music. But now money's entered into things. Wan buys Mulqueen's loyalty. And now someone's wining and dining Shao's father. No one spends that kind of cash without a reason."

THE SOUND OF the phone is rude beyond belief, a disturbance close to sacrilege. Such an unmusical little sound. Purely to silence it Letitia Wheatley-Craven snatches the receiver.

She is naked, conscious of the scratchy feel of a blanket on her bare skin, a feeling with which, after almost five years, she's beginning to reacquaint herself. During that time she's retired each night wearing her nightgown, with no need to remove it, no warm masculine hands to reach under it and draw it up, no muscled arms to hold her and press hard flesh to hers. Now her bareness reasserts itself, along with a score of tiny signals of bliss she's forgotten. The warm breath on the back of her neck, the delightful rills of sweat down a masculine shoulder, the slowly waning pulsation between her thighs, the sheer weight and presence of another body in the bed, the superb feeling of having all the pent-up frustration pummeled out of her by a man. And what a man.

"Hello?"

"Letitia?"

"Yes."

"This is Twinkie Choi. I was wondering if you could answer a question."

That woman again.

"What sort of question?"

"About Shao Din-yan."

She closes her eyes. "Wait a minute, please," she says. Then she grabs her nightie, takes the portable receiver into the bathroom, closes the door.

"What is it?"

"You interviewed Shao a few times. Did he ever mention his father?"

"His father? What's this about?"

"Nothing, probably. Do you know anything about him?"

"I don't know whether I should tell you anything, really. First you try to ruin his reputation, and now you're going after the family ..."

"Letitia, you know that's not true. I'm just reporting what the orchestra says. I let the management comment too, you know. Fair is fair."

She's unconvinced. Still ... "Well, at least what I tell you will be the truth. His father's a vice minister at the State Economic and Trade Commission. He's posted in Shenzhen now. He sent Din-yan to study music in the UK in the 1980s."

"Do you know his name?"

"No. Why?"

"Never mind. Does he ever come to visit? I'd like to meet him."

"I have no idea. But you could ask Maestro Shao, I suppose."

"I might do that. Thanks." The phone goes dead.

Letitia washes up, brushes her teeth, dabs a bit of cologne behind her ears, and walks back to the bedroom, still carrying the nightgown. For a second she considers slipping it on, returning to the familiar comforts of being clothed. Then she changes her mind, tosses the nightie back on the chair, and burrows quietly under the covers.

The figure in bed stirs. His head, bald but for a few wisps of hair on the side, moves to the crook of her neck, and then between her breasts.

"Mmm, it's my *dai san poh*." Big hill woman.

She laughs. "Oh, Maestro ..."

CHAPTER 36

LOK HAD NOT intended to be in Fatman Leung's office today. This morning he'd been looking over the toxicology report, which denied the existence of poisons or other foreign substances in Milkie's body. Nothing to point specifically to murder other than the way she was dressed. She wasn't poisoned, wasn't shot, wasn't stabbed. Almost as if she were still alive.

Then Pang walked into his office, holding a stack of credit card slips from Milkie's steady Wednesday night customer, one Leung Hing-kwok. He'd traced the man's English name, and it was a familiar one: Fatman Leung, film producer and liar. One of those bits of efficient police work that can instantly change the way a case is going.

There's no shooting today, so they're in Fatman's office in Sham Shui Po. For a film director, the space is businesslike and empty of glitter, apart from a wall full of posters from his films. File folders everywhere. Papers, DVDs, casting photos, and storyboards smother every horizontal surface. A fish tank in one corner, and on top of it, a small ceramic turtle, obviously placed there for *feng shui* reasons. No proprietor would ever keep a real turtle—it slows down business.

Lok and Big Pang sit opposite Fatman Leung's desk. Lok lays out a VISA slip. $3489, VSOP Club, including drinks and a $2500 charge marked Entertainment.

Fatman doesn't touch the receipt. He looks away from the policemen, whether in shame or fear, Lok can't tell.

Finally he speaks, almost a whisper.

"What do you want to know?"

"Where and when did you first meet Milkie Tang?"

"At VSOP. Last October, I think."

"And you saw her a lot after that."

"A few times a month. Two, three, maybe." A woman throws open the door. She carries a tray bearing three glasses of tea. Fatman shakes his head, and she retreats.

"Always on Wednesday, I understand."

Fatman's eyebrows twitter behind his lenses, probably at the realization that his private life is hanging open in the breeze, like the breasts of one of his stars. "That's right. When I'm free. "

"Where did you go?"

"Took her to my place."

"Always?'

"Always."

"Why were you seeing her?"

He looks genuinely startled. "Why do you think?"

"I'd think a film producer could get all the girls he wanted ..."

Fatman shrugs good naturedly. "You know what they say, Inspector. I'm not paying them to sleep with me. I'm paying them to go home afterwards. It makes for a less complicated life." A bit of swagger has returned to his voice.

"Why did you lie about knowing her?"

He gestures toward the posters on the wall. On each one a female form predominates, usually baring impressive cleavage.

Hard to be Sexy. Sexy Ghost. Waitress and Wife. "The stuff I do isn't obscene—I stick to the category guidelines. I still have to haggle with the censors, but I stay in business. But news like this—the death of an actress—could attract the wrong kind of attention."

"I thought you people liked a good scandal."

"That might have been true before '97. But you know how it is. One day Beijing could pass the word down that our film industry is getting out of hand, and it's time to root out corruption and filth. Who would come to my aid? The newspapers? The human rights groups? No, I prefer to keep a low profile nowadays." He smiles faintly, the smile of one making the best of things.

"Did Yip Tak-tak introduce you to Milkie?" asks Lok.

He drops the smile abruptly. "Yes." He loathes the man, Lok can tell.

"How do you know Yip?"

"You know how it is. We all have to deal with them." He lowers his voice again. "I had to pay some triad bastard twenty thousand to use that street the other day. If I didn't do it, lights would start toppling and breaking, equipment trucks would get stuck in traffic, the grips would call in sick. You get the idea. And that's just the day-to-day stuff. Occasionally one of the bosses decides he wants to fuck a movie star. His assistant just calls me up and says, 'My boss would like the pleasure of Mona Chang's presence tonight at dinner.' What can I do?"

"Are you paying protection money to Yip?" Lok asks.

"No. I just know he's triad. You can always tell. *Sun Yee On*, I think."

"Mona Chang, eh?" says Big Pang.

"Don't say I told you," says Fatman. "Anyway, it's not only her."

Lok: "What happened when you met Yip?"

"He said he knew a girl who wanted to be an actress, that's all.

It's easier just to say yes to these people. There's always an extra part somewhere for them, even if they're no good, which is almost always the case. Better than having them pissed at you, right?"

"And how good was Milkie?"

Fatman pauses. "She'd have had a career, eventually."

"Could she act? Really?" asks Big Pang, surprised.

"No, not well. She was average. But she had drive. You need that more than anything."

Lok again: "Where did you go when you took Milkie out?"

"Nightclubs, mostly. Sometimes the movies. You can ask my friends. We all go around together nights, after shooting's done.

"Can you tell us who would want to kill her?"

For a second a genuine look of puzzlement comes over Fatman's face. "She was a tough girl," he says to Lok. "But she was soft inside. I know how corny that sounds—like one of my films. You've seen *Stay Off My Heart*?"

Both men shake their heads.

"Well, anyway, she never wanted to hurt anyone, I know that. She wanted to make good, to make people proud of her. She was like a kid, really. I think she wanted to be a success so that she could please someone."

"Yip?"

A sneer. "Him. No. She didn't think much of that one. Yes, I know Milkie was his personal property, but she was using him too."

"Was she using you?"

That stops him.

"Maybe," he says. "But I was using her. Fair enough, right?"

———

OUTSIDE, WAITING FOR the van to pull up, Big Pang says, "He looked nervous."

"Could be natural," Lok says.

"You'd think he'd be a bit more embarrassed about whoring around. He looks a bit high class for that kind of thing."

"Who can tell?"

"So you think he's telling the truth."

"No, I think he's still lying," says Lok "But I don't know what the lie is, exactly. I wonder about his relationship with Yip, if it's as casual as he says. How about you keep an eye on him for a while? Maybe get Airport to help." WPC Carrion Kwok, known throughout the CID as *fei gei cheung*, or "airport," thanks to a chest as flat as a concrete runway.

"Surveillance on two people? And informal? Aren't we spreading ourselves thin?"

"Yes, but I want to get rid of this case soon, before it's as rotten as that girl in the drawer. If nothing turns up in a couple of days we'll drop Fatman, at least. But not till we find out just what kind of a mess Milkie made for herself."

ANOTHER DOOR, ANOTHER face, this one a man, maybe fifty, slightly confused and nervous, guarded by a metal gate he won't open.

Million Man shows his identification through the bars. "Sir, we're from CID. I'd like to ask you about the woman who lived in 3F."

"3F? Who's that?"

"The girl who died."

"Ah, yes. Sorry, I don't know anything."

Such a quick denial would be suspicious anywhere but China. Here people are taught not to meddle, and the Chinese definition of meddling is vast.

"Did you know the woman in 3F?"

"No."

"Did you ever see anyone enter or leave her flat?"

"No."

"Did you ever hear any arguments from her flat?"

"No."

"Any unusual noises?"

"Don't remember. No."

The door swings shut.

"That's it for the floor," says Million Man. "Eight flats, two empty, six people who saw and heard nothing." He walks to the elevator, punches the button. "No one who even knew the victim. Either Milkie Tang lived a quiet home life, or the whole floor is like most people in this city, deaf and blind."

Across the corridor the door to 3A cracks open, and a weathered face peers out. Then the door silently closes.

"Let's go get lunch," says Million Man. "There's a good curry club near here."

Ears looks at the door.

"You go. I'll call you." The elevator door shudders open.

Million Man shrugs, steps in. "Suit yourself."

Ears walks to 3A, knocks gingerly, hears the clatter of some kitchen utensils, then the click of a door latch.

"*Wai?*" The old woman peers through the gate.

"I spoke to you a half hour ago. About the girl?"

"I told you, I don't know anything."

"I understand. But I want to learn a little more about the building. May I come in for a minute?"

Without much enthusiasm, Mrs. Liu opens the gate and then pads back to the kitchen. Her flat is the same layout as Milkie's but less modern. No stove, just an LPG cooker, a few shabby chairs, and a dining room table, set for one. On a 25-inch TV in the living room a woman is begging her lover to leave his wife.

"Have you lived here a long time?" Ears asks.

"Nineteen years ago, we bought the place."

"You're married?"

"My husband's dead."

"Children?"

"Three. Grown."

"You're making *bo tong*, aren't you? Smells good."

"Like some? I've got plenty."

"I don't think …"

"Oh, come on. Have some. You look too skinny." She plucks another bowl from the drain board by the sink and places it on the table. Then she ladles some steaming soup into the bowls, her hands brown and gnarled as banyan roots, but steady.

"Sit down," she says.

"This smells good," he says. "My mother makes a good *bo tong*."

"Does she use north and south almonds?"

"No, no, raw cashews."

"Try this, then. You'll see. My son likes this a lot."

Ears can see some bean curd and watercress. He blows on a spoonful of the boiling-hot broth and then slurps it carefully. It's not nearly as good as his mother's—not enough salt—but he smiles and compliments her.

"Do you like this building?" he asks. "I think it's kind of noisy, myself." Earlier today, Ears had seen Mrs. Liu's nose poke through the gate every time he entered or left a flat. It's obvious she watches everyone and everything on the floor.

"You're right, it is noisy," she says. "Too much going on here. And that girl was the worst."

"Worse than that couple with the two teenage boys?"

"Much. She had visitors at night, the whore. Different men. Three different men!" She holds out three fingers.

His heart begins to beat like a dragon boat's drummer. "Can you describe them?"

She shrugs. "Bah! I don't concern myself with other people's business."

CHAPTER 37

AT THE SYMPHONY office Hector is about to announce himself when Yip, bookended by his minions, emerges from a back office and charges toward the door. When Hector speaks, he freezes.

"I'd like a favor from you."

"You what?" Yip turns to face Hector.

"I'd like to talk to the guy who's fixing my bass."

"No need," Yip says. He pulls out a cellphone, presses a number.

"It would help."

"He knows his job."

"Sure. But I'd like to meet him just the same."

A flash of irritation in his eyes. "He's very busy."

"Good. But ..."

"What are you so worried about? You worry too much, *See-fat*."

"Look, Yip. It's my bass. I agreed to go with a local repairman to save the orchestra money. It's my responsibility to ensure that the bass is repaired correctly." Words carefully chosen to give Yip face.

A woman at the desk across the aisle calls to Hector. "Mr. *See-fat*, you can see Mr. Ng now." From a cubicle somewhere a stifled giggle squeaks.

Yip tells whoever's on the phone to wait, then looks at his watch, a plump Rolex in gold the color of frozen piss. "460 Caine Road," he says. "Fifth floor. Two o'clock." Then he walks out, ear to phone.

Hector walks into Bonson's Ng's office. Bonson is seated behind his desk, a look of seriousness approaching agony on his boyish face. He's dressed in a blue cashmere blazer and burgundy tie. Drawn blinds deflect the gaze of outer office keyboard tappers.

Hector is dressed in jeans and red Balinese batik shirt. He flops idly in the guest chair to dispel the impression of fear or even interest. It's his third appearance in the Symphony office this season, his first by actual invitation.

"Hector, it's come to my attention that you've been harassing a member of the General Committee."

"Says who?" He faces Bonson square on.

"Don't interrupt. John Mulqueen called me last night. He was absolutely furious. I've never known anyone so angry in my entire working life. He wants you fired immediately, and threatened to have my job if I didn't do it. He is outraged that anyone would make such malicious accusations without the slightest proof or foundation."

We've shaken him up, Hector thinks. *He's striking out in panic.*

"So, I'm fired?"

Bonson folds his delicate hands on the desk. "No. It took a while on the phone—and it was not fun, believe me—but I managed to convince him that you weren't intending him any harm by posing as a photographer."

"Just what was I intending, then?"

"I'd be careful what I say right now, Hector. Your job is hanging by a thread. And I know that the American orchestral world is not exactly ready to welcome you."

So Bonson knows. Interesting.

"Hector, if I hear another word about you, another rumor, anything that suggests that you're making things difficult for the orchestra, then you are finished. Your work visa goes, and you'll be deported within three days of my phone call to Immigration.

Hector nods, eyes now on the ceiling. Bonson continues.

"You are not to sign any more petitions, talk to the press, agitate the orchestra, or misbehave in any way. Do you understand?"

Hector nods again.

"Just what were you trying to do with Mr. Mulqueen?"

Hector leans forward and says, "I was trying to find out why Ambrose Wan bribed Mulqueen so that Shao would end up as our conductor."

He watches carefully for Bonson's reaction, and is rewarded with a beauty. The man shrivels like a prawn on a bed of coals.

"Get out," croaks Bonson, the last shred of his buoyant tenor gone.

On the street Hector hails a minibus into Central. From there he catches the escalator that ascends into the Mid-levels. Standing on the moving steps, watching second-floor tenement windows glide past, he ponders what he's learned today: that Bonson is even more shit-scared than Mulqueen. Mentioning Ambrose Wan and Shao in the same sentence petrifies them. What could be at stake? There isn't enough money in all of Hong Kong's classical music business to get anyone excited, much less frightened. And if there's no money in it, what else is there?

Yip is waiting when he arrives at 460 Caine Road. Neither man greets the other. They mount five flights in a musty stairwell to reach the top of the old, high-ceilinged building. Yip knocks on the first door they see. Hosell Lai opens it, ushers the pair into the main room.

Hosell Lai Man-kit is probably in his late fifties, with a dark, oily complexion. He's wearing a vinyl apron over cheap Chinese-made shirt and trousers.

The world of the workshop is a familiar one to Hector. The smells of maplewood and pine. A tin pot warming on a hot plate, full of glue made from animal hides. A workbench against the wall, and behind it a neat rack of primitive-looking tools: rasps, planes, awls.

Above all, there is the serenity, the sublime sense that, at least in this room, nothing is ever rushed. Several jobs are in progress, each frozen in time until Hosell can get back to it. A cello fingerboard, ready to be contoured. A violin locked in the tight embrace of wooden clamps till the seams dry. Another violin, its belly stripped to reveal the unfinished wood inside.

Across the room is another workbench, on which lies the headless corpse of Hector's bass.

Hosell speaks in strangely-accented Cantonese to Yip, who translates.

"He says he'll replace the ..." he points to where the fingerboard should be.

"The neck," says Hector.

"Yes. He's ordering one from Germany, and he'll fit it when it arrives. When that's done, he'll fit it to the bass."

Hector scans the violin that's open on the bench. A crack has been glued and reinforced, and the wooden splints conscientiously sanded down to add the least mass possible to the instrument.

"This is good work," Hector says. "He's been at this for a long time, I take it."

Yip translates, listens, and answers. "He learned in Shanghai. Worked there for many years. He makes his own instruments as well."

"Violins?"

A pause for translations. "Violins and ...*chung tai kam*." Yip doesn't know the English word for viola.

Hector is ushered to another room, where Hosell's violins and violas are on display. They look pretty impressive.

"When will it be ready?" he asks.

Yip doesn't bother translating, but answers right away. "Six months," he says.

"That long?"

"I told you, he's very busy."

CHAPTER 38

IN THE HOT ROOM, Old Ko and Big Pang are reporting informally on their surveillance of Yip Tak-tak. Nothing is in writing at this point.

"He leaves his flat yesterday at 8:45 a.m. A bit early for a Red Pole, wouldn't you say? Drives to Hong Kong Cultural Centre, spends the morning and early afternoon in the company of what appear to be a crew of workers, all male. Doesn't do any work himself."

That's no surprise," says Lok. "Know anything about the crew?"

"Yes. He's staying true to form. Two of the men are Lo Wai-ho—that's Small Eyes Lo—and Skinwic Sze. Don't know the third one."

"*Gow jais*?" 49s, or *gow jais*, are a Red Pole's henchmen.

"Maybe," says Big Pang. "Nothing much on them. Some minor juvenile offenses for Small Eyes. Skinwic Sze was interrogated a couple of times, most recently for that chopping in the Yee Foon restaurant last April. He was near the scene and knew the victim, but no witnesses or evidence, so he wasn't brought to trial. He does have a record for assault, from around five years back. There was an argument over a woman, he punched the man. I've got a bad feeling about him. Small Eyes doesn't look too bright, but I wouldn't trust him either."

"It gets better," says Old Ko. "Yip goes home, then out to Club VSOP at 10, back with a girl at midnight. Then, out again at two in the morning."

"Looks like you've been earning your money."

"He meets a man named Hosell Lai. He's got a history, nothing recent. Some kind of woodworker. He fixes violins."

"Violins? Could Yip and this Hosell have had legitimate business?"

"At two in the morning?" asks Old Ko.

"All right, good work. Keep on him another day. What about our movie director?"

"Nothing yet. He was on the set all day till late, and went home afterwards," says Million Man.

"Well, keep on that," Lok says. "Fatman knew the victim, had sex with her regularly." In murder cases, you always look at husbands and lovers first. For whores, pimps and regular customers are as close as you get.

A shout, resonating on tile, interrupts them. Old Ko and Big Pang rush next door to the bathroom, where Station Sergeant Fu stands over the sink, cursing and flinging a Styrofoam coffee cup against the wall.

In the sink are twelve .38 cartridges and the remains of a cup of coffee.

"What prick did this?" he screams, loud enough to address every Crime team on the floor.

"Found your ammunition, did you?" says Old Ko.

"Who was it? Who's trying to fuck me up?"

Pang shrugs, shakes his head. They back out and move a safe distance away before bursting into laughter.

THE FACE THAT peers out the door of Flat 9E possesses a look of queasiness that turns to dread at the sight of a policeman.

"Alvin Yau?" Sinbad holds up his warrant card. "Sinbad Ho, Traffic Accident Investigation Unit"

"Yes?"

"I need to speak with you for a minute. It's about your blue 1996 Jaguar Sovereign."

At the mention of the car the owner lurches back a step, then finds his balance again.

"You want ... what's this about?"

"We're making some inquiries. This will only take a minute. May I see your car, please?"

"Who's that?" a woman calls from a back room.

"Nothing," he answers. Then, softer, to Sinbad Ho: "May I know what this is about?"

"May I see it, please?"

"That's not possible. I'm sorry. It's not here."

"Can you tell us where it is?" Sinbad asks.

Alvin pauses for a few seconds, lets his eyes wander the room. "It's being repaired. It's not here now."

"Which repair shop? We'll need the address."

A woman enters carrying a baby not more than six months old. Behind her a toddler, another boy, ducks behind his mother, then peeks out from behind her trouser leg.

"What's this about?" she asks.

"Nothing important, Sonya," Alvin says to her.

"Yau *sin-sahng*, could we see your carpark?" asks Sinbad.

"Yes, yes!" With his wife in the room he appears only too happy to agree. "I'm just going down to show this man the carpark," he

says, as if she hadn't heard. "Something he's checking. I'll be back."
Bewildered, Sonya watches them leave.

Alvin ushers Sinbad out and shuts the door as if the place were
on fire. On the elevator he speaks.

"I lied to you," he says. "I apologize. The Jaguar isn't at the
repair shop. It's gone." The door opens, and they walk past the
parked cars to a gap marked with a 9E in yellow paint.

"Gone?" says Sinbad.

"Yes. I sold it. My wife doesn't know."

Sinbad says nothing. Alvin surveys the emptiness of his parking space, then leans listlessly against 9F's teal BMW. "Mahjong.
I've been losing for months. I did all right last year, but this year
there are some new players in the office, and they're too good. I'm
in debt a hundred fifty thousand. Last week I sold the car to pay
the loan shark."

After taking a few notes, Sinbad says, "We'll need to find out
who you sold it to."

"Of course. I'll write it down. Just don't …"

"Your wife won't find out from us," says Sinbad.

CHAPTER 39

THE ISLAND OF Cheung Chau looks different than it did in old days, at least to Lok's eyes, but it smells the same—sea air freshened by kapok trees, the aromas of steamed pork dumplings, incense, diesel oil, and cigarettes—and for that he's grateful. Later on will come new smells: smoldering mosquito coils, deep-fried cuttlefish, roast pigeon and beer in the outdoor restaurants.

Lok and Dora, and their children Kelvin and Kitty file through San Hing Street, making slow progress through the waist of the island, which is cinched to a bare five-hundred-foot width. Lok and Dora, laden with bundles of food for *Yeh Yeh* and *Ma Ma*, are mired in the Sunday crush, so the two children slip easily ahead of them and melt into the crowd.

Shops spill out into the alley, obstructing the thoroughfare on both sides with cartons and shelves full of toys, clothing, candy, bottled water, charcoal, and forks for barbecuing. Old friends call out greetings on the way—Ah Ping, who sells cheap prefab furniture from his shop, Fat Mary at the hardware store, Limpy at the Western coffee shop.

Lok was born on Cheung Chau back when it dozed, almost untouched by the economic typhoon that was sweeping a way of life out from under their kinsmen eight miles away in Hong Kong. The tiny island was a base for the fishing boats that plied the South China Sea, bringing snapper, prawns, and eel to the colony's markets and restaurants. The launching and mooring of boats and the tides set the island's rhythm. Grateful offerings of fruit and incense to Pak Tai, god of fishermen, sustained the rhythm and staved off calamity.

Today there are still no cars—no roads, in fact, only footpaths. However, the jungle of rickety shacks by the dock that once served as a market is gone, replaced by a park in the Hong Kong urban style: benches and planters on flat concrete. Nowadays inhabitants buy their meat and vegetables at a sanitary tiled structure down the street.

Lok and family pause at a fruit stand. Old So, the proprietor, isn't around. His teenage grandson, slick and fashionable with spiky hair and a lean, muscular tank-topped frame, nods at them without recognition. The boy weighs the oranges that Dora has chosen and dumps them into a plastic bag. Decades ago a hand-balance let Old So short-weight every sale. Now the government prescribes easy-to-read scales, dial poised outward toward customers by law.

They reach the shop where Lok's father has been selling housewares for as long as any of the family can remember. The shop is a warren of shelves and cubbyholes overflowing with teakettles, knives, adhesive hooks, wooden cutting boards, woks, chopsticks, corks, bottle openers, rice cookers, rattan mats. Every morning *Yeh Yeh* rolls onto the street a few carts with his most attractive goods onto the street. In the evening he wheels them back inside and rolls down the gate.

Lok enters and says "Hello, *Ba Ba*." To the kids he's *Yeh Yeh*, or grandfather, to Dora *Gnok Fu*, or husband's father.

Lok senior has a meager frame, slightly stooped, and dyed black hair and spectacles. He wears an oversized cotton jacket over a white singlet, and baggy brown trousers. He keeps his left hand concealed in the pocket of his jacket. A pulley savaged it when he was fourteen, retiring him from the boats forever.

Still, he's a fisherman at heart. He was named according to fishermen's custom: Lok Sam-gan, or "three catties," his weight at birth.

"I told you not to bring anything," he says. The children have parked themselves in front of a TV that glows and babbles on the floor. They've already found the candy box that *Yeh Yeh* keeps for them.

"No trouble," says Lok. "Just some cakes and things. How's the cold?"

"Gone. Yap gave me some good herbs."

Lok nods. He pays close attention to the health of his father, who takes orders from his herbalist and no one else.

A herd of teenage girls descends upon the shop. Lok looks them over, all backpacks, earbuds, and giggles, much like the girl who would have spotted Milkie Tang's body in the harbor.

They buy a mosquito coil. *Yeh Yeh* places the coins in a blue bucket that dangles from a disused light fixture.

"Business good?" Lok asks.

"Could be better. Supermarkets are right near the ferry, they get most of the holiday people first." In Lok's day a supermarket or a Watson's chain store on Cheung Chau would have been laughable. Now they're thriving. Still, *Yeh Yeh* has no reason to complain. He owns his store and the flat above, and another flat besides.

Ma Ma enters the store and draws Kitty and Kelvin to her generous body. *Ma Ma* is *Ba Ba's* height, but she's stockier and more carefully dressed, in a purple pantsuit and gold pendant.

"Where's Edna?" she asks.

"She's coming on the next ferry," says Lok.

"Couldn't she ride with the family?"

"She has a boyfriend now, didn't you know?"

Ma Ma arches her eyebrows. "A boyfriend? Did you allow it?"

Lok says nothing, aware that his wife is better at this.

"We don't know anything about him yet," says Dora. "He's coming with her today. We'll meet him for dinner."

Later they're sitting on a *kaido*, chugging past the moored junks that serve as houses as well as workplaces for the fishing people. On one junk's roof a tiny girl plays with a superhero doll, oblivious to the rope around her waist, her only babysitter. That might have been his childhood, had *Ba Ba* not tried to steady a net full of garoupa by grabbing the pulley one windy evening. Would it have been so bad? Sailing out each morning before dawn, unloading a catch an evening or two later, opposing currents and storms instead of Chief Superintendents and killers?

———

AT SUNSET, THREE generations of Loks convene at an outdoor restaurant near Tung Wan Beach. Lok and his father drink beer, the women *bo lei* tea, the kids Sprite from chilled cans pearled with moisture. Behind a veil of dangling roast pigeons a chain-smoking cook conjures meals over a thundering gas jet. From above them windows broadcast the clatter and crash of mahjong tiles; there are probably ten games going on within earshot, and twenty more up and down the street. Some residents sit down at the table after work on Friday and keep going through Sunday night.

When Edna arrives, the sight of her once again hits him like a well-directed slap. It's as if someone has worked up a blonde-haired parody of his daughter just to rankle him.

Standing next to Edna is a *gweilo* of medium height, mid-twenties, with indifferently-combed red hair and a silver cross dangling from his left ear.

Edna greets her grandparents warmly, gives her parents a cautious but friendly hello. "This is Julian," she says in English. Smiling, Julian extends a diffident greeting to the family, one by one. The table is quiet for a minute, as they adjust to the presence of a Westerner among them.

"The *gweilo* has red hair like a cat," whispers Kitty to Kelvin.

"Say *sai yan*, it's more polite," says Edna. *Westerner* instead of *ghost man*.

"Julian," says Lok. "What do you do?"

"I work at the Chute," he says.

The name doesn't register with Lok.

"It's a bar in Lan Kwai Fong. I've been there for four months."

"I see. And before that?"

"In the UK." He appears to notice that his measure is being taken, however politely, and he speaks up to be heard through the island din. "I did different things. Sold cars, worked in a record shop. My plan is to be a DJ here."

"He's really good," Edna says.

"A DJ? You play records in a bar?" Lok had seen the lone figures, perched in their booths above the crowd, bent over their turntables. He doesn't have an opinion about DJs, but he does have thoughts about bars and the people who run them.

The dishes arrive. Salt-and-pepper squid, beef and broccoli, steamed prawns, all born in a barrage of steam and sizzle from two enormous woks in the open kitchen. The meal is a welcome distraction from the stalled conversation. Lok, Dora, and Edna speak English well, Kitty and Kelvin poorly, *Ma Ma* and *Yeh Yeh* not at all.

"Edna says you're a policeman," says Julian.

"That's right."

"Have you ever shot anyone?"

Lok halts his chopsticks, which hold a prawn, in mid-air. "No," he says. "There are not too many guns here." He places the prawn on his plate, grabs it in his hand and dismembers it.

"It's not like the movies here, then."

Lok shakes his head.

Silence now. Julian, across from Lok, is attempting to spear a piece of tofu from Lok's side of the plate. Edna, conscious of the rudeness, looks down at the table. Finally he hooks the bean curd, only to drop it on the table by his bowl.

"Fuck," he says. He picks up the tofu in two fingers and pops it in his mouth. Kitty watches, then looks at Kelvin. They both laugh.

Then silence. The cook, still toiling behind the roast pigeons, pauses to hear the Mark 6 lottery results on the radio. Finally Julian speaks.

"Edna tells me you grew up here."

"That's right," Lok says. "I was born on the island."

"Amazing."

Lok sees nothing amazing about it. In any case he should be doing the interrogating, not Julian. *What are your intentions? Do you take drugs?* A little pressure and he'd have the kid sorted out. But this is Edna's so-called boyfriend at Bor-Kee seafood restaurant in Cheung Chau, not a murderer in a Yau Tsim interrogation room, so he has to brook the lies and chatter of a man on his best behavior.

"What a place," says Julian. "Lots of energy."

"It used to be much quieter," says Dora, pouncing on a neutral topic. "When my husband was younger, the ferry wasn't so frequent. There were no hoverferries, so you had to take the full hour's journey on a slow boat. Much more remote."

"It's still pretty wild," Julian says. "I saw a rat over there by the garbage. Kids peeing into the open rain gutters. Don't know that I could take it."

"We survived," says Lok.

After the dishes are cleared Lok pays the bill—Julian doesn't protest—and Dora says, "Kelvin, Kitty, don't wander. We want to catch the 9:30 back." They gather their things. Edna says, "We're not taking this ferry. You go ahead."

A thought flashes through Lok's mind. "You'd better come with us," he says. He finds he's looking into her eyes, rather than at her face with its crown of bleached hair, to recapture the beauty that was once a fount of pride.

"I'll be fine, *Ba Ba*."

He's tempted to cast a look at Julian, who hasn't understood a word of the Cantonese. But instead he ignores them both. After exchanging good-bys with *Yeh Yeh* and *Ma Ma*, he herds his remaining family to the ferry.

CHAPTER 40

WILL I FIND *release from boredom today?*

He almost never finds it. Not in bars of .999 gold plucked from broken jeweler's windows, nor in the sputter of an AK-47 stock against his chest, nor in the feel of banknotes seized from frightened drunks in Mongkok alleys. Not in the tense half minute between drilling the lock to hot-wire a Lotus and peeling out into traffic. Not inside the Jockey Club betting the horses, nor between the thighs of whores who never, ever do business with him a second time.

Will I find release from boredom today? To Skinwic Sze life has always been a procession of stultifying rules and inane chores, imposed to the accompaniment of hateful sounds: orders from assholes, whines from cowards, squeals from stupid women.

Time itself is cursed. Second after second, minute into hour into day into week, with nothing to do, no relief from the unimaginable tedium of life. Watching people fill their gullets, talk their nonsense, promote their pathetic dreams. Waiting for something to happen, and instead finding the same bullshit on the news, on the street, in every building, and in the face of every stupid sucker he meets.

Today the cops called, told him to come down, told him it's confidential, his employers won't know. That means they don't know a thing. They're wasting their time, and watching people waste their time is a bore.

He's alone, seated in an interrogation room. Interview room, they call it. No tapes are running, no warnings given, so he knows they're not expecting a confession. They're just fishing.

Skinwic's mind flees the present, races back to one early morning in Shanghai's Minhang district when, as a child, he stumbled upon a pig being slaughtered for market.

I hear the pig's cries, like the shriek of a braking train. I hear the spatter of blood on concrete, I see the river of red swish down a flume. Staring in the pig's eyes, imagining that the beast is transfixed by my stare as well, I feel a foot taller.

To this day it's the only kind of purity he knows, the only feeling that fully transports him from this monotonous world—a holy fire kindled by torment that's absolute and final. He can look forever into the eye of a creature in pain.

But dying doesn't take forever. The moment slips away, and the boredom returns.

The moment came again five years later, when a fellow student stole a 50-fen coin from his pocket while he was swimming.

There it is—that look, fixed in his oh-so-wide eyes as my fingers open and he drops ninety feet onto the roof of a cement truck. I run down six floors to catch one last glimpse of those eyes before the anguish leaves them forever.

Four years later he made it to Hong Kong with nothing but a few contraband U.S. dollars and a linoleum knife. In Hong Kong, he knew, there were people who could use him. People with money who needed a man with strong fists and a strong stomach.

He would make a decent living here. He would have a job, food, money, women.

That left only the boredom.

———————

HAVING STUDIED SKINWIC'S face for ten minutes through the one-way-mirror, Lok is prepared for a close-up as he walks in and sits down. Still, it's enough to scare him. *Wonder why we need police? Look into that face.*

"What is your name?" he says.

"Sze Mun-to."

"Age?"

"Not sure. Forty-one, I think."

Shanghainese, Lok concludes. His Cantonese is good, but you can't hide the accent. The Shanghainese dialect has maybe eleven tones, even more than Cantonese. To Lok it's always sounded like singing. Peculiar to hear a song from a face like that.

"Address?"

"211 Lung Kong Road."

"Where's that?"

"Near Kowloon City."

"Your work?"

"Mover."

"Where?"

"Tsim Sha Tsui. Cultural Centre."

None of Yip's calculated groveling, Lok notes.

"Do you know Yip Tak-tak?"

"Work for him."

"How long?"

"Six, seven years. Don't remember."

"What do you do for him?"

"What I said. Mover."

"Before that."

"Different things. I help Yip with his business."

"What does he do?"

"Consultant. Restaurants, bars, that kind of thing."

"Do you know why we brought you here for questioning?"

"No."

Lok searches his face for a sign that he's concealing something. But Skinwic's face was designed to conceal everything. It's a curtain masking some wicked drama he acts out in his own mind. Something as small as a woman's death couldn't ignite a spark of meaning in that dead thing.

"Do you know Tang Yee-fun?"

"No."

"Milkie Tang."

"No."

"Yip knows her."

"I don't."

"Do you go to the VSOP Nightclub?"

"Been there. Not often."

"Did you kill Milkie Tang?"

Slowly Skinwic, who has been staring listlessly at nothing in particular, looks at Lok.

"No," Skinwic says. "I said I don't know her."

"Tell me about Yip's girlfriend."

"Don't know."

"He doesn't have any?"

"I didn't say that. We don't socialize. He hangs out with women on his own time."

"A lot of women?"

"How would I know?"

"You work for him. You see him every day. You must know something about his women."

"No."

"Does he have a lot of them? Does he change them often?"

"Couldn't tell you."

"Does he get tired of them? Happens, doesn't it? After a while the old girl's like yesterday's meal. Did he like the fresh stuff?"

"Most guys do, don't they?"

"Did Yip kill Milkie Tang?"

"What are you asking me for? Ask him." His eyes drift off again.

"Did Yip ever visit Milkie at her flat?"

Skinwic shrugs.

"Answer please."

"I don't know."

"Did you ever go with him to visit a woman?"

"What are you talking about?"

"Ever been to 72 Woosung Street?"

"No. That her flat?"

"I'll ask the questions. Did you know Milkie Tang was a whore?"

"I didn't know her, I told you."

"You don't like whores, do you, Skinwic?"

"What do you mean?"

"You know what I mean. You don't like prostitutes. The girls at the bar. They don't like you, either, do they?"

"I don't give a shit."

"Do they avoid you?"

"No."

"So you spend a lot of time with them."

"Didn't say that." Skinwic reaches in his pocket.

"Got a girlfriend, Skinwic?"

Skinwic returns Lok's stare. Then he places a small black object in his teeth, bites down. A sunflower seed.

LOK JOINS BIG PANG in the chamber that adjoins the interview room. Through the one-way mirror they see that Skinwic hasn't stirred, hasn't raised his eyes to look at the painted cinderblock walls. Only his left hand twitches, the blunt, callused knuckles in slow, steady motion against one another, like cogs in some mechanical contraption.

What were those fingers telling him? Was Skinwic nervous? Angry? If he didn't know better, he'd swear the man was bored out of his skull.

"Get permission to search his flat," he says. "Get rid of him. Then meet me in my office." It's been a long time since the presence of a *lan jai* has awakened any kind of fear in Lok. But Lok feels it now. Not for his own safety, but for the defenseless, the Milkies of the world, and God help him, the Ednas and the Doras, too.

A few minutes later Big Pang returns, grabs a threadbare seat that Lok was going to replace until he realized it discouraged long visits.

"What do you think?" asks Lok. Normally the DPCs are the ones asking his thoughts, but Skinwic has upset even this order.

"If he did it," Big Pang says, "he's not going to confess."

"I don't see it anyway. Milkie was with Yip. Why would his 49 kill her?"

"On his orders, perhaps?"

Lok shakes his head. "Triad killings are either for business or honor. In neither case are women involved.

"Unless someone stole his girl."

"Even then, the man would get the chopper. Women just don't count.

"So what do we have? A girl from a miserable home, with the foolish dream of becoming a star. She's not particularly good in school, but she has some sense. She knows she needs a plan.

"First, she thinks, you have to look like a movie star. Big round eyes, big tits. That means an operation. A girl like that, a laborer for a father, Chinese writing and math poor, no English—where is she going to get the money to pay a plastic surgeon? It has to be whoring. She starts working at VSOP, then hooks Yip, the Red Pole who controls the protection for the club. Yip decides there's money in a movie actress, so he bankrolls her operation. He could twist a producer's arm to get her in films, then take most of her salary, who knows?

"Meanwhile, Yip is onto a new enterprise. He's taking a job supervising movers at this big orchestra. Is there money in that? Must be, or why would he be doing it?"

"What's that got to do with Milkie?"

Lok shakes his head. "Don't know," he says. "Forget the music band for now. Suppose Yip got tired of Milkie, kicked her out, went back on his agreement to make her a star? The average bimbo wouldn't do much but pout, but we know what Milkie's capable of. Remember how she treated Yorks? A woman like that wouldn't let Yip dump her."

"She wouldn't have a choice," says Pang. "Yip's a Red Pole. She'd have known what she was getting into."

"Normally, yes. But this girl is different. Think about what Fatman said about her one-track mind. Say she was angry about being dumped. She threatened Yip, told him she'd go to the police, testify about things he's into, his protection, extortion, who knows what else. Yip would never take that. He'd get Skinwic to kill her, dress her up, dump her in the water."

The theory dangles before them, flimsy as a wraith.

"No chance of a confession from those two," says Pang.

"Not without evidence. But one of them might give up the other to save himself if we made a case." It's a hope as fragile as their theory. The Department of Justice scorns anything that smells of bargaining. They want full, honest confessions without any promises in return. Lok would have to build up a case good enough to make one of them give up hope, confess, and turn the other in.

"Big Pang," Lok says, "I'm going ask you a favor. Yip is going across the border for a couple of days. We need to follow him unofficially and see what's going on."

"To the mainland? How will I write this up?"

"You won't, for now. This is informal. We need to find out what Yip is up to, see why he's meeting that Shanghainese Hosell Lai, and employing those 49s as movers. There might be something going on in China."

"We won't be able to use anything we find there."

"Not in court, no, but it might give us a line of questioning. Meet me tomorrow morning at eight at the ferry terminal."

Pang nods.

Lok continues. "One thing. I have no authority to do this. If the CI finds out, he'll roast me alive, and you with me. So I can't order you to go."

"Any chance of some golf while we're there, sir?"

CHAPTER 41

THE LION WRITHES as if in flames, each thrash propelled by a volley of drums and cymbals. It's chaos, and Hector surrenders to it as he always does, engulfed by the sound. He's tried to apply his musical mind to the lion dance, but remains a helpless captive of the ritual. Just when he thinks he's fathomed the relationship between the moves and the beat, something changes—the lion head flails out in a new direction, the pulse shifts, the cymbal crashes overlap on one another till the din is felt not as sound but as an exquisite pain. Leo told him not to try to understand. *Just give in to it, Hec. You think a meteorologist in a typhoon doesn't get blown away like everyone else?*

The consecration of the tour was supposed to wait until Ambrose Wan came and spoke, but he's late, so the show has gone on without him. Bonson has spoken words of pride and painted dots in the eyes of the lion. Now the lion dances to bring fortune to the tour. The words for dancing lion—*mo si*—sounds like "no trouble."

Hector is contemplating the irony—the dancers, attired in glowing yellow, red, and black, are performing a stylized version of Yip's warning—when Twinkie approaches. She's carrying a small travel bag and her memo recorder.

"What happened with Bonson?" she asks. "I heard you were in his office."

"He told me to keep out of orchestra business. Threatened to fire me if I went near Mulqueen again." He eyes her travel bag. "Are you coming with us?"

"I cover the orchestra, right?" They take off toward the seawall, a promenade for tourists, families, and lovers to catch the harbor breeze and ignore the harbor stench.

"Bonson is afraid," he says. "I've never seen him that furious."

"He's protecting Mulqueen. He must know it's triad-connected. They're probably paying him to take part in this."

"Who's paying him? Take part in *what*? We don't even know what they're involved in." They move away from the tourists.

"We'll know soon," Twinkie says. She looks to both sides, sees no one close, speaks. "I found out about Shao's father. He works for the State Economic and Trade Commission. He's a vice chairman, stationed in Shenzhen. He has a lot of power there. Nothing's more important in China than trade."

"Go on." A tug blasts its horn. *G-sharp*

"Let's say Wan is behind it all, which is probably true, since he's put the real money into it. Wan's spending cash wining and dining—really bribing—Shao's father. Why would he do that? What's in it for him?"

"He wants something done in China—something he can't do legally."

"It's not that simple, Hector. If someone wants something from the SETC, why not just show up at Shao's father's house with a suitcase full of money? Why force Bonson to hire Yip, why start kidnapping and coercing? There has to be more to it than a simple business deal. There's a reason the orchestra is involved."

Hector ponders this. "We don't do anything important except play music," he says. "And that's not important in Hong Kong, because it doesn't make money."

"Well then, think about this," Twinkie says. "As soon as the petition came out, Chiu got hit by a car, and Shao started to purge the orchestra. That's got everyone petrified, and stopped the Anti-Shao movement. There's some reason they don't want Shao out of the orchestra."

"So is all this a conspiracy to launch Shao's conducting career?"

"I don't know."

Across the harbor a yellowish haze hangs above the rooftops, a nimbus of dust, smoke, and sulphur dioxide darkening Hong Kong lungs and lives.

"All right then, explain this to me," says Hector. "Ambrose Wan is a legitimate businessman. What's he doing with triads?"

"Are you kidding? This is Hong Kong. Business and organized crime are old friends here. Most of the great old firms have shady histories. Wan married Octavius Wu's daughter. Do you know Wu's company?"

"Goldway International, right? Shipping, manufacturing ..."

"Importing, leasing, food processing. They're gigantic. And Octavius Wu is a crook from way back. So was his father. I don't mean bending safety regulations and evading taxes. I mean smuggling, blackmail, theft, and probably murder, too."

Figures, Hector thinks. In Hong Kong, money is the only passport to respectability. You can do anything if you have it. No one asks how you got it, or cares how you treat people who don't have it. "So Wan would be close to the triads?"

"Not directly. As you say, he's legitimate. But if Wan does business in Hong Kong, he's paying triads. You need them to get things done."

"So, what do you think?."

"I think that something's going to happen. It might happen in China. So keep your eyes open."

Hector turns, watches as a Black Mercedes pulls up to the Cultural Centre. Ambrose Wan, most likely, with a little speech of encouragement.

CHAPTER 42

"YOU'RE THINKING ABOUT Edna, aren't you?" Dora, in her bathrobe, dabs her dripping hair with a towel.

Lok: "How did you know?"

"I saw you look at the picture while you were getting your socks."

Lok glances at the photo in the teak frame on his dresser. "Remember when that picture was taken?" In the photo a younger Lok and a ravishing Dora flank a six-year-old smiling imp: Edna, the eldest, the first. Kelvin, in Dora's arms, is a bewildered tyke with a thick mop of black hair. Kitty hasn't been conceived yet.

"On Cheung Chau, that little shop. *Gnok Fu* and *Yeh Yeh* wouldn't be photographed." Lok's parents never will: for them, photographs are for funeral displays.

"Have you spoken with Edna?"

"Since Cheung Chau, you mean? Yes."

"So how did she meet this Julian character? Is it serious?"

"What does 'serious' mean at her age, Herman? She doesn't know enough to be serious."

"You know what I mean."

"I presume she's sleeping with him. It's done nowadays."

Instantly he regrets having pressed Dora.

"He didn't look like much to me."

"He wasn't trying to impress you, I suppose."

"He didn't."

"No. But she says there's a tender side to him."

"I'll bet." He slides open a closet door, pulls out a shirt. "And I suppose my disapproval isn't going to matter."

Dora walks over to Lok, places her hand gently on her arm. "Women have a way of getting around their fathers' disapproval, don't they?" He understands immediately. Dora's parents had much grander plans for their daughter than marriage to a policeman.

"Where are you going?" Dora asks. "China or Macau?"

Lok stops in mid-comb, thinks. Living with the world's greatest detective can get eerie at times. "I'm wearing a polo shirt, right?" he says.

"Right. And you checked your wallet for cash. Why would you do that if you were going to the office?."

"I'm going to Shenzhen. But it's informal, so don't say anything."

"Of course," she says, picking up her hair dryer. "And try not to worry about Edna."

"I always worry about Edna. You married a cop with a career ahead of him. She's picked up some *gweilo* bartender."

"DJ."

"DJ, whatever."

———————

TRAVEL BAGS ASWAY on their shoulders, Lok and Big Pang look like salarymen off to China for a quick eighteen holes, one of the pack of casually-dressed travelers whose golf clubs are piled in the front by the gangway.

Golf is the crack cocaine of the travel industry. The users are Japanese executives, Korean tourists, American middle managers who will pay any price to swat a ball across a well-kept lawn. As a result, grass seed, fertilizer, and sprinklers are the raw materials of economic freedom for third-world countries. Golf courses have propagated like a green rash across the face of Southern China. Well-off Hong Kong residents, tourists, convention participants, and business travelers regularly hop ferries to the Mainland to play, since the city is starved of green space for fairways.

"Where's Yip now?" asks Big Pang.

"On the orchestra truck. We should arrive a few hours ahead."

"Do we check in with local authorities?"

"Not now. This is unofficial. It might just end up being a holiday. I have a friend in the PSB we can contact if we need to. Can't say how much help he'll be, but it's something."

They'll have to board a bus to the city center at the port of Wenjindu. Had Lok taken the more direct train route, he'd have risked encountering a friend from the force and having to explain his trip. Reflexively he scans the passengers on the boat, looking for a familiar face. A few of his colleagues have holiday flats on the mainland, getaway places.

Then he realizes where his colleagues are.

"Shit."

"What is it?"

Lok says nothing. His subordinate does not need to know that, as they glide on murky waters toward Shenzhen, someone is noticing the absence of Herman Lok at a seminar entitled *Teamwork in the 21st Century*.

CHAPTER 43

LOCKED IN TRAFFIC, the Mercedes inches down Salisbury Road to Star Ferry, Kowloon side. The Rolls Silver Shadow, his father-in-law's preference, is too ostentatious for the younger man. "Is that what they taught you at Harvard?" Octavius Wu said. "To be ashamed of your money?" In fact, Ambrose Wan is deeply attached to money and all it can buy. But to flaunt it prematurely would be tempting the gods.

Beside him is Winsome, and between the two of them on the leather seat a copy of today's *Post*. Facing up is a front page story which also serves as Ambrose's horoscope.

Wan Industries Lawsuit Overturned—Elkon to Pay

In a decision that some regard as unexpected, the Shenzhen People's Municipal Court today ruled against Elkon Industries of San Francisco, California. The company had brought suit against Wan Industries, its joint venture partner in the construction of Valiant Plaza, a multi-purpose residential/commercial complex in Shenzhen.

The American company accused Wan Industries of pro-

*viding substandard construction. In his ruling, Judge Wong
Man-yiu cleared Wan Industries of wrongdoing and ordered
Elkon Industries to pay for rebuilding the property to proper
construction codes.*

*A spokesman for Elkon said he was " … flabbergasted.
This ruling is totally incomprehensible to us."*

It's been a month of undiluted misery. True, the noose is off
his neck now. Greeny Ma fixed that, albeit in return for his own
balls on a silk cushion. Cash flow, moreover, is tight right now.
His Hong Kong rental properties, thought to be foolproof investments, are half-empty.

And Octavius is asking about grandchildren again.

"How long will this take?" Ambrose asks Winsome, who is
seated next to him, decked out in her charcoal grey skirt and jacket.
Koo is navigating the Mercedes expertly through Kowloon traffic.

"Fifteen minutes. Not long. You just need to pose with the
General Manager and say a few words."

"What's his name again?"

"Bonson Ng."

"Oh, right. What will I say?"

"Here." She hands him a set of three index cards with a few
neatly printed paragraphs. He reads. *A special day … important
for the arts, and Hong Kong as well … proud to have you as Hong
Kong's representatives on the mainland, and ambassadors overseas
…* Good thinking, he remarks to himself. If she'd written "ambassadors on the mainland," and implied that Hong Kong wasn't part
of China, he'd hear about it later. Thank the gods for Winsome.

Koo approaches the Cultural Centre and turns into the drive,
past a crowd of musicians dressed in cheap and motley wear.
They're waiting for some inspiring words from Ambrose Wan,

industrialist and Chairman of the General Committee, son-in-law of Octavius Wu, whose name is chiseled on plaques in every hospital and orphanage in Hong Kong. The chattering mob gathered at Star Ferry Pier has no idea what it is part of. May that never change, Ambrose thinks.

PART III

Go away. Go back to your own country.
All the cemeteries are full here.
We have enough madmen of our own.
We don't need any foreign madmen.

GIUSEPPE ADAMA AND RENATO SIMONI,
LIBRETTO TO *TURANDOT*, ACT *I*

CHAPTER 44

LOK AND BIG PANG are parked half a block from the stage entrance of the Shenzhen Grand Theatre on Hongling Road.Lok focuses the binoculars on Yip, whose men are opening a 24-foot box truck with Hong Kong Symphony Orchestra emblazoned on the sides. They begin unloading. Several trunks come first, then larger boxes, and finally some tall, coffin-like cases.

"Look at the size of them," says Pang. "Cellos?"

"Bigger. Those are the biggest fiddles. I forget what they're called."

"They have enough of them."

Yip is standing over his men, directing, pointing, coaching, probably threatening. Through the lenses Lok sees a copper-colored drum, obviously heavy, being eased down the ramp by Skinwic and another of Yip's men.

"That's the first time I've seen Skinwic do any work," says Lok.

"A lot of trouble for a couple of performances," says Big Pang.

While the truck is being emptied they sit in the car, moving little to avoid attracting attention. In a couple of hours the musicians begin arriving, most of them carrying weirdly-shaped cases of their own. Lok recognizes the fiddles and the trombones, but some of the other cases mystify him. How many instruments are there in an orchestra, anyway?

"Do you listen to this kind of music?" Lok asks.

"Classical? No. Went to a concert once with my school." They watch the stage door swallow up musicians. "Why aren't they wearing suits?" Lok asks.

"Must be a practice. The poster says the performances are tonight and tomorrow night."

"Then back to Hong Kong? Seems a waste."

"Back for a couple of weeks, then to Europe, Japan, and the USA."

Lok watches the last few musicians stray into the theater. The door closes.

In the course of the next two hours they see Yip emerge from the theater twice to smoke and once to use his cellphone. At six the musicians trail out for a dinner break. Yip and his men take a delivery of rice boxes backstage, presumably so they can keep watch on the instruments while they eat.

Once during the watch Lok's cellphone beeps. Yau Tsim station, says the message window. *Probably wanting to know where in hell I am.* He pockets the phone and continues his surveillance.

They sit in silence, broken once when Pang praises the rented Camry, which offers enough foot room for his large frame.

"Back when I started," says Lok, "the unmarked police cars were green Ford Cortinas. Problem is, no one besides a cop in Hong Kong would even know where to buy a green Cortina, so they weren't very effective for surveillance."

"Plus they kept a copy of *Offbeat* on the dashboard, so Traffic wouldn't ticket them, right?"

"Right, but that wasn't the worst of it. They had no air-conditioning. Remember I was on Ronnie Kan's team for a couple of years? He had to drive around Tsim Sha Tsui in summer, and all the 14K triads on his beat knew his Cortina. Rather than lose face and admit that he had no A/C, he kept the windows closed. I think he sweated off fifteen pounds every summer."

The musicians come back from dinner break at seven-thirty, the men now dapper in tails, women in black dresses and pantsuits.

"No sign of Yip," Big Pang says. "They must be keeping him busy."

"Or they're just guarding the instruments. How much are they worth, anyway?"

"I think the violins are expensive. I saw one in the paper that sold for millions."

Lok shakes his head. A thought occurs to him. "How long is this thing supposed to be?" he asks.

"The man at the box office said it'll go three hours."

Lok says nothing.

"Do we wait?" Big Pang asks.

"You do," says Lok, popping the door. "I'm going to buy a ticket."

———————

HALF AN HOUR later the stage door cracks open. Yip appears, lights a cigarette, and vanishes around the corner. Pang slips out of his car after him. He follows Yip along Shennan Road, and watches him disappear down a Metro entrance.

With no idea where he'll end up, Pang buys a maximum-fare card and sticks as close as he can to Yip. The only thing worse than losing him would be to let Yip discover him. A tail is the easiest thing in the world to detect if you suspect one's on you. Just head into a shopping mall, dash up a crowded escalator till you're out of sight, and then wait at the top, watching. The cop will come charging up a few seconds later and look right into your eyes.

So Big Pang hangs back, sits in the next train car, watches carefully for Yip's form. When Yip hops out at Zhuzilin, Pang hurries after him, concealing himself behind another body whenever he can. Tall as he is, Pang is not the best choice for tailing suspects.

Yip passes into some kind of industrial business park. These are all over Shenzhen; they are, in fact, its purpose. Lured by whorishly favorable terms, businesses from all over the world flock to Special Economic Zones like Shenzhen to build factories and offices. Once a backwater turning out pesticides and farming tools, Shenzhen is now China's leader in infotech and financial services.

The smell of cash draws people as well as companies. Fewer than a third of Shenzhen's five million have legal residency permits. The rest are schemers of one kind or another, doing their best to dip into the troughs while they're still full.

Yip approaches a row of squat factory buildings, slows down and waves discreetly. That's when Big Pang notices a second man lingering in the shadows by the door to Unit 510. Pang starts to memorize his dress, gait, haircut, glasses, assembling a picture of him to give Lok. A moment later he discards the details, for the picture is no longer necessary; he recognizes the face, a Hong Kong face. It's Hosell Lai, the man who repairs instruments, the man Yip met at two in the morning.

The pair enter the building. Pang aches to know what floor they're on, but windows are aglow throughout the building— people working crazy hours, just like in Hong Kong.

Pang withdraws behind a vacated guard's shed across the street. *In this job you have to know how to wait*, Lok taught him. *Nothing happens when you want it to. It happens when it hap-*

pens, and you'd better have your eyes open.

Pang has memorized the configuration of the building, the number of floors, the number of windows that are lit. He's checked the parked cars and trucks on the street for occupants, the windows for movement, the streets for passersby.

In the doorway of adjacent building, a shadow shifts. A man? Possibly. It moves again. Someone is there, definitely. Shorter than Yip or Hosell, dressed in dark clothes. Now Pang has two doorways to watch.

Whoever's hiding there might have taken lessons from Lok as well. The figure doesn't move more than two or three times in the fifty minutes Pang has the factory under surveillance. A couple of times he suspects he imagined it.

Yip and Hosell appear again. Pang scans them for bags, packages, bulging pockets, but sees nothing. The two men part ways silently, Hosell taking off south down an alley, hands tucked in his waist-length jacket, and Yip returning to the Metro. Pang waits for Yip to pass him. Then, instead of stepping into the now-empty street, he holds back.

Out of the second doorway, where he'd seen movement before, a woman appears. She's in her mid-twenties, good-looking. She hangs at the corner to let Yip gain some ground, and takes off after him.

———

IT'S CERTAINLY GRAND, even grander than the colorful Cantonese operas Lok saw with his grandparents in his youth during festivals on Cheung Chau. The stage seethes with action, light, and color, and the auditorium booms with the sound of a hundred musicians.

But this show, this *Turandot*, doesn't resemble those mannered Cantonese tales. This story is just as peculiar and unreal, but in a different way. The characters sing in Italian, not a word of which Lok understands, while a Chinese translation is projected simultaneously above the proscenium. The costumes are Chinese, but the attitudes and movements come from some faraway place he can't divine. Commoners and courtiers talk to royalty without bowing their heads. Characters stare at one another rudely and sing long songs. It's all so strange, sometimes beautiful, sometimes boring.

From a balcony seat, Lok can see the musicians too, blowing and stroking away while the leader waves a stick. How can so many people play together and make it sound so good? This Shao must be a sorcerer.

Lok's knowledge of operatic voices extends to a performance of *The Three Tenors* he and his wife watched on television some years back. Dora was enchanted. Lok found it pleasing, but he can't see how people get caught up in music the way they do.

The show is about a woman, the princess Turandot. She hates men, and yet men risk death to have her. Those who want to marry the princess must answer three riddles, and if they fail, they die. One prince solves the three riddles and wins her.

Lok thinks: nothing like a riddle to make life interesting, eh, Prince?

CHAPTER 45

"WHAT DID YOU FIND?" Hector asks Twinkie. They're walking toward the hotel on a road bathed in sodium lamplight. After the last curtain call Hector slipped out of the theater to meet her. Most of his colleagues are out on the town or in the hotel bar.

"Yip met another man out at an industrial park. They visited a factory building of some kind. They went in, spent almost an hour, then Yip went back to the concert hall."

"Did you hear them talking?"

She shakes her head. "They didn't say much."

"So what do you think?"

"Hard to say. If Yip is as crooked as he looks, it could be anything."

"Heroin," says Hector. "They could be producing it up there."

She shakes her head. "No. We cover the heroin trade. You can smell an opium refinery before you can see it. Those people have to pay a lot of bribes to keep themselves in business. You'd never find one in such a populated area."

"Okay, they're doing something illegal. How does Shao fit into it?"

"That's what we need to find out. My guess is that Leo did find out."

When they reach Hector's hotel room he finds that his room-mate Clem has come and gone, judging by the black trousers and tails hung up in the closet.

Hector hasn't spoken since Twinkie mentioned Leo. "Look, Hector," she says, "I know Leo is your friend, but you have to face that he might be dead."

The words prick something in his gut.

Twinkie moves over to him, sits beside him on the bed, and pats his hand.

"I'm sorry," she says. "I hope it isn't true."

He looks in her eyes to accept the comfort she's offering, and moves his head closer till their foreheads touch. He draws his lips slowly toward hers.

A beep, a click, and the door flies open. Clem walks in.

"Hec, listen ... oh, sorry," he says. As if to reassure him, Twinkie beams, stands up, and reaches for her bag. "I'll talk to you tomorrow," she says. She's out the door.

"Sorry ..." Clem says. He looks distracted, anxious.

"Forget it."

"I just heard Chiu died today."

CHAPTER 46

LATER THAT NIGHT Lok and Big Pang compare notes over beers at a restaurant near the Shenzhen police station.

"So Yip meets this fiddle repairman at an industrial flat," Lok says, as he pours a beer from the bottle. "He spends an hour there, and then they split up. Right?"

"Right," says Big Pang. "Then Yip goes back to the concert hall, and stays busy with the instruments. But that's not all. Listen to this—someone else was following Yip."

Lok halts his beer halfway to his mouth. "You're sure?"

"Yes. Woman, Chinese, mid-twenties. She was doing her own surveillance, no doubt about that. She hid in another doorway on the same block, took off after Yip when he left."

"Did she follow Yip to the building, too, or was she waiting there already?"

"Don't know. To tell the truth, I wasn't looking out for anyone else on the way to the factory."

"Did she spot you?"

"No. When she trailed Yip she didn't even look behind her."

It made no sense. "How about the building they went to?"

Pang reads from his notepad, not his official one but a

recently-purchased supplement for off-the-radar use. "Hong Wah Industrial Park, Unit 510. Happy Charm Herbal Medicine Company."

"I'll call the PSB tomorrow." Lok wipes his mouth, tosses the napkin on the table.

Big Pang signals the waiter. "How was the show?" he asks.

Lok thinks. "Not bad, actually. Tell me, what's born every night, and dies each day?"

"What?"

"It's a riddle."

Pang nods. "I know these ... let's see ..." He gazes out the restaurant window.

"Neon?"

Lok laughs. "No, it's 'hope.' If you were the Prince, you'd be dead."

"What?"

The waiter arrives with the check. Lok tosses a bill in the tray. "Never mind," he says, rising to his feet. "I liked your answer better anyway."

———

THIS TIME IT'S fish-head soup. Ears has finished his bowl, declined a second, and is chatting with old Liu *tai-tai* in 3A. Down the hall Milkie's flat is still marked with a crime scene notice.

Ears got as far as he could on the last visit, withdrew, and showed up again today. After discussing her children, the price of gold, and the proper way to make winter melon soup, he's gradually worked the conversation around to the neighbors, none of whom amount to much by Mrs. Liu's standards.

"Did the girl in 3F complain about them?"

The old lady laughs. "Her? She didn't talk to us. Too good for us, understand? She just had those men."

"You know, I should try to find those men. Ask them what they know. Her murderer is still out there. Maybe they could identify him."

"None of my business."

Ears says nothing, waits.

"One was a short man with glasses and a beard. One had a pony tail. And the other one was the one with the TV."

"The TV?"

"He took her TV away one night. Don't ask me why. I'm surprised she didn't call the police herself."

"He carried away her TV?"

"One of those big ones, this big," she says, holding her hands out as far as she can. "At two in the morning, he walks out, pushing this box into the elevator."

His breathing halts at the mention of the box, but he makes his next question sound casual.

"What did the man with the TV look like?"

She wrinkles up her nose. "Not very pleasant looking. Tall, thin. The rough type."

"Do you think you could identify him from a picture?"

She shrugs. "I think so. I could probably remember all of their faces. I've got sharp eyes."

"Indeed you do, Liu *tai-tai*." She's probably witnessed every entrance and exit on the third floor since her husband died and freed her to the life of surveillance she was born to. Suddenly he has the urge to pull out his notebook and write it all down. He stands up, thanks her for the soup and hands her a card.

"I'll drop by again tomorrow, if it's all right."

"Come at lunchtime," she says. "I'll make my pork and pearl greens soup."

"I can't wait. Meanwhile, please call this number if you remember anything else about those men."

"Nothing to remember," she says, unlocking the door. "I mind my own business."

———

THE PUBLIC SECURITY BUREAU, Shenzhen Municipal Division, looks newer and better equipped than most of the police stations Lok has seen in China. A lot of money here, he reminds himself.

Inspector Xue must be about fifty. He has a thick head of black hair and glasses like Old Ko's. Lok met him at a command course a few years back.

"You're not here officially, are you?" asks Xue.

"No. We're investigating a murder in Hong Kong, a floater. We have a suspect, but no evidence yet. We're looking around, trying to get a feel for the lifestyle of our suspect. It turns out he's spending some time at a factory here."

Xue has already seen the paper in Lok's hand, sees that Lok is politely waiting to be asked for it.

"Is that the address?"

"Yes. I understand that you must be pressed for time ..."

"Who isn't?" He takes the paper from Lok and reads it. "Herbal medicine ... doesn't mean anything to me. Any mainland people involved?"

"So far none that we can tell. We haven't been inside the factory."

"Well, I'll check on it," Xue says. "I hope you don't expect much, though. We don't have the resources to take on this kind of thing."

"I'd be grateful for anything you can do." Lok thanks him for his time, gives him a card with his cell number circled, and they leave for the ferry.

CHAPTER 47

HECTOR AWAKES, TOO early and joylessly drunk. Last night he'd drifted like a ghost through the second performance of *Turandot*. His hands animated themselves like zombies, pulled him through the bass part note by note, without a trace of feeling. The music sounded vague and distant, as if the orchestra were underwater.

Chiu is dead, he kept thinking. *And I'm playing notes on a bass fiddle.*

All of the players seemed numbed, listless, aware of their impotence against death. Only Shao moved with energy on the second night. After the opera Hector and Porvin found a bar full of white-shirted businessmen. There they toasted their dead friend till the bartender sent them home.

Hector rises, feeling the full weight of his head, and ransacks his bag till he finds some pills he bought during his last hangover. He showers, throws his clothes in his bag, goes downstairs for coffee.

Outside Clem Farraday leans against the hotel wall, eyes open and focused across the street. The orchestra bus has not yet arrived.

"You all right?" Clem asks.

Hector nods, sips his coffee.

"What time did you get back?"

"Don't know."

"How did you get back, for that matter?"

"Don't remember. Woke up in my room, though."

"I know. I tried to wake you an hour ago. You told me to go to hell."

"Yeah, well, I probably meant it. Sorry."

"Can't blame you. Poor Chiu."

Poor Chiu, Hector thinks. *What a wretched vocabulary we have for death.*

Clem hasn't looked at Hector. His eyes are still trained across the road, where Yip watches his flunkies reload the HKSO truck.

"He'd look at home with a cat-o'-nine-tails in his hand, wouldn't you say?" Yip seems poised to flay anyone who gets out of line.

"Keeping an eye on him?" Hector asks.

"Ever since they dropped your bass. Those bozos are carrying my Testore around too, so I'm watching them from over here. Don't want to make them nervous."

"Suppose they drop it, and you're across the street? What good will that do?"

"Nothing. You're right, it's pointless. Like your getting drunk last night. But at least I'm keeping busy." A pause. "Did you get back together with Twinkie?"

"Not yet. She's gone back to Hong Kong already."

"She's writing about the tour for the paper?"

"I think so." Hector hasn't told anyone about the real reason she came—to follow Yip.

"Sorry about last night, barging in ..."

"Don't be. If it works, it works. There's time."

They watch Yip and his men for a while. Clem says, "What's Amy going to do?"

"Without Chiu? I don't know. They'd talked about marriage, I know. Chiu wanted to wait until he was more settled, maybe in an orchestra in Germany. I just don't know."

Clem says nothing for a minute, just watches the activity in front of the theater. Finally: "Hec, I have a question for you. The orchestra has nine basses, right?"

"Right."

Clem scratches his chin, narrows his eyes.

"Then why did Yip and his men just load eleven bass cases onto the truck?"

CHAPTER 48

"**I MEANT TO** be there, but there was too much going on, sir."

"Then tell me why Bing in team six can find time to go." K.K. Kwan is livid. "He has the rape murder in Yaumatei and the wife killer, and he's up to his eyeballs with the Golden Tower Disco chopping court case. But he was able to make it to the seminar."

"I was busy ..."

"With an informer, no doubt," Kwan says. They both know that, in the Twenty-first Century, you're never "too busy" to be a team player, to pitch in, to better yourself. No longer can you evade any obligation by claiming you had to "meet an informer." The Hong Kong Police have been modernized, coordinated, networked, humanized.

"Herman, I'm not going to say what you think I will. I'm not going to talk about this year's promotion exercise." He doesn't have to mention that the ones on the fast track, men like Sam Bing, with their degrees and their networking skills, are never too busy to make an appearance at a seminar or pose for a photo in *Offbeat*, the cops' newspaper.

Kwan continues. "But I am going to advise you that whatever happens as a result of this, I won't pull you out of it."

Lok's cellphone beeps. They ignore it.

Kwan lightens his tone slightly. "Well, since you've been on the case this weekend, what have you to report?"

It's too early to let on about the China trip, at least directly. So he must be silent about the medicine factory, Yip's meeting with Hosell or the girl in the doorway.

"Nothing yet, sir," he says.

Lok's cellphone beeps again. Kwan looks at Lok, shakes his head, waves him off. Out in the hall Lok reaches for his phone.

"Inspector Lok?" Lok takes a minute to place the voice. It's Xue, calling from China.

"Thanks for calling back," Lok says. He starts down the hall to the Hot Room to meet the team.

"About that matter we spoke of yesterday ..."

"Yes."

"Nothing to report on it."

"Did you find out about the factory? Who owns it?"

"I made some enquiries, but there's nothing of interest to you there. It would be too complicated to follow up. It's not in my district, and anyway, the factory is owned by a Beijing entity. I have no authorization ..."

Lok listens, thanks him and kills the phone. You don't have to be an expert on PSB terminology to know when someone's telling you to mind your own business. Either the Happy Charm Herbal Medicine factory is already under investigation, in which case he'll hear about it someday, or else it's under protection, in which case he could expect nothing but trouble.

———————

IN THE HOT ROOM Million Man is the first to speak about their surveillance. "Fatman is nervous, I can tell you that," he says. "He's in the habit of taking quick glances around him before he exits buildings."

"Worried about being followed, you think?" Lok says.

"No, he doesn't do anything evasive," says Ko. "More like he's afraid he'll be seen by someone he knows."

"Any activity?"

"Sunday Brunch at a place in Lan Kwai Fong. Meetings with his studio, his bank. Nothing strange."

Ears is silent, but during the report on Fatman Leung his body writhes with what is clearly impatience. Finally Lok looks his way, nods.

"Sir, I think I know the date of the murder. August 18th."

Old Ko laughs dismissively. "What happened, you got your fortune told at the Wong Tai Sin Temple?" No one else laughs this time; Ears's face betrays an excitement that one rarely sees in the Hot Room.

"There's an old lady in a flat at the end of the hall—she has a view of Milkie Tang's place. Whenever I did anything, the woman peeked out. She's obviously the nosy type, keeping tabs on everything that happens in the place."

"She said she didn't see anything," says Million Man.

"I went back and got her talking. It took a while." He lowers his head slightly; it's a loss of face for Million Man. "Turns out she saw someone haul a large TV box out of Milkie's flat in the middle of the night."

"You're saying Milkie was killed in her flat, and they brought out the body in a TV box? All right. How did she remember the date?"

"She didn't. But she remembered the box." He pauses, a bit flummoxed by the silence in the room. "Suppose that the murder isn't planned in advance—it just happens during a fight, say. Now the killer needs a way to get her out of the building. So he looks around, finds a discarded TV box, and hauls her away. It's worth checking out. So I spoke with all of the residents from the second through fourth floors.

"You asked everyone if they've bought a TV recently?"

"Right. It would have to be a wide-screen job. It turns out that a man in 4F, directly above Milkie Tang, bought a new Panasonic 42-inch on August 18th. The owner threw the box into the stairwell, planning to get rid of it on the weekend. But it was gone the next day."

"And he's sure about the date?"

"He kept the receipt for the warranty." Ears brandishes a photocopy. Lok scans the document, nods. Ears continues. "He was nervous at first—thought I was after him for blocking a fire exit with the box.

Lok nods again. "Any description of the man who hauled out the box?"

"Tall, thin, ugly face. She might be able to identify him from a photo."

"One of Yip's 49s matches that description," says Old Ko. "The dirtbag."

"Skinwic Sze," says Pang.

"She also saw two other men there from time to time," says Ears. "A guy with a pony tail, no description beyond that, and a short man with glasses and a beard."

Pang and Lok look at each other. Pang excuses himself, and Lok turns back to Ears.

"The short one is Fatman Leung, obviously. You know what you're doing now?"

"Mrs. Liu is coming down today to look at pictures," says Ears.

"She's all yours. This could be introduced in evidence, so are the photos all in the same format?"

"Yes, sir. Color pictures, same size. Nothing to prejudice her."

A minute later Pang returns. "I checked with Mary, our foul-mouthed mama-san. Good news. Turns out Yip Tak-tak had a pony tail until recently. Probably cut it off for the new job with the music band."

"Let's wait and see if we get an ID on Skinwic," says Lok. "Then we can charge him. He might confess, or he might tell us it was all Yip's idea. Then we have them both."

Million Man gives Ears the thumbs up. Big Pang pats him on the shoulder. Old Ko says nothing, but hints at a smile. Thanks to their attention, Ears's face is pomegranate-red.

"Nice police work," says Lok. If only he had had this information a half hour ago, in K.K. Kwan's office.

CHAPTER 49

"HECTOR, WHAT ARE you doing here?" Twinkie asks. Wearing the photographer's ID he'd used with Mulqueen, Hector has shown up at Twinkie's cubicle at the *Post*. His presence has clearly thrown her off.

"We need to talk. You haven't been returning calls."

She pulls out her cellphone, taps on the buttons, shoves it into a cradle on her desk.

"Stupid battery. Still, I wish you'd waited. I'm really busy." She's angry, distracted.

"I found out something. Two extra bass cases are traveling with the Symphony."

"Those big things?" She gestures a height somewhere above her head.

"Yes. There's no reason for them to be there. There's supposed to be one for each bass, that's it."

She thinks for a moment. In the background, the sound of feet on carpet, fingers on keyboards, phones chirping, reporters mumbling into headsets. Finally she says, "You've done it."

"It's drugs, isn't it?"

She begins to whisper. "Has to be. From China to here, and

then maybe to other places when the orchestra tours."

"Jesus," he says. "So Ambrose Wan ..."

"Quiet," she says.

They leave the offices, race down the escalator, and half-run down the street, slowing down only when the traffic of Quarry Bay has absorbed them. Ten minutes later they're settled on a bench in a children's playground near the towers of Taikoo Shing. This time of day, it's almost empty.

"It makes sense now," Twinkie says. "We had it backwards. All this time we were wondering about Shao—why did they want to keep him as the conductor? It was the tour they were trying to protect, not Shao. Your friend Chiu and his petition were stirring up people and endangering the tour. Without that, there's no operation."

"And Shao?"

"His father's an official, remember? He has to be the connection on the other side."

"Are you going to put the story in tomorrow's paper?"

She shakes her head. "That would be crazy. No proof." She thinks for a second. "Do you know where the cases are now?"

"No. They might still be in the truck. But won't a story just blow things open?"

"Maybe, but my editor would never print it without proof— *Hong Kong Symphony Personnel Smuggle Drugs During Tour.* Except we don't know that it's drugs, or what kind, or how many people are involved, or where the drugs are. We'd have a libel suit on our hands."

"So let's go to the police."

She thinks for a minute. "No."

"No? Look what's happened already. Chiu's dead, probably because he tried to stop the tour. Leo was snooping around the office, and he's disappeared. We've got to see that Yip's put away."

"Hector, if you call the police now, you'll ruin everything. Suppose they've already disposed of the stuff in the bass case. The police come in, see nothing, and go away thinking we're crazy. Yip knows he's being watched, so the operation closes down and he covers his tracks. He goes free, and we never find out what happened to Leo."

"So what should we do?"

"Find the stuff, if it's still there. Take it for evidence."

"Jesus, Twinkie!"

"Then I contact Yip, tell him I'll make a deal. My silence for the truth about what happened to Leo."

"You're not serious!"

"It'll work, I'm sure of it."

"It's absolutely insane. Suppose he tells you where Leo is, then what?"

"Then I write the story, incriminate him."

"What about the drugs?"

She thinks for a second. "We'll turn them in to the police anonymously, naming Yip. I know a safe way to do that. So legally we're in the clear."

A Day-Glo orange ball rolls near Hector's foot. He plucks it off the ground, tosses it gently near the toddler who's been chasing it. Far enough away to keep the child and her minder at a distance.

"I don't believe you're saying this, Twinkie. You're risking your life. Our lives."

"It's the only way to put pressure on Yip. You want to find out about Leo, don't you?"

"You're not doing it for Leo. You want the story."

"I'm a reporter, Hector. This is what I do. If I can trap a

murderer and put my name on a great story at the same time, why shouldn't I?"

"It's dangerous, that's why."

"It's dangerous anyway. Being in the orchestra with people like Yip is dangerous. If you call the police before you have the evidence, and Yip goes free—how safe do you think you'll be?"

Hector thinks not of Yip but of Skinwic, his cold stare and sour breath. "We could tell the police everything anonymously right now," he says.

"Then you'll never find Leo."

"And you wouldn't get your story."

"Right."

Hector feels as if he's just awakened from a dream to find himself in freefall, cannonballing toward earth, his hands clutching desperately for a parachute. The enterprise he's contemplating is illegal, immoral, and insane.

Yet he knows he's being impelled by a force as inevitable as gravity. In a way, his actions had already been decided before he discovered the smuggling, before Leo disappeared, even before Hector boarded a plane for Hong Kong. The plan kicked off nineteen years ago when a cherished older brother left Hector's home and his world. All his life Hector has been assembling pieces of Oscar around him. Leo was perhaps the biggest piece of his lost brother, the one he's held closest to him the longest, and now Hector is about to throw his life away to get him back. Nothing insane about it.

"So where do we look for the drugs?" he says.

"Let's start with the obvious. Where do they usually take the truck?"

"They unload it at the Cultural Center. The truck's stored in a depot at Hung Hom."

"Okay. If you know the address of the depot, I'll go there."

"No. The depot's sure to be protected. Video cameras, all that stuff. We won't get in."

She thinks again. "Then it's probably not there. I can't see someone hiding drugs under the lens of a video camera."

"I can. It's so unlikely it's perfect."

"You might be right, but that's too Sherlock Holmes for me. I say they're already off the truck. People like to move this stuff quickly. Maybe it's already in the distributor's hands, depending on what it is and how much processing and packaging is needed. I wish I knew who his partner is."

"What partner?"

"The man he met in Shenzhen. Chinese, middle age, medium height."

"Oh, right. The one with black hair, right?"

"Very funny, *gau bang*."

"Did you just call me 'dog biscuit?'"

"Yes. It means a jerk."

"I know what it means. Why is it 'dog biscuit' anyway?"

"I don't know. Why 'jerk'?"

"Never mind. Who is this partner? Where did you see him?"

"He was waiting at that factory place. They split up afterwards, and I followed Yip back to the theater. I should have followed the partner probably."

"Did they say anything?"

"Not much. I caught an accent. Shanghainese."

"Christ, Twinkie. I know who it is. And I think I know where the drugs are."

CHAPTER 50

A REASSURANCE: HE can leave by the front door, if he doesn't die first. But the front door is an unfathomably remote luxury right now, as he clutches a rope tied to a drainpipe five floors above the ground, dressed like a cartoon burglar in stocking cap and leather jacket. The rope is tied around his waist, to save him from death if he loses his grip. But once saved, he'll hang like a pressed duck till the police take him away.

It's no great acrobatic leap, just a hop of maybe five feet from the roof to a balcony railing and over to a nearby window ledge. But his stomach is twisted as taut as the rope in his hands.

He eases himself down the pipe. Using a flange in the pipe for a foothold, he steps down, and is halfway there. He has to jump the rest. Just two feet or so.

He utters a quick curse and jumps.

He alights on the balcony railing and grabs the pipe for stability. From there he hops to the kitchen window ledge and kicks in the window grille, shattering one thin rusty bar along with the glass and bending another enough to slip inside. A hexagonal *ba gua* mirror, placed in the window to frighten away spirits, clatters to the floor. He shucks the rope and is free.

It's dark. He recognizes the smell, though: wood, glue, old things. The flat is empty. Hector watched Hosell take off to chase a diversion he and Twinkie cooked up.

In the beam of his penlight, the main workshop is just as he saw it last: Hector's bass on one bench, some violins on another. Nothing out of place. He curses to himself. What if he'd been wrong, and the Shanghainese man Yip had been talking to wasn't Hosell?

His idea makes sense, though. Some customs officer could easily snap open a bass trunk for a random check. If it were stuffed full of contraband, that would be it. But if there were a bass inside, chances are the inspector would close it and move on. All you'd need is someone who could conceal something inside a bass fiddle. Not hard if you know how.

To the side of the main workshop is a storage room. That's where he sees them: two white Stevenson fiberglass bass trunks. Looking entirely comfortable among the musical instruments and cases in the room.

He snaps the locks on one of the cases and opens it. Inside is a nondescript bass, a Chinese plywood instrument from the looks of it. Not something a professional symphony orchestra would be hauling around, but how would a customs man know that?

Hector unbuckles the straps and tries to lift the instrument, striking a string in the process—*E-flat, way too low for the g string*—and suddenly he knows he was right. The thing weighs more than the heaviest bass he's ever hefted. At least thirty pounds too much.

He prods inside the f-holes. The instrument should be hollow, but it isn't. There's wood where wood shouldn't be. Some kind of compartment. It's well-glued—no way to budge it with his fingers.

He looks around for something to pry the compartment wall with, something small enough to insert in the f-hole without damaging the top of the bass. Nothing. Hector starts toward the workshop, to find a tool, then stops.

What in hell am I doing?

He walks back to the thing that isn't a musical instrument and kicks its belly in with a sharp thrust of his hiking-booted foot. He flings aside the splinters to uncover dozens of snugly-packed cellophane bags, each the size a hardback book, each filled with some kind of crystals.

In one swift motion he's unfastened the duffel that's tied around his waist and placed some of the bags of crystals inside it. Five. Ten. *This needs to be dramatic*, Twinkie had said. *Take as much as you can carry so they know we mean business. Enough so they won't be able to write it off easily.*

Thirty. Thirty-five. He's emptied out the bass entirely.

Dramatic.

He pulls open the other bass case, staves in its top, and begins pulling out more bags, all of them identical, none of them belonging in a double bass, even a cheap Chinese plywood model that has a stiff action and dull sound.

He stops to listen.

The elevator door. Footsteps.

Twinkie had given Hosell an address a good distance away, across the harbor in Sham Shui Po. He shouldn't be back so soon. What if he's changed his mind, figured out that he's been sent on a wild goose chase?

Hector can't leave by the front door. And drainpipes are harder to climb up than down, especially with bags full of drugs on your shoulder. And there's no way he'll leave without his bargaining chip. If Leo's alive, the drugs could get him back.

Hector zips up the bag and strides into the workshop. He spots a hammer, seizes it, swings it twice. Two pounds, perhaps. Not ideal, but he can knock Hosell out and be gone before anyone sees him.

He waits to one side of the door, stocking cap pulled low over his brow. The footsteps approach the door.

They fade a second later. A latch clicks somewhere down the hall. Hector expels a long breath.

He jogs back to the storage room, fills the duffel with every remaining bag of crystals. In just over a minute he's out of the building.

Only when he's exited the taxi and is back on the familiar ground of Portland Street does the numb panic dissipate and his senses begin to reawaken. Shouldering the duffel bag as casually as one can a fifty-pound burden, he walks past the aquarium shop and the walk-up brothel into his building lobby. Triumphantly he slaps the elevator button, as if high-fiving the earth itself for his safe return.

"Looks like a heavy bag," says a voice behind him in Cantonese. He wheels around, sirens wailing in his brain. It's Mrs. Lam, his neighbor, her Pomeranian leashed and compliant at ankle height.

"Another vacation?" she says.

"*Mai yeh*," says Hector. Shopping.

The Pomeranian sniffs at the bag, which rests against Hector's leg. The door opens, and they enter. Mrs. Lam presses 15 eight times, her lucky number. While the car ascends Hector regards the furry beast, then studies the numbers above their head as if they're the day's headlines. After an eternity the doors open, and they walk to their flats.

"What did you buy that's so heavy?" asks Mrs. Lam.

Realizing a slow answer is a suspicious one, Hector parts his lips and the first words that fly into his head.

"*Gau bang*," he says. Dog biscuits.

THE CRYSTALS ARE large, chunky, yellow-white.

"Ice," Twinkie says. "Pure stuff. Thirty or forty kilos. You're a strong guy to carry it all the way here."

"Ice ..." He turns the bag over in his hand.

"Freebased methamphetamine, made for smoking. It's terrible stuff, Hector. And expensive. Each of these bags is ... I don't know, a half kilo, worth maybe fifteen thousand U.S. How much was there altogether?"

"This is it. All of it. Yip had rigged two basses with false compartments. I emptied both of them."

She takes it in slowly. "This must be worth a couple of million dollars U.S., at least. You've cleaned out his whole stash, made a fool of him."

He looks at the duffel bag, at the stuff that killed Chiu, that drove Leo from his life. The stuff that makes Yip a bastard, Bonson a wreck.

That's the way of the world, Hector. On one hand, there are opportunists, on the other, fools like us. In the middle, more fools. Humankind is nothing but a disappointment to Leo.

Hector presents a bag to Twinkie, who steps back, hands in the air. "No thanks, I don't even want to touch that stuff. Think of what it does to people."

"It's addictive, right?"

"Insanely addictive. It stimulates the reward center of your brain, giving you a euphoric high. After a while, it takes away every other goal in life. The high becomes the only prize that's worth going after."

"It's the ice that sets you on fire. It makes you a slave as it makes you king."

"What are you talking about?"

"That's the third riddle in *Turandot*."

She ponders that, eyes still on the bag in his hand. "What's the answer to the riddle?"

"Turandot. The princess herself. But it sounds just like this stuff."

"This ice makes you paranoid, causes hallucinations, kills you with a heart attack or stroke."

He replaces the bag alongside the rest of them and washes his hands.

"I didn't know they made ice in China," he says. "I always think more of heroin, opium."

"Hector, there's a saying. 'Wherever there are drugs there are Chinese.'"

"That true?"

"I'm ashamed to say yes."

"You're not smuggling this stuff, you're helping to put Yip in prison. Ready to call?"

"Give them some time to realize it's gone," says Twinkie.

She moves closer to him, closer than she's ever been, and looks in his eyes. "You were very brave tonight." Her hands curl around his neck while she plants a silent kiss on his cheek. Then another. Their lips melt together, and for the second time tonight there's fire in his blood.

His hands move on her gently, almost timidly, so reluctant is he to scare her off and shatter the mood. But she isn't frightened; she moves closer, till their bodies are against one another and each breath is a caress.

She pulls back and looks in his eyes and at her hands, which glisten with his sweat.

"Sorry," Hector says. It dawns on him how filthy he is. Twinkie begins to laugh, points to his sodden shirt and grimy jeans, matted hair. "I think I'll take a shower," he says.

"Just for me?" she says, unbuttoning her blouse. Right now he'd pull a jumbo jet up Nathan Road with his teeth just for her, but he only nods.

"Then hurry up!" She plucks open the last button, unveiling smooth flesh and a web of lace.

He races into the bathroom and jumps into the shower, basking for a few moments in the cleansing torrent. He soaps himself, trying not to anticipate too closely those same motions performed by Twinkie's soft hands.

A pair of white lace panties sails over the shower door. "What's taking you so long?" Twinkie says. He catches them, laughs, tosses them back out. A Vivaldi concerto fills the apartment. She's fired up the stereo.

Clean and somewhat dry, he considers entering the bedroom with a towel around his waist, but discards the idea. Enough coyness. He walks out, naked, rampant.

Not finding Twinkie in the bed, Hector walks to the living room.

No Twinkie. No bag of ice. Just a gaping front door, through which he can hear the sound of slow footsteps approaching.

Mrs. Lam plods by with a bag of *choi sum*, sees Hector, blinks, walks on.

"Better feed your dog," she says from down the hall. "It looks hungry."

CHAPTER 51

HOSELL LAI MUTTERS under his breath as the minibus deposits him a block from his building, minus a few good hours of his life. What in hell is going on?

On the phone the woman seemed sincere. Her husband died, leaving her a violin, the worth of which she couldn't guess. She wanted to sell it, get the cash before his family started asking for things.

Her late husband, a heart surgeon, had said it was an Albas, Alba, something like that. Doctors can afford good fiddles, he knows, so it might well be an Albanesi, worth a quarter million U.S.

What if you come over now, she'd said, and take it with you if we agree on a price? I never cared for the sound of the violin, anyway, she'd said. Beautiful.

It was worth a trip out to Sham Shui Po. If it turned out to be an Albanesi, he's ready to show her an old Sotheby's sale report listing violins by a lesser maker named Joseph Albani. He'd demonstrate that the Albanis went at auction for twelve thousand U.S. He'd offer close to that—- he had to make some profit, after all. This would have been a great moneymaker, a way to clear a hunk of cash before Yip's deal went through.

But no one by that name existed out in that godforsaken block of flats in Sham Shui Po.

He enters his flat and, prodded by a sudden uneasiness, walks to the back room. He flips on the light and cries out at the sight of both basses torn open, like carcasses ravaged by a lion.

The image of the carcass stays in his mind as his trembling fingers punch the phone number of Yip Tak-tak.

CHAPTER 52

"LEUNG SIN-SAHNG, you haven't been honest with us."

Lok has deliberately chosen a mild accusation, but he can't tell whether Fatman Leung is showing panic or relief. The little man says nothing. He sulks like a chastened schoolboy caught writing dirty words on the blackboard.

"Yesterday you went to a public bathroom on lower Wyndham Street, a known pick-up spot for the male homosexual community in Hong Kong. You waited outside at the bus stop opposite until a young man named ..." he glances at his notes " ... Damian Mo walked to the stop, then crossed the street and entered the bathroom. You followed him."

"I didn't know there was anything illegal ..."

"I didn't say there was, Leung *sin-sahng*. It's been decriminalized, as you know. But the picture you gave us of your relationship with Milkie Tang was false. Wasn't it?"

Fatman narrows his eyes. "Who says? I go both ways. Ever heard of that?"

Lok waits, says nothing.

"I haven't broken any laws. What is the relevance of all this?" His voice has an edge now. He shifts in his seat. "It's ... important that

I be careful. My image. Do you know what image is, Inspector?"

He does. The word, always in English, appears in conversations, lectures, memoranda all the time. *The force needs to maintain its image ... needs to modernize its image.* Fatman's probably as tired of it as he is.

The silence works on Fatman for another thirty seconds. Finally he says, "So what was I really doing with Milkie? Is that what you want to know?"

Lok nods gently.

He takes a breath, expels it, lets his eyes rest on the floor between them. "I met her at VSOP, as I told you before. I'd been going there to pick up girls, take them to dinner, go somewhere just to be seen with them. Helps the image, as I said. I'd only go out with a girl once or twice. Most of them were pretty dull, to tell the truth."

Yes, tell the truth, for a change, Lok thinks.

"That changed when I met Milkie. She wasn't going to let go of me till she got her movie contract. I didn't mind, really. Most of the girls are pretty dull, you know? She was kind of, well ... she was clever, and up front about what she wanted. We became friends. I went to her place once a week or so."

"What did you do?"

"We watched movies, Inspector. Old ones, usually. She was really sentimental, did you know that? She liked the big romances: *In the Mood for Love, Autumn's Tale*, Hollywood films like *Titanic, Somewhere in Time*—she'd even watch black-and-white movies with me. You don't get too many people her age who will, at least, not outside film school."

"Is that all?"

"You mean, is that all I did with her? Yes. I'd take her out and treat her like dirt in front of people, and then we'd go home and watch men and women find true love against impossible odds."

"Was she happy with this arrangement?"

"Very. I warned her that film was a tough business, did what I could for her. And she was good-looking enough. Who got hurt? What did I do wrong?"

"You lied to us, Leung *sin-sahng*." Lok lets that sink in for a second. "Why did you lie? Did she threaten to expose you?"

Fatman starts, but doesn't answer.

"Did she want more than a bit part from you, Fatman? A starring role in one of your movies?"

"Is that what you think?"

"You know how insistent she could be. Is that right, Fatman?"

"No," he says, regaining some composure. "No, it's not."

"Milkie told you she wanted star billing, maybe a nice pile of money, and if you didn't give in, she'd tell the world that Fatman Leung, the big sex movie man, was a queer."

"No ... no."

"You befriended her, then she turned on you."

Fatman's regained some of his cool. "Inspector, I admit it might be a setback to see my private life in the gossip magazines. But I'd survive. You'd be surprised who's a *gay lo* in the entertainment business."

"Why should we believe you, Fatman? What are you holding back now?"

"Listen, Inspector. I liked Milkie. She wasn't easy to like, but my heart went out to her. She didn't have much to work with, no money, no family, and she wasn't the lucky type either. But she was brave, and she didn't give up. I respected that. My father came from Guangdong with nothing but the clothes on his back. He could barely read or write, but he wouldn't take shit from anyone. Milkie was like that. "

"She wouldn't take shit from you either, then," says Lok.

"I told you what we did, Inspector. We met at her flat, and we'd watch old movies and talk about the people in them, talk about them as if they were real people." He removes a handkerchief from his pocket and dabs a tear, composes himself. "Look," he says. "Milkie was clever enough to know she couldn't get anywhere by hurting my career. Who would touch her after that? Everyone has secrets, as you know. No, she never threatened me. And if she had, I wouldn't have hurt her. I do comedy, Inspector—not tragedy."

———————

"DO YOU BELIEVE him, sir?" asks Million Man.

Lok does. But as usual, the truth raises more questions than it answers. Up to now he'd seen Milkie as a calculating devil. And she was, but Fatman's shown him a new side to this troubled girl. She was a dreamer as well as a schemer, capable of making a sucker of Yorks Ma, blackmailing him to use his cars, but sniffling at smarmy love stories. He tells this to Million Man.

"I still don't know if I trust Fatman."

"Why not?" asks Lok.

"You know, sir ..."

Lok shakes his head. "Million Man, in this job, you're going to meet every kind of person. Some will be like you, some different. It's your job to understand their motivations, not judge their lives. Ever hear of Ivan Lee?"

Million Man shakes his head.

"He was a television newspaper reporter, and he was queer. That was back when it was a criminal offense. One morning they found him hanging in his office by a lamp cord. The CID came and went through the motions, declared it a suicide. Didn't bother bagging his hands, checking under his nails for evidence of a struggle. As far as they were concerned, it was just another dead *gay lo*, nothing to bother about.

"The only problem was, people knew he'd been preparing a feature about gay life in Hong Kong, and his notes had disappeared. Maybe he'd erased them before he died. That's what we figured. But a lot of people said it was a cover-up, that his article was going to reveal that he had gay friends in the police department.

"The point is, we should have done our jobs. Instead, we wanted him to disappear because he was homosexual. And the police department got a black eye because of it. Understand?"

Million Man nods.

Lok glances at his watch. Eleven-thirty, and the Hot Room should be hotter by now. One anomaly points up another: street sounds, which seem wrong to him. *Why is that wrong?* He glances over Million Man's shoulder.

"The window's open!" he shouts. Across the room, the blinds are up and the room's sole window is open wide, a *feng shui* violation.

"Shit!"

Million Man whirls around and shuts it with a bang that almost shatters the glass. "Must have been the new room boy." He snaps the latch, draws the blinds, and smooths them. "Now we're in for it." He runs off to scream at the room boy and make an offering to Kwan Dai.

CHAPTER 53

HECTOR SLOUCHES ON the frayed and sprung sofa in his living room. He stares at the door, which is now closed, though he doesn't remember closing it. He doesn't recall getting dressed either, but he's wearing a pair of jeans and a sweatshirt. Since Twinkie vanished he's been hearing only muffled sounds, seeing indistinct shapes, and moving slowly, as if someone had pumped the room full of a viscous liquid.

Facts, he thinks. *Start with facts.* Twinkie set him up. No, that's an assumption. Fact: Twinkie left, and took the drugs. Fact: she used Hector to get them.

She's been after the drugs all along, that much is clear. But how much did she know when they first met? Did she know what kind of drugs were involved, and how they were hidden? Probably not. That was Hector's role, finding that out. She got him to sneak her into the orchestra's office, learn about Yip and Mulqueen, figure out who Hosell Lai was and how he fit into it.

Fact: Twinkie lies.

Where did the lies begin? Had Leo really spoken to Twinkie before he'd disappeared, told her something was going on in the orchestra?

Fact: he doesn't know a goddam thing.

His head careens from one unanswered question to the next. If she was always after the drugs, how did she find out about them in the first place? Not from anyone in the orchestra. Did Leo find out and tell her? Or did she invent all the stuff about Leo to get him enrolled in her little treasure hunt?

Fact: Twinkie is one big lie.

And that was why I was picked. Because I'm a faithful friend. I am a prize sucker, a dupe, a gull of the first order.

Fact: Twinkie is a good judge of character.

A siren. For a moment his body stiffens, then slumps when it retreats, as if the sound itself were a distillation of panic. It's not over, he thinks. What's the next move? Go to the police? And say what? *Hi there. I stole some fifty pounds of crystal meth and brought it to my flat, only it's gone now, sorry. You see, my friend Twinkie was going to report the whole thing after she wrote up the story and won a journalism prize.*

Fact: act like a Siefert, people will treat you like a Siefert.

Stage one of the decision process: make a drink. He walks to the cabinet but stops when a knocker clangs on the steel bars of a gate. *C-sharp.* There's someone at the door. Twinkie, no doubt, duffel bag and explanation in hand. He crosses the room and opens the door.

The doorway is empty.

He unlatches the gate to peer outside, and Skinwic Sze appears from nowhere and shoves him back inside his flat.

"*Hai bin-do ah*?" he says, staring into Hector's eyes. *Where?*

"What?"

"No bullshit. Where is it? You took it!" Hector recognizes the accent now, Shanghainese, like Hosell.

"Take a look yourself. I don't have, I uh …" Skinwic grips a handful of his shirt and pulls him closer together so their breaths mingle, Skinwic's a blend of onion, Marlboros, dental plaque, sunflower seeds.

"*See-fat!*" he hisses, delivering a sharp slap across Hector's face. Before Hector can react Skinwic thrusts Hector backwards till he hits the wall and drops onto the sofa. His ears ring from the slap. *C-natural.*

"You took it!"

"It's gone," Hector says, instantly regretting the words.

"Gone? Where?"

"I don't know."

The wrong thing to say. Skinwic punches Hector in the ribs, sending darts of pain through him. *Got to fight back.*

From his position on the sofa he scans the room for a weapon, but the only one he sees is in Skinwic's hand: a linoleum knife, held sideways, its hooked blade parallel to Hector's throat. *Got to get help.*

"Okay, okay, you win!" He hopes Skinwic will withdraw a little, but he doesn't—the knife stays at his throat. With nothing to lose, Hector throws himself backwards and topples the sofa. The move throws Skinwic off long enough for him to scramble to his feet and run to the balcony. Someone will see him. Someone will call the police.

Before Hector can shout anything coherent Skinwic reaches Hector and pins him with an arm lock. Paralyzed with pain, Hector falls to his knees, and there comes more pain as Skinwic presses the blade into his ribs. Hector inches away, and Skinwic jabs the blade into him again.

He's prodding me. Pushing me somewhere. Why doesn't he just kill me?

They're by the glass door now. In the reflection he sees Skinwic's knife move to his throat. Hector twists his head away from the door. Skinwic pulls it back. Their eyes meet in the reflection.

He wants to see me die.

Again he turns away. Skinwic grabs Hector's hair and forces him to face the glass door once again.

He wants to look into my eyes as I die.

Hector snaps his head back and smashes Skinwic's chin, and he breaks free. Grasping Skinwic's legs, he hugs tight and shoves upward with every ounce of his strength. Maybe he can get Skinwic on his back, stomp on his stomach and make it to the door.

Skinwic slips out of his arms. Suddenly it's quiet.

Did he run? Where is he?

Confusion. Wherever Skinwic went, he's gone.

When he can finally hear something over the rasp of his own breath, it's a woman's voice in the distance. A shriek, far below on Portland Street. He peers over the railing at a man on the ground, head and limbs splayed like a five-pointed star. At first it's a just an image, pale and meaningless, unable to compete with the reality he's just faced. Then his mind connects the man below with Skinwic. He recoils from the railing.

This isn't my life, it's someone else's. I'm here by mistake.

Hector shoves his keys, cellphone, wallet in his pocket, navigating once again as if underwater, seeing only shadows and shapes, hearing only miscued sound effects instead of anguished voices and the crescendo of sirens in the street below.

Twinkie. He must find Twinkie.

PART IV

Whoever gives you milk is your mother.

—CHINESE PROVERB

CHAPTER 54

BY NOW PORTLAND Street traffic will be choked by police vans, the pavement garlanded in yellow tape, the corridors of the fifteenth floor jammed with gossiping neighbors trading fragments of misinformation like black market gold. Hector has used the night hours to move in the only direction he can comprehend: away from his flat, as far as possible.

He's spent most of the night lurking in a place with the unlikely name of Knutsford Terrace, a strip of jaunty nightspots channeled between two Kowloon shopping streets. Bars are not where he does his best thinking, but dumb white faces—tourists, businessmen, party people—are handy camouflage. Ironic, since he's never felt less kinship with his race, or the human race, for that matter.

At three a.m., in a Caribbean-style bar where a dreadlocked bartender juggles glasses and waiters wear loud print shirts, he sees the story break on TV: a roadblock on Portland Street, yellow crime scene tape, no comment from the police.

No more news after that. Eventually the bars close, and by four the street traffic thins, and the crowds have dispersed. Somehow he makes it through the rest of the night. A sudden impulse to max out his ATM card leaves him flush with cash. No one has blocked his account yet.

Now the sun is high, but a cool breeze off Tolo Harbour postpones the mounting heat. Hector rests on a bench outside the Ten Thousand Buddhas Monastery in Sha Tin, melting into a landscape of comfortably-dressed Westerners and staring at idols who stare back with preposterous serenity. Skinwic Sze's death has trapped him in an endless loop of deliberation, from which every exit is a nightmare in itself.

He should call the police and give himself up. They already know it's him, after all. He can explain it was self-defense. This isn't a fascist state, after all. The law rules.

But how does he tell the cops why Skinwic attacked him? Mistaken identity? The police must know Skinwic is smuggling drugs, or they'll find out shortly. No, they'll assume it's drug-related, and if the police trace the ice, the path will lead to him. Maybe he was even spotted at Hosell's place.

They'll have it wrapped up in no time: *gweilo* steals a million dollars worth of ice, triad thug gets wise and attacks him, *gweilo* gets lucky. Self-defense, but it happened during a crime. What would he get? Fifteen years in Stanley Prison?

He could get out of Hong Kong, back to New York. But there's probably some kind of extradition agreement. Within a week some guy in a dark suit and white socks would turn up at the door, flashing his ID.

A tune chirps from his pocket. *William Tell Overture transposed to B-flat.* The melody cycles through, entertaining no one, and then cuts out.

He considers Mexico, Brazil, Bali, then shakes his head. *What am I, fucking Adolf Eichmann? I've done nothing wrong, and I'm contemplating lifelong exile?*

Done nothing wrong—perhaps an overstatement.

He checks his voice-mail.

"Hec, where are you? We need a sectional for the Bartok. You up for it? Give me a shout."

Clem, calling from a life that's as far away as childhood now, wants to rehearse for the next concert.

The second message. *"Mr. Siefert, this is WPC Catherine So from the Hong Kong Police, Yau Tsim District. Inspector Will Pullman would like to speak to you."*

A number follows. Hector waits patiently for the third message. A voice he doesn't recognize at first.

"Answer your phone. I'll call in fifteen minutes."

The phone clicks off.

He places a face to the voice: Yip Tak-tak. Instinctively he glances from side to side, as if Yip's very presence on the phone is dangerous.

The next time the phone sings out, Hector presses the green button.

"Yes?"

"Bring it to me tonight," says Yip, without prologue. "The carpark under the Mai Sun Shopping Center, level P5. Don't tell anyone."

"I don't have it."

"Don't bullshit me, *See-fat*. Nine o'clock."

"I said I don't ..."

"Hector ..." A different voice, female, taut with panic. Is it Twinkie?

"Who ..."

"Hector, please. Do what he says."

It's Zenobia.

Yip speaks again. "I have a knife like Skinwic's, *See-fat*. You know what I'll do to her?"

"No, please ... don't hurt her."

"Nine o'clock." The connection cuts off. He tries to redial the number, but the caller ID's been blocked.

Not Zen. Anyone but her.

Where is Twinkie now, he wonders. Out of Hong Kong already? Is there a buyer somewhere, some sleazy triad ready to take delivery, bundles of cash packed up? Or is it more sophisticated these days, all electronic transfers and key codes? Has she already made a fat deposit in one of Hong Kong's handy banks, and hopped a plane to God knows where?

That possibility is too horrible to grasp, so he discards it. As far as he knows, there's time to get back the ice, satisfy Yip, get Zen back, and get the hell out of Hong Kong. Steal a tourist's passport and sneak through immigration. It can be done. *You all look alike to us*, Twinkie said.

Did Leo do the same thing? Slither out of Hong Kong before Yip could grab him? Am I a lemming following my best friend off a cliff?

Time to think. Nine-forty a.m., just over eleven hours till he meets Yip. Eleven hours to find Twinkie, get the ice, and while he's at it, keep himself from getting arrested for murder.

Where in hell is Twinkie?

CHAPTER 55

"**MISS TWINKIE CHOI,** is that right?"

"Yes, it is."

"I'm sorry about the inconvenience," says Lok. Talking to someone decent for a change, someone not under suspicion, he finds himself savoring his own politeness. The team is out right now, leaving this fetching reporter to himself. "And I apologize about this hot room. We shouldn't be long." She nods agreeably.

"You probably know about Milkie Tang," he continues. "Your paper ran an item about her a couple of days ago. While investigating her death, we also came upon this piece about her, from June" He slides a clipping across the desk to her. She reads it, smiles in recognition. What a smile. Like an ocean breeze in the Hot Room.

"I've moved on from there, Inspector. I cover news now, not entertainment."

"I understand. But you did meet her, didn't you?"

"Yes. I didn't know her well, though. Assignments like that, well …" They share a look of understanding about less-than-perfect jobs. "Anyway, what would you like to know?"

"When did you meet her?"

"It was just once. I was on the entertainment beat for about three months, and she came toward the end of that … let's see … probably it was mid-June, a few days before the piece came out."

"What was she like?"

"I liked her, actually. Generally, I'm not too impressed with the starlets. Some of the real actors are bright people, but the cute ones who just want to get into films … well, you know …"

Lok nods.

"Milkie could only talk about one thing—what she was going to do in films. How big a star she was going to be."

"Did she seem to be nervous or troubled about anything?"

She looks to the ceiling, gathers her thoughts. "She seemed okay to me. But remember, people put on a face for reporters."

A lot of good it does us, Lok thinks. Reporters still print whatever they want. "Did she mention any men?"

She cocks her head to one side, thinks. Lok finds himself reflexively tilting his own head to keep eye contact. Nice shape to those eyes. "No, sorry. We didn't do any girl-talk. It was all about Milkie, all about her new film."

"What did she think about Fatman Leung?"

Again, a pause for thought. "It was a while back, let me see … just that he liked her, recognized her talent. That's about it. Sorry. Would you like me to try to dig up my notes? There might be something there I forgot about."

"Would you do that? It might help."

"Absolutely." She accepts Lok's thanks and walks out, breezing by Big Pang and Million Man, who have just entered.

"She's not bad," says Million Man. "We seem to be getting a better class of woman at the station lately."

"Twinkie Choi, reporter from the *Post*," Lok answers. "She wrote the piece on Milkie Tang."

"How did you find her?" asks Big Pang. He looks thunderstruck.

"What do you mean? I called the *Post* a couple of days ago, asked her to come here."

"Sir, I mean, how did you know it was her?"

"What are you talking about, Pang?"

Big Pang wheels around, dashes out the door and disappears into the stairwell, leaving Lok and Million Man to stare at each other.

Five minutes later he's back, frustration knitting his brow. "Couldn't find her," he says.

"What's going on?" says Lok. "What the hell are you talking about?"

"Remember the girl I saw following Yip in Shenzhen? That's her. I thought you'd picked her up."

"You're joking," Lok says, but Pang isn't a joker.

"What was she doing here?"

"Let's think this through," Lok says. "The girl goes to Shenzhen and follows Yip, same as us. We're doing it because we think he's linked to Milkie's murder. Why is she there?"

"She's a reporter," says Million Man. "She's doing a story, whatever."

"So we're both interested in Yip, but for different reasons?" says Pang.

"I don't believe it." Lok says. "She knew Milkie. Yip knew Milkie. Too much of a coincidence."

"Say she's made the connection. Maybe she's planning a story naming Yip as the killer, telling how the police didn't pick up the clues. They love to make us look stupid."

"Call the *Post*, get her back."

Lok ponders the balls that this woman has, to come in and chat with him as if she's uninvolved and innocent. Kwan is going to love hearing about this.

At that moment Ears ushers in a small, elderly woman waving a mug shot of Skinwic Sze in her weathered talons.

"This is the man," she says. "He dragged the TV box out of that girl's flat."

"Good," Lok says. "Thank you, Liu *tai-tai*." Finally something is going well. He can pick Skinwic up and charge him.

"But I really don't understand," she says. "All this fuss because he took the girl's TV?"

"We appreciate your help. Ears, have a constable take Mrs. Liu home." Ears leads her away, nodding as she invites the team over for cabbage and dried shrimp soup.

Before Lok can pick up the phone Will Pullman walks into the office and tosses an ID photo on his desk. "This your man?"

It's the same photo of Skinwic Sze that Mrs. Liu clutched in her bony hand a moment ago. This time the expression pulls Lok in. A mug shot is taken when a *lan jai* is at his lowest. He's been caught, charged, thrown in a cell, tossed around the system like a mullet at the fish market. By the time he's shoved in front of the camera his face is usually a mask of confusion and fatigue. Even some of the tough ones look as if they'd just been awakened from a bad dream.

Skinwic's isn't like that. He's oblivious to the camera. *The son of a bitch is bored.*

"We're just about to pick him up," Lok says. "Know where to find him?"

"Easy one. The fridge," says Pullman. "He was the one thrown off the balcony on Portland Street last night. Fingerprints match."

"Shit." Lok drops the photo.

"We're doing a search of the flat now," says Pullman. "It was rented out to a Westerner named Hector Siefert."

"*See-fat*? This a joke?"

Will beams. He's been asked that twice already. "No, it's a German name. Anyway, he hasn't shown up since last night. Didn't show up for work today, probably panicked and ran. There was a wicked little knife on the balcony with Sze's fingerprints on it. He probably came at *See-fat*, who got lucky. But that's a guess at this point."

"Any blood? Chance he's wounded?"

"Don't think so. There was a struggle, no doubt about that."

"Where does this *See-fat* work?" Despite the trouble this man has caused, his name has lifted Lok's spirits.

"The same place the victim did. At the Hong Kong Symphony. And that's the reason that you're getting this. Kwan's orders."

His smile vanishes. It figures. Lose one suspect, gain another. Wait till the Chinese papers get hold of that name. *Police unable to locate see-fat, probe to follow ...*

"We've got the man's employer in Room Two," says Pullman. "Name's Bonson Ng."

"*See-fat*'s employer, and the dead one's as well."

"Yes, one big happy. Miserable piece of luck about this Skin-wic, though."

It's true. He'd gone farther with the case than he had any right to expect. Did the footwork, got some breaks. And now someone's shoved his case out a Mongkok window.

Pang returns. "Sir, I called the Post. Twinkie Choi is on holiday, starting today."

Will picks up the photo, now a meaningless exhibit in a dead rogue's gallery. "What did you do to bring this on?"

An image flies into Lok's mind: the Hot Room last night, its windows thrown wide open to the ghosts.

———————

"INSPECTOR, I DON'T know what to say. This is truly awful." Bonson Ng looks ill, his skin gray, his hair limp, an expression on his face that hints at some anguish even deeper than the bad news could account for.

"What can you tell me about Hector Siefert?" Lok asks.

"I never would have thought him capable of something like this. He plays double bass in the symphony. He's been here three years. There was that incident in his past that I told the constable about, but I never dreamed that there would be violence here."

"What incident?"

"A woman constable called me a week or so ago. It seems Mr. Siefert reported his friend missing." His tone of voice suggests surprise that Lok doesn't already know this.

"What friend?"

"His name is Leo Stern. Another orchestra player, an American. He apparently left right before the season, never showed up for work. I'm pretty sure he just quit abruptly without giving notice, but Mr. Siefert was worried that something had happened to him. I told the constable that Mr. Siefert's opinion wasn't terribly reliable, that he himself assaulted someone in the States when he worked there."

"Is this true?"

Bonson's eyeballs seem to inflate. "Yes, of course! I wouldn't make up something like that."

"Do you know the nature of that assault?"

"It was an artistic disagreement. In Tulsa, Oklahoma. I don't know much else."

Lok nodded, made a note. "Does Siefert take drugs, do you know?"

"No, I doubt that. You can talk to his colleagues, but I'd be surprised."

"What about Skinwic Sze? Did you know he had a police record?"

Bonson shakes his head, and his jaw seems to drop loose. "Oh, my God, you're joking." Then: "I apologize. Of course you're not joking. I had no idea, Inspector. He was hired by my stage manager, Yip Tak-tak. I had nothing to do with it. Is it serious, uh, I mean, is he, is the police record ..."

"You'll get the details later. What did Skinwic Sze do?"

"Do?" Bonson looks away from Lok, absorbed in something. There's that feeling again, that Bonson's distress comes from something else beyond a dead employee.

"What was his job?" Lok says.

Bonson snaps back to the present. "He moved instruments," he says.

"What about Yip Tak-tak?"

Bonson pauses, gulps. A mist begins to form on his forehead. The man was made to order for interrogators. "He's the stage manager, Skinwic's direct superior. He's in charge of the moving crew."

"Do you know where Yip is now?"

"No. I left a message, but he hasn't got back to me." These last words spoken softly, almost mumbled.

"What led you to hire Yip Tak-tak in the first place?"

"He was qualified. I can show you his resume."

Lok suppresses a laugh. A Red Pole with a resume, that's a new one. *Education: Sun Yee On triad society. Experience: VSOP Nightclub. Other interests: murder, extortion, pimping.*

"And you don't know where Yip is now."

Bonson hesitates slightly. "No."

The phone rings. Lok answers it, and then takes off for a few minutes. He returns bearing a photocopy of a newspaper clipping.

Bonson begins to squirm as if sitting on a heated wok. "Is there anything else I can do, Inspector?" He's begging to leave, Lok knows.

"Just one thing."

"And that is?"

"Stop lying. Now."

The words hit Bonson like a blow to the gut.

"We know about your baby," Lok says. He pulls a news clipping from a folder and reads. "*Vancouver Sun*, March 10th. A seven-month-old girl is returned to her mother several hours after being kidnapped ... the police have no idea who it was or why they did it ... they conclude that kidnappers panicked after stealing the baby, leaving it in a basket in the lobby of the mother's building ... .the mother, one Tina Ng, is relieved to have her daughter back ... the husband, Bonson Ng, works in Hong Kong and is not available for comment."

Silence.

Lok lays the clipping on the table gently. "It's nothing new, Ng *sin-sahng*. It's standard triad practice. They like to let you know they're in control." Lok has seen the message many times—*we can do it if we need to, don't forget that.*"

Bonson stares at the floor like a chastised schoolboy.

"You must be suffering," says Lok. "All this time, no one to talk to about your fear. Your colleagues mustn't know about it. Your bosses don't care. You have to reassure your wife, but no one can reassure you. You must feel like the loneliest man alive."

Bonson begins to weep.

CHAPTER 56

HECTOR WALKS INTO the cavernous lobby of the *Post's* editorial offices, conscious that somewhere above him reporters are waving his photo around and writing up his crimes.

In the elevator he's joined by a man and a woman, deep in conversation, Cantonese peppered with English words. Hector pulls out the photo ID Twinkie gave him.

When the couple emerges Hector trails a few steps behind them, nodding as the man speaks, pretending to listen and agree as they pass the security check. Leaving the couple, he plies a maze of cubicle dividers and enters the immense main room with its acreage of desks. Twinkie's is empty, her terminal dark.

Her home address is still a mystery. Somewhere on her desk could be a notebook, a receipt, something he could use to find her. Casually he walks to the side of the desk, lowers himself in a seat alongside, like a visitor waiting for an interview, and inches his hand around toward her desk drawer.

"She's not in, you know ..."

He jerks his hand back. The words come from a Western woman at the next desk. She barely looks up at him. "Twinkie went on leave," she says, then picks up a phone. The reporter is in her thirties, long dirty blond hair pinned up carelessly. Hector can't place the accent. South African, possibly.

"Leave?" he says.

"Yes, she'll be back in three weeks. Randy? Felicia here. I can't locate the venue for Gary Chong's speech. Is it at the Convention Centre again? Thanks, I'll wait ... ."

Twinkie has set things up beautifully. By the time she's missed she could be anywhere.

"I must have the wrong day, then," he says. "I'll just leave her a note." He stands, grabs a pen, and begins to scribble on a pad. With his other hand, he eases open her middle desk drawer. It's empty, just a pack of staples.

He covers the page in gibberish, makes a show of tearing it off the pad and folding it. Meanwhile he scans the desk for anything that might tell him where Twinkie is. But it's hopeless, as nondescript a station as anyone ever toiled at.

He lays the note ostentatiously on the desk, weighs it down with a steel rule. As he does so, he sees something in the trash bin. As gracefully as he can he dips his hand into the bin, takes hold of the paper, and gets up to leave.

"Hey!"

The reporter's caught him.

"Come back here!"

Hector smiles, gives the woman the thumbs-up, begins to stride away.

"You can't take that. It's not your property!" The woman hits the speaker button on her phone and punches a three-digit number. "Security, Felicia Gorey on the third floor ..."

A few other faces look up now, to watch Hector disappear around a partition. He picks up speed, ducks into a stairwell, runs down to the main lobby, and jogs out to the street. He leaps into a taxi just as a couple of security guards, radios in hand, emerge from the building. "Star Ferry," he tells the driver, for something to say, and then unfolds the paper that he stole from Twinkie's trash.

It's a drawing, maybe ten years old or more, judging by the faded crayon lines and limp paper. A child drew it. One with talent, he judges, because it's a very good crayon drawing of Yip Tak-tak.

At Star Ferry he crosses back to Kowloon, merging with a family of German tourists at the exit in case the police are searching for lone Westerners. The one constable he sees doesn't seem to be watching the crowd too carefully.

Nine hours left, according to the old Star Ferry clock tower. Should he bolt now? He has no passport, just his Hong Kong ID, which isn't the type that can get him into China or Macau without more documentation. The airport, of course, is out of the question. Security, immigration, computers.

He could make it to an island called Ling Ding, under mainland jurisdiction, where locals go for cheap prostitutes and cheaper beer. One time he took a boat there illegally, just to look around. Maybe at Ling Ding he could pay a fisherman a couple of thousand to take him to Thailand, say.

It's no use. They'd take his money and then turn him in for a reward. As a *gweilo* on the Mainland he's too exposed, too conspicuous. And anyway, they've been keeping people inside their borders for fifty years now. For a *gweilo*, Hong Kong is an air-tight box.

And there's Zen.

He has to face Yip and make him believe what happened. If he can just buy some time he can find Twinkie, turn her and the ice into the police, and clear his name. With the ice they might believe him. Without it, he's just a dirtbag who threw a guy off his balcony.

The midday heat and smog suffuse the city's air. The temperature should mellow out in autumn, but someone forgot to arrange it this time around. Sweat trickles down Hector's neck and onto his shirt, which hasn't been off his back since yesterday morning. He needs a place to rest, to clean up, to think.

Hotels are out, at this point. They all check ID.

You really did it this time, See-fat. All because you wouldn't let go of Leo.

Then he thinks of a hiding place.

CHAPTER 57

"WHAT IS YIP TAK-TAK doing, Bonson?"

"I don't know."

"I think you do," says Lok.

Now they're in the interview room, at a table shaped like an isosceles triangle, Bonson sitting along one side, Lok on another, Bonson' s lawyer at the hypotenuse, each place labeled to keep them in the correct seats: Interviewee, Police, Lawyer. Chairs are chained to the floor to prevent anyone from whacking a cop or suspect if things get out of hand.

A microphone dangles above them. Behind Bonson, close enough to be visible in the video they're shooting, is a clock. Should anyone try to edit footage out of the video later on, the sweep second hand will jump. A mirror, also visible on tape, assures the viewer that no one is behind Lok, gun in hand, coercing the confession.

Behind Lok a bank of VCRs is making duplicates of the tape for the police, the court, and the lawyer, imprinting the unique room number YT01 on each one. The tapes are all brand new and blank. Shoving a used tape in one of the specially-configured machines would set off an alarm.

Bonson speaks. "Yes, I know what he's doing. He's bringing in something from China."

"Drugs?"

"I suppose so. I don't have anything to do with it."

Lok says nothing.

"I mean, I did what Yip told me to do. I hired Skinwic and his crew to keep an eye on things."

"What things?"

"The smuggling. They're using two large bass trunks. Unless you're looking for them, you won't notice them. They even have instruments inside them. The instruments are full of whatever's being smuggled. They were brought back to Hong Kong from Shenzhen. On our next tour Yip was planning on taking shipments to Europe as well."

"What kind of drugs?"

"I told you, I don't know. I don't even know if it is drugs, I just presume so. I've never even seen an illegal drug. Whatever it is, it's made in a factory north of Shenzhen. While the orchestra is performing, they load up the cases, and take them back over the border with the other instruments."

"And your job?"

"My job is my job. I manage the orchestra. See that concerts go on, and people get paid. I'm not part of it. Don't you see, there was nothing I could do? They'd take my child away!"

"I understand, Ng *sin-sahng*. Let's go back to the beginning. When did the operation start?"

"Last year, in March. we needed a conductor, and Ambrose Wan suggested Shao Din-yan. I said I preferred someone more experienced. That weekend my wife called to tell me our baby had disappeared. You can imagine what we went through.

"Ambrose Wan phoned soon after, said that he could use his influence to get my baby back, but I'd have to do what he said. What could I do? At first, I thought he was just being kind to me. Eventually I realized that he was the one behind it all. As soon as my baby was returned, Wan gave me the order to get Shao appointed conductor."

"Did you have the power to do that?"

"No, but another CG member, John Mulqueen, was also very persuasive. Shao was taken on. Then Wan told me to hire Yip, and that Yip was effectively my boss." Revealing this shames him, Lok can tell.

"Who else knew about this?"

"In the orchestra? No one."

"What about the conductor Shao?"

He shakes his head. "I doubt it. He's clueless."

It was still confusing, and even Bonson seemed to be bewildered by the mess he'd found himself in.

"I'm not sure I follow this, Ng *sin-sahng*. Why did Ambrose Wan want you to make Shao conductor?"

"Shao was the key to everything. His father is a vice minister at the State Economic and Trade Commission. He helped smooth the way for the tour, made it his pet project, an important cultural exchange. That's how we got through customs easily."

"Is the father getting paid off, too?"

"In a way. His son gets a music career. That's no mean accomplishment, given the competitive symphonic world. And when he comes to Hong Kong, we take him to bars, give him a night out, buy him Russian whores. He loves it, the filthy bastard."

"Where is he now?"

"Back in Shenzhen, I think."

A cadre of that rank would be a delicate matter. Better to wait with him.

"Tell me about Hector Siefert."

"He's a bass player in the orchestra, a good fellow. I lied to the police when I said he was unreliable."

"Why did you lie?"

"A police constable called a couple of weeks ago, said that Mr. Siefert had reported a friend missing. The idea of police looking around the orchestra frightened me, for obvious reasons. So I did my best to discredit him. He has nothing to do with this."

"He wasn't involved in your smuggling operation, then?"

Bonson jumps to his feet. "It's Ambrose Wan's smuggling operation. It's Yip's. Not mine!"

"Very well," says Lok. "Please sit down. You're saying Hector Siefert wasn't part of Yip's operation?"

"Not so far as I know," Bonson says, a little more calmly.

"How did he find out about it?"

"I don't know. He did visit Hosell Lai. Maybe he figured it out. I really don't know."

"Tell us about Hosell Lai."

"He's an instrument maker. Yip hired him to hide whatever's inside the bass fiddles, make them look good. He's getting a cut of the money."

"Are you?"

"No! I said I didn't want anything to do with it! I just want my family safe."

"Why did Hector Siefert visit Hosell Lai?"

"A legitimate reason, I think. The movers dropped his bass

and broke it, and he was checking on the repair. Maybe he found something out there."

Lok excuses himself, walks to the next room, where the team is watching on a monitor.

"Get ready," he says. "As soon as we have this all on tape, we're picking up Hosell Lai."

CHAPTER 58

HECTOR QUIETLY UNLOCKS the door and slips into the welcoming darkness of Leo's flat. The air is warm and stale. He flips on a desk lamp.

First things first. Before he can think, he must shower. And before he showers, he must have a drink. Grabbing the Wild Turkey bottle from the shelf, he pops out the cork. *B-flat.* Normally a tune would come to him immediately, but fatigue and fear have locked up the immense library of melodies in his brain. *To this you've come, Hec. You can't play in the orchestra, and you can't even make music in your head anymore. B-flat's about as easy as they come, too. Schubert Trio. Beethoven Horn Sonata. What else ...*

B-flat.

He replaces the cork, pulls it out again, hears the same muted plunk.

For a moment he stays still as a corpse, bottle in hand. Then, pouring a generous slug of bourbon, he speaks.

"All right, Leo. Come out."

More silence.

A hinge squeaks. Then a door opens, and a man emerges from the back room to stand in the door frame.

He looks more gaunt, and seems not to have slept since they last saw each other, so pronounced is his pallor. He's wearing the same T-shirt with the torn-off sleeves.

"My man Hec," Leo says, welcoming an old friend into his home. "Nice going. How the hell did you know?"

Hector raises the bottle. "Last time I came, it was a D-flat. It's gone down a few tones. Who else would be drinking this stuff?"

"Who else would have remembered the pitch? You're something, Hec. Haven't got a cigarette, by any chance? I ran out an hour ago."

"Why, Leo?"

"Why, what?"

"Don't bullshit me. Why did you disappear?"

Leo sighs, sounding as tired as he looks. "Because I didn't want to be around the orchestra when the shit hit the fan. As far as anyone but you is concerned, I'm gone."

"You knew this was going to happen?"

Leo approaches him, grabs a glass from atop the cabinet, takes the bottle from Hector, pours a double. "Not exactly. It didn't happen the way we planned it."

"'We?' Who's 'we,' Leo?"

"Twinkie and me. Who do you think?"

Maybe it's the mention of her name, maybe it's a night without sleep, but Hector's knees suddenly loosen, and he staggers. Leo catches him. "Easy man. Sit down, have some of this." He hands Hector his drink, guides him to the sofa, then goes back to grab his own.

"What the hell are you ..."

"Don't, Hec. I need you to listen to me. It's all fucked up now. I apologize, man. You weren't supposed to get hurt. I made her promise that."

Leo takes a seat cross-legged on the floor, as if they've just finished playing a string duet. "I met her in the summer, while you were gone," he says. "In no time she'd gotten into my brain and wouldn't let go. You understand. You're hot for her, too."

Hector looks away.

"Hey, it's okay. Nothing to be ashamed of. She wanted it that way."

Hector's face cooks with humiliation.

"I was here, dead broke," Leo continues. 'She was doing a story, had been poking around the orchestra, said she'd found out something scary. We got to talking, and hit it off. It took me, like, weeks to get into her pants, but I wouldn't give up." As if he's talking about a difficult passage in a sonata that he finally nailed.

"I've never met anyone like her, Hec. No one's ever made me feel like that. She just sets me on fire. When I'm with her I can't think. No, that's not right, I *am* thinking. I'm thinking about things that I wouldn't dream of without her. I think about greatness, Hec. About taking the big chance, doing something wild and risky. With her next to me, I can do it. I know I won't crash. It's like flying, Hec. You must have felt that just a little. Remember *Turandot*, the second riddle? "If you despair it grows cold. Dream of conquest, it catches fire."

The answer is blood.

"They were just words till I met her, Hec. Now I know what it's like to have my blood catch fire."

"Yeah, okay, Leo."

He sighs again. "I'm getting weird now, I know."

"Forget it." To keep from exploding, Hector has to wrestle

down the pack of demons pounding inside his chest: anger, frustration, despair, and envy of the most shameful kind. Suppressing them all, he asks, "What was the scary thing she found out?"

"That the orchestra had hired a real criminal, a triad guy named Yip Tak-tak, to take charge of the moving crew. She said Yip had to be using the orchestra for something, that no one like him would take such a lame job without a scheme of some kind."

"She knew about Yip?"

"All about him, yeah. She'd been investigating."

I'll bet she had, he thinks.

"We didn't know what he was up to. Twinkie asked me to help her out, do a little amateur detective work. I got a job in the orchestra library, got in the files, learned a little. Twinkie figured it out."

Hector's head begins to swim. "She figured it out? When?"

"We had the general idea that he was smuggling drugs before you came back from your summer break. We decided to rip the bastard off and get out of here. Twinkie knew some Taiwanese triads who'd buy the stuff. But first we needed to figure out what it was, how much, and how it was being moved, so we could steal it."

She knew it all when she met me. All those discoveries, she was leading me on, getting my juices going.

Hector looks at his friend, for the first time wonders who he really is. "I still don't get it. You want to steal ice from the triads and get yourselves killed, fine. But why did you get me involved?"

"Oh, man, that's fucked up, I know," he says, taking a good gulp of whiskey. "That's why I wanted you out of here. Even lined up a job in Switzerland. But you wouldn't go—you had to be a good guy and honor your contract. So later on, when we needed someone, you were around. Twinkie said you wouldn't get hurt or arrested or anything."

"Why did you need me?"

"Because the job wasn't finished. We needed to find out where the ice was, but I couldn't just go looking around, asking questions, and then disappear with the stuff. Yip would send his goons after me. So we decided I'd disappear at the beginning of the season. That did two things. It got me out of the orchestra, away from Yip, so he wouldn't suspect me when the ice got lifted. And it got you interested."

"And you knew if you disappeared, I'd look for you. And while I looked for you, I'd find out what Twinkie needed to know."

Leo nods, a bit sheepishly.

"Especially if I thought you were in trouble, or been kidnapped or murdered by Yip."

Leo nods again. "It all happened fast. Remember we were playing duets that day? I called Twinkie while you were in the bathroom. She didn't know I was at your place. When I told her, she threw a fit, told me to get out that minute. She said I had to sever myself from the orchestra completely or it wouldn't work."

"You had to leave your viola?"

"You were about to come out of the bathroom. I made a choice, man. With two million bucks, what do I need the viola for?"

And once I'd convinced myself he was in trouble, Hector thinks, *she could get me to do anything. Break into the Symphony office, steal drugs. She'd played us both like a pipe organ.*

"She said that you and Yip had a fight. You were looking around in back of the Cultural Centre, and he caught you."

Leo nods. "We cooked that up to get you interested. I've never met the guy."

"Those sunflower seed shells on the floor above you ..."

"Twinkie's idea. Same with making this place look like it'd been searched, hiding the documents in the dehumidifier. Shit, I probably shouldn't be telling you this. You're not even supposed to be here."

Leo's sheer cruelty amazes him. But perhaps he deserves it for being so vulnerable, for being so petrified of abandonment in the first place. A feeling of satisfaction settles over Hector, as if this betrayal is the solution to an age-old mystery, the last blank in a crossword puzzle he's been doing since birth. *Act like a See-Fat...*

"So you got me to steal the ice," he says, "and now I'm in the shit."

The comment seems to agitate Leo. "That's not the way it was supposed to happen. You've got to believe me, Hec. You're my man. The way we arranged it, you'd take the stuff, deliver it to Twinkie, and show up for work the next day. Who'd guess it was you? Nothing pointed to you, right?"

"Safe? Skinwic tried to fucking kill me!" All at once he sees Skinwic's face, his dive off the balcony, the faraway shriek of a passerby.

Leo shrugs. "Hec, man, I just don't understand that. There was no reason for him to come after you."

"Oh no? Twinkie took me with her when she taunted Mulqueen. Mulqueen would have gone back to Yip, and told him that Twinkie and I were a problem. But Yip would never have found Twinkie—I sure as hell couldn't. So Yip would have to have come after me, Leo."

"How would he have known you two were hanging out together?"

"He recognized me from a concert. Bonson also saw us together. So don't tell me Twinkie didn't know she was putting me in danger."

"She wouldn't have done that on purpose. She knows we're friends, man."

"You were friends with Chiu as well. Look what happened to him."

That knocks Leo back. "No, Hec. She's not responsible for that. No way. If I thought Chiu was in danger I'd have warned him."

"So he wouldn't get in the way of your big score, right? You know, Leo, you still haven't answered my question. Why did you do this? You're the one guy I know who lived for the music. You never cared about money. What got into you?"

Leo twiddles his empty glass, gets up, pours another drink.

"I think you know, Hec. You know what it's like being cut to pieces by the thing you love most of all."

They look at each other.

"I spent all my life chasing beauty," Leo says. "And believe me, that's one fucking hard thing to do. Not a lot of people get that."

Hector says nothing. Leo takes a sip of the bourbon, then another.

"You know about Bo Ya, Hec?"

Hector shakes his head.

"He was a musician in China, long ago. They say he just played for himself, until one day he found a woodcutter who understood his music. After that, Bo Ya lived just to play for that man. He played for him every day. Then one day the woodcutter died. And Bo Ya stopped playing.

"Well, Hec, I've been playing for twenty years, and I haven't even met the goddam woodcutter yet. I have nothing to show for it. No reputation, no recognition, not a goddam dime. Everywhere I've lived I've been low man on the totem pole. It's as bad in America as it is in Hong Kong—they tell you how wonderful art is, then they treat artists like shit. Every other fucker in the world gets the big blowjob for owning a factory that makes fly swatters, for trading stocks or designing bikinis, but not for playing Mozart.

Not even Mozart. I'm tired of it, Hec. And Twinkie has shown me the way out."

The smells in Leo's flat seems to thicken, transforming the air into a miasma so putrid that Hector's lungs want to reject it altogether.

"Don't you care how you get your money?" Hector says.

Leo's green eyes flash. "Does Ambrose Wan care how he gets his? Does Hong Kong care? All that matters is you get it."

Twinkie is deep in Leo's blood, polluting his desires, distorting his judgment. She's found a way to use his passionate nature to her own ends.

"So what will you do with the ice?"

"Sell it, transfer the money out of here, set up an investment company where they can't touch it. Twinkie's got some ideas about China trade. They've got more than a billion people, and all of them want telephones, computers, cars, gadgets. We've taught a whole world how to want stuff, and no place wants it more than China."

Hector feels drained, numb. "Okay, you win," he says. "Do what you want. But I'm in deep shit, and so is Zen. You need to help us out of this."

"Zen? What's she got to do with this?"

"Yip has her. He'll kill her if I don't deliver the ice to the parking garage at the Mai Sun Shopping Center tonight."

That shuts Leo up. For a couple of minutes he thinks, finishes his drink. Hector hoped that the threat would jar Leo back to the real world, but he's too far gone. It's just a high-stakes mahjong game now, and Leo's figuring out which tile to play.

"Stay here," Leo says. "It's probably the safest place for you. I'll take care of it."

Hec stands. "Forget it. I'm coming with you."

"Won't work, Hec."

"You've already fucked me over. You think I'm going to let you walk out and decide on your own what to do with me?"

"I said forget it. I can handle Twinkie, you can't. Wait here."

"I don't trust you."

"You don't have a choice, Hec."

Leo walks out the door.

CHAPTER 59

"**HOSELL LAI IS** waiting to be questioned, sir," says Ears. "Are you going to notify Narcotics as well?"

"No," says Lok. "This is still a murder investigation. We can hand him to Narcotics on a plate after we've sorted things out." And there is plenty to sort. If Skinwic killed Milkie Tang, Lok still has to establish a motive. If he didn't, then Yip is still a good bet. And in any case, Skinwic's killer is still at large, so it's best to keep a tight rein on the case.

Narcotics will have to be brought in eventually. A bag of pure methamphetamine hydrochloride—ice, what some call *shabu*—was found behind a bookcase in *See-fat's* apartment. *See-fat's* fingerprints are on it. It stands to reason he was dealing the stuff, perhaps to support his own habit. He must have fallen afoul of Yip, who sent Skinwic to take care of him. Lok has a hard time imagining a different chain of events. It would take a pretty stupid *gweilo* to attack a Red Pole's follower and expect to live. But it takes a pretty stupid *gweilo* to deal drugs in Hong Kong in the first place. In any case, *See-fat* is no innocent who's been dragged down in someone else's dirt.

Big Pang fills the doorframe with his body. He's holding a

transcript of a phone report. "Sir, *See-fat's* been sighted."

"Where?"

"At the offices of the *South China Morning Post*, around ten this morning. A reporter says he stole something from a rubbish bin."

"What's that supposed to mean?"

"He was poking around the desk of one Twinkie Choi."

That girl again. She's turning up everywhere.

"Did you check with Million Man? He's looking her up."

"I just asked him. She hasn't taken a flight or ferry out of Hong Kong, as far as we can tell."

Wonderful, Lok thinks. *Everyone who could give us info about our case has disappeared.*

CHAPTER 60

AT FIVE P.M. a key rattles in the door lock. For a moment Hector considers hiding, but dismisses the thought. Leo enters, carrying the duffel. He lays it on the floor with a solid thump that strikes Hector in the soles of his feet.

"Here you go, man," Leo says. "Signed, sealed, and delivered."

It's the same dull grey bag, bulging like a well-fed leech.

"What did Twinkie say?"

"She understands. She doesn't want anything to happen to Zen." He pushes the bag of poison to one side, stands it against the wall.

"That's it? After all this she's giving it up?"

"She has another plan."

"I'll bet she does."

"Never mind. Let me handle Twinkie. Underneath she's good."

Right.

"Are you sure you want to do this?" Leo says. "Yip is one dangerous fucker."

"No choice. I can't just let Zen die."

"Well, you're dangerous too, man. You proved that." He turns to leave. "Take care and watch yourself." And once again, Leo's gone.

He checks his cellphone for the time. With just under four hours to go, Leo has delivered a plan of sorts into Hector's lap. He shoves the duffel in a closet and takes off.

CHAPTER 61

HOSELL LAI LOOKS up at Lok, his eyes wide, his large, fleshy mouth agape, his hair wrung into an oily tangle by his own trembling fingers. The two are alone in the interview room.

"I've never heard of Milkie Tang!" Hosell says. "I've never heard of the girl! Who is she?

"I'll ask the questions," says Lok. "Did you ever see Yip Tak-tak with a bar girl at VSOP?"

"No. I don't socialize with him. I'm just a fiddle maker. He's the big man."

"Can you tell me where the big man is now, Hosell?"

He shakes his head.

"Please speak out loud."

"No, I can't."

"When did you last talk to him?"

"I called him last night, around midnight."

"Why?"

"Just business."

"Do you know who Twinkie Choi is?

"Who?

"A reporter for the *Post*. She followed you in Shenzhen."

He says nothing, but the sweat on his forehead betrays a new, deeper fear.

"Do you know Skinwic Sze?"

"Yes."

"What can you tell me about him?"

"He works for Yip. I don't know him too well."

Lok sits and looks at Hosell, says nothing for a minute. The silence drains another cup of sweat from him.

"Hosell," he says. "Think carefully. Why did you call Yip last night?

"I told you, it was just business."

"Did it have to do with the broken instruments in your workshop?"

"I ..."

Lok cuts him off. "Think carefully before you answer, Hosell."

"I told him something was missing from my studio."

"Drugs? *Shabu*?"

His hands begin to tremble.

"Yes, Hosell, we know. You'd better tell us."

Cornered, Hosell starts to talk. He tells how he was brought in to help Yip smuggle ice into Hong Kong and out to Europe. How he visited the storehouse in Shenzhen that night to get an idea of the weight and quantity of drugs he'd have to conceal.

"Later, Hosell. Right now I'm concerned with Skinwic. He's dead. Did you know that?"

In answer, Hosell turns as white as a rice dumpling.

"Did you kill him?" Lok asks.

Absurd as the accusation is, it has the intended effect on Hosell. "No, I didn't know anything about it, I swear! I told Yip the *shabu* was gone, and he just hung up on me!"

"Where was he when you called?"

"I don't know. I called his cellphone."

"Think back, Hosell. Do you remember a man named *See-fat*?"

"I know who he is. A bass player. I'm working on his bass." Said as if he plans to return to his workshop later and take up where he left off.

"What's his connection to this? Did he see the *shabu* at your place?"

Hosell shakes his head. "Impossible. It was in the back room, in the cases. He couldn't have known about it."

"Who do you think stole it, then?"

He shrugs. "Someone crazy. Someone who wants to die."

Lok had hoped Hosell would tie things together, but he hasn't. One person is still an enigma. Sure, he'll find out that *See-fat* lives up to his name, an asshole who tried to cheat a *Sun Yee On* Red Pole. Skinwic will be a dead crook with a history of greed and violence. Nothing new there. Yip will be a thief and possibly a murderer.

But who will Twinkie Choi turn out to be? How is she part of this bloodbath? No one knows her, no one has a thing to say about her. Yet she's involved with everyone. Until he finds Twinkie—or finds out who she really is—this case will not close for him.

CHAPTER 62

AT EIGHT FIFTY-EIGHT P.M. Hector walks down the ramp beneath the Mai Sun Shopping Center, treading gingerly to muffle the sound of his own footsteps. They'll have privacy—at this time of day the carpark is less than half full, so no cars will be going all the way to the bottom level to find a space. Hector rounds the bend to P5 and sees Yip and two of his men posted by a gold Benz. Across from him are the only other vehicles on that parking level, a blue Camry and a white Nissan van.

Hector has walked here from Leo's flat, maybe a mile away, and his shirt is soaked with sweat, his skin chafed from rubbing against clammy underwear.

He stops well away from Yip and his henchman, whom he recognizes from the orchestra moving crew. One is slim and a couple of inches shorter than Yip. He's wearing a flat-top and a camel-hair blazer over a blue silk shirt. The other is stockier, outfitted in fashionable black. They're better dressed than they usually appear at work, if what they do for the orchestra is work.

"Where's Zenobia?" Hector calls to Yip, words resonating on filthy concrete. He scans the whole level, sees no other human. A security camera dangles from the ceiling, but someone's probably done a vasectomy on it. Either that, or Yip has given security the evening off.

Yip: "You have it?"

"Right here," Hector says, nodding toward the bag on his shoulder. "Where is she?"

"You'll get her. Give me the bag."

"Not till I see her."

"She's not here."

"Then forget it!"

Hector turns to walk away, hoping that his insulting gesture will unsettle Yip, make him think he's not fully in control. Instead, he hears another voice shout "*See-fat!*"

Hector looks back, sees flat-top holding an automatic, dashes toward the nearest pillar. A shot fires, loud as a bomb blast, reverberating on the concrete walls. Flat-top sprawls on the pavement. Fashionable black draws his own gun, starts to aim it well to Hector's right. Another blast, and the henchman dances backward and collapses on his mate.

The Benz roars to life. Yip backs up and tears up the ramp, tires shrieking.

The two henchmen's bodies haven't moved. The air smells of cordite.

Khan jumps out of the white van, holding his shotgun barrel up, finger on trigger, ready to shoot. "Are you all right, Mr. Hector?"

"I think so. What ..."

"Wait here. We need the boss." With surprising speed for such a beefy man Khan charges up the ramp and into the stairwell. Hector stares at the carnage once again. A crimson halo now encircles the bodies on the pavement.

Another squeal echoes through the carpark as Yip rounds the second corner, out of sight. Then comes a metallic smash, obviously Yip clipping a fender on the turn. Forgetting Khan's order, Hector takes off up the ramp. On P4 he finds Khan running toward him.

"Jesus, Khan. What's happened?"

Khan is breathing heavily from his sprint. "What I was afraid of. I made a bad mistake. We should have hidden the bag till we were shown Miss Zenobia." For the first time Hector sees something like doubt in Khan's face.

Two hours ago Khan's nephew Mohammed had driven the van in, parked it, and walked away, leaving Khan hidden inside. He'd been waiting, silently listening and watching through a pinhole he'd drilled through the Nissan emblem. Yip had checked the van earlier through its window, seen nothing but a pile of Pakistani rugs.

"Quickly now, Mr. Hector." He whistles a long, keening tune and jogs back to where the two henchmen lie. By the time he reaches the bodies a boy has joined him. He has dark skin and wavy hair—obviously Mohammed. The two of them roll the bodies in rugs and dump them in the truck. A cellphone drops from flat-top's pocket and bounces off Khan's foot. Hector grabs it.

"You'd better not keep anything, sir." He plucks the phone from Hector's hand and tosses it in the back.

Mohammed hastily wipes up the worst of the blood with some rags, shoves them in a plastic bag, tosses them in the back of the van. "Get in, please," he says. He's probably eighteen but looks fourteen.

Before Hector can close the door the van is shooting up the ramp, Khan at the wheel, Mohammed in the middle, the bag of ice stuffed between Hector's knees and the dashboard. No one glances at the cargo in back.

"We must find Yip," says Khan. "Make him the same offer. This time we'll see that he doesn't get away. He's frightened of us now. We just need to keep him from getting the bag until we're sure Miss Zenobia is safe."

"Shit, I'm sorry I got you into this."

"We need to find Miss Zenobia. I hoped to take care of the two followers and catch Yip, but I was not fast enough.

"They were going to kill me."

Khan is silent. The Pushtun drives slowly, carefully, yielding to the taxis that flow through the traffic stream like overagitated red corpuscles.

Khan seems untroubled by the bloodbath in the carpark. His face is the same serene mask he wears in front of the jewelry store while scanning passersby for the robber who never comes. Had Khan ever fired his gun with intent to kill? Hector has no idea. Though he was raised in the traditions of the great Pushtun tribe, Khan had lived all his life in Hong Kong, far from his Wazir kin and the Mahsud tribesmen whom his grandfather reveled in shooting at from time to time.

Hector takes stock of what he has left. His life, thanks to Khan. That, and his one bargaining chip: the bag between his knees.

"Khan," Hector says, "let me see that cellphone." Khan gestures to Mohammed, who climbs over the seat into the back and returns with the phone. Hector studies it for a minute.

"He probably has his boss on speed dial," he says. But which number? He tries the first. From underneath the bodies in the back pipes On Top of Old Smokey. *F-Major.*

"Getting close," he says, pushing 2.

"*Wai?*"

It's Yip.

"Where is she?" Hector says.

From the earpiece comes a string of Chinese curses.

In Cantonese, Hector says, "You give me girl, I give you bag." Little better than pidgin, but understandable.

Yip switches to English, mentions a time—four a.m.—a place, some directions. The last thing he says is, "Leave Ah Singh at home, or she dies." Then he hangs up.

Ah Singh, from the Indian surname, is a typical derogatory term for anyone from India, Pakistan, or Sri Lanka.

"It's set up," says Hector to Khan. "He's really mad now."

"Where are you meeting him, sir?"

"On the waterfront, near Yau Ma Tei, where the typhoon shelter used to be. On the other side of the Harbour Tunnel road. What's there?"

"Not much, Mr. Hector. It's all reclaimed land. No one's built on it. Tonight I'll take a look, arrange a place to make the trade. This time we'll ..."

"No, Khan. You've done enough. I can't involve you anymore."

"Mr. Hector, I told you, I'm doing this for Miss Zenobia. I have to get her back."

"The best way to get her back is to let me do the trade. If he sees you again, he'll kill her. That's what he just told me."

"I'm worried, Mr. Hector."

"So am I."

"Take my shotgun."

"No. He'd see it."

He says something to Muhammad, who reaches in his jacket, pulls out camel hair's automatic. He checks the magazine, replaces it, cocks it as casually as a shopkeeper works a cash register.

Hector shakes his head. "It would only get me killed, Khan. I can't shoot guns. The only thing that might work is to convince him I'm no threat, that I'll leave him alone if we get Zenobia back."

Muhammad replaces the pistol in his jacket.

They drive through the tunnel, back to Hong Kong Island, now ablaze in neon. At a streetlight a taxi driver pulls up alongside, sees Khan, yells *"ga le gai fan!"*—chicken curry!—then cackles to himself. Khan ignores him.

"Mister Hector, you should understand. My grandfather, great-grandfather, they all fought the British. My father joined the British, held a rifle on the Hong Kong border. Now there are no British to fight against, and no British to fight with. So now I fight for a Chinese family, the Chans, who are good to me, and who I have promised to protect."

Hector nods. "Just let me try this one, Khan. If I end up dead, then you can do whatever you have to."

The van slows down and stops at a corner in North Point. Hector steps out, then leans in and clasps Khan's hand one more time.

"What'll you do with … ?" Hector gestures to the corpses in the back.

Khan smiles, for the first time tonight. "Don't worry about that, Mr. Hector. Just take care of yourself."

CHAPTER 63

MILLION MAN WALKS into the Hot Room and joins the others.

"We've found something," he says. Hector Siefert booked a flight to Mexico City for the twenty-first. That's three days from now."

"Anyone still think he's innocent?" asks Old Ko.

"When was the booking made?" asks Lok.

"Two weeks ago."

"Just one passenger?"

Million Man nods and hands the report to Lok, who checks it over. "Have them advise us if the reservation is changed," Lok says. "He's reserved 19A. Check the rest of the plane. He might be alone, but there might be someone else who's keeping a distance to avoid attracting attention. And find out what other reservations were made to Mexico City within three days on either side."

"Looks pretty obvious," says Old Ko. "He planned to rip off the drugs from Yip and take off to Mexico."

Lok made the same inference, but isn't convinced. "This man *See-fat* isn't doing what he's supposed to. He's on the run. He's been dealing drugs, he's just killed a pretty frightening character in his own house, and we're after him. So where does he go? Does he give himself up? Try to catch the first flight out before we can even figure out whose flat Skinwic fell from? No, he goes to the offices of the *Post*, to look for a reporter named Twinkie Choi. Why?"

"Maybe we have it wrong," says Pang. "Suppose he's innocent, and needs this reporter to prove it. She's been investigating Yip herself. Maybe she knows something about Yip's operation."

"How do you explain Mexico?" says Lok

"Not against the law to go to Mexico, is it?"

"We found the ice in his flat," says Old Ko.

"Maybe Skinwic put it there. Maybe that's what the fight was about." Pang's voice is fading. He doesn't even believe it himself.

"Then why didn't he get rid of it after Skinwic went over?"

"He could have panicked."

Lok nods, unconvinced.

Ears: "Why did he go to the *Post*, sir?"

"He wasn't going to the *Post*," says Lok. "He was going to Twinkie Choi. He avoided everyone else. This wasn't about making a big declaration of innocence. He needed her and her alone. That suggests he's not clean."

"So she's in on the smuggling too?" asks Ears.

"Well, she's gone. That should tell you something," says Old Ko.

Million man returns later on with a list of flight bookings. Lok reads the list, stops halfway down, at 19B. The seat next to *See-fat* has been reserved under the name Jenny Choi Loi-tai. Both seats were booked within ten minutes of each another.

Jenny Choi. The name illuminates some long-dark chamber in Lok's memory. Perhaps it's a corridor that will lead him home.

"It seems *See-fat* has booked a flight with a dead girl," he says.

CHAPTER 64

HOW DOES SHE do it, Leo thinks—sense how worried he is, second-guess his fears and calm them. She has her own way of helping him forget the perils of this insane adventure. They're sprawled naked on the floor, glazed with sweat, in the flat of a *Post* photographer who's on holiday for a couple of weeks.

The sex has long left the realm of intimacy, crossed the pale into a hot and frantic kingdom of pain and release. No one can do what Twinkie does, not that sweet torment with her fingers and tongue that makes him breathe like a marathon runner, then beg like a condemned prisoner, then moan like a man being flayed alive. Where did she learn that stuff? She won't tell.

He burrows his face in the nape of her neck, licks the salty sweat, runs his hands over her body one more time, as if trying to convince himself that this perfect human form is truly his alone to ravish.

"It's time to call," she says. She bites him gently on the shoulder.

"Suppose so." He grabs the phone, which sits by a potted schefflera whose leaves are shriveling. Twinkie borrowed the flat on the condition that she water the plants.

Leo makes the call.

"Hec? That you? What the fuck happened?"

"You tell me, Leo."

"What's that supposed to mean? Did you get Zen back?"

"No. They didn't have her. I tried to walk away, and they pulled guns on me."

"Jesus, Hec. Are you okay?"

"Yeah. Let me talk to Twinkie."

"Forget it, Hec."

"My name's on TV. They're officially looking for me now. They found a bag of ice with my fingerprints on it."

"Where?"

"Where do you think? At my flat. Your girlfriend planted it. 'Think of what it does to people,' she said. Well, she's right about that."

"Twinkie didn't plant it."

"Don't bullshit me, Leo."

"What are you going to do now?"

"I called Yip and set it up for tomorrow morning."

"How do you know he won't pull the gun again?"

"I don't. I'm going to hide the stuff, try to get him alone somehow. I don't know."

"Sounds stupid."

"Won't be the first stupid thing I've done."

"Where are you now? You safe? We need to talk."

"Doesn't matter."

"Where?"

"Never mind." The phone clicks off.

"Hec? Hec?" He slams down the phone. "Shit!"

"What happened?" asks Twinkie.

"I'm not sure. He has another meeting set up with Yip. I think he's going to try to get the upper hand."

"Where is he now?"

"He wouldn't say."

She clutches his arm with a vehemence that startles him. "That's all you had to find out, where he was! Why couldn't you do that?"

"We've lost him. He doesn't trust me anymore."

"Then what good are you?" Her voice cuts him like a razor. "You were supposed to shoot Yip and his men after the handoff, after the girl was safe."

"He says you planted a bag of ice with his fingerprints on it for the cops to find."

"That's bullshit! He's out of his mind! Listen—I let you give him the ice for one reason."

"Because Zenobia was in trouble."

"No. Because Zenobia is a witness to all this. We need to get to her, buy her off. You were supposed to get the ice."

"He never gave it to Yip! What was I supposed to do, shoot Hec?"

She doesn't answer.

Leo had seen the whole thing. Crouching behind a pillar one level up, he waited for the handoff, a Black Star 9mm in his belt. Then Khan, this crazy Pushtun who guards Zen's family shop, jumped out from a panel truck and blasted Yip's men. Yip saved his own ass, took off without the bag. Leo dived behind a Lexus before Yip streaked by. He stayed out of sight when Khan tried to chase Yip up the ramp.

If Hec and Zen had been alone, he'd have taken back the ice. But with Khan there, no way.

Twinkie places her hands on Leo's shoulders, stares into his face, forces him to stare back. The affection has drained from her face now. "We need to find him," she says. "Get him before he does something really stupid and ruins it all. Now, think! Where is he?"

He's shaken by her fury. "Listen ... let me think. He was in a public place. I heard the TV, the races on in the background."

"What else?"

He closes his eyes, tries to remember the conversation, the sounds behind Hector's tired voice. "Dishes. Some dishes being collected, stacked. You know the way they bang together."

"What else?"

There is something else. A funny sound. Not exactly rhythmic, but steady, insistent. *Click ... click ... click ...* he closes his eyes, tries to put a place, a time to the sound.

Click ... click ... click ...

"Christ, Twinkie. He's at Poon's. Those chess players."

"Where?"

"A restaurant, North Point!"

"Well, come on. We have to follow him to the meeting." She's grabbing her underwear off the floor.

"He won't get hurt, will he?"

He feels her arm snake around his waist. "No, baby. We're here to protect him. And the plan's still good, Leo. We can do this."

CHAPTER 65

"SHOULD WE WAIT for Big Pang?" asks Old Ko. Lok has gathered most of the team to learn what information Old Ko could dig up on Jenny Choi, the girl whose name is on the ticket to Mexico.

"No need," says Lok. "He's at the VSOP Club. I sent him there to sweat our friend Steinway Fung. Steinway does business with Yip, probably has a way to contact him."

"Okay, here we go." Old Ko adjusts his glasses and reads. "Jenny Choi Loi-tai, 21, found dead in her flat in TST. Worked at Lucky Man Topless on Hankow Road. Found by her roommate, Lydia Mo, another bar girl. She closed off the doors and windows, fired up a charcoal barbecue, then took a drink and went to sleep. Died of carbon monoxide poisoning, ruled a suicide. Questioned co-workers at the club, including Yip Tak-tak, who had the bouncership—unofficially, of course. Yip had an alibi for the entire day, but it was pretty clearly suicide anyway."

Death by barbecue is a favorite of young people these days. The charcoal gradually eats up the air and replaces it with an asphyxiating gas. Lovesick teenagers and pressured honor students rent rooms on Lok's home island of Cheung Chau to make their final exit, thinking they've found a painless, quiet way to die.

Lok knows better. He's seen the agony in their faces, the blood on their hands from trying to claw open locked doors.

Lok takes the sheet from Ko, scans the summaries of the interviews. "Here it is," he says.

Yip said that he introduced the victim to the club eleven months previous. He had met her through Tang Yee-fun, another of the bar hostesses.

Tang Yee-fun. Milkie Tang. That's two-thirds of the connection. The final third is printed on the bottom of the sheet.

Parents deceased. One sister, Choi Dai-tai, is studying in Canada.

Milkie Tang, Jenny Choi, and now Choi Dai-tai—English name Twinkie Choi. Three women connected to Yip Tak-tak. Two, Milkie and Jenny, were lured into prostitution by him, and are dead. The other, Twinkie, has been following him secretly.

Something occurs to Lok. "Ears, ask your girlfriend Mrs. Liu if she ever saw a woman visit Milkie Tang."

"Description?"

"Early twenties, attractive, 160 to 162 centimeters, hair about this long. No glasses."

Ears nods and dashes back to the big room to make the call.

"You think Twinkie Choi is connected to Milkie?" asks Old Ko.

"Yes. Twinkie Choi has a grudge against Milkie Tang and Yip Tak-tak. They started her sister whoring. They're the ones she'd blame for Jenny's death." Rightfully, he could add. So many girls succeed in quitting their life of prostitution by quitting their life. "And just as Yip's follower is killed and his associates arrested, she goes on a three-week leave. Reporters don't do that when they're covering a story. It doesn't add up. Old Ko, I want you to pick up this Twinkie Choi, see what we can get out of her. No charge yet. We don't have proof she had anything to do with Milkie's death. Maybe we can get her on our side, make her understand we're after Yip."

"I'll dig up her address," says Old Ko. He leaves.

Ten minutes later an unsmiling Big Pang walks in.

"No cooperation," he says. "I tried to put some fear into Steinway, but he's got plenty of that anyway. Yip has him by the balls."

"I expected that," says Lok, easing Big Pang's loss of face.

"It was crowded," Pang continues, "and Steinway stayed where the music was loudest, trying to keep me off guard. Said he didn't know where Yip was. Wouldn't tell me anything. He's good and scared."

If Big Pang can't get anything out of him, he must be scared, Lok thinks.

"Maybe you should talk to him, sir."

"No, I wouldn't do any better," Lok says. He picks up his phone and punches an extension.

"Fu, I need you."

Million Man gives Lok a startled look. "Sir, if you want, I'll give Steinway a scare he'll never forget."

"Big Pang," Lok says, replacing the receiver. "Could you leave us for a moment?" Pang disappears.

"Million Man," Lok says after Pang departs, "I'm sending you with Fu, and for a reason. You're about to learn who Fu is, and why some jobs can only be done by a Station Sergeant. Follow him, but stay back, let him do the talking. Learn something."

"Yes, sir."

"And I don't want any more practical jokes, got it?"

Million Man, his tongue cinched, merely nods. Lok is about to leave when Ears approaches.

"Mrs. Liu remembers a girl matching Twinkie's description," says Ears. "She visited Milkie from time to time. She was there the night of the murder."

CHAPTER 66

FU DESCENDS THE red-carpeted stairs and walks into the turbulent fertility rite that plays in the booths of VSOP after sundown, seven days a week. A tuxedoed Filipino quartet fills the air with a jaunty version of *I Just Called to Say I Love You*. The place is jammed with Chinese businessmen in pearl-grey suits, Americans and Germans in polo shirts, all grinning and laughing as they toast blonde Ukrainians and pat coffee-colored Filipino thighs.

Flanked by Million Man and Big Pang, Fu walks toward the bar in a straight line, ignoring the door hostess's greeting. The bartender raises his eyebrows to him, expecting an order. He gets one.

"Tell Steinway to get his stinking ass out here now."

The bartender gives him a look and disappears.

"What do you want?" says the bouncer, six-two, a body of pure muscle hidden under a sport jacket. The man rocks gently on the balls of his feet, ready to launch himself like an arrow from a crossbow if Fu so much as taps his chest with a finger.

"I'm here to see Steinway, not you."

"He's busy."

"Give him these." Fu reaches in his trouser pocket, then slams his hand down hard on the bar. He pulls it away to reveal three tiny yellow chips on the wood counter. The bouncer reaches for them, halts his hand in mid-air before touching them. Big Pang and Million Man look on silently.

"Do it," Fu says.

The bouncer glares at Fu, sweeps up the objects, melts into the crowd.

It takes another minute for the manager to appear, time Fu uses to ignore the bartender's existence. Behind him a Brit and a Yank are deep in a discussion.

"Why don't you go to Delhi? That's where we run our customer care centers."

"Good English there."

"Right. We'd do it here, even with the wages, but the English standard's just not high enough. It's the way they teach it here, I think."

"Just laziness, if you want my opinion."

A minute later Steinway emerges. When he sees Fu he freezes, then whispers a few words to the bartender, who turns up the lights and silences the band. All at once the club's magic dissolves, replaced by halogen-illuminated trashiness. Couples and groups, knocked off guard by the change, fall mute. The VSOP Nightclub is about as sexy as a school gym.

Steinway Fung approaches Fu, passes him, and loops around the bar to keep a distance, real and symbolic, between them. Fu leans forward till his face is an inch from the manager's.

"Get me Yip."

Steinway stands still. His fear fills the room like the reek of a water buffalo.

"Don't know where he is." He flashes his teeth, whose brilliant whiteness sets off the gaps between them. They're both ignoring Million Man and Big Pang.

Fu grabs a handful of polo shirt, jerks him close, asks again.

"Where is he?"

"I told you ..."

"Did you get my present, Steinway?"

Steinway says nothing.

"I gave you one nickname. Do you want another? Right now, in front of your customers?"

"Listen, I ..."

"No, you listen. I'm going in the back room. You're going to follow me in, and then you're going to tell me exactly where Yip is. If you don't, I'll walk home with your balls in my left pocket." Signaling his men to stay, Fu begins to move slowly to the back.

Steinway gulps and follows Fu, an arm's length away. When they're both in his office, door closed, the manager speaks.

"I'm not supposed to tell you. I'm not even supposed to know."

Fu says nothing.

"Look ... Yip has an arrangement with a coach rental company that stores buses near the Yau Ma Tei waterfront. On the reclamation, where the Typhoon Shelter used to be. There's an old container he uses for an office, a couple of sheds." They both know what the arrangement is. The company gives Yip the space, in return keeping the buses' tires and headlights intact from month to month.

Steinway continues. "A few months ago Yip took delivery of a load of DVD players. He needed help unloading them, so he took me there, just that once. Told me to forget I saw the place."

"So what makes you think he's there now?"

Steinway looks down at the floor. Fu waits, skewering Steinway with his eyes.

"You can't say where you found out," he says, finally.

Again Fu is silent.

"I heard that a shipment of photocopiers came in today from China. He'd be out there today to supervise. I don't know if he's still there, but ..."

Fu turns to leave. Steinway grabs his arm.

"Wait. Please, don't tell him I talked to you."

Fu shakes off the arm. "Keep the teeth," he says. "But get out of line, and I'll come back for your balls."

He moves through the club as the lights once again dim. The band starts up, and Million Man and Pang fall in behind Fu. By the door Pang passes Mary Ma.

"Get Yip," she whispers to him. "My girls want him gone."

CHAPTER 67

HECTOR STARES ACROSS the eight lanes of the West Kowloon Highway, sees nothing but a grey-black void in the distance. A taxi could take him across, but the driver would remember delivering a *gweilo* to such an obscure location. The only alternative seems like madness. Shouldering the bag, he embraces the madness and steps into the road.

Traffic is sparse at this hour, so he clears the first five lanes easily. When a Kowloon Dairy truck hurtles into view, Hector picks up his pace.

A horn blasts like a trumpeting elephant. *F-natural.* The driver slows, and Hector reaches the railing, chucks the bag over and leaps after it. Behind him, the horn's wail Dopplers down to E before it cuts off.

Hector studies the terrain in the sodium light. The reclamation is nothing more than flat earth dotted with patches of wild grass, new ground that hasn't settled enough to be built on yet. In any other city these neglected lots would be found everywhere. Here they have to be newly built. Every scrap of land larger than a ping-pong table is already turning a profit for someone.

For decades the Chinese border and Mao's army prevented

expansion to the north, so the Hong Kong Chinese built into the ocean. Much of the city's most valuable land was created by mammoth developers, minor gods who flattened mountains and parted the seas.

Hector's eyes adjust to the light, revealing some chain link fencing, and behind it a row of motor coaches. Nearby is a landscaping machine, a pile of bricks, a truck.

The container near the bus lot by the water, Yip had said.

And there it is, a 20-foot container parked across the field, the faded COSCO letters on its side.

Instinctively Hector crouches as he walks, sticking close to anything that will give him cover: a bulldozer, a pile of rusting reinforcement bars. He reaches a wooden shed in which a security guard might have dozed and read girlie magazines during the construction of the new shoreline.

Further on, the ground opens into a cement-lined hole, from which protrudes a steel ladder. He peers in, sees what looks like a pile of clothes. Then he has to fight the sudden rush of bile that charges up his throat as a pair of lifeless eyes meet his. Khan's eyes.

Stringing muttered words into some kind of incoherent prayer, Hector descends into the hole, which is really the mouth of some kind of tunnel, and which smells of damp earth and the sea. Khan is indeed dead, judging from his blood-drenched shirt and the gash in his throat.

CHAPTER 68

THE TEAM IS together now. Old Ko and Million Man have returned from Twinkie Choi's empty flat, having posted a UB man there in case she returns. Calls have been made to the airlines and immigration to see if she's made it out somehow, but now Yip is the more pressing matter. Either Yip killed Milkie, or he can pin it on Skinwic. Either way, the case is cleared.

Fu did what was asked of him. Like many of the old Station Sergeants, he's tough as they come, the oldest shark in the water. He's explained to Lok where the hangout is, why it's likely Yip would be holed up there now.

Lok phones K.K. Kwan, who had been asleep, to let him know the next step: pick up Yip at a location where he's known to seek refuge with his followers.

Kwan says to proceed, watch out, report back.

Lok has never been to that part of the waterfront—it was nothing but water when Yau Ma Tei was his beat as a constable—but his driver will know how to get there. Like the place where Milkie's body was found, it's a white expanse on the station map labeled No Beat Defined. This case is ending right where it began, in a place that doesn't exist, where no one belongs.

CHAPTER 69

THIS CITY NEVER darkens. Where once a lonely moon shimmered above the Tang Dynasty poets, office towers glow like paper lanterns, and neon beer logos jostle one another in a silent aerial turf war.

Hector shrinks from the betraying light, tries to blend into the rough surface of a sewer pipe that's as tall as he is.

Suppressing the thought of Khan's nearby corpse, he scopes the terrain for a place to hide the bag. Facing Yip while carrying the dope would be suicide.

He's aware of a dull warmth creeping up his body as he crouches. Eight hours after sunset the noontime heat still leaches out from the gravel beneath him. There's not even a wisp of sea breeze to cool a sweaty brow, wash away the exhaust-filled air, dispel the reek of the harbor.

The white shipping container lies some three hundred yards away. Hector edges along a pile of sandbags till he comes upon a cart-mounted cement mixer. He stashes the ice and sets out toward the container.

A rustle of gravel freezes him.

A hundred feet away, near the water, a man is taking a seat on a waist-high pile of steel beams. He's young, Chinese, dressed in chinos and a dark jacket, his head down as if praying. He has to be a guard. No one wears a jacket outside in the subtropical inferno, except to hide a gun.

The man glances toward Hector, but apparently he sees nothing, for he lowers his head again to study something in his hands, something small and metallic.

Hector silently retraces his steps to the pile of steel reinforcement bars—rebars, they're called. He grabs one that's about three feet long and as thick as his thumb.

No way can he jump the sentry, not from here. He'd walk right into a bullet. But there is a way to get behind the guard.

He pads back to the hole by the shed, eases down the ladder, and slips into the black throat of the tunnel, pausing for a last glance at Khan's body. His goal is the patch of moonlight at the other end.

The walls of the tunnel are new cinderblock, strung with still-shiny pipes, cables, and junction boxes. Hector walks slowly, cushioning every step, conscious that sound is his worst enemy now. One good echo and the sentry will peer in the tunnel to find the easiest shot a killer could want.

He's about ten feet from the exit when he hears the tattoo of wavelets slapping against pilings. The tunnel is a storm drain, funneling the wash from typhoons into the harbor.

He emerges from the drain at the seawall and scales a steel ladder without making a sound. The guard is a mere fifteen feet from him, still hunched over, oblivious to the world.

Hector grips the rebar tightly enough to make his fingers ache, closes in on the sentry in swift, silent steps. He raises the bar and brings it down with a sharp thump on the man's head.

"That's for Khan, motherfucker!"

The man topples over, unconscious. His Gameboy skitters on the gravel.

Hector leaves him and moves in a wide circle towards the shipping container.

Containers look solid from far away, but ones stashed on land soon become pocked with holes—rust holes, improvised ventilation holes, holes from bolts gone astray. Interior light bleeds through the box, mapping a constellation of flaws. Hector moves close and peers inside.

Yip is there, half-sitting on a cheap metal desk, below a bare wire-hung bulb. Japanese electronics are stacked everywhere. Zenobia sits on the floor against the wall, hands behind her. Hector looks to her eyes for a sign of life, but they're closed.

Quietly Hector draws away and slips between two motor coaches parked on the far side of the container. He palms a cellphone—the one Muhammad retrieved from the body in Khan's truck—and hits the redial. He's too far away to hear the ring inside the container, but he knows the voice.

"*Wai.*"

"I've got the bag," he says softly. "Where's Zen?"

"She's here. You have to come and get her."

"I want proof that she's alive."

"You can talk to her."

"How do I know where you are? Maybe you're both together on the Peak, and you've left a couple of your men inside to shoot me."

"You're a clever man, *See-fat.* Come here and see for yourself."

"Not yet. Come out with the girl, show me she's okay. I have binoculars. Open the door. I want to make sure no one else is waiting to ambush me. Then you can have the stuff."

A pause. "Okay, but no more bullshit. I see Ah Singh, I shoot the girl, got it?"

The comment throws Hector. Maybe Yip thinks he has an army of Pushtuns. If only he did.

Tossing the cellphone, he moves back to the container, dives into in the shadows, clutches the rebar, and waits.

Nothing at first. Just a breeze, and the smell of diesel oil wafting in from the harbor. Rivulets of sweat drip down the back of his neck, unable to evaporate in the saturated air. More sweat pools under his arms and back, dripping from his balls like water from a stalactite.

The container door opens with a metallic shriek. Yip walks out, dragging Zen by the collar in one hand, gripping a 9mm automatic in the other. Zen responds to Yip's pulling and poking with limp quiescence, like a marionette.

Yip scans the terrain for the glint of binoculars. Seeing nothing, he turns back to the container and shoves Zen inside. For a second he lets down the gun's muzzle.

In that second Hector leaps from behind and swings the rebar at Yip with every ounce of strength he can muster, missing his head but connecting solidly with his collarbone. Yip bellows in pain as it snaps.

Hector lands a second blow on Yip's kneecap, a third on his gun arm. Yip grunts in agony, curses, clutches his wounded arm. Hector drops the rebar and grabs Yip's hand, working it until the weapon falls to the ground.

Then Yip comes back from nowhere with a kick to his chest that empties Hector's lungs. With the next blow the ground rears up, rushes toward his face, and smacks him hard. His hands flail in search of the rebar, but Yip kicks him one last time in his kidney and it's over.

He rolls on his back, opens his eyes to a blurred moon in a blue-black sky. He's aware of sounds: first a boat's horn, placid and far off, then his own breathing, finally the sharp, percussive sobs of a woman shorn of hope. Hector wants to crawl to Zen, stroke her soft arms and beg forgiveness. But he can't move his body for the pain.

His eyes finally focus upon the barrel of a gun. He stares up the steel shaft, past Yip's arm to a face contorted with rage, one eye battered closed in a gruesome parody of a wink.

"Where's *Ah Singh*?" Yip says. A drop of blood beads at his earlobe, falls onto his shoulder. With his free hand he clutches his caved-in collarbone.

Hector hears the words, but understands nothing.

"Where's *Ah Singh*?" Yip repeats. "The Indian! Is he coming to get the girl?" Yip looks from side to side, trying to make out movement in the shadows, attuned to the possibility of ambush.

For a moment the words race around Hector's skull, too fast catch. Then he understands. He laughs, awakening new pain in his chest and back.

"What's so funny, *See-fat*?"

"You didn't kill Khan."

"Who?"

"Ah Singh. You didn't kill him and leave him in the hole."

"Kill him? What are you talking about? No more bullshit, *See-fat*." He pronounces it *boo-shit*. "Give me the *shabu*."

"All right," Hector says. "You can have your goddam *shabu*." Then louder, to the sobbing woman inside the container: "Hang on, Zen. This'll be over soon, I promise."

Hector leads the way back toward the highway, limping and stumbling, Yip training his automatic on Hector's back the entire way. They trudge to a pile of sandbags heaped on a wooden pallet.

Hector shoves aside a couple of sacks and extracts the duffel bag.

"Here. Now I'm going to get Zen," he says. "I left word where I was. If I don't return with Zenobia, the police will be all over this place." It sounds contrived even to his own desperate ears.

"Open the bag," Yip says, flexing his fingers on the automatic's grip.

"It's all there."

"Open it."

"Whatever you say." Hector stoops, rolls the bag to expose the zipper.

Immediately a blast hammers his right eardrum and knocks him off balance. He dives down to the gravel.

Twinkie walks up, flings away Khan's shotgun, and pulls a 9mm from her belt. With her toe she prods Yip, who's still breathing in heaving gasps, hands joined over the wound in his belly.

She bends over Yip, looks him in the eyes. "Remember me?" She pulls something from her pocket, holds it in front of his deadening eyes. A red disc, about the size of a beer coaster. "Number 64," she says. "Remember me?" She shoves it in his mouth, jams it further down with the heel of her shoe.

"God, Twinkie ..."

"Don't waste your breath, Hec," says another voice. Leo appears from behind the motor coaches, jogs up to where Yip lies. "The pimp deserved it."

"I told you to stay out of sight!" says Twinkie to Leo. Nervously she fingers the automatic at her side.

Hector says nothing. He's out of words. He stumbles to his feet, looks at his friend, then at the lifeless Yip. The red disc in the gangster's mouth forms a grotesque caricature of a tongue.

"Don't worry about me," says Leo. "I know what I'm doing. Don't waste any tears for Yip either. He's a piece of shit."

"He made me into a whore," Twinkie says. "He took Jenny from me."

"What? Who's ... ?"

"When I was fourteen, *Ba Ba* sold my sister Jenny and me to Yip to pay a loan shark. I didn't know his name then—he was just a man with a pony tail. Yip drugged us, raped us, made us both work in a Bangkok whorehouse. Do you know what that was like, Hector? There was a man there, a filthy old man who gave us lessons for two weeks, so we'd be good with the customers."

He wants to say something, but words catch in his throat.

"We spent our days sitting in front of a TV in a glass-walled room. We were in a display case, Hector. Like cakes in a bakery. Men looked in and picked us by number. I was 64, Jenny was 65."

Hector glances at the red disc in Yip's mouth, the button she wore every day in the glass-walled room.

"People traveled the world to rape Jenny and me. Americans, Germans, Hong Kong and Taiwan Chinese, Japanese, Thais, everyone had us. Sometimes they walked in drunk and confident, sometimes they were nervous first-timers. But they all did it, Hector. They did the same thing you wanted to do."

"Twinkie, I'm sorry, I didn't know ..."

"Back home Jenny loved to draw. I thought she'd be an artist some day. But in the whorehouse she hid her talent—she knew they'd put her in a sex show, make her draw pictures with a marker stuck up her if they found out. For the rest of her life Jenny only drew one more picture. It was of Yip. She wanted to remember his face so she could hurt him back one day."

The crayon portrait he stole from the wastebasket. It could have been drawn by a kid.

"What happened to her?" he says. He needs to keep some

control of the conversation. But she's a thousand miles away, in Bangkok.

"We held on for a year and a half, while I figured out how to get us out of Bangkok before we got killed by AIDS or something else. One night some Australian bastard called my number. I persuaded him to take Jenny, too. He was drunk, and when he lay down on the bed to rest, I hit him with a chair. We slipped out, found a mission in Banglampoo district that took in bar girls, no questions asked. That's how we got back to Hong Kong."

"What about Jenny? What happened then?"

"I went to Canada to study. Jenny stayed in Hong Kong, but Bangkok had done something to her. She couldn't concentrate on school, couldn't keep a job, couldn't even pay her phone bill regularly. We lost touch. I didn't realize she'd gone back to whoring until they told me she'd killed herself.

"That's when I decided to come back to find the man with the pony tail. I got a job on the *Post*, one that would take me all over Hong Kong. Six million people, three million men. Every day I looked at the faces of a hundred men. Three thousand faces a month. Times a hundred is three million.

"It took years, but I found him, found out his name." She glances with contempt at Yip's body. "He still had his whores, of course, and Jenny had been one of them. A bitch named Milkie Tang had brought my sister back to him."

"Why didn't you call the police?"

"Police? I wanted Yip to die."

It dawns on Hector that he's never spoken to Twinkie, not really. His voice could never overcome the clamor of rage and bloodlust inside her head. The woman that captivated him was a mask, a puppet. In Twinkie's drama he played the part of a servile dunce.

"Okay," Hector says. "You've got your stuff now. Enjoy your-selves. Send me a postcard from Tahiti or whatever." He starts to turn away.

Twinkie levels the automatic at Hector.

"Twinkie!" Leo says. "Leave him out of this!"

"Out of this?" Twinkie shouts. "He knows both of us! He'll call the police the moment he's safe!"

"I never did you any harm, Twinkie," Hector says.

She glares at him, shakes her head. "You haven't done me any harm? *Ba Ba* sold me when I was fourteen. Suppose I'd been a boy, do you think he would have done it? But girls are disposable. They're just a disappointment.

"The Chinese hate women, did you know that? 'May you have many sons,' they say when you get married. 'May your first child be a boy.' When people ask 'how many children do you have?' they answer, 'we have three sons,' as if girls are nothing."

Hector utters her name softly, but she ignores him.

"You know what my mother's grandmother's name was?" she says. "They called her 'eldest daughter.' I found it written on the back of the one photograph that was ever taken of her. She was known only as a daughter, until she got married. Then it was 'wife of Leung.'"

"My sister and I would never have been born if they did ultra-sounds back then. Now in China they bribe doctors to tell them the sex of their baby, so they can abort girls. One carton of ciga-rettes, that's what my life is worth."

"Things are getting better, Twinkie," Hector says. "Women's rights are improving ..."

"Don't give me women's rights, you piece of shit! Twenty years from now China won't have any young women, thanks to all the parents who are aborting girls now. Almost no women, and animals like you who'll do anything for a fuck. Can you imagine how rich the pimps will be then? Do you think I'd let Yip live to see that?"

"Twinkie ..."

"You're no different, are you, *See-fat?*"

CHAPTER 70

LOK IS CLOSE enough to hear the blast. Shotgun, from the sound of it. Reflexively he draws his .38. Pang has done the same, and the others follow. Lok orders the driver to stop, and they pile out, dispersing and taking cover while the driver radios for backup. Lok will wait till they arrive if he can. But first he has to move closer, find out if anyone's been hurt and what in hell is going on.

"Sir, you need to see this." It's Old Ko.

The DPC leads Lok to a storm drain manhole. At the base of the pit lies a dark-skinned man, head resting on one blood-covered arm.

"I recognize him," Lok says, sizing up his clothes, his wound, his position. Years back one of Lok's duties was to ferry some of the city's Sikh and Pushtun guards to the Smuggler's Ridge firing range, to make sure they could still hit a target with their ancient Remington single-shots. This man was pretty sharp, Lok remembered. He could handle his weapon.

"Whoever did this took him by complete surprise. No other way."

They move on.

CHAPTER 71

"TWINKIE," LEO SAYS, a tremor in his voice. "You said nothing would happen to Hec."

She casts a malevolent glance at Leo, then Hector, then she scans the terrain behind them. Her eyes betray a mind that's racing ahead, planning move after move.

"Get the bag," she says to Leo, pointing toward a housing estate beyond a wire fence. "This way."

"Check it first," says Hector.

"What?"

"Check the bag."

She motions to Leo, who yanks the zipper open to reveal a couple of tough paper sacks. From an open gash in one of them bleeds a trickle of sand.

Twinkie bares her teeth like a wolf. "Where's the ice?" she says to Hector.

"I'll make the same deal I was going to make with Yip. Let Zen go, and I'll give it to you."

"I'll blow your head off."

"And then what do you have?"

"I don't trust you."

"I give you my word I won't call the police."

"The girl will," she says, nodding toward the container.

"Zenobia? After you killed Khan? She'll be too scared. I can convince her to keep quiet."

Something seems to take hold of Leo. He turns slowly to Twinkie.

"You … killed Khan?"

Hector ignores him. "At first I thought it was you, Leo, but you're no killer, just an asshole in love. How did you do it, Twinkie? A small woman like you? Did you run up to him, fear in your eyes, begging him to protect you? A frightened woman, out of nowhere? He'd never turn you away. Did you lure him near the tunnel entrance? Somehow you had to get behind him to cut his throat. But you figured out a way. You're a clever girl."

Twinkie keeps her gun trained on Hector, but shifts her gaze between the two men, watching for a move. "The knife was to stab Yip in the heart," she says. "But the Indian showed up. He would have stopped me."

"My God … Twinkie …"

She ignores Leo, speaks to Hector. "Okay, how do we do this?"

Hector can see she's spinning out of control. He says nothing.

"You'd better start talking …"

"New deal, Twinkie. Zen goes free, you take the ice, but one other thing. Leo leaves right now."

Leo: "Hec, for fuck's sake …"

"He'll go to the police," Twinkie says.

"Leo? No way. They'd send him away for twenty years. Let them go, and you'll get the ice. Deal?"

A pause. "Okay," she says. "Get it now."

"Take off, Leo," Hector says.

"Hec, don't you get it? As soon as you hand it over to her you're dead."

"Leave while you can, Leo," says Hector.

"The bitch is crazy, Hec. She killed Khan and Yip! What do you think she'll do to you?"

"Just get the fuck out of here!"

A sudden burst of daylight hits them straight on.

"Get your hands up!"

The voice is a man's, amplified by a bullhorn. "Twinkie Choi, lay the gun down on the ground and step away from it. Now."

Instinctively, the two men raise their hands and back away from Twinkie.

"Do it now, Twinkie. You're under arrest! I am Inspector Herman Lok from the Hong Kong Police"

"What the fuck?" says Leo. "How did they find us?"

"It's not you, it's me," says Twinkie, squinting at the light.

"What?"

"They want me for killing a whore."

"Oh Christ, what are you saying?" Leo's losing it, Hector can tell. Twinkie speaks calmly, eyes diverted from the blinding beams.

"Jenny didn't go back to Yip on her own. She was lured by Yip's girlfriend, a stupid, calculating whore who wanted to get into the movies. I got to know her, made her trust me. Then one night, after Yip left her flat, I did it. Nothing easier to kill than a whore."

The voice from the bullhorn barks out again. "Drop the weapon! Do it now!"

She ignores the command, continues speaking as if they're alone. "I left the door open, figured someone would see her dead and call the cops. They'd find Yip's sperm inside her. Having him rot in prison for the rest of his life would have satisfied me. I even planned to cover the trial. But nothing happened. Yip must have found the body first and covered it up."

Leo looks sick now. He turns to Hector. "Christ, Hec. I didn't know this. I swear."

"Yip was smarter than I thought," Twinkie says, heeding neither man, intent on getting to the end of the story. "I needed to find out what he was doing. I wanted to destroy Yip and live off his body. And I found a way, with you two."

Leo looks drugged by defeat. "Hec ... I really fucked up. She said that no one would get hurt but bad guys." The searchlight's beam streaks his face, throws a glint of silver in his green eyes. *It's the ice that sets you on fire. It makes you a slave as it makes you king.* That was Twinkie. But Leo answered the riddle too damn late.

Leo moves slowly toward the source of the light.

"Hey, can you hear me?" he shouts. "Hector Siefert isn't part of this, all right? He's innocent. Twinkie planted the ice in his house. She tricked him. Hec didn't do any of this. It was Twinkie and me, underst ..."

Twinkie fires. Leo bucks like a kite in a gale, and falls.

Hector shouts his friend's name. Twinkie levels the automatic carefully between Hector's eyes.

Another shot explodes, this one from the darkness. The bullet rings off the fence pole to Twinkie's left. *E-natural.* Twinkie dives behind the sandbags and takes off toward the container. As soon as she's out of sight some policemen sprint into view, guns ready.

Hector is kneeling beside Leo, cradling his head in his arms. A cop with big ears wrenches Hector him away, drags him across the dirt to the van, handcuffs him behind his back. He radios for an ambulance, struggling to make himself heard over the curses and wails of his prisoner.

Before he left Leo's side Hector heard four last words. "Sorry about Zen, man."

CHAPTER 72

MISSING THE SHOT both relieves and worries Lok. He has no desire to be the first Hong Kong policeman to shoot a woman. But neither does he like the odds with her alive and armed out in this shitty place. The Emergency Unit is on the way, but this girl might know the area better than they do, and might escape before they arrive.

He decides he can't wait for the EU team. No telling what's on the other side of the coach lot, how many cracks she can slip through. "Let's go," he says. "Ears, stay with the prisoner, make sure he's safe. You three spread out, and watch yourselves." Million Man, Big Pang and Old Ko take off toward the motor coaches. It's a Great Wall of Buses, five aisles wide, and only four men to search them.

Lok moves swiftly through the middle aisle, checking around corners, sweeping his light back and forth underneath the buses in case Twinkie is crouching there. But there are too many buses, too many shadows to light them all.

Lok is the first to reach the end of the lot. Nothing. Million Man, Old Ko, Big Pang emerge one by one within seconds of each other, guns raised. This side of the lot is a chain link fifteen feet high, topped with razor wire, with no breaches in sight.

Then a shot rings out from over by the van.

"Shit," Lok says. "She tricked us. Back!"

FOR NO REASON but instinct Hector tugs at the handcuffs. They're staying on, for what that's worth.

Two men are with him now, the driver and the cop with a serious expression and ears that jut from his head like teacup handles. The cop is on the radio, reporting that the *sai yan*, the Westerner, is safely locked up, when the seat explodes beside him. The driver clutches his side and howls in pain. Instinctively the cop leaps in front of Hector, shouts "Down!" in Cantonese, and draws his gun.

Hector reaches for the door handle, can't get near it with his cuffed hands. "Christ! Unhook me!" he shouts.

Instead, the policeman pushes him down, aims and fires at the shed, then shouts something into the radio. Hector catches the Chinese word for "ambulance."

The driver is still breathing. The bullet has cut a divot into his flesh below his ribcage, but it isn't too deep. The cop with the ears reaches for the first aid kit. Another shot hits the van, rips through the side window and slams through the floor.

"Jesus!" Hector shouts. Twinkie is out to kill him, no question.

"Keep down!" the cop says. He puts one shot through the wall of the shed, and one through the window, shattering it. They need to get out of the van, but the only escape route is directly into the line of fire.

Then a pungent smell seeps into the van: the fuel tank's been shot out, leaving them parked in a pool of gasoline. Anything could ignite it. The friction from a bullet hitting steel at a thousand miles per hour will do just fine.

A siren approaches. *Continuous rising and falling pitch topping off at A-natural.* A van marked Emergency Unit barrels up, bounces to a halt in a spray of gravel, and disgorges six uniformed men, pistols in hand. The newly-arrived cops take positions crouching behind their truck. The cop with the ears is about to fire back again when they hear a voice on the radio.

Hector concentrates on the Cantonese, desperate to find out what's going on, but the words from the speaker are too fast, too garbled. The cop answers that the driver is not too bad.

"She has us pinned down," the cop says to Hector in English. "My team is going to draw her fire so we can get out of here."

LOK AND HIS men move through the reclamation, keeping out of sight. A wall of sewer piping brings them up short.

Lok grabs his radio. "This way's blocked," he says. "We're coming back. Ears, you need to hold on."

"What? Repeat."

"There's no way to get behind the shed from here."

A static-filled pause.

"There's a tunnel," says Ears.

"What?"

"The *gweilo* says there's a tunnel that leads behind the shed."

"What the hell ..." And then Lok sees the ladder poking up, near the bodies of Yip and that other *gweilo*. He scans the terrain, finds the hole that the Pakistani was dumped in. That must be the entrance.

Another gunshot, and the van sits in a pool of flames.

"Shit!" Lok says. "Let's go!"

Lok leads them through the tunnel, out onto the seawall. He

tells Million Man and Old Ko to take cover behind some bags of cement and sand. They can see the girl, crouched behind the shed, holding a 9mm pistol the length of her forearm. Lok shouts through the bullhorn.

"Twinkie! Hands up now!"

She turns, fires at them, a wide shot, then dashes behind a backhoe. Million Man and Old Ko return her fire. "Ears!" Lok shouts through the radio. "Go! Now!"

The *gweilo*, now unchained, leaps through the smoke and tears around the van. Ears pulls the driver from behind the wheel. Thirty seconds later they collapse behind the EU van, heaving and coughing.

Lok gives the order to cease fire and raises the bullhorn. He repeats the order for Twinkie to come out, tells her it's over.

For a moment, nothing.

Then Twinkie steps out into the light, haloed in patchy yellow radiance from the flames. She still grips the automatic.

"Put the gun down, very slowly," says Lok.

She freezes, halfway between the shed and the flaming van.

"Put the gun down," Lok repeats.

She calls over to where Hector is huddled behind the EU team. "You know what my Chinese name is? It's *Dai-tai*. That means 'bring a brother.' Jenny was *Loi-tai*. That's 'brother on the way.'"

She looks back at the carnage by the water. "And what was I to Yip? And Leo?" She turns toward the EU vans and shouts louder. "And what about you, Hector?"

She points the automatic toward the EU team that shields the *gweilo*. "Was I anything to you but a … ?"

"No, drop it!" shouts Million Man.

But it's Lok's shot that brings her down.

CHAPTER 73

IT COULD BE the outer reception room for hell. No aircon to speak of, and the policeman seems unaware that the windows are shut tight. Hector recognizes the cop as the one who shot Twinkie.

The Inspector wastes no time with preliminaries. "You were arrested for manslaughter," Lok says. "That's a serious charge. However, I was in charge of preparing the file for the Department of Justice. In it I was able to point out that you have no criminal record and no history of drug use. Moreover, Skinwic Sze was known to be violent and unstable."

The cop speaks a little too fast for Hector, whose mind is creaky from nights of foiled sleep on a prison cot. Yet he suspects he's hearing good news.

Lok continues, "The Department has decided that it would not be in the public interest to prosecute."

Hector starts to speak. Lok cuts him off.

"There is, however, the charge under CAP 134, which deals with possession of dangerous drugs. This is a more difficult matter. You knew about the drugs but didn't report them. You also transported them."

Hector knows enough not to speak.

"The ice was found in the cement mixer, where you said you'd hidden it to keep it from Yip Tak-tak and Twinkie Choi. Zenobia Chan has vouched that you'd come to save her life, and that Yip Tak-tak had threatened her with death if you called the police. Also, there's this."

Lok lets an American passport fall to the table.

"This was found among Leo Stern's effects. Either he or Twinkie Choi must have stolen it from you. Stern was going to fly to Mexico with it. If we hadn't had the alert out on you, he would have left Hong Kong under your name. Twinkie had an altered passport as well. That explains the flight reservations we thought you booked."

Hector flips open the document to face a younger, even stupider Hector looking back at him. Just a couple of eyes and a beard. It might have worked. *You all look alike to us.*

"That passport more or less exonerates you. It proves that Leo and Twinkie were conspiring to escape Hong Kong, probably with money or drugs."

Hector nods, taps the passport as if to thank it.

"Which doesn't mean you weren't extremely foolish. You could have reported the drugs when you first had suspicions."

Hector nods meekly.

"There are other matters too. You broke into Hosell Lai's studio. He's in no position to make a complaint, of course, but once in possession of the ice, you were duty bound to call the police."

Again Hector is silent. It seems so sensible now, so obvious. How do you explain what it's like to have every tissue in your body yearn for Twinkie Choi? What it's like to shed every civilizing force, every code, to wish into oblivion every barrier that stands between you and a woman? Can Lok know? He doesn't look as if he's ever had an irrational impulse in his life.

"There's also the matter of Mr. Daud Khan."

Impressions dart into his mind. Two tiger eyes set in a swarthy brow. Gentle words gruffly spoken, a callused hand enfolding his own. Khan, whose very memory accuses Hector. It was Khan who delivered him from death, then died on his account. Hector owes him two lives. The debt's going to crush him.

"In your statement," Lok continues, "you said you spoke to Mr. Khan the day of your meeting with Yip Tak-tak. Did you ask him to go after Yip?"

"No. I asked him not to."

"So you were surprised that he went to the reclamation site?"

Hector nods. That much at least is true.

Lok nods as well, as if Hector's statement merely confirms what he knows. "The evidence you've given will help convict Hosell Lai," he says. "While the others involved are dead, your statements have helped us clear up the case. Because of that, and because your motive was not personal gain, the Department of Justice is not pursuing that case either."

Hector's head seems to fill with something lighter than air.

Lok sits back in his chair. "I gave you your passport for a reason," he says. "You're to use it. In forty-eight hours you are to be out of Hong Kong. Your employment visa has been revoked. Your employer is going to withhold any salaries and bonuses against taxes you might owe. Do not ever come back. Good-by, Mr. *See-fat*."

———

HE TEARS OFF the yellow tape and enters his flat. Hector hasn't been here since Skinwic's death, and it still feels like a crime scene to him. The police have left drawers and closets gaping open like pillaged tombs. Now he knows what a search really looks like.

His bass, still broken, is leaning in one corner, where Clem has placed it. Once he gets some money he'll have it repaired in the States. Hosell won't be doing much work for fifteen or twenty years.

Packing takes no time, just a few clothes in a backpack. He'll get the first plane out. There isn't forty-eight hours of business left for him in Hong Kong.

The downstairs buzzer rings. *G-natural.* He presses the button and continues to pack. A minute later he opens the door to find Zen peering through at the gate.

"You're going, they told me."

"The sheriff told me to get out of town." He opens the gate and ushers her in.

"I came to apologize, Hector."

"I'm the one who should apologize. Khan's dead because of me. It was my stupidity that got you kidnapped. I almost got you killed."

"It's not that. I meant before."

"No need. Your family was right. I wouldn't have been much of a husband. And father? Forget it. What would I teach a kid? No, Zen, you made a wise choice. I'm sorry you ever met me."

"Hector, the baby ..."

"You had every right."

"The baby wasn't yours. It was Leo's."

The room falls silent. He starts to ask her why, and then realizes he doesn't care. Why is no more interesting than how, at this point. Leo betrayed him. Zen betrayed him, then lied to cover her own guilt. He even betrayed himself. Why should he expect anything else? If there's one thing he learned from all this, it's the cost of loyalty. He's paid in full, gotten nothing in return.

Sorry about Zen, man: Leo's words, as he bled to death.

"It doesn't matter."

"It does, Hector. You think I wouldn't marry you because you weren't good enough. I'm the one who's not good enough. Leo came after me late last year. At first I told him to stop, but I suppose I liked it. He ..." She searches for the words. "You loved me for who I am, but he made me feel like someone ... I wanted to be. I can't explain it better."

"Fine. You'd better go, Zen."

"Hector, my father wants to see you."

"I'm leaving. Isn't that enough?"

"You don't understand. He wants to give you a reward. You saved me, that's how he sees it. You need to let him reward you."

"I need to? Thanks, Zen, but forget it. I brought all this on you. Tell him we're even."

"Hec, it's a lot of money. My father is wealthy."

"Just leave, Zen, now. Please."

She stares at him, shakes her head.

"*Ba ba* was right. You *gweilos*..." She turns and walks out the door. Her footsteps are lost in the clang of the steel gate as it shuts.

He zips up his bag, takes a last walk through at the flat. Floor pillows, bed, bookshelves, lamp, nothing but meaningless junk. The landlord can have it. In the kitchen he pauses to look at a postcard stuck to the refrigerator door. He pulls it free, flips it over, reads the words one more time. *Hi, Hec. You should be here. Love, Oscar.*

He tosses the card on the counter, walks back to the living room where his bag and his bass are waiting. "No, Oscar, you should have been here," he says to the empty room. Then he leaves.

CHAPTER 74

"NOT A LOT to show for it, is it, Herman?"

"Suppose not, sir." It's nighttime. The team is gone except for Lok, the Hot Room empty and dark. K.K. Kwan and Lok are alone in Kwan's office. "The musician who took care of Skinwic did a service to Hong Kong, as far as I'm concerned. Do they still give a citizenship award?"

Kwan almost smiles. "It's really your word that the girl Twinkie killed the actress."

"She was the only one with the motive. She told *See-fat* that she strangled Milkie, left her body to be discovered in the flat. Yip would naturally get the blame. We figure Yip came back that night, found her, and moved fast. He hunted up a box in the stairwell, called Skinwic to dump the body."

"Would have been nice to get the confession on tape."

"Do you think I shot her to make things easy for myself?" The coroner's court will take six months to issue a report. Lok will spend that time wondering if he did the right thing. Even if it's ruled a lawful killing, as he suspects it will, the Chinese gossip rags have already made their own killing from it. A spokesman had told reporters that Lok was satisfied that he'd done his duty and had moved on. The next day, the City Pages printed their version.

According to his superiors, Inspector Lok has been tortured by the shock of shooting a female suspect. Several times he has burst into tears during meetings, and he has recently sought the help of a counselor. "She was so beautiful," Lok told one of his fellow officers. "It was so tragic."

Will Pullman had cursed aloud when he read that. *Where do they get this shit,* he'd asked. *Do they make it up?* Westerners just don't understand how the Chinese press works. The papers aren't there to report the facts. Facts are pretty uninteresting things anyway; *gweilos* are welcome to them. News stories are there to reassure people that the world works the way it ought to. They bring stability, not upheaval.

"Bonson Ng's out, I understand," Kwan says.

"He'll probably get off lightly, since he was being coerced into this. Hosell Lai is out of luck, though. He's been handed over to Narcotics Bureau.

"Can't say I feel sorry for him. What about the Irishman?"

"Mulqueen? He claims he knows nothing, was just returning Wan's generosity. Who knows? Let Narcotics sort that out. The true innocent here seems to be the conductor Shao."

"Even with his father involved in it?"

"His father's a different story. He's been recalled to Beijing, from what I hear. No doubt Mrs. Shao will be buying a bullet soon. The man has seen his last Russian whore, in any case."

Kwan nods. *Making your family pay for a bullet when you're executed—we Chinese love our symbols.*

"By the way," Lok says, "you might be interested to know that

Ambrose Wan is not to be found. His office says he's on holiday, and they're trying to contact him."

"Trying ..."

"That's what they said. Should be interesting to hear what he has to say."

"He's covering his tracks, no doubt. This thing is probably connected to someone like Kung Chi-wan, Greeny Ma, Sammy Kung. Until we get Wan in for questioning, there's nothing to pursue."

Kwan nods, turns, stares out his window, as he did the night he took a call about an unknown floater, female.

"Good night, Herman."

Lok walks back to his office to kill the light, glances at his desk, notices a sheet of paper that wasn't there earlier.

TO:DI Herman Lok
Re:Service Enhancement Campaign
Phase III: Adding Value Through Motivation

On 16 October the Department Commissioner's Office will hold a seminar on Adding Value Through Motivation. This offering will enable participants to gain new insights into motivation strategies that bring greater productivity and job satisfaction.

The seminar addresses key factors in motivating staff, and demonstrates how applying a consistent philosophy of motivation is more successful than the traditional incentive/disincentive matrix.

Topics Covered:
— What motivates you motivates them
— Job Description—getting it right from the start
— Self-esteem—cause and effect

— Tailoring a recognition system

— 10 Motivation Mantras

Seminar will be held at the Police Training School at Wong Chuk Hang, 9am to 4pm. All are expected to attend. Please arrange your schedules accordingly.

———

THE LIVING ROOM and kitchen are dark. One light, a yellow brilliance, draws Lok to the bedroom. Dora is in bed, studying a sheaf of papers she's brought home from one of the charities she volunteers for.

"The children asleep?"

"Yes. Esmeralda too."

"Spoken to Edna lately?"

"Yes, today. We'll see her next Sunday. She says that Julian liked us. What do you think of that?"

A few minutes later Lok has emerged from the shower, wet and clean. He returns to the bedroom, dons some pajama bottoms. As he stretches out beside her Dora taps the switch. Blackness.

"Dora ..."

She turns toward him.

Words hastily composed in his mind scatter like rats. Observation and memory must lead to understanding if they're of any use at all. But what right has he to ask for understanding if he doesn't offer it? If he doesn't even possess it?

"Dora, a while ago an old man told me that our generation of Chinese were the unluckiest of all. We gave everything to our parents and get nothing from our children."

"Do you feel that way?"

"I don't know. But I wish Edna were ..."

He searches for the word.

"More obedient?" she suggests.

"Happier."

"So do I," she says. "Edna doesn't know what she wants yet. She has too many choices. That's what our modern world does to us. I watch how Western parents let their children decide everything for themselves. Do you want to eat here? Which jacket do you want to buy? And I want to ask them, don't you know what's best for your child?"

"They're trying to teach independence."

"I know. That's the Western way. Like her professors from England who urge her to speak up, challenge her classmates."

"So that's where she's learning it."

"We worked hard to give her choices. But now I realize that having choices doesn't give you happiness. Edna's a child, and in this modern city we tell children to choose who they are. It used to be Chinese kids understood who they were from birth."

"Isn't that good? To be who you want to be?" He thinks of *Ba Ba*, whose career was set by a mangled hand. Of Ears, who still fights against the jeers of Old Ko and Million Man to make himself into a detective.

"It's just too big a decision for her. She's frightened. You can feel it every time she comes in the flat. Going to university has made her more aware of herself and her feelings than most kids. She's afraid that we'll rob her of that."

"Why does she have to make it so difficult?"

"Give her time, Herman. Let her get over her fear. She'll choose, and I think she'll choose well."

"Why?"

"Because her mother did."

Somehow Lok is aware they're both smiling.

"Dora, I'd like ..."

"What would you like?"

His eyes are slowly getting accustomed to the dark. Just now he realizes that he never falls asleep till his eyes can see shapes in the darkness. The dresser, the lamp, the frame of the curtained window that both hides and confirms the existence of the inextinguishable lights of Hong Kong. The reassuring form next to him, rising and falling gently with each breath.

"A soft chair. For the living room. Like the one that used to be there."

"Then you'll have one."

They kiss.

CHAPTER 75

AMBROSE WAN SIPS a margarita and pats the thigh of the wispy maiden lying next to him. The girl, whose name is Au, flips the page of the magazine, which is peppered with tiny pictures of handsome people and tinier blocks of Thai text explaining who they are and why they're happy.

Rai Lei Beach is far enough away to grant him a feeling of safety. He's young, fit, and handsome, after all, and he needs a few good sexual outlets. But if his father-in-law finds out he's cheating on his daughter, he's done for. Here in Thailand he can keep a low profile, as long as he stays away from places like Phuket where the world's aristocrats go, where the gossips and photographers follow.

And when he gets back, who knows? Maybe he'll give the old bastard a few grandchildren. About time to have a son to carry on his name.

"Are you sure you don't want to go topless?" he says. Au smiles and turns back to her magazine. Conversation isn't included in the rental.

He doesn't care if she's topless anyway. There are Western girls sunning themselves, their breasts bared and oiled, and he can look at them if he wants. When they go back to his shack, though, Au does what he tells her to. That is included in the rental.

Enjoy it while you can, he thinks. *Sooner or later you'll have to return to Hong Kong, face the inquiry, pay the lawyers to help you pry your way out of this one.* They're working on it now, trying to establish alibis, manufacture proof of ignorance, place all the blame on that fool Mulqueen.

He was consumed with dread at first, but Greeny told him to calm down. *After all, Ambrose, I'm the one who's in the tough spot here. I'm the one they'll want to get at. If I'm not prepared to go to prison, why should you worry? It'll be taken care of. Trust me.*

Greeny should know. He had the connections and know-how to buy the judge in Shenzhen. And Wan had fulfilled his part of the bargain, setting up the tour and installing Shao's son as conductor. Greeny had a powerful state agency behind his smuggling operation, Shao Senior had a career for his son, and Wan had a winning verdict for his lawsuit. He'd done his part well. Why should he suffer just because Yip couldn't control the musicians?

"Swim?" Ambrose says. She shakes her head and flips another page. What is in those magazines that's so damn interesting?

Wan rises, stretches, and saunters to the water's edge. He wades into the foam, then launches himself into the sea with the grace of a seal. In a few moments he's far from shore. He has the ocean to himself, apart from two young men who entered the water just after he did.

He turns, starts to make his way to shore, when he feels a scratch on his thigh. Then another. At first he thinks he might have scraped a rock or a piece of driftwood. But it's painful, more painful than a scrape.

The young swimmers are close by now, but they're moving away in forceful strokes. *How did they get here?*

Strange, this pain on the inside of his leg. But no cause comes to him, simply because his head is emptying of thoughts, emptying of everything, becoming light as the clouds that dot the blue Asian sky. By the time he sees the pink sea darkening to red, he can make no sense of it.

EPILOGUE

MONG RINGS THE BELL. The door is opened by a woman, *gweipoh*, blonde, early middle age, attractive if you like the type. She offers him a pleasant if distracted smile.

He reads from the sheet. "Mrs. Wheatley-Craven?"

"Yes?"

"I'm from the Traffic Accident Investigation Unit." He produces his ID, which seems to rob her eyes of their focus. "You own a Jaguar Sovereign?"

She doesn't answer. Her face is rigid.

"Mrs. Wheatley-Craven?"

"They wouldn't leave him alone," she says, her words half-chanted like some atonal dirge. "He's an artist, but they wouldn't leave him alone. Who do they think they are?"

"Excuse me?"

"You can't imagine what it's like. To find someone who understands me, who feels as I do about real art, and see those horrid players slander him. They tried to get him fired, can you imagine? And that horn player was the worst of them, talking to the papers like that."

Mong is as puzzled by *gweilos'* reactions as the next Chinese man, but this makes no sense at all. "May I see your motorcar?"

"The Maestro conducted wonderfully, brilliantly. You should have seen his hands. And then after the concert I drove home and there he was, the horn player, right in front of me. All I could think of was how cruel he'd been to my Din-yan. Cruel and selfish. And I stepped down hard on the pedal ..."

"I think it would be best if we go to the garage," says Mong. He pulls out his radio and mumbles something into it. Then he takes Letitia Wheatley-Craven's arm and they descend the car-park stairs.

"Do you understand music, Constable?" she asks, looking not at him but ahead, at the bleakest of imaginable futures.

"No, not really."

"Pity. I don't know how I can explain, then. There are some things that only a musician can understand."

ACKNOWLEDGEMENTS: My thanks go to the many people from the Royal Hong Kong Police (pre-1997), and the Hong Kong Police (post-1997), who were extremely kind, patient and helpful, and who, if I revealed their names, would shoot me.

Thanks also go to Esther Lowe for her skillful and patient Cantonese instruction; to Callas Cheu and Carol Leung for their insights into Chinese culture and slang; to Marcel Lam for the insider's tour of Mongkok; and to Ute Zahn for the lowdown on violins and their makers.

To my readers: Harry Rolnick, Lincoln Potter, Ron McMillan, Colette Martin-Wilde, Susanna Martin, Mary-Anne Martin, Lynn Bump, Conrad Wesselhoeft, and Eva de Souza.

Eric Spain's excellent reminiscence *The Way of the Pathans* was instructive on the history and character of the Pushtuns.

Thanks go to my dear friend Michael Campbell, who has been for decades a source of colorful and acute observations on music and musicians, as well as a cheerful and willing boniface on nights I missed the ferry.

I am grateful to Barbara Lowenstein for her kindness and encouragement. Joe Pittman deserves an extra measure of thanks for his brilliant insights and masterly editorial touch, as well eternal gratitude for taking my book, and my ambitions, seriously.

I thank Cathy and Toby for everything else there is.